ria Lewis is an author, screenwriter and journalist based
Sydney, Australia. A reporter for over 15 years, her writing has appeared in publications such as the *New York
Post, Guardian, Penthouse, Daily Mail, Empire Magazine,
Gizmodo, Huffington Post, Daily* and *Sunday Telegraph,
i09, Junkee* and many more. Previously seen as a presenter,
writer and producer on SBS Viceland's nightly news
program *The Feed* and as the host of *Cleverfan* on ABC,
she has worked extensively in scripted film and television.
Her best-selling first novel *Who's Afraid?* was published
i 2016, followed by its sequel *Who's Afraid Too?* in
017, which was nominated for Best Horror Novel at the
urealis Awards in 2018, and her Young Adult debut *It
ame From The Deep*. Her fourth novel in the shared
pernatural universe, *The Witch Who Courted Death*,
on the Aurealis Award for Best Fantasy Novel in 2019.
ho's Afraid? is currently being adapted for television by
FTA and Emmy Award-winning production company
odlum Entertainment.

Visit Maria Lewis online:
www.marialewis.com.au/
www.facebook.com/marialewiswriter
Twitter: @MovieMazz
Instagram: @Maria___Lewis

Also by Maria Lewis

Who's Afraid?
Who's Afraid Too?
The Witch Who Courted Death
It Came From The Deep

THE
WAILING
WOMAN

MARIA
LEWIS

piatkus

PIATKUS

First published in Great Britain in 2019 by Piatkus

1 3 5 7 9 10 8 6 4 2

A CIP catalogue record for this book
is available from the British Library.

TPB ISBN 978-0-349-42130-8

Typeset in Sabon by Hewer Text UK Ltd, Edinburgh
Printed and bound in Great Britain by Clays Ltd, Elcograf S.p.A.

Papers used by Piatkus are from well-managed forests
and other responsible sources.

Piatkus
An imprint of
Little, Brown Book Group
Carmelite House
50 Victoria Embankment
London EC4Y 0DZ

An Hachette UK Company
www.hachette.co.uk

www.littlebrown.co.uk

This book is dedicated to Mariah Carey.
Seriously.

Prologue

TEXAS

Sadie Burke hadn't meant to scream. He could tell that just by looking at the startled expression on the girl's face as she'd hit the sand. She had been playing on the second level of a jungle gym, laughing at something one of her sisters had said, when she'd slipped.

Texas Contos had been watching from the shade of a nearby tree when it happened, his legs spread over each side of a branch and his toes brushing the tips of the grass. He had learned that when the Burke sisters visited, it was safer to watch from a distance as a mass of red hair and freckles descended on his beloved playground equipment. He was an only child and he usually navigated that kingdom alone, talking to imaginary friends and diving down the slide without a single one of the seven Burke siblings to get in his way.

When they showed up, he preferred to watch. If he wasn't in the mix, the girls would fight each other. If he dared step into the invisible arena they occupied, suddenly they would turn on him – the lone boy – and present a united front as they tormented him. The Burke sisters made the kids at school look delicate as they punched, scratched, yelled, and pinched any moving target. He wasn't sure if it was because they were fiery in nature, because they were banshees, because they were sisters, or a combination of the three. As far as Texas knew, this was just how females behaved. So he preferred to stay quiet, stay away, and stay still.

'Their vision is based on movement,' he had been whispering to himself, pretending he was Doctor Alan Grant from his favourite book and movie, *Jurassic Park*. He had been hoping one of the Burke sisters might play with him as Ellie Sattler, but he was too afraid to ask. They more closely resembled the velociraptors: deadly; vicious; working together as a team. It was a surprise to him that Sadie fell at all, her hand clutching the air, trying to grab the pole as she slipped backwards. He expected any one of the siblings to see what was happening and catch her at the last minute: especially the middle one, Sorcha, who never seemed far from Sadie's side. Yet none of them noticed until it was too late.

The youngest of the Burke sisters screamed as she fell, the sound starting off as something normal before the pitch and volume increased exponentially. He slammed his hands over his ears in order to block out her cry, but it was as if it penetrated flesh. Texas slipped off the tree as he watched her land with a thud on the orange sand at the base of the jungle gym, her scream finally cutting out. It took him a moment to understand what had happened. His ears were ringing and his vision was blurry as he stumbled, collapsing to his knees on the grass. It felt like everything disappeared momentarily, as white cut through his mind and replaced the scene in his backyard. When it faded, he knew something was terribly wrong. It was like a bizarre game of statues: all of the Burke sisters were frozen still in the positions they had been just seconds before Sadie fell. They didn't move, just stared at their youngest in shocked horror. As Tex's eyes poured over them, not missing a detail, he noticed the only one who didn't look completely surprised was Sorcha. Rather, she looked frightened.

There was a shout behind him and he twisted around to watch as the adults spilled from the house, diving off the veranda and landing in the backyard at pace. *What happened to the windows?* Tex idly thought, noting the sliding door to his house – in fact, every glass surface – was now a gaping hole. The glass that had previously been there was shattered, instead laying on the ground in tiny, reflective shards. As full control of his senses began to return, he noted the neighbour's dogs barking in the distance and, beyond that, car alarms ringing like high-pitched sirens. His two uncles rushed towards him, David getting there first as he pulled Tex to his feet. Gavino was asking him if he was 'okay', repeating the question over and over again.

Yet Tex couldn't answer: his eyes were fixed on his father, Andres, as he walked slowly towards Sadie Burke. She sat up, a pained grimace on her face as she dusted the sand from her chest and looked at the commotion around her. She was confused, he could see it, but his father looked strangely exhilarated. He was hovering closest to the girl, just a few metres back, watching her with newfound interest.

Tex knew that expression. He'd seen his father's eyes light up with it countless times when he had been taken out into the field with him, his parent recognising a threat no one else could see: it was fear. Sadie's own mother was hanging at the back of the group, her thin hands gripping the wooden railing of the veranda for support. If you squinted, you could maybe see Máire Burke's resemblance to her daughters. But the reality was she looked more like a faded photograph version of her offspring, who moved through life in full colour. Her previously vibrant red hair was now streaked with white, making her look closer to the folklore banshees from which she hailed.

Maybe that's what made Tex do it; he truly couldn't be sure. As he watched another type of resigned grief pass over Máire Burke, her body going weak as her sister Aoife rushed forward to support her, twelve-year-old Texas Contos did something he knew that he absolutely, positively should not do. Pivoting in his uncle's arms, he warned her.

'RUN!' he yelled.

His father whirled around, shock replaced by anger as he realised who the words had come from. David's grip tightened on his nephew's arms, shaking him slightly as he scolded him.

'Be quiet, boy!' he hissed.

'Texas . . .' Uncle Gavino said, his tone more sympathetic. That didn't deter him one bit.

'RUN, SADIE!' he repeated, not understanding why they were all still standing around.

His second warning seemed to do the trick, with the Burke sisters springing into action, like gargoyles that had just awoken from slumber. The two eldest – Shannon and Nora – had been 'too cool' to actively play with the others and had instead been sitting on the slide, legs draped across it as they gossiped. They leapt from the playground and landed in front of his father, effectively blocking the man's view of Sadie. They were not large women, but neither was his dad as the man tried to rush past them. He was reminded of dinosaurs once again as he watched the two sisters scratch and kick and spit at his dad, the man having a) never fought women and b) never fought women *like that*. The four other sisters descended on Sadie in a flurry of movement, the nine-year-old disappearing beneath them entirely.

Tex was desperate to join them, but he didn't strain against his uncle's grip: he already knew he was in trouble for the warning cry. He felt his fingers twitch with the need to grab the young girl's hand and pull her towards all the best hiding spots. After all, this was *his* backyard. He saw Ina, Keavy and Catriona sprint off towards the cluster of mango trees that ran along the fence line. Everyone's eyes followed the girls and his father shouted at some of the other supernatural folk to go after them. Gavino did, leaving just David with Tex as the young boy watched Sorcha and Sadie slip away in the other direction. He said nothing, hoping that if they were quick enough they could wiggle under the small gap next to the frangipani tree and make it out on to the street.

It was right in the middle of Australian summer, dusk only just starting to take effect as it ticked past 7 p.m. If the sisters were lucky, night would cloak them. Their gathering was small, just the Burke family and a few others who worked within the supernatural government known as the Treize, like his father and uncles.

None of them were particularly adept at tracking given they worked for a sub-group called the Askari, who were more like secretaries and office workers just with a higher fatality rate. There wasn't an immortal among them and Tex wondered if that would count for something as he listened to the cries of

Sadie's mother mixing with those of her sisters. His father returned from the fence line, dragging several of the Burke girls with him by the collars of their shirts and dresses. The man looked agitated and he flashed Tex a deathly stare. The boy knew that once this was over he would cop a beating.

You will not be forgiven, the look said. *I will remember this.*

His father was right, of course. He had done the wrong thing and he would deserve whatever punishment would be dealt.

As he sat there on the lawn, guarded by an uncle and plucking bindis from the grass as dusk turned to night, Tex let himself feel a morsel of hope. It had been more than an hour now, creeping closer to two, and his father had just returned to the backyard for the second time empty-handed. The meat they had barbecued for dinner had long gone cold, with flies buzzing around the discarded meal and a sunken pavlova sitting untouched in the middle of the table. The scent of mosquito spray mixed with Citronella candles burned into Tex's mind as he was dragged into the house, then dumped in his bedroom and the door locked behind him. He'd looked into the sad eyes of the Burke women as he passed them in the lounge, all of the sisters and Máire and Aoife and her two daughters clustered together as if bound with invisible restraints. He knew a look of defeat when he saw it. The rage he'd seen them display earlier as they fought for their youngest sister was not the norm. Banshees were weak. Banshees were obedient. Banshees were a dying breed. Fighting back was not the banshee way.

With his ear pressed to the door, Tex continued to eavesdrop as more Askari came and went. He was only able to distinguish the voices of his immediate family, not recognising those that belonged to women called in to assist as his father expanded the search into neighbouring suburbs. It was nearly midnight and the adrenaline was beginning to wear off, with a swirling anxiety deep within his stomach the replacement. The full reality of what Texas had done was starting to sink in. There had never been any question of what he would end up doing when he was old enough to have a career: he would be an Askari, just like his father and just like his uncles and just like the other men in his family before him. Despite not yet being a teenager, he had already started the intense training. Where most boys his age would have toys or video game consoles lining the shelves, Tex's room was filled with texts on supernatural law and governmental structures. Where there should have been superhero posters, there were charts detailing the complex hierarchy of paranormal beings. When other kids had play dates or joined sports teams, he was enlisted in an extra class on conflict management techniques.

It wasn't enough for a Contos man to be an Askari: he had to be the *best* Askari. It was an honour, a life calling, and – as his father always told him – if they just worked hard enough they could 'proceed upwards'. He wasn't sure what 'upwards' was yet, but he was certain of the fact he had embarrassed his father very publicly that afternoon. Even worse, he had done so in front of other supernatural beings and gone against everything he had been trained to do. He felt the material of his shirt stick to his skin as he thought about it, beads of sweat springing up as Tex realised one beating wasn't going to be enough. There would be a greater punishment in store, he just wasn't certain what it would be.

His heartbeat raced as he recognised the footfalls of his father coming down the hall, the short yet purposeful strides of Andres Contos unmistakable. He was coming for him. Tex took several steps away from the door, waiting for it to be flung open and his father's stocky frame illuminated in the dead space. He imagined his hand reaching for the doorknob, Tex willing himself not to cry, when suddenly there was a rhythmic ringing through the house. His father swore under his breath, marching away from the bedroom and further down the hall towards one of the phones that hung on the wall. Tex dared to rush back, pressing his ear to the wood as he listened.

'Hello?' he barked. 'Took you fucking long enough. No, not yet: that's what my message was about. I need you to get the werewolves.'

Tex scuttled backwards, not even worried about the sound the floorboards made underneath him. *The werewolves.* If he thought things had gone badly that evening, they were only about to get worse.

The alchemist arrived not long before dawn, the woman's face only partially visible beneath a hooded cloak. The only thing that told Tex she was human were elegant hands that escaped the sleeves, each finger marked with symbols he didn't understand. His Uncle David had come to retrieve him shortly 'before the ceremony', which made the young boy's blood run cold. He couldn't stop shivering despite the sweltering heat, even though it was four in the morning. This was the right thing, though. His family knew what needed to be done. He was pulled into a line alongside David and Gavino, with other members of the Askari positioned further down the queue. They were easily identifiable to folks within the paranormal community by the symbol tattooed at their wrist: a split line followed by three circles at the tip. It was a long-forgotten alchemist symbol for wood, meaning that's what they were: the strong foundation holding up the rest of the house by gathering information, monitoring supernaturals, collecting ground truth and doing what had to be done.

His fingers ran over the skin at his own wrist, which was bare for now. When he was old enough and had passed the necessary tests, that's where he would be marked. Even now, he would use a black texta pen to draw a wobbly version of the symbol on his skin, desperate to show his dedication to the ruling supernatural government. Casting a sneaky look at his father who stood at the head of the line, observing the alchemist work, Tex knew he couldn't afford to disappoint him again. And he wouldn't. He'd be as strong of a foundation as every Contos man before him.

There was a small gap among the line of his people, just large enough for two figures to walk down, and on the other side were the Burkes. The mother was leaning hard against the shoulder of her sister, whose arm was slinked around her as a measure of support. The rest of the girls were assembled by age: the two cousins Bridie and Colleen first, then Sadie's sisters Shannon, Nora, Ina, Keavy and Catriona. Later in life, his survival would depend on being able to read people more dangerous than he was. And he could read what was on the women's faces as if a spotlight was shining on them: sadness, grief, and resignation. There was something else among Sadie's sisters though, clear in the hard line of their lips as they pressed them together and waited. It was anger, he realised, an emotion the older women seemed to have let go of like an untethered balloon on a windy day.

His eyes flicked towards the veranda where some internal instinct told him someone was coming even though there hadn't been a noise. The hairs on his arms prickled, as if sensing danger. He didn't quite believe it at first, even though he had heard his dad utter the words 'the werewolves'. They were here and they did not look happy about it, several members of the local pack moving silently through the night like the predators they were. The lights inside his house were off, plunging everyone else into a darkness that was only broken by the altar of candles constructed by the alchemist and her assistant. Some of the Askari were holding candles in their hands that flickered as the werewolves moved by them, not bothering with their own illumination since they could see perfectly in the dark. They unnerved him and Tex couldn't help but gawk as they formed a second line behind the banshees.

The message wasn't lost on him and from the way his uncles stiffened, he guessed it wasn't lost on them either. *We're here because we have no other choice*, their glowing, yellow eyes said. *And we stand with our supernatural sisters*, their positioning confirmed, quite literally as they formed a united front at the rear of the grieving women. It didn't matter that banshees as a species had no fight: the werewolves had plenty of it to go around. The rift between their community was stark, with werewolves and banshees on one side, Askari on the other. The gap between them might have been physically small, yet Tex wasn't stupid. He doubted there was anything that could bridge it, even obedience. There were a series of grunts and pants, with Sorcha appearing at the back of the group as she struggled against the two female werewolves who were dragging her towards the crowd.

She twisted in their grip, legs off the ground as she kicked wildly through the air and attempted to bite one of her captors. Tex sucked in a breath, worried about what the werewolf would do: they were not known for their even tempers. Instead, the woman looked down at her affectionately, as if she was tickled by the fact a teenager had tried to bite *her*, a werewolf! Both women readjusted their grips, taking Sorcha to the front of the line next to her mother where she would have the best vantage point. Tex wasn't aware of the specifics of what was about to happen, but as he watched his father give the women a stiff nod, he knew immediately that it was Andres Contos' idea.

Sadie was next, silent as the new head of the Kapoor werewolf pack led her down the line of bodies and towards the alchemist waiting patiently beneath her hood. All of the houses in the surrounding area were occupied by Askari and Treize officials just like the Contos family, so Sorcha's continued sobs and muttering of Sadie's name was of little significance. They were heard, certainly, but not by people who would do anything to help her: everyone knew their place, including Tex. He had embarrassed his family once. He wouldn't do it again. For her part, Sadie was quiet. Tears streaked down her cheeks and she was shaking, but it was the only clue as to how she was really feeling. *Of course they hadn't gotten away*, Tex thought. No one could track them better than werewolves and once they'd got involved, it had only been a matter of time before they were caught and brought back to the residence.

Just like the pack he ruled, alpha werewolf Ben Kapoor did not look happy. He was as young as half of the Burke sisters, but he appeared older as his hands guided the nine-year-old girl past her family and to the altar.

'Is that—'

'Yes,' his Uncle David said, answering his brother Gavino's question before it was even properly verbalised.

'He's young,' he whispered.

'Nineteen.'

'Too young to lead a pack.'

'What choice does he have? His sister was the previous alpha and now that she's locked up in Vankila . . .'

'Bloody Outskirt Pack bullshit,' the man cursed, shaking his head. 'They're lucky the Treize even left them standing, given how close they were to the Ihi clan.'

A low, deep growl cut through the hush of the assembled parties and the uncles fell silent immediately. A normal human being wouldn't have been able to make out David and Gavino's conversation, but with their superior sense of hearing the werewolves had heard it all. Texas could almost smell his family's fear as the lone growl was met with a chorus of others, the werewolves of the Kapoor pack gently reminding the Contos brothers and every other Askari present that although they couldn't do anything about it, they had heard what was said, and they would remember it.

'Hello there, Sadie,' Andres Contos said, drawing Tex's

attention back to the front of the line. Even though he wasn't a tall man, his father had crouched down so he was at a similar height to the young girl.

'*Please*,' Sorcha murmured through sobs, having stopped struggling against the female werewolves and resorted to begging now instead.

His father continued on, as if he didn't hear her at all. 'I understand you must be scared, but I promise you this is the best course of action for everyone.'

There was a significant pause before Sadie's small voice could be heard.

'Why?' she squeaked.

'A banshee wail is a dangerous thing, sweetie. It's deadly. Now I know you've been having death visions for a long time, haven't you?'

Tex saw the ginger hair of her head bob up and down as she nodded.

'Right, so that's your one ability. No banshee is allowed to have more than that and *especially* not a wail. It's a powerful and dangerous thing: you saw all the damage you did from just a little fall and you didn't even mean to. Can you recite The Covenant for me, Sadie?'

'Please don't do this,' Sorcha continued to cry, her voice barely above a whisper. One of the werewolves ran a soothing hand down the girl's arm to try and calm her.

Sadie's head jerked, as if she was about to turn around when Andres reached out and gripped her chin between his fingers so that she was forced to stare at him.

'The Covenant,' his father stated. 'Repeat it for me, Sadie. I'm trying to save your life.'

'Per the Treize's order of seventeen ninety-one,' the girl started. 'No banshee is to leave the penal colony of Terra Australis, upon penalty of death. No banshee is to change their surname, lest they forget the shame of what generations before them have done. No banshee can hide or carry more than one predicative ability, upon penalty of death. No banshee is to forewarn others about their impending doom, upon penalty of death. No banshee may intervene with fate's plan, upon penalty of death.'

'These rules are in place for a reason,' Andres Contos said, taking a step backwards as he stood up and addressed the gathered parties. 'They have kept your people alive since you were first banished from Ireland centuries ago. They keep you safe. They keep us all safe.'

Even at his full height, his father was still a head shorter than Ben Kapoor, Tex noted. And he knew the boy was still growing into a man.

'Now, I suspect you didn't know about your wail, did you?' His tone shifted to one that mirrored understanding. Sadie shook her head quickly and mumbled a hasty 'no' in response.

'You didn't know you had two abilities. Since your gift to foresee the last few minutes of someone's life came first, I have to take away your second gift.'

'Take away?' Sadie questioned, the girl casting a worried look over her shoulder at her family. Her eyes ran down the line of women before flicking over to him, Tex feeling the pressure of her gaze as she stared at him with a mix of confusion and fear.

'It's either that or Vankila for you, Sadie,' his father said, as if giving her a choice Tex knew didn't exist. 'Do you know what it would be like for a little girl in a big, supernatural prison like that? Surrounded by the biggest and scariest monsters our kind has to offer?'

Tex watched the fingers of Ben Kapoor as they dangled at his side, his eyes widening as they morphed from human to elongated werewolf claws and back again like it was *nothing*. Something about the gesture felt like the supernatural equivalent of clenching and unclenching a fist.

'It's okay,' Sadie whispered. 'You can take it. It . . . it hurts people. I don't want to hurt people.'

'Thank you, sweetie. You're a very brave little girl and the banshee wail is not something you should be burdened with.'

His father moved further away, standing at the head of the line of Askari so that for the first time Tex got a better look at the altar the alchemist had constructed. It scared him, everything he saw there. He didn't truly understand the difference between witches and alchemists except that one had a powerful, natural gift while the other had a learned ability steeped in science and symbolism. The woman had her back to them, leaning over a dish that was heated with an open flame. Symbols that would haunt his nightmares for years to come were marked into the ceramics, with hot wax bubbling over layers of the altar and mixing with granules of something that seemed to singe his nostrils as he breathed it in. When the alchemist turned around, she was holding an arched dagger that looked comically small to him.

Her cloak billowed over the tips of the grass as she walked towards Sadie, hands now hidden under two thick gloves that cradled the handle of the weapon. At first he didn't understand why. Yet as the alchemist passed his father and the illumination from the candle he was holding, Tex understood. The blade was dripping with liquid silver, a burning sound coming from the grass as droplets landed on it. The woman moved the blade to one hand, gripping the handle as her other extended and a finger gently touched a place on Sadie's forehead just between her two eyes. The girl looked almost hypnotised by the alchemist's movements, not watching as the handle was moved into position closer to her shoulder and Ben Kapoor's grip tightened ever so slightly.

He couldn't recognise the specific words she was speaking, but Tex knew enough Latin to know that's what the woman was muttering. The pace was quick and her tone feverish as she built an invisible rhythm. There was another alchemist standing nearby, having not earned the right to be fully covered so his face was exposed to the group. Tex wanted to focus on his anxious expression instead, rather than what was about to happen, as the man gripped a cloth of red silk in his hand and waited. In a movement so swift he thought he'd missed it at first, the female alchemist's hand dashed forward in a sweeping gesture from left to right. A hand was clamped over Sorcha's mouth to stop her from screaming as Sadie lurched forwards, blood spraying from her throat in a gruesome shower that landed on the altar like raindrops. The werewolf caught the girl as her knees gave out, holding her up by the armpits as the alchemist leaned forward to examine her handiwork.

She repeated a final phrase that Tex was too shocked to comprehend, his breathing rapid as he realised his friend's throat had just been slit in front of him. *It's the only way,* he thought to himself, glancing up at the faces of his uncles on either side of him. Their expressions were confident, assured, and it helped quell the unease he felt swirling in his stomach.

It had been centuries since a banshee wail had been heard by mortal ears and it was too dangerous not to be contained. *This was the only way to spare her.*

The alchemist reached behind her for a bowl of powder, removing her gloves before using her long nails to collect a portion of it and tossing it towards Sadie Burke like it was confetti. With a flick of her wrist, the assistant with the silk came forward and, per the woman's instructions, pressed it to the girl's throat like a bandage. She had passed out fully and Tex thought he might too, his uncle propping him up as his windpipe constricted and he gulped air greedily. Like she weighed nothing at all, the alpha of the Kapoor pack lifted the child into his arms and cradled her there as the two alchemists inspected her. The woman turned to Andres Contos, who was leaning forward to see if the ritual was complete.

'It is done,' the alchemist said, speaking English for the first time. Her tone was clipped and almost singsong, something so specific Tex was sure he would never forget it.

'She'll live?' he heard Máire Burke say, but he was unable to take his eyes off the alchemist. The woman nodded, before her dark eyes turned back to stare at his father.

'Do not ask me to do this again.'

She seemed to float from his backyard, her cloak mixing with the night sky as she disappeared into the house. Her assistant was left behind to pack up the altar, cases clinking and bottles bumping against each other as he worked quickly. A Paranormal Practitioner was on hand and they nervously crept forward to examine the child. There was an audible exhale among the gathered Askari, his father even breaking into a smile as a colleague patted him on the shoulder.

'Job well done, matey,' one of them said.

'Expertly handled, Andres,' added another.

They had done a good thing, everyone agreed. They had spared Sadie's life with their quick thinking. Tex listened to them talk about how their superiors would be impressed, they were all *so* impressed, and now no one would be at risk. All the while, a werewolf continued to cradle the bleeding body of nine-year-old Sadie Burke. She didn't know it yet, but her entire life had just been changed because she had the misfortune to fall off a jungle gym.

10 YEARS LATER

Chapter 1

SADIE

Sadie Burke was doing her best to eavesdrop on a conversation, but it was difficult when she was supposed to be dedicating all of her energy to cleaning a woman's bodily fluids out of the carpet. From the corner of her eye, she watched as the subject of her attention paced in the kitchen, his shoes clicking over the tiles. She was on her hands and knees in the living room, scrubbing feverishly. The bottom half of her face was obscured by a white, respiratory mask that meant she was able to breathe while she worked without inhaling any of the toxic chemicals in her cleaning products.

Her hazel eyes peered out from under the line of her fringe, which was long enough she could feel it every time she blinked. She didn't care, she liked it that way, feeling like it was some kind of protective visor. A sponge hit her back, before bouncing off and landing on the floor in the middle of the fluids she was in the process of cleaning up. She sat on her heels, spinning around angrily to face her eldest sister.

'Eyes on the job,' Shannon said. She threw a pointed stare at Denton Boys, just to let Sadie know that she hadn't missed exactly where her sister's focus had been targeted. He was in his early forties and ordinary in every way, except for the fact he worked for the local supernatural government as an Askari. For the past few years, he had been the officer assigned to liaise between the Burke sisters and whatever supernatural crime scene needed cleaning up. He was never rude to them, never overly friendly either, but there was something about Denton's demeanour *today* that had drawn Sadie's attention. Her older sister had clearly mistaken it for attraction, thinking she had been caught perving on the clock. Even though she was wearing thick, plastic gloves, Sadie's fingers moved rapidly through the air as she used the Australian sign language alphabet – Auslan – to communicate her frustration.

'We're on a tight budget,' she signed. 'We're not going to be able to reuse that sponge now.'

'And we're not going to make our quoted timeline if you keep gawking,' her sister snapped. 'We need to be out of here by six o'clock.'

Annoyed, she got to her feet while her hands continued to move. 'We'll make the damn timeline.'

'Bitch,' Shannon muttered as Sadie walked past.

'Mole,' she signed, in response.

She heard her sister's appreciative snicker as her white booties marched over the shag pile carpet and into the other room where her siblings Catriona and Keavy were working. They had been born just eleven months apart, her auntie dubbing them 'Irish twins' with a knowing smirk. For all intents and purposes, they acted pretty much like twins: always working together; hanging together; scheming together. They even went on double dates, which Sadie found entirely gross.

Catriona looked up just as she entered what had once been a bedroom, most of the furniture now moved out so the sisters could give the space the forensic clean it truly needed.

'Look, Sades,' Catriona said, her face cracking into a smile as she pulled down her mask. 'I found a finger!'

She held up a dismembered digit, a ring still visible on the greying flesh as her sister waggled it through the air.

'*ET phone hoooome*,' she croaked, Keavy giggling in response as Sadie rolled her eyes.

Two cousins had once lived in this house, with the girl-friend they shared. Sadie could only imagine what had caused her to 'snap' – as she often heard the cops call it – hacking both of the men to death in the most gruesome of fashions. She had chosen a much less violent end for herself, taking several sleeping pills and washing them down with a bottle of cough syrup before dying in the living room. It had been several days before anyone found them, despite the fact that Sadie had seen the cousins' final moments play out in a horri-fying vision. Yet this trio had been off the radar, with outdated and incorrect government records and no identifying land-marks in the scene for her to pinpoint exactly *where* the murder was taking place.

So she had passed on what she recalled to Ina, one of her other sisters, who maintained the family's books and moni-tored emergency channels for jobs that may slip through their net. There had been nothing for nearly a week, until Ina picked up a report on the police scanner that junior officers were being sent out to perform a welfare check on Cypher Ikkoye and his cousin Lino James after strange smells had been coming from their home. There had been enough indicators in the job callout that Ina had recognised it as the crime Sadie had seen in her vision.

The sisters had assembled as quickly as they could, five of them piling into the Burke Forensic Cleaning Services van and arriving at the scene just minutes after the officers had. Their knack for being in the wrong place at the right time had long baffled the local police. There was no reasonable explanation as to why they seemed to know exactly where they needed to be and when, but the Burke sisters were a familiar sight at most crime scenes in Sydney – not just the supernatural ones. They would be there, the door to their van open as they sat around and waited until a detective gave them a wave that meant they were needed.

Forensic cleaning wasn't a lucrative business, but there were few jobs as perfectly suited to the predicative abilities of a banshee family than this. Besides, Sadie's sisters had all tried to pursue regular careers at one point or another. It was hard to blend in a workplace and stay under the radar when you might foretell someone's death at a moment's notice. Those who knew exactly when a colleague's father was going to die so rarely received an 'employee of the month' certificate. Like their mothers and aunties before them, they'd given up on professional dreams and stuck with what they knew: death. At least at that, the Burke sisters were succeeding out of sheer force of will. And maybe a little supernatural help.

'What's that look on your face?' Keavy asked.

'What look?' Sadie signed. 'You can't even see most of my face.'

'You do have that look though,' Catriona agreed.

Keavy nodded. 'That look as if we're going to go over our scheduled clean.'

'The body was there too long,' Sadie signed to them both,

annoyed they had read her so well. 'It has eroded through. We're going to have to pull up the carpet.'

'Faaaaark,' Catriona moaned, climbing to her feet. 'Here, Keavy, take my lucky finger will you.'

'Ew, gross.'

Sadie spun around, almost colliding directly with Denton who was watching her from a nearby doorway. She hadn't even heard him hang up the phone, his heated conversation with someone down the line clearly having ended minutes ago.

'How's it going in here?' he asked, his gaze shifting from her to her sisters as he waited for an answer.

'The carpet has to go,' Catriona said, interpreting Sadie's message as she signed at her. 'Both in the bedroom and the living room.'

'Really? Huh, I didn't think this job looked that bad ... all things considered.'

The last job he had called the Burke sisters to had been a showdown between goblins and shifters in a share house. This crime scene was like comparing a Monet to a Pollock. Denton had been forced to run outside at one point, vomiting into the garden bed on his hands and knees. It seemed Sadie wasn't the only one who remembered that display of squeamishness.

'Body fluids are like acid,' Keavy told him, getting unnecessarily descriptive as she continued to scrub. 'Especially when they've been left long enough: they'll eat through anything. None of us are comfortable saying this is a job well done if those carpets are still in the house. Also, finger.'

She tossed it to him, Denton catching it with a grimace. His face went greenish almost immediately as he realised what he was holding.

'Ah!'

He rushed from the room, muttering excuses about needing to 'bag the evidence' and taking the finger with him.

'Need a hand?' Catriona called, the two sisters chuckling with amusement. Sadie thought she heard the front door bang open and the sound of retching follow shortly after. Denton didn't come back inside, her sisters having achieved their mission of getting rid of him one well-placed gory detail at a time. There was little else left to do besides finish the job. It took a few more hours, but with their combined efforts the Burke sisters were soon assembled around an industrial skip that had most of the house's furniture and carpet now dumped inside of it. The outside air was cool on their faces, a relief to all of them as they took off their masks and rested them on their heads.

'Someone should go tell the vomitron we're done,' Shannon said, turning to her younger siblings. Nora had her hands firmly crossed across her chest. She had been twenty-one and Ina eighteen when Andres Contos had orchestrated the slitting of Sadie's throat when she'd been just nine. He'd had her vocal cords severed, rendering her unable to speak and therefore unable to use the banshee wail the Treize seemed to fear so much. That event had defined much of their life afterwards, changing all of the Burke family in different ways. For Nora and Ina, that meant their own cone of silence. If the Askari had taken their sister's voice, then they had taken theirs too: neither women had spoken to *any* Treize official ever again. As banshees, they had very little power they could practically flex. Yet that was the way two of her sisters chose to use theirs. Keavy and Catriona were more of the perpetually annoy and torment variety, Shannon was the most mature and maintained civility, while Sorcha . . . Sadie couldn't even think about her without feeling a pang of sadness.

'I'll go,' she signed.

'How?' Keavy snapped, reading her gestures. 'None of them know Auslan, Sadie. He's not going to understand what you're saying.'

'He can read lips,' she replied. 'Just like you can.'

'But—'

'Fine,' Shannon answered, cutting Keavy off and ending a potential argument before it had a chance to begin. 'Sadie, go tell him. The rest of us, let's get this shit packed up. Skip collection is in half an hour.'

Sadie marched around the side of the house, slipping through the backyard fence so she didn't have to enter the interior again. Dealing with the smell of detergent every day started to drive you a little mad and it didn't matter how much of her favourite Marc Jacobs perfume she used, *Daisy* could never seem to drown out the smell of industrial cleaning products. He had his back to her and at first she thought Denton was on the phone again, the tension in his voice matching that of his earlier calls. But as she approached him, she saw who he was talking to. And she froze. The man had been about to reply, yet he cut himself off when he realised they had company.

'Hello, Sadie.'

Gavino Contos. He was one of the more senior Askari in Sydney, maybe all of Australia. He was also the uncle of her childhood friend, Texas, and the brother of Andres, the man who had maimed her forever. The latter had been promoted after the incident, his actions enough to warrant a permanent place overseas among supernatural counsellors the Custodians, who could choose immortality as a gift if they so desired it. He had. Texas had been shipped off almost immediately after; one of Sadie's last memories of him was a yelled warning as he'd told her to run. She'd heard hushed conversations among her sisters about exactly where he'd been sent to, but a strict Askari training school in Romania had been the general consensus.

His uncles, Gavino and David, had remained in Sydney and it wasn't unusual to view them from a distance every now and again if they were overseeing a major crime scene. This, however, wasn't that. This wasn't even a supernatural scene, with Denton's presence at the job purely because the Burkes had shown up and someone had to be monitoring them at all times. And yet, Gavino was there. Just being in the same physical proximity as him was enough to bring back horrible memories. Even if she could have, she would have said nothing. As it was, she could manage little more than a curt nod by way of greeting. Denton looked flustered by her sudden arrival, Sadie unable to shake the feeling that she had caught them in the middle of something.

'You done?' Denton asked abruptly.

She nodded again.

'Good, good.'

'I have to get to the airport,' Gavino told the man, shaking his hand as a form of farewell. 'We can discuss the details later.'

'Definitely, yes, of course.'

He paused as he was about to turn away, looking back at her with interest. 'It was good to see you, Sadie. You look well.'

She had to resist the compulsion to add to Denton's growing pile of puke on the front lawn as she watched him march to his car nearby. The Askari observed him as well and Sadie knew that he shared her discomfort, albeit for very different reasons. She cast him a sideways glance, her sharp eyes not missing anything as she assessed the clammy pallor of his skin and the constant twitch of his eyebrows. Something was up. And she didn't like it one bit.

It was a little after 7 p.m. when the Burke siblings finally returned home, Nora letting the others out of the vehicle while she drove the van around the back. Like all of the houses in the suburb of Inner West Sydney where they lived, there was an alley running at the rear of their residential street with garages opening up at the back of each property. Their mother was sitting in her usual position on the second-storey balcony, a shawl over her lap despite the heat. She slowly rocked backwards and forwards in her chair, the chatter of talkback radio just audible as Sadie glanced up and threw her a wave. Máire never waved back: she barely responded to any of her daughters any more, not even the grandchildren Shannon and Ina had given her over the last four years. From the outside, it looked like a degenerative brain disease despite it coming on a little early. Her mother wasn't yet sixty, having just celebrated her fifty-eighth birthday in October.

The sisters knew what it was, and so did their auntie Aoife. It was a particular type of sickness that took hold of their women. Most banshees reached a tipping point when they had just seen too much, experienced too much death, and too much loss. Sadie could never quite determine exactly when it had happened, when her mother had sunken in to herself. Truthfully, she had always known her that way. Her father, Hobart Bosworth, had been the love of Máire's life apparently. Sadie had never met him: he had died in a construction accident while her mother was pregnant with her. The tragedy of it all was Máire knew it was going to happen. Yet due to The Covenant which dictated all banshee lives, she had been unable to verbalise this horror or intervene. All the while, her last child Sadie had been growing inside of her, belly swelling as the woman carried both the baby and the knowledge that Hobart would never live to see the face of his seventh daughter.

When they had taken Sadie's voice as a child, she guessed that had been the final straw, the final 'too much'. She had fleeting memories of her mother smiling before that. As it was, she hadn't seen an expression on Máire's face in nearly a decade. She watched the tendrils of smoke from a cigarette resting in her mother's ashtray mingle with that of a lit mosquito coil, the two grey strands intertwining in the sky and weaving up off the balcony. Máire's older sister Aoife was sitting there by her side – as she always was – reading a romance novel. Sadie couldn't help but wonder which one of her own siblings she would have to do that for one day. Or which one of them would have to do it for her. Her auntie stirred as the girls arrived at the front door, peeking over the railing of the balcony and blowing them a kiss.

'Darlings,' she crooned, 'Bridie and Colleen have cooked dinner; it will be ready in twenty minutes so you have enough time to wash off.'

'Where are the kids?' Ina called up.

'Isn't that what husbands are for?' Aoife replied, before settling back in her chair. As far as her auntie was concerned, the only thing men were good for was giving you babies and then taking care of them. In that order.

'That means they're at my place,' Shannon muttered, hitching the handle of her bag further up her shoulder. 'I'll head over there first and meet you lot back here.'

'I'm coming with you,' Ina agreed, before holding the front door open for the others. 'See you soon.'

Sadie could smell the marinating meat from the moment she crossed the threshold and her stomach rumbled. She was so hungry that she didn't doubt whether she had the capability to consume one of her nieces or nephews if they were running around at her feet. Before she could even think about food though, she had to tidy up. The van and the maintenance of it was Nora's responsibility, but Sadie was in charge of making sure that every cleaning kit was fully stocked and replenished after each job. They could get called out to another at any moment and there were few things worse than being tasked with getting rid of black mould without enough borax to do so.

Besides, the shower pecking order had been established long before she was born. Since Shannon and Ina lived in their own homes just three doors down on the same street, that meant Nora was up first, then Keavy, then Catriona, then Sadie had to scrounge for whatever hot water was left. Heading into summer it didn't matter so much, as she preferred a cold shower. But in winter it was hell.

The sisters walked through the living room, which was thin and long, like most of the house. It had three storeys – plus an attic – and was one of the first homes built in the area back in the eighteen hundreds. Sadie knew this because it had been in their family since then, with the generations of Burke women before her having lived and loved and died in this same tall, skinny house. It had been added to over the years, yet the core structure was still the same with high ceilings, light switches that were just as likely to give an electric shock as they were to illuminate the room, and floorboards that continuously creaked. Aoife lived directly next door, with her two daughters Bridie and Colleen: all three of them helped keep the forensic cleaning business running. While other banshee families had died off or been bred out, the Burkes were one of the few that had survived *because* they stuck together. Heck, there were so few of them plenty of supernaturals thought the species had gone extinct.

Keavy and Catriona peeled off, racing up the stairs to dump their stuff and get to the second-storey bathroom first. That was the nicest. The loser would end up downstairs as they took the consolation prize and showered just metres away from the loo. Sadie marched straight for the backyard, where she could already hear the sound of water splashing off metal as Nora hosed the van down. Her cousins were tinkering in the kitchen, putting the finishing touches on dinner, and she planted a kiss on each of their cheeks as she passed. Unlike their neighbours, there was no grass in their backyard: it wasn't big enough to have a proper garden anyway. It was just large enough to fit the van and a small shed, which housed most of their back-up supplies. As a teenager she had helped her sisters pave it, even fitting in a small drain so the water would run off into the alley.

'Jan's all yours,' Nora said, turning off the hose and placing it back on its hook. 'I checked the water and oil, vacuumed the inside, she's good.'

She gave her sister a thumbs up as they switched positions, Nora heading back into the house and Sadie towards the shed. She wasn't sure which of her sisters had named the van 'Jan', but it was going on six years now and the name had stuck. Rolling back the door, she worked as quickly as she could, gently shaking each bottle to establish how much liquid was left as she moved through all nine of the cleaning kits. Each one was a different colour, making it easy for her to track. The same equipment was in each, the idea being that it wouldn't matter which one you used because they all stocked the same tools. Slapping a mosquito as it landed on her arm and attempted to drink her blood, she ran a hand through her hair and jogged back into the house.

'Dinner in five, Sadie,' Colleen called, 'don't be late.'

She nodded, knowing that it truly wouldn't matter. Her cousins always insisted on punctuality, but Sadie would be at the back of the line anyway: the oldest got their plates first, with the servings working their way back to the youngest. It was a wonder she wasn't thin, given how hard she had to fight for food in this rowdy household. Sadie felt like she couldn't truly exhale until she had the second-storey bathroom door closed at her back. The cool surface of the black and white checkered tiles under her feet like a soothing balm after the thirteen hours they'd spent cleaning up the crime scene. Her muscles hurt, her back ached, her hair was lank and oily after a day of sweating, and she smelled. Stank, actually. There was an uncomfortable twist just below her belly button followed by a cramp that took her breath away.

Great, she thought, *I'm getting my period as well.*

Yet as she stepped under the cool water coming from the shower head, not surprised at all by the fact the hot tap had nil to offer, Sadie focused on the positive things. She was exhausted, so she would sleep like the dead tonight. It was Thursday, which meant she had her one day off tomorrow. If she was lucky, they wouldn't catch a job until late Saturday afternoon so she could sleep in. And downstairs, bickering over what the correct portion of lamb shank was per person, was an entire house full of women who loved her fiercely. In that moment, it was enough.

Dried and dressed in a pair of floral, satin pyjamas, she towelled off her hair as she skipped down the stairs. She was sure to leap over the second last one, as it had partially collapsed years ago and had an uneven divot that could cause you to trip if you weren't careful. She did it by instinct now and paused just as there was a knock at the door. The sounds of her family were coming from the kitchen, cutlery and utensils clanging together, so she knew most of them were gathered. *No Burke would bother knocking,* she thought to herself with a smirk as she twisted the handle.

It wasn't a Burke. Sadie felt the towel slip from her fingers and land in a crumpled pile on the floor as she stared at the party assembled in front of her. Gavino and David Contos were standing there formally, hands grasped in front of them, with a younger man positioned at the centre. Her eyes skimmed every inch of him, from the pale-blue business shirt with two buttons undone to the glimpse of an Askari tattoo *just* visible on his wrist. His skin was paler than that of his uncles, but his gelled hair was the exact same shade of inky black. Sadie recognised some features – like his big, wonky nose they had teased him about as kids – while others seemed completely foreign to her, namely the broad set of his shoulders. If she thought she had seen a glimmer of excitement in his eyes, it was dashed as her shaking hand went straight to her throat. There was a choker there, one she always wore to hide the scar that swept from one side of her neck to the other. She felt the old injury burn beneath her skin as she heard the words of a boy, only three years older than her, pleading with her to run. He was a man now.

'Sadie Burke,' said Texas Contos. 'It has been a while.'

Chapter 2

TEXAS

He didn't know what he expected to find when he arrived at the Burke family home almost a decade after his family had irrevocably changed their lives. He'd been to their house to play a few times as a kid, but his memories were clearly rose-tinted as he observed the somewhat rundown exterior of their terrace house. They all looked like this, he reasoned, the narrow streets having bled into each other as his uncles drove him straight to the address. They'd been waiting for him at the airport, proud as punch when he arrived back home on Australian soil as a fully qualified Askari at just twenty-two. Some might have expected his father to be there. Tex didn't. It had been years since he'd heard from the man outside of a cordial 'Sincerely, your father' written in an email.

On the flip side, it seemed the Burkes' familial connections had grown stronger than ever in his absence. He watched with interest as the many redheads of the family swarmed protectively around the youngest, Sadie, who seemed frozen at the very sight of him. She wasn't what he was expecting either, even though he knew the family's file off by heart. Once he'd gotten enough security clearance on his eighteenth birthday, that was the first thing he did: request the Burke documents. In it were up-to-date records on each of the sisters, including Sorcha who had broken The Covenant many years later and attempted to flee Australia. It was strange, catching up with people who had been such a seminal part of his childhood through the medium of case files meticulously maintained by Denton Boys.

Yet seeing them in the flesh was just as strange, his uncles stepping over the threshold of the front door and pushing their way into the house like they belonged there. It wasn't necessarily how Tex would have done it, but it was better than waiting outside for an invitation that might never come. As a protective unit, they worked quickly. Gone were the days when their friendly, neighbourhood Askari weren't seen as a threat. Aoife, the auntie, was ordered to take the children from the room: nieces and nephews Tex knew belonged to Shannon and Ina. Several of the other sisters left too: all except Shannon, Sadie, and Keavy. *Three on three,* he thought, unable to help the tactical math that popped into his head thanks to years upon years of training.

'We're sorry to interrupt your Thursday evening,' David said formally. 'Especially after such a long day at the deceased's property.'

'We don't usually deal with you,' Shannon replied, cutting straight to the point. 'Where's Denton? He's our assigned contact.'

'Denton Boys has been relieved of his post.'

Tex's eyes had barely strayed from Sadie since he arrived, fascinated by the young woman she had grown into. Her sisters might have been more conspicuous on the surface, but she was the pearl among them: soft, beautiful, and with ginger hair hanging in a wavy bob that framed the painting of her face. Her nose was dotted with freckles and huge eyes blinked back at him, Tex's gaze lingering on her lips. She couldn't physically speak, but she didn't need to. As his uncle and her sister been talking, Sadie's hands had been moving to communicate her own message.

'Ask them why,' she signed, clearly used to the fact none of the local Askari had bothered to learn Australian sign language. She expected her messages to go unnoticed by them, using their ignorance as a way to shield the content of her conversations. Tex, unbeknownst to her, had learned.

'Getting taken out of the field and assigned to a desk is a demotion,' she continued, her sisters both reading what she told them with their eyes.

'Why has he been relieved?' Shannon said to the room, using their terminology back at them. 'We just saw him a few hours ago; we weren't informed of this.'

'These requests take time, you see,' David explained. 'He's about to have his second child and wanted a more stable situation.'

'One where he's less likely to vomit?' Keavy asked, ignoring the elbow from Shannon.

'One where he can be more present for his family,' Tex's uncle answered.

'Bullshit,' Sadie signed, frowning slightly as she noticed Tex watching her.

'Thankfully, you're already familiar with his replacement. Young Texas here is more than capable of taking over from

Denton and has familiarised himself with the case notes. He'll be your new liaison from now on and taking a much more hands-on approach.'

'We've seen what the men in your family can do with their hands,' Shannon said, voice neutral. 'The implication is received and understood.'

'Good.' David smiled, everyone clearly done with pretence. 'Well, there's not much more for us to say then, is there, Texas?'

'I'll be stopping by periodically over the course of the next few days,' he said, speaking up. 'I'd like to conduct some preliminary interviews with each of you, discern how you all worked with Denton and what's the best way to proceed forward. If you have any questions in the meantime, here's my card. I'm contactable twenty-four hours a day, seven days a week.'

There was a pause, before Sadie signed a barb that he wasn't expecting.

'The ultimate Treize bitch,' her hands said, earning a smirk from Shannon and a laugh that was attempted to be disguised as a cough by Keavy. Her eyes were watching him as she did it and he couldn't be sure, but Tex suspected it was a test to see if he reacted. He kept his face composed, giving away nothing.

The card was left on the table between them, untouched, as the three Contos men got up to leave. Everyone was silent, except Sadie, whose hands were moving at a rapid rate once again. He didn't catch what she was saying, but he couldn't help glance back at her as he stepped out the door.

'It's good to see you again,' he said, directing the comment at her before he clarified further. 'All of you.'

Shutting the door behind him, he and his uncles remained quiet until they were in the sanctuary of Gavino's company issue Mercedes-Benz sedan.

'Phwoar, what do you think?' David asked, letting out a chuckle. 'Miserable bunch, aren't they?'

'That house is in disrepair,' Tex replied, still somewhat shocked by that detail.

'What did you expect? Those banshees breed like rabbits; there's so many mouths to feed and they barely make enough with that cleaning business.'

'*Body* cleaning business,' Gavino corrected. 'Don't leave out the crucial detail.'

'They're doing better than some banshee families,' Tex said, not immediately sure why he felt protective of the Burkes. A banshee wail was a deadly, uncontrollable thing that hadn't been documented in existence for over one hundred years before Sadie. Another Askari might have killed her, permanently removing the risk forever. It may have appeared cruel from the outside, but if there was anything he had learned in his decade of training within their supernatural world it's that Andres Contos had shown a small mercy. Sadie could be dead, probably should be. His father and uncles had spared her life, even if the Burkes would hate them forever for it.

'Can you drop me at the apartment?' Tex asked, suddenly very tired after his fifteen-hour flight and journey straight from the airport.

'No can do,' Gavino replied. 'You've gotta head into the office.'

'What? Now? It's nearly—'

'Nearly time for the first official meeting of the VCC at nine p.m. It's an honour, you know, getting to spearhead such an important task.'

'It's the Vampire Conservation Committee,' Tex said, over the laughter of his uncles who were enjoying making fun of him. 'It's a deadbeat gig and you both know it, occupied by Askari who have aged out of doing anything else. I'm going to be the youngest person there by at least fifty years.'

That just made them laugh harder, his relatives having long passed the point in their careers where they had to participate in symbolic sub-committees. Pulling up next to Hyde Park, Tex sighed as he bent down in the backseat and grabbed his satchel full of work files. His uncles told him they'd drop the rest of his luggage at the Rose Bay apartment he'd now be occupying under a Treize lease, with David tossing him a key and a residual 'you're going to be late, mate'.

If the situation was reversed, if it was Tex's nephew returning to Australian Treize headquarters for the first time since they were twelve, he would have gone with them. But the Contos family were not the type for handholding or even the most basic forms of affection. He'd learned that early on in life and had made his peace with it. Their love was saved for the job and the job alone. Thankfully, he didn't need their help. He'd memorised the route he needed to take and mentally checked off the landmark of Archibald Fountain as he passed its jetting streams.

Picking up his pace just a little, he crossed a gaggle of tourists who were open-mouthed and pointing up at the sky as enormous bats flew overhead. The sound of their screeches mixed with the native birds to form an unholy racket. There were so many this time of year that their silhouettes dotted the skyline like a scene from Alfred Hitchcock's *The Birds*. Tex paid little attention to it, skirting around the walking path and into a structure that wasn't much bigger than a phone booth from the outside. It was a staircase that led down into the bowels of St James train station, this entry and exit point rarely used by commuters unless it was by accident and they stumbled out into Hyde Park, surprised at why they were among the foliage and not on the main road at Elizabeth Street.

In fact, most of this place was rarely used, which is why he guessed the Treize had chosen it as their Australian base of operations. They'd previously been situated on Goat Island just off Simmons Point, but as the world had gotten bigger, they had needed to go underground: literally. When the city of Sydney had grown, the once pivotal St James Station had begun to empty out. There were better stops for workers heading to the city: more central routes being catered to at Town Hall or Museum Station. It left entire tunnels and platforms abandoned deep within the bowels of the main structure. They had been used as bunkers during World War II, yet now they had an entirely different purpose.

As his hands skimmed down the dark-green railing of the staircase and his feet hit the main platform, Tex couldn't help but think how perfect this place was. The Treize had dug deeper, expanding the networks and infrastructure that was already there. He had been in a lot of Treize buildings at different points, from the Bierpinsel in Berlin to the Clock Tower in Hong Kong, but this preserved train station was unique even by their standards. The walls were white and tiled, with a pair of dark-green stripes that wrapped along the length of the station. It was the same shade as the bannisters, the benches, even the words that spelled out exactly where you were to anyone who bothered to look.

It didn't seem like a normal, modern train station; it was like stepping back into the thirties, he imagined. All of the fittings and designs were from another era. Given the sheer number of employees who hailed from the same period, he wasn't at all surprised the Treize had paid good money to keep it that way, thanks to well-placed donations and political manoeuvres within the state government that meant this site was heritage listed and could not be touched.

Tex headed towards the southern end of the station, walking further down the platform until he neared an elderly man in a Sydney Trains uniform. The gent was holding a fluorescent orange signalling flag and leaning against a glass cabinet that was built into the wall. Inside it was the original St James Station sign, along with historic photos and a collection of other random mementos. He leaned forward, pretending to inspect them.

'Texas Contos,' he said, loud enough for the man to hear him. 'Here for the VCC.'

'Fresh off the boat, ey.'

The man unhooked one of several swipe cards that hung from a utility belt around his waist and handed it to Tex.

'Don't lose this. It's your access in and out. I assume you know your way?'

'I've studied the blueprints.'

'Good, 'cos those that get lost down there stay lost. If you know what I mean.'

Tex turned his head to the side, meeting the gaze of the old gent. From the outside, he appeared completely normal and unassuming. However, just as they made eye contact his eyes flashed ever-so-slightly. *Demon,* he decided. *And the real security mechanism.* Whatever this creature's abilities were, they had been used to assess whether Texas Contos was clear to pass through the entry point. With a nod, he was given the permission he had been waiting for. He swiped the pass in front of what looked like an old, rusting mechanical lock. There was a subtle *beep,* followed by a click as the cabinet popped out of the wall. Tex stepped through, the light changing immediately as he began the descent down yet another staircase.

It would continue for a solid thirty metres, jagged rock on either side and other staircases visible as people ascended and descended them non-stop, twenty-four hours a day, every day of the year. An elevator shaft was at the centre of it all, the carriage moving slowly down to the main floor and the start of Treize headquarters, which ran unbeknownst to most below the entirety of Hyde Park, mirroring the layout of what was on the surface but underground. The ceilings curved overhead, and the area extended in a long, graceful arc just like the train tunnels that were intended to fill this void. In his mind, this was something much more impressive. Glancing at his wristwatch, Tex increased his pace to a light jog past two tunnels dedicated to his people – the Askari – on his left. There were three for the enforcers of their outfit, the Praetorian Guard, who were soldiers gifted with immortality and sent out by the Treize whenever a peaceful resolution couldn't be reached.

The Custodians had just one tunnel, but they sometimes shared desks with the Askari if they needed to. They were above him in rank and supposed to be valued as much as the Praetorian Guard, with Custodians choosing immortality as a reward only if they wanted it. They were the peacemakers, those employed within the supernatural hierarchy to look after those who had no one else: the rogue werewolves, the lost witches, the creatures vulnerable to attack outside of their preordained groupings. Unbeknownst to him at the time, it had been the job his father had been mercilessly working towards when he decided a small girl's fate with the *swish* of an alchemist's blade. Hopping up a raised platform and dashing through a thick, wooden door as quickly as he could, the heads of everyone in the room swivelled as Tex entered.

'Young mister Contos,' one of them said; 'we were just wondering where you might be.'

'My sincerest apologies to the committee,' he replied, taking the empty seat allocated to him at the table. 'I came straight from the airport and straight from Romania before that.'

'Ah, the old office,' one of them remarked with a nod. 'I remember the days fresh out of Askari training, so eager, so keen to be part of it. 'Course, most of my classmates are dead now . . .'

'Here we go again with the mortality.'

'Askari don't live long; we're the front line when it comes to dealing with nasty beasties. All I'm saying is that our contribution should be respected a bit more.'

A deadbeat gig, he thought again, sliding out his laptop and some of the paperwork. He didn't want to be rude, but he wanted to get through this as quickly as he could. If they started off talking nonsense, that set a bad precedent.

'Shall we get started?' Tex said, speaking up over the chatter of the eight other members of the committee. 'I know we all have limited time and we've been entrusted with this important issue, so let's not waste it.'

His pandering to their egos appeared to work, with a few of the men and women at the table puffing up at the use of the word 'entrusted'.

'So,' he continued, consulting his notes, 'the first issue at hand is a habitat for those vampires that can be sourced free of disease. Do we have any proposed locations?'

The truth was, the entire purpose of the committee was meaningless to him. Tex couldn't give a shit whether the vampire species went extinct next week or next decade: he loathed the nasty, cat-like creatures. With their hunched-over bodies that exposed the lumps in their vertebrae, and the horrific, high-pitched squeals they made, vampires reminded him of Tasmanian devils more than anything. They were even considered below ghouls, which were part of a lower tier of supernatural creature that didn't have any kind of cognitive behaviour or quantifiable intelligence.

This was just one of several new duties he was required to take on now that he was out of probation and in the field. It was another box to tick, albeit a very boring one compared to the Burkes, yet it allowed for his mind to wander. He knew generally speaking banshee families were rarely well off, their abilities restricting them from pursuing even the most basic jobs. The descent into poverty wasn't an uncommon one, with many of the original bloodlines having died out or been driven mad in the centuries since they were banished to Australia. Maybe it was because he had known them personally, been terrorised by the Burke sisters and entertained by them simultaneously, but Tex had never filed them into that category in his mind.

Even years after his father had him sent off to the most remote Askari training post he could find, leaving him free to accept his new job with the Custodians sans the anchor of a child, Tex had thought back on the Burkes in Sydney with a nostalgic affection. To him, they had always looked like how a *real* family unit should operate, unlike the fractured and oddly sterile one in which he had grown up.

Seeing them that evening, however, had shifted the reality. They had multiplied, sure, but they were struggling to hang on. They were a family defined by the absences: the absence of the mind of their matriarch, Máire; the absence of their sister, Sorcha; the absence of a way out; and the absence of Sadie's voice. There had been an overwhelming absence of hope, despite them putting on a firmly 'making the best of it' front that he recognised as classically Aussie.

He wasn't sure what he had expected to be greeted with when he was given the assignment, but it wasn't that. A rumbling snore snapped him back to the present, along with several members of the committee as they chuckled at the sleeping secretary among them. Tex ordered someone to gently wake the man up, before calling an end to their first session. Packing up, he assured them he would email a condensed version of the minutes from that evening's meeting out to everyone before they resumed again next week. He received a gentle pat on the shoulder, telling him he was 'a good lad' as the others exited one of the dozens of meeting rooms spread around Treize headquarters for purposes just like this.

47

Well, purposes of more importance probably, he thought. He rubbed his face, fighting exhaustion as he began to make his way out of the building. It was just past midnight and he guessed that between the travel and the time difference, he had been awake for over twenty-four hours. The prospect of his bed in a strange apartment, however, didn't seem particularly appealing to him.

He paused, coming to a stop in front of another enormous tunnel as an idea popped into his mind. This one contained the largest Treize library in the Southern Hemisphere. It was alluring to Tex as he thought about all the volumes he would be able to get his hands on in there that he couldn't access anywhere else. Then he thought about the Askari diaries, those handed in yearly by former officers in his position once they moved on or were killed. He was extremely keen for more information about exactly what had happened to the Burkes in the years since he had been gone and if there was anywhere he would find it outside of the case files, it was in one of those journals.

There were only a few people milling about inside and most of them were positioned close to the oak doors that served as the entrance. It was the kind of space that made Tex feel immediately warm as he strolled deeper, passing shelves that started at the floor and extended hundreds of metres in the air. There were staircases leading to three balconies that cut around the perimeter, but even they couldn't get you close to the volumes stacked in the arched ceiling that curved above him. They had to maximise every inch of space and he watched with wonder as the librarian appeared to affix herself to a zip-line cable and zoomed across the shelves in order to retrieve a book.

Ankles crossed and her feet resting on one of the shelves, she dangled upside down. She was inspecting something he couldn't see from that distance, but his gaze must have been sensed. Her neck craned back and she gave him a small wave. He returned it, knowing better than to call out a 'hello' and break the precious silence Treize librarians maintained through a combination of intimidation and icy stares. He would introduce himself later. Taking a space at the table furthest away from anyone else, he set down his things and switched on one of the lamps that was angled to directly illuminate whatever was beneath it. It took him some time to find the reference numbers for the journals he needed, before he snaked through the standing aisles of books and came to a stop in front of the restricted section.

He swiped his entry pass in front of the reader, the electronic beep allowing him access to the tomes kept safely within this caged area of the building. Loading up with the journals he knew covered the corresponding dates, he reopened the door with his foot before settling down at the spot he staked out firmly as *his*. Most Askari preferred to pass on the titles and code numbers of what they needed to a clerk, those volumes arriving at the comfort of their desk a short time later. Yet there was no privacy there and Tex had just arrived in town. There was no reason for everyone else to know what he was looking into unless he wanted them to.

He started right at the beginning, opening a journal from a decade ago and trying not to feel anything as his fingers ran over paper filled with his father's handwriting. There were more words on one page of Andres Contos' journal than inside all of the birthday or Christmas cards Tex had received from him combined. That was before they had stopped coming, of course. Before his father had been elevated to the position of a Custodian and taken the gift of immortality, happily leaving his son and his brothers behind. His father was a triplet, with Andres, David and Gavino all looking like slightly different versions of the same person depending on their weight or whose Greek skin darkened the most with a tan. All three of them shared a similar type of burning ambition – something they valued, which Tex had come to view with caution in the years he'd grown up away from that family structure.

His eyes skimmed the pages until he settled on a date that was burned into his mind: January seventh. It was the night his father had an alchemist perform the ritual that stripped Sadie Burke of her banshee wail and – ultimately – her ability to talk. It was bizarre, viewing an evening he had lived through in written form, but he couldn't deny it was interesting to observe it via his father's lens. There were a lot of notes about the specifics, the ritual being performed in the early hours of a Monday morning, January eighth, while the moon had been in its third quarter and visible. These were all elements that corresponded with silver in alchemical practices, with the metal being a key part of whatever had been done to Sadie according to Andres' annotations. It wasn't just the physical act of slitting her throat and the scar she'd been left with; it was about the magic that bound the ritual in place.

'Silver's a pure metal.'

He jumped, not hearing the librarian as she had approached him from behind.

'Uh, really?' he asked, resisting the urge to slam the journal shut and shove it off the table in a panic. If you didn't act guilty, sometimes people wouldn't think you were.

'One of the few,' she continued, walking around him and pulling out the chair opposite. 'They call its correspondence with the moon the "call of silver".'

'Is that where the myth about werewolves and silver comes from?' he questioned, unable to help his curiosity.

'Probably.' She shrugged, sitting down. 'But that's also why it doesn't work on werewolves. Contrary to the *Malleus Maleficarum*, they are not impure creatures.'

'*The Hammer of Witches*,' he translated, referring to the book that been published in the fifteenth century as a handy guide on how to identify, hunt and exterminate witches. There was a little-known section on werewolves as well, with the two species being persecuted side by side for centuries by the humans.

'Please tell me you're working on something interesting,' she pleaded. 'Everyone else here bores me.'

He chuckled, not entirely surprised as his eyes swept over the other occupants of the library.

'I'm Fairuza,' she said, extending a hand. He shook it politely, observing the small set of tusks that emerged from either side of her nostrils. She was a demon, then, and had chosen to file down her identifiable markers to make them as discreet as possible.

'When I go out into the human world, I have a prosthetic I slip over them to make it look like a septum piercing to the casual eye.'

'Sorry?'

'My tusks, what you're staring at.'

'I, uh, my apologies, I didn't mean t—'

'It fits with my earthy aesthetic,' she continued, gesturing to several real piercings visible along her ears. 'Work with the disguise you've got, you know?'

'Regular human,' he said, gesturing at himself. 'My disguises are limited.'

'Askari though, so your knowledge can be a disguise if you want it to be.'

'How did you know that?' he wondered, curious as to whether his credentials were so obvious from a distance.

She whistled softly and pointed at the ceiling. 'You met my father upstairs, Burt.'

'*Burt*?!' He didn't mean to chuckle, but he'd never met someone less suited to the name 'Burt' in his life.

'The human tongue can't pronounce his real name without splitting in two. He chose Burt instead.'

He smiled, leaning back against his chair as he observed this interestingly chatty creature before him.

'So you know my name, then? Everything about me?'

'Texas Contos, fresh out of Askari training. Son of Andres, nephew of David and Gavino, none of whom ever spend much time in here, mind you.'

'If you know so much about me, let me ask something about you then.'

'Shoot.' She grinned, clearly delighted to play this game.

'How old are you?' Despite looking barely a day over thirty, demons rarely presented their chorological age and he assumed she was no different.

'Let's just say over two hundred,' she started, 'but under three. I've been the sole guardian of this library for as long as it's been here.'

In the supernatural scale of things, two hundred wasn't exactly *old* but it wasn't youthful either. Tex had heard of Praetorian Guard soldiers rumoured to be in the thousands. If she was closer to two centuries and a demon, that meant she retained almost as much information about their world as the books around them did. Almost.

'Do you remember when the banshees arrived?' he asked her, finally voicing the question that had been on his mind.

She fiddled with one of her piercings as she thought, her eyes squinting just enough so that Tex knew her keen mind was stretching back. 'They came on six prison ships,' she said, 'carrying about fifteen hundred women between each of them, with another three store ships in support.'

'Were you there?'

She nodded. 'They unloaded them at The Dead House.'

Tex knew the place she spoke of: it was Sydney's first morgue and given its macabre nickname for obvious reasons. It was one of several warehouses that jutted out over the water, ships docking alongside them originally.

'It's called Pier 8 now,' Fairuza continued. 'Prime real estate, trendy office spaces, I think the Sydney Theatre Company is nearby . . .'

'At Pier 4.' Texas smiled. 'I've done my research to get reacquainted with this city.'

'Huh, well, it wasn't like that then. These women were brought out thin, pale, smelling like piss and shit. Some of them were wearing a Scold's bridle.'

His expression must have told her he had no idea what that was, because she got up from the table and retrieved a volume nearby. She was flicking through it as she walked, finding the page she was after and placing it down in front of him. The image was horrific, to say the least, with a full-page illustration depicting a woman in a bonnet whose mouth was covered with a grim, metal harness that stretched over her head and fastened on the other side. Texas couldn't tear himself away from the woman's sad, pleading eyes. He read the annotation under the diagram, blood running cold.

'To prevent the banshee's wail, make sure the screws are fully fastened at the sides of the bridle and the lock is firmly secure in place. It is the most effective way.'

'History is not pleasant,' Fairuza commented. 'Especially in this country.'

'How many were like this?' he asked.

'More than there are now: fifteen hundred doesn't seem like very many, but they left Ireland with just over two thousand.'

'What happened?'

'Selkies took them down, along with the two accompanying guard ships.'

He frowned. 'So . . . they drowned?'

'The soldiers definitely did. No one knows what happened to the banshees: they were marked as lost at sea.'

'Why make them wear a Scold's bridle?' he said, mostly to himself as he thought out loud. 'Why not just have *more* alchemists perform *more* rituals?'

'Maybe they tried,' she murmured.

He met her gaze, intrigued by the twinkle that seemed to dance there. Alchemist rituals were old and they endured as they were passed down from mentor to apprentice. Elements might change or evolve, but the core practice should be the same. If they'd tried a ceremony similar to what was performed on Sadie back then – and settled on a Scold's bridle anyway – maybe it was because the former wasn't sufficient. *It is the most effective way.* The words on the page echoed through his mind as he carefully considered what had been omitted.

Texas made a 'hmmm' sound as he flicked through further pages of the tome Fairuza had handed him, searching for an answer. It didn't look familiar; in fact, he'd made a conscious effort to try and read as much material on banshees as there was over the years. There were so few texts, he'd had to resort to reading human academic resources instead. He flipped over the book, inspecting the tattered leather cover that indicated this tome had seen some shit.

'*The Collected Banshee Histories*,' he murmured, looking up at Fairuza with confusion. 'How have I never seen this?'

'Have you looked?' she countered, raising one bushy eyebrow.

'Yes, repeatedly, for years.'

'I guess your hard work paid off then.'

He opened his mouth to ask her another question, but stopped when she slid a very ordinary book jacket towards him. Without another word, Fairuza got to her feet and left. Blinking, he inspected the jacket between his fingers, realising with shock that it had been taken from *Advanced Askari Training Methods: Volume Twelve*. That was a text *every* Askari owned and most importantly, it was one that could be taken anywhere. He slipped it over *The Collected Banshee Histories*, noting that it fitted perfectly and cloaked the original book underneath. Texas felt that he could safely leave the library with it, no one any wiser about what was really tucked into the satchel at his side.

He had only been at the desk for an hour and although he believed no one was watching him, if he left so quickly after his interaction with Fairuza it would look suspicious. His mind whirring with questions, he slipped the book into his bag and returned to the pages of his father's journal.

When it neared 2 a.m., and he eventually powered down his laptop, feeling as if he had sketched out more details of the ritual performed on Sadie, there was a certain urgency to his steps as he left the library. He was desperate to leave the building and take his new finding home where he could inspect it thoroughly. With a glance upwards, he made eye contact with Fairuza who was leaning against the railing of the second level. She was stacking books, two volumes clutched in her hand, but she had paused as her dark eyes tracked his movements. He could have imagined it, yet Texas thought he saw the faintest trace of a smile on her lips. Coming from a demon, he had no idea whether that was a good thing or the sealing of his doom.

Chapter 3

SADIE

The footpath beneath her was hot in the summer sun, the day already beginning to heat up despite the fact it hadn't hit midday yet. She trailed behind her sisters in a line, Shannon at the front and all of the others at her back as they made their way down Coogee hill. Most of those around them with towels draped over their shoulders and eskies in hand would continue down to the main beach, totally unaware of the slice of paradise tucked into the rocks nearby. Shannon took a sharp right turn, Sadie watching the other people with pity as they pressed on. The entrance to McIver's Ladies Baths was discreet, looking like little more than a narrow trail that veered off the main one and towards a public bathroom. Yet as they each donated a gold coin into the bucket being held by a smiling volunteer, it was as if the world opened up when they turned the corner.

Cerulean-blue waters stretched out towards the horizon, far as the eye could see, with the occasional splash of white as foam broke along the surface. She could taste the salt on the air, watching as surf splashed against the rocks down below, the jagged brown edges jutting up towards the sky like outstretched hands. A particularly large wave broke on the rocks, frothy foam crossing an immense distance before landing in the waters of a pool that wasn't immediately visible from above. The further you strolled past the change rooms and two small lawn areas where women lay sprawled out on towels, the more you could see the large rectangular shape full of water so green and lush and tropical that it didn't look as if it could be real life.

After the unexpected arrival of Texas Contos and his uncles the night before, it had been Shannon's idea for *everyone* to take the day off. Sadie knew what she was doing: her older sister was trying to distract the family and divert any niggling worries they had about the return of Andres Contos' son. The best way to do that, was the ladies baths. It was somewhere she only ever came with her sisters: all of them if possible. Usually as soon as one Burke woman learned another was heading to the baths, they all wanted to go. They had been coming here since she was at least twelve, it feeling like something sacred shared between not just the women in her family but the women of her city. On warm days like today, every spare inch of space was covered with the female body. All shapes, all ages, all sizes, there was no judgement or uniform way a woman was supposed to look here. Because of that, almost every person Sadie passed on her way down the rocks to their spot near the water's edge had their breasts exposed. A lady that crossed her path was in her fifties and completely naked, her skin dripping with sea water after a recent dip in the pool. Another squeezed past her, a green patterned hijab matching the material of a long-sleeved swimsuit perfectly.

Sadie had called it Themyscira once, referring to the female-only island of Amazons in *Wonder Woman* and her sisters had ribbed her for it ever since. As she threw her towel down on the rocks, Keavy and Catriona seeking out positions in the shade just under an outcrop, Sadie still thought of it that way as she glanced around and saw women – only women – everywhere she looked. Nora was rubbing SPF50+ sunscreen on her fiancée Deepika's back, all of the Burke sisters having applied theirs hours earlier to protect their fair, Irish skin from the sun's harmful rays. Shannon was unpacking an esky full of snacks, while Ina had the one full of booze. She passed out ice cold ciders to all of them, Sadie clinking hers with her cousin Colleen in cheers and thinking not for the first time that she wished Sorcha was here.

'Who's coming for a dip first?' Bridie asked, getting to her feet and untwisting the sarong at her waist to reveal a red and white polka-dot swimsuit. She had a pair of cat-eye sunglasses on her face and a floppy, wide-brimmed hat to really complete her 'Lucille Ball at the beach' aesthetic.

'I am!' Catriona answered, taking her cousin's hand for balance as she leaped across the rocks. Naturally, Keavy followed and then Ina and Nora and Deepika, so that it was just Shannon and her left minding their things. Everyone was doing a very good job of pretending things were fine. They were smiling. They were chipper.

'This was a good idea,' Sadie signed, before taking a sip of her drink and enjoying the warmth of the sun on her skin as she stripped off.

'That's all I have,' Shannon replied. 'Great ideas and a mediocre set of tits.'

Sadie had been in the process of taking another sip when she snorted her drink, her chest moving with laughter as she wiped her lips.

'I think you have a great rack,' she told her, face solemn with respect.

'Not like yours,' Shannon replied, giving her an appreciative nod. 'When you eventually lose your V plates, those are gonna make someone very happy.'

Sadie slapped her sister on the arm, mouthing at her to shut up as she looked around to see if anyone had overheard Shannon.

'Oh, chill out,' her sister chuckled. 'No one cares that you're a virgin except for you.'

'Doesn't mean the whole east coast of Australia needs to know. And besides, my boobs come from the ten kilogram difference between us, so—'

'I got Dad's lankiness and flat chest.' Her sister shrugged. 'You got Mum's curves and boobs before seven kids sucked them dry.'

Shannon looked down at her own chest, prodding what sat there in her low-cut full piece.

'Actually my pregnancy boobs were pretty great, I'll give them that.'

Shannon and her fell into an easy silence, the chatter of bathers around them ambient background noise. Just because this was an orchestrated distraction didn't mean she couldn't enjoy it. And Sadie didn't want to be left alone with her thoughts, which were plagued with worries her sisters were pretending they didn't have. She had no opinion about Denton Boys either way, good or bad, but over the years they had worked out how to navigate him. They knew how to get by with Denton as their liaison. Texas was an unknown entity and one that came loaded with a complicated personal history intertwined with her family.

She didn't buy the line about Denton requesting a transfer, not for a moment, which meant he'd either fucked up or they wanted a sharper eye on the Burkes.

Neither scenario was good. In her head, a supercut began playing of the Texas Contos she'd known: the stocky young boy who'd grown into a stocky young man. All the afternoons, all the mornings, all the play dates, all the times she'd pretended to be interested in dinosaurs just so he'd hang out with her rather than her sisters. Sorcha had teased her relentlessly when she learned about Sadie's epic crush, telling her boys were 'totally festy'. Her older sister had turned out to be gay, so that hadn't been a lie on her part. In adult form though, the grown Texas was anything but.

She felt angry for a moment, at what should have been. They should have spent the past decade as neighbours, that childhood crush developing into resentment and then all the way back around to a teen romance based on sheer proximity. Instead, the night she'd lost her voice she'd also lost one of her favourite people. When she'd finally learned about his father shipping him overseas, it had been weeks later. There was no way to contact each other or even write letters, regardless of the fact her family would have destroyed them the second they were discovered. It was just another possibility, another potential future, that had swung shut on her like a door caught in a gust of wind.

She didn't know the Texas Contos who had returned. And yet, at the house last night she had the strangest sense that he was watching her, understanding what she was saying as she signed to her sisters. Logically she knew that didn't make sense: there were many different forms of sign language and just because you knew one, American Sign Language, didn't mean you knew another, like Auslan, Australia's sign language. Some symbols were universal – such as bullshit, her favourite – but there were intricacies it took years to learn and constant study if you wanted to be fluent. Aoife had everyone in the family take beginners and then moderate classes in Auslan after the incident, which got all the Burkes up to at least conversational levels.

There were specialist classes after that, usually filled with aspiring legal clerks or adults pursuing specific types of jobs. The Burke sisters were always an oddity in those, with Shannon and Nora old enough to slip under the radar but the remaining siblings varying from late to early teens. They'd done it though, all of them, making sure Sadie would never be isolated in terms of communication. Sorcha had been the sister to lead the charge when it came to catch-up courses, ones that only lasted a few hours but took you through updated vocabulary and symbols. Nothing could beat constantly using them though, it was the only way to increase your speed and confidence. If Texas could understand what she was saying, without the added assist of her mouthing the words as she signed them, that meant he had learned Auslan at some point. And was competent. The question was, why?

Yet another thing she didn't have an answer for, at least not yet. She wanted to get to the bottom of the Denton Boys situation too and she had a rough idea about how she could tackle that *and* the pressing case of Texas Contos simultaneously. It meant sneaking out, because if her sisters knew her intentions they would never let her try to do either thing a) at all and b) alone. But if there was a threat coming, the least she could do was anticipate it, give her family the heads up, so they could navigate it together.

Sadie glanced down at her bikini, which was a shade of auburn that matched her hair perfectly. It had daises patterned all over it, with white piping lining the bralette and high waist of the bottoms. If she was going to go where she needed to that evening, she'd have to ditch the florals or she'd be eaten alive. Maybe literally. She felt the smallest surge of excitement charge through her veins, enjoying the prospect of being able to do something useful even if it was slightly dangerous. She let that energy carry her down from the rocks as she carefully navigated the route to the pool, gripping the chain that ran around the perimeter for support as she felt the cool and slippery surface beneath her. The women she loved were half submerged, laying on rocks at the far end of the baths and looking more like selkies than the banshees they were. Goosebumps had sprung up on her skin as she made contact with the chilling, turquoise water and she watched the surface shimmer in front of her. With a deep breath, she closed her eyes and plunged.

The Wisdom was not the kind of establishment you could just stumble upon. Like all of the coolest bars in Sydney, you had to know exactly where you were going: down Clarence Street in the CBD, left into the always open doorway of what looked like a dodgy office building, up two flights of stairs and into a tiny elevator that had only one button and one destination. Unlike the other cool bars in Sydney, this one was run by wombat shifters. And the clientele? Strictly supernatural.

Sadie had never actually been there before, but she knew it was *the* place when it came to paranormal hot spots, thanks to years of eavesdropping on other people's conversations. Because she couldn't physically speak, that made her invisible in the eyes of a few assholes and she was able to blend in well, listening to conversations she shouldn't and learning about the delicate supernatural hierarchy of Sydney despite rarely experiencing it first-hand. It was Denton who spoke about The Wisdom a lot, usually when he didn't think Sadie was listening, and that's how she knew he came there. Alone. With his wedding ring in his pocket.

If there was any night an adulterous Askari with a pregnant wife at home would be out on the town attempting to pick up, it was a Friday. So Sadie had waited in the shadows of an alleyway that overlooked the first of The Wisdom's many entrances, dressed in a velvet green dress that hugged her curves and Spanx that hugged her ribs. Businessmen walked by, briefcases in hand, and women whose heels clicked and clacked over the path as they rushed to make their train, normal folks clocking off for the weekend just as it ticked past 7 p.m. It didn't take long for her to spot a cluster of supernaturals, however, namely because the person spearheading their group was so striking. He was tall and lithe, attracting the gaze of everyone around him as he strolled in the direction of The Wisdom's hidden doorway. He was thin, almost painstakingly so, with bones jutting out from underneath his denim overalls.

He's an arachnia, she realised, shocked to see one in such a social setting. Other supernaturals had only learned of their existence relatively late, all things considered – a few hundred years back – and when they were in their natural, spider-like form, apparently they were truly something to behold. Their human shape wasn't bad either, she noted, albeit a runway model not necessarily being her type.

When she had learned about arachnia, Sadie had been excited at first, wondering what other paranormal creatures might exist in the world unbeknownst to their own kind. Sorcha had always thought gargoyles were a thing, but she was semi-sure that was because her sister had a crush on Demona from the animated nineties show rather than actual, tangible proof. Her money was on fairies, purely because they featured in too many human stories and too much folklore. It was her experience that the basis for most legends came from somewhere.

Stay hidden, she thought. *That's what I'd do.* Instead, she did the exact opposite. She pushed herself off the wall and joined the tail end of their group, following them into the corridor, up the stairs, and smiling politely as she squeezed into the elevator with them. Looking like she was part of their group was the easiest way to get in and blend. When the arachnia knocked on a non-descript door after they filed out of the lift and were greeted by the bouncer, Sadie slipped in with their posse. She wasn't sure what she was expecting, but it wasn't necessarily this.

For all intents and purposes, The Wisdom looked like the inside of a circus. Draped red and white fabric hung from the ceiling, making it appear as if they were inside a giant tent. People were laughing as they tossed balls into the rotating mouths of clowns with one hand, while their other clasped elaborate cocktails garnished with multi-coloured, swirling straws. Big, flashing light bulbs were placed around a sign on the wall that read 'The Wisdom' in classic sideshow font. There was a six-piece band on a small stage, the music best described as country-horror. There was even a guy *playing* the chains, whacking long, metal links against the ground rhythmically and in time with the beat. The band was called Graveyard Train and she figured that was pretty damn appropriate.

It was packed wall-to-wall with supernaturals, Sadie inching her way towards the bar and past a waitress juggling several limes intended for drinks. The Wisdom was owned and operated by a family of wombat shifters, which sounded cute on the surface. Yet as soon as you met the Petershams, all notions of human-looking people with big eyes, long whiskers, and adorable, wet noses went flying out the window – *fast*.

They all looked like variations of circus strongmen from the early nineteen hundreds, men and women, which she figured was venue appropriate now that she'd seen the place. Swole under their crisp, red-and-white striped shirts with braces that looked they could barely contain the muscles underneath them as they criss-crossed over their backs, she didn't think a single member of the family was over five foot four. Yet she knew for a fact they could carry at least ten times their weight. As if on cue, a woman descended a set of stairs across the space, carrying an entire keg on her shoulders like it weighed little more than a toddler. She could only guess what the rest of their abilities were, not interacting with shifters enough as a species to know little more than they took on some of the traits of the animal they were affiliated with.

As publicans, they were not to be messed with. Not that this was the kind of place you expected a lot of trouble to go down, what, with the bougie carnival aesthetic and all. Yet with so many different breeds of supernaturals in the one space, not to mention officers from the governmental structure who tried to control them, all of the embers were there waiting to ignite. Sadie spotted one such flammable material through the crowd, Denton Boys, and to her surprise he was alone. If she hadn't been purposefully searching for him, she wasn't sure she would have found him among the haze of cigarette smoke in the corner. He was lurking just near the hallway that led to the bathrooms, clearly waiting for someone, and she carefully began picking her way through the crowd so she could get herself into a better vantage point.

As she was drawing closer, a woman showed up looking like every bit the Bettie Page devotee with hair assembled in perfect victory rolls. With a subtle jerk of her head, Denton followed her into the bathroom. She wasn't the type of bird Sadie would have expected him to go for, with his whole private schoolboy-turned-real estate agent aesthetic. Appearances could be deceiving, however, and she watched as he clutched at her waist and pulled her into the loo, the door slamming shut behind them. Each toilet cubicle door had a different, demented clown painted on it as if John Wayne Gacy had been the interior designer. Slipping out of her heels, she tried to ignore the thought of whatever germs would be on the surface of the bathroom floor as her feet skimmed across it silently in stockings. She could already hear the pants coming from the stall and she was about to turn away, feeling gross about the whole thing, when the noises suddenly stopped.

'You think that will do it?'

'Go out and check.'

The sound of the lock twisting back was the only warning Sadie had as she dashed into the open cubicle next door, holding her breath as Denton checked to see whether they were alone. With a satisfied huff, he returned to his companion. Gently, Sadie closed the door of her own cubicle.

'No one,' he whispered.

'Be quick then, what was so important that we had to meet?'

Sadie had to strain to hear them over the combined noise of the live band and rabble from the club, which she guessed had been the whole point of this location.

'I've been taken off the Burkes,' Denton said.

'What? When?'

'Last night. They replaced me with Andres' son, Texas.'

'Shit.'

'I know.'

'Did they say why?'

'No, but someone is clearly suspicious. They know the leaks are coming from somewhere and I guess they just figured out where.'

'I don't know,' she replied. 'If they knew it was you, you'd be dead already.'

'Is that supposed to be comforting?'

'No, that's just a fact. Whatever they want from you, they haven't got it yet. It might be your network.'

'You're a part of that too, you know. Hogan and—'

'Hogan and the goblins are underground, literally,' the woman snapped. 'When the Treize abandoned Berlin, it was only a matter of time before they came for 1984. The bar and operations are dismantled, for now, which is why I'm here.'

'To help me?'

'To help our werewolf friends, actually. You weren't supposed to need help.'

'Listen, Ginger, I have a second kid on the way. If I'm killed, I need to know Lin and the babies will—'

'We'll take care of her, you have our promise. But what you're doing is important.'

'I know.'

'Supernatural lives dep—'

She cut herself off, a flurry of voices echoing off the tiles as several people came in, loudly peed, reapplied their lipstick and left. Sadie edged herself further into the cubicle she was hiding in, grateful the toilet seat was already down as she carefully lifted one leg, and then the other, to crouch on top of it. She was glad she did, with a few more beats passing before she heard Denton scrambling on his hands and knees to check under the stalls for any remaining feet. Satisfied they were alone once more, he returned to standing.

'Listen, they've downgraded my security clearance.'

'I'd expect that.'

'What else am I supposed to do?'

'Maintain the course. I'll help you when I can, but it's almost better if I don't. I'm not as known around here as the Berlin scene. That's not to say I'm inconspicuous either.'

With that, she left. Sadie risked peering through the crack in the stall door to get a better look at her, lips moving in a soundless gasp as she watched the woman named Ginger readjust her hair in the mirror. One of her victory rolls had unravelled slightly, revealing a small yet perfectly curved horn that sat out from her skull. With two bobby pins clenched between her teeth, Sadie watched with fascination as the demon wrapped a strand of hair neatly around the shape and clipped it in place.

Satisfied with the result, she readjusted her cleavage and strutted from the bathroom.

It was a whole five minutes later before Denton emerged, risking getting caught in the women's toilets by taking another moment to splash his face with water. He stared at himself in the mirror, his usually confident façade completely cracked as Sadie observed him in silence. There was a flash of panic on his face and he looked as if he was about to cry. She almost felt sorry for him. Then it was gone, the man straightening up and resettling himself with a puffed exhale. She heard him make a suggestive comment to a woman as he passed her in the hallway, the recipient of the 'compliment' calling him a cockwomble as she continued her own path to the bathroom.

Legs folded up underneath her on the toilet lid, high heels clenched in her hands, Sadie had come here looking for answers. Instead, she felt like she might be about to leave with more questions. Wandering back out into the main section of The Wisdom a few minutes later felt completely different, with just the hem of a curtain having been lifted to reveal something to her she didn't quite understand. In fact, she was so caught up in replaying every word she had overheard so she wouldn't forget them later that she didn't notice the person tracking her through the increased throng of bodies until he was right behind her.

There was a hand on the bare skin of her shoulder, directing her into a small enclave that was tucked between arcade machines. It was a relief to be out of the mass of people at first. That feeling lasted all but two seconds as another body squeezed into her space, forcing Sadie against the wall. She went to sign angrily at him, having to stop herself mid-sentence when she realised of course the odds of this guy being able to read her signals were slim – probably non-existent.

'Hey there, great hiding place,' the man said, his eyes not entirely visible under a set of hipster glasses. She wondered if the frames were even fitted with a prescription lens or if they were just for show. She threw him a thumbs up, making sure the annoyed look on her face was transparent.

'You know, it's the perfect place to cosy up.'

He inched closer towards her, the hair of his moustache bristling as she realised that he was inhaling deeply.

'Nice and quiet.'

She couldn't back up any further, the wall at her rear as she pressed harder against it to keep as much space between them as possible. He was going to touch her, she could tell by the way his fingers were twitching as they moved through the air towards her, and the skin on her shoulder where he had first made contact itched. Of course, Sadie wasn't going to be able to scream. Instead, she braced her left knee, ready to lunge it forward and into his crotch, hoping that she was strong enough to throw him backwards and charge her way out.

'I like you, pretty, pretty thing,' he hissed.

He *literally* hissed, a forked tongue emerging from between his lips and flicking at her as he tasted the air. She turned her head away from him, not wanting to look, just as two hands sunk down hard into his shoulders. The man hissed again, this time in pain, trying to twist around before he was yanked free from the enclave and hurled into the crowd. He was positively hurled, there was no other word for it, and she was left to gape in shock as Texas Contos stood in front of her, a lethal look in his eyes. He held out a hand, Sadie staring at it sceptically.

'You okay?'

She shook her head, gaze flicking from his hand to his face, which was set in a stony expression. Over his shoulder, the creeper was being shoved from group to group, further and further away from her.

'Come on, I can get us out of the crush.'

Impulsively, she threw her hand in his as sweaty fingers closed around hers, dragging her into the mass of people. She was taller than him at five foot eight, but Tex knew how to use his stockiness to his advantage as he braced his body around Sadie, arms almost forming a cage as he guided them through the sea of paranormal beings. People parted for him, she noted. He nudged somebody out of the way and they snapped around, eyes blazing with orange flames, but he didn't seem fazed by the fire elemental. She guessed he'd been trained for all kinds of situations over the past ten years, those skills coming in handy now as he tugged her on to the metal steps of a spiral staircase after him.

She let go of his hand, gripping the railing instead as she climbed in a circle until suddenly miraculous fresh air was stroking every one of her pores as she looked out at the Sydney skyline. She was on a rooftop, a few people milling about and smoking cigarettes, but the area was mostly empty as she stumbled and took a moment to get her bearings. Tex had taken several steps back, as if knowing she needed the illusion of distance. The door he had barged through closed behind them, but it burst open again as one of the Petershams barrelled through it.

'Wus going on?' she asked, eyes touching on Sadie for only a moment before they glanced back at the Askari.

'Fucking snakes,' Texas replied, voice calm while his eyes raged. 'Tried to have a crack at her.'

'Which one?'

'Glasses,' he replied, looking back at Sadie. She made a gesture at her top lip, Texas nodding before he added: 'Moustache.'

'Red-bellied black, that is. I'll sort 'em, take 'em down to the basement.'

The two shared a significant glance that Sadie didn't miss, before the shifter turned their attention to her.

'Sorry about that, love, don't want any funny business on my property if I can help it. Can I get youse both drinks to make up for it?'

Her mind stumbled to come up with an answer that sounded cool in the present company. A shandy was the only thing she could think of, knowing immediately that it was the wrong choice. She started to sign, realising too late once again that it was useless among people who didn't know Auslan. She shook her head, reaching for the notebook she had tucked in her handbag when Tex stepped in.

'An Old Fashioned for me,' he said, 'and a lemon, lime and bitters for my friend, right?'

She felt her mouth pop open with shock, the knowing smirk on Tex's face telling her that his recollection of Sadie's favourite drink wasn't an accident. Well, it had been that and a fire engine when they were kids, but the lemon, lime and bitters suited her adult tastes much more.

'Coming right up,' she said, throwing out a hand to Sadie. 'Name's Sharon Petersham by the way, but just call me Shazza.'

She met this gesture with her own, feeling the strength in the woman's grip and the tendons and muscles practically rippling below the skin.

'Back in a jiffy.'

Suddenly she and Texas were left alone, the strangeness of the past series of events swirling in her head.

'Smells like jazz cabbage up here,' he muttered, seemingly to himself.

When the Askari pointed in the direction of an iron table and chairs nearby, she shrugged because there was little else to do. Her legs felt wobbly as she slumped into the seat, staring out at the blinking lights of the cityscape because it was less awkward than staring at him. He didn't seem to mind the latter, however, and when she looked back Sadie was unsurprised to find his eyes focused on her.

'Did he hurt you?' Texas asked quietly.

She shook her head, holding out her limbs for inspection when he looked at her sceptically.

'You had no idea, did you? He was slithering his way through the crowd towards you. I wouldn't be surprised if he could smell that you were prey the moment you walked through the doors.'

'Prey?' she mouthed.

'Yes, prey. Despite what that dress says. What are you doing here, Sadie? The Wisdom isn't a place for people like you.'

She snatched her notepad up, scribbling a response quickly. It read: 'People like me?!?'

'Nice, decent people,' he replied, his dark-brown, almost black eyes glinting. 'Innocent.'

She felt her nostrils flare as she undid the chain at the back of her necklace, the plain black choker she always wore with a moonstone at the centre dropping into her lap. He couldn't see the scar that was there with it on, couldn't see the line of raised flesh that seemed to run from the base of one ear to the other. Sadie made sure no one could, always covering her neck with not just that choker but several necklaces as well so that it wasn't easily visible. It wasn't an ugly scar. In fact, she had thought it was rather beautiful as she had stared at it in the mirror countless times over the years, her fingernails gently brushing against it. Right then, however, it was a rebuttal as she gestured at her throat. Her eyes said what she couldn't.

'Innocent?'

His lips pressed into a hard line and she swore she could hear his teeth grinding. She scribbled in the notebook.

'I had my "innocence" taken a long time ago, wouldn't you say?'

There was a vein in his forehead that jutted out for a moment and Sadie was certain she saw the flash of something in his eyes. He frowned, his mouth opening and closing as he tried to formulate words. Texas looked conflicted and she could almost hear what he was going to say before he said it: *It was that or kill you.* Instead, what he actually said was more shocking.

'They didn't know any other way,' he murmured, the words barely audible.

His response confused her, not just because it was entirely unexpected.

'And you do?' she signed. His eyes watched her movements, before flicking to the untouched notepad and back again. He was deciding whether or not to continue the pretence of not being able to understand her, she guessed.

'I might,' he replied, the words cementing his choice.

Ha, I knew it! Her face cracked into a grin, Sadie unable to help the 'gotcha!' feeling that spread through her like adrenaline. There was an amused flash in his eyes and for the first time, she felt like the kid she knew was still there, just under the surface. Her smile faded the longer she looked at him, the years weighing heavily on the both of them.

'I'm suffocated by the guilt of men around me,' she signed.

Texas opened his mouth to reply, but was interrupted by the squeak of the door as it revealed Shazza with their drinks.

'Here ya go.' She smiled, setting them down on the table with coasters. 'On the house.'

As the shifter's arm crossed her field of vision, Sadie didn't miss the smear of blood on her wrist. Heck, she cleaned it up for a living: she'd recognise it anywhere. She could tell Texas saw it too. He gave Shazza a pointed look and the woman discreetly wiped her arm with a tea towel hanging from her waist. Sadie decided to break the tension, writing down 'thank you' in her notepad.

'Thank you?' Shazza said, reading out loud. 'Oh, thank you!'

She made the same gesture in Auslan, her four fingers moving outwards from her chin.

'She's saying thank you in response,' Texas said, watching Sadie out of the corner of his eye as she nodded enthusiastically.

'Ah, thank you,' Shazza repeated, imitating her gesture in a manner that was entirely over the top. Her chest moved with laughter, the wombat shifter backing away as she left them to it. When they were alone again, Sadie took a hearty sip of her lemon, lime and bitters, downing a third of it in one go. Several minutes passed in silence as they sipped their beverages, neither one wanting to break the impasse they had reached. She watched multi-coloured bunting flutter in the wind, the small paper triangles lining the edge of The Wisdom's rooftop. In the distance, Sadie heard the loud, blaring horn of a taxi as it sped through the CBD looking for its next customer.

'You know why they call this place The Wisdom?' Texas said, a clear attempt to lighten the mood.

'It's the collective noun for wombats,' she signed.

'I'm impressed.'

She rolled her eyes at him. 'Please, they taught us that in school. Well, maybe not Askari schools, but definitely in the regular kind. My question is how do you know . . .?'

'Shazza?'

She smirked, nodding to confirm that's what she meant. Besides spelling her name out letter for letter, she hadn't quite sussed out how to sign who she was talking about. Texas seemed to know this.

'My – what do you call it – work experience? This isn't my first time back in Australia; it's just my first time back in Sydney. A few years ago I did a three-month stint in south Victoria, my first proper time in the field unassisted. It's a trial period, really, and it's supposed to be top secret. None of your family, your friends, no one is allowed to know where you're stationed. It's a big old test.'

'Everything with them is a test,' she signed, wishing there was a way to add sarcastic infliction physically. She would have '*them*'ed to the moon and back, otherwise.

'I get why you'd think that.'

'So you met her then, in Victoria?'

'I met her sister, actually. And brothers. That's where the Petershams are from originally and I was sent there as their temporary liaison. They roll deep as a family, very tight network, so if you get in with one you're in with them all: kind of like you and your sisters.'

She frowned, confused by the jerk of something in her chest. It took her a moment to realise what it was: jealousy. Sadie had never really felt it before, at least not directed towards a man, and the idea of Texas 'getting in' with Shazza's wombat-shifter sister made her feel irrationally annoyed.

'Have you ever seen a wombat shifter in action?' he asked, having missed her vibe completely. Or maybe he was doing a good job at changing the subject, because despite her feelings Sadie was suddenly bloody curious.

'It's unbelievable, I swear to God. There are demons I'd rather fuck with than the Petershams. Their claws are as sharp as a werewolf, with the power in their jaws close to a ghoul. And they're just . . .' He struggled for the right word, eventually tossing his arms wide. 'Impenetrable! They can take a lot of damage, more than you'd think. And despite the fact they all look like front row props, they can *move* when they want to.'

'How fast?' she signed. 'Werewolf fast?'

'No, but fast enough. You wouldn't want one in pursuit of you.'

She huffed appreciatively, taking another sip of her drink. He sculled the remainder of his, setting down the empty glass on the table between them.

'Come on, I should get you out of here.'

'Get me out of here?' she bristled. 'You're not my parent.'

He paused in the act of getting up and she could almost see the cogs in his mind whirring into gear as he backtracked through the conversation to understand what he'd said that had offended her.

'I watched you,' he replied, tone gentler. 'You're very good at making yourself invisible, Sadie. But I've known you for a long time and I see you. You came here alone and you're never alone, your sisters are always nearby, which makes me think they don't know you're here right now.'

Damn it, she thought. *He was right.*

'Given this whole town hasn't been turned upside down yet, I guess that means they don't know you're gone. With the added element of my uncles and me being back in your lives, I figure your absence would be cause for greater alarm than usual.'

She crossed her arms over her chest, saying nothing. Sadie knew the defeated expression on her face would say everything.

'So how about I drive you home, make sure you sneak back in safely, then no one has to know about this: not your sisters, not the Treize, not anyone.'

'Not your uncles?'

There was a significant pause before he answered her. 'Not anyone.'

She made him wait a few more seconds before she started gathering her things, Sadie getting the smallest bit of pleasure out of Texas having to go by *her* schedule.

'Fine,' she mouthed, reaching for her choker as she fastened it back up around her neck. He was watching her intently, as if transfixed by the mark. She caught him staring, but he didn't look away.

'Your scar glints under the stars, did you know that?'

She hesitated before responding with one, solemn nod. Sadie did know that. She had studied the mark there for hours upon hours those first few years, until she eventually grew used to it. It didn't heal like a normal scar and it didn't look like one either if you examined it close enough. There was a line of silver that seemed to run through the raised flesh, something she thought she had imagined at first. But it was there, just as real as all her other imperfections were.

Getting to her feet, she went to make her way towards the staircase they had come up before Texas placed a hand gently on her elbow and steered her in a different direction.

'Not through there,' he said, thumbs flying over the screen of his phone as he texted someone at the same time. 'I know another way.'

Why not through there? she wondered, taking advantage of her height and his lack of by peering over his shoulder as they walked. He was messaging Shazza.

'Using the fire exit,' his first message read. 'Don't have anyone attack us, please.'

'You leaving with your friend?' came the shifter's reply.

'She was never here.'

'Got it.'

She quickly looked away as Texas slipped his phone into his back pocket, pretending to be entranced by the skyscrapers that towered over the open-air rooftop they were on like tombstones at a grave.

'Down here,' he said, pushing back several enormous plants that had been purposefully placed to cover a doorway. She ducked under the giant leaf of a potted palm, wiggling the doorhandle before slipping through it and into a dark stairwell. The lights were motion sensitive, so as they began to descend each level was illuminated with their movement. It was slow going at first, with Sadie gripping the handrails as she navigated the concrete stairs in her stilettos. About halfway down, she gave the fuck up and slipped out of them, carrying the heels in her hands instead and enjoying the lack of wince-inducing pressure on her toes. This wasn't the classiest look, but on a Friday night in Sydney city she didn't appear out of place.

A woman nodded at her in solidarity as she passed her on the street, her own pair of heels gripped in her hands and bare feet slapping the pavement. Texas was parked just around the corner. Out of everything she'd seen that night, getting a park in the CBD was perhaps the most supernatural of them all. There was a police label hanging from his mirror as she got inside, Sadie figuring that's how he had secured such a mint spot. To her surprise, she recognised the song that was playing out of his car stereo.

'You like The Dardi Shades,' she signed, when they stopped at a traffic light and he could see her hand movements.

'Huh? Oh, yeah, just discovered them.'

The look of scepticism on her face must have been potent. 'What?'

'You've been in Askari boarding school for a decade and you "just discovered" an indie rock band from Camden?'

'Yeah, sure, why's that so unbelievable?'

She shrugged. 'I dunno. Just figured you'd be playing Romanian folk music or something.'

He laughed, the burst of warmth all-encompassing in the small space. The light switched to green and he accelerated, chuckling for another few kilometres at her comment. They didn't speak again until they drew closer to her house, Sadie directing him through a labyrinth of back alleys that ran behind the terrace homes so she could safely sneak inside without being spotted.

'Okay,' he admitted. 'They were on an Australian music playlist.'

'Who, The Dardi Shades?'

'Them and a bunch of others: Moof de Vah, The Stained Daisies, Fairchild. I've been listening to it for months, trying to get better acquainted before I came back to Australia.'

She grimaced. 'Ugh, how do you take the fun out of music? Studying it to assimilate is such an Askari move.'

He smiled, the gesture not quite reaching his eyes. There was something sad about it, actually. They sat there in the dark for a few minutes longer, there being no light down this narrow lane that was littered with garbage bins and a prime fighting ground for the stray cats of the neighbourhood.

'Are you sure you're going to be okay getting in?' he asked.

She pointed, gesturing to the back of a house just a few metres down. It was plunged in darkness too, all of her family likely asleep at this hour. Sadie didn't need the light; she could find her way into that house blindfolded if she needed to. Thankfully, she didn't need to. She unclipped her seatbelt, making a move to get out of the car when Texas reached out to stop her.

'I know you were following Denton.'

His hand stayed on the bare skin of her forearm for what felt like forever. Sadie was torn between dashing from the car in a panic over the fact she had been sprung and wanting to stay there, with him, in this tiny pocket of safety. His car was like a sensory deprivation tank, all of their messy backstories and family drama unable to break through into the sanctuary of that pine-scented interior.

'I couldn't follow him in there, either of you, but I need to know what you heard.'

She slumped against the seat, the illusion properly shattered now. Did she tell him, word for word? The Contos family and Askari in general already held so much power over her, she didn't like the idea of enabling them with more. And yet, it was becoming clearer and clearer that Texas was not like them. Plus, there were things she couldn't make sense of without another perspective and he was that, if nothing else.

'He's in trouble,' she signed, feeling weirdly disloyal despite she and Denton never having been friends. But it was clear he was doing something to undercut the Treize and, in a way, that made them allies. 'And he knows you're on to him.'

'Huh,' Texas said, releasing his hand from her arm as he looked out the car window, forehead creased in thought. She tugged on the material of his jacket, making sure he could see her hands as she asked him the next question.

'Were you sent here to watch us or to watch him?'

'Both,' he replied, the quickness and honesty of his answer surprising. 'I think.'

'Why? I mean, I get him but … why us? Banshees aren't powerful in the grand scheme of things. Even if some of us are, well, your dad took care of that. We're no threat.'

'Maybe,' he murmured, mind clearly somewhere else. She reached for the doorhandle, this time really taking her cue to leave when he stopped her again.

'Hey, do you know a demon called Fairuza? She's a Treize librarian, black skin, small—'

'Tusks,' Sadie signed, cutting him off.

'Yeah, that's the one. You know her?'

She bit her lip, unsure of what she should and shouldn't say. 'Why?'

Understanding crossed his features as his mouth popped open in a small 'oh' as he processed her hesitation.

'She's not in trouble or anything,' he rushed to say. 'This conversation isn't going anywhere outside of this car. I just . . . I met her at Treize headquarters last night and she was helpful. I think. I don't know. It's hard to navigate who's a friend and who's a foe, you know?'

She snorted, rolling her eyes at his statement. *Boy*, did she know.

'Ah, right. Sorry, I guess you understand that better than anyone. I didn't—'

'She's a friend of Sorcha's,' Sadie signed, correcting herself immediately. 'Was, anyway. I could never work out how they knew each other at first, I thought they might have dated. But after everything that happened, I went poking around and there was a whole side of Sorcha's life I never knew about. She was a dancer at this club that had drag acts, strippers, burlesque, you name it. I think that's where they met.'

'Do . . . do any of your sisters know about this?'

'About Sorcha stripping? No. Not that they'd care, but just bringing her up is . . . hard. It hurts them.'

'It hurts you too,' he whispered, clearly reading her face.

'I just miss her, that's all. She was my best friend.'

'I know.'

There was little else to be said and the direction the conversation was heading in made Sadie uncomfortable. It was too honest, too revealing, and angling towards territory too deeply personal. She heard the sound of surprise escape his lips as she jumped out of the car suddenly, offering no form of farewell as she jogged down the alley and started climbing the lattice that would get her over the neighbour's back fence. From there, she just had to scale the ladder they always had propped against the side of the house, balance on the gutter for a few seconds, and then climb in through the window to what had once been Sorcha's bedroom. No one else liked to go in there.

Once she was safely inside, she peered out at Texas' parked car below. He stayed sitting at the wheel for another ten minutes, Sadie wondering if he would ever leave.

Eventually he did, dropping the handbrake and letting the car roll a few houses down before he switched on the lights and started the ignition. Glancing around at the darkened space of her sibling's now neglected bedroom, everything left exactly the way it had been, Sadie felt uncomfortable there for the first time. It wasn't the setting; it was the night. The list of things she thought she knew? Out the damn window, trailing behind Texas' car as he drove through Sydney.

Chapter 4

TEXAS

Texas hated his Rose Bay apartment. He hated the endless chrome surfaces that spanned from the kitchen to the lounge room and back again. He hated the harsh, white lighting. He hated the minimalist aesthetic, with the space coming fully furnished with cold, black and grey furniture. He'd spent his formative years sharing a clustered room with a rotating roster of other Askari recruits, so he wasn't sure what to do with this much space and this little human company to fill it.

So he'd spent time with the book instead. It was a sufficient replacement for a person and weirdly felt like the only bit of company he had. He propped it on his stomach and attempted to find a comfortable position on a couch that seemed to be plated with steel, it was that unforgiving. The Scold's bridle thing had bothered him more than he liked as it planted a seed that seemed to grow of its own accord. He'd turned to the volume looking for answers and with each page he read and re-read, he was getting them. Unexpected ones, even for someone who had done a whole semester on banshee studies.

In class, he'd learned that banshees and the legend surrounding them were deeply significant to Irish culture. He'd even written a paper on an extract from *Táin Bó Fráich*, a piece of eighth-century prose that said hero Fraoch mac Idath's impending death was heralded by the cries of 'the otherworld women'. The phrase was the literal translation of *bean sí* – now spoken as banshee. What he had been taught by the Treize though, what he was told by his father and his uncles, was turning out to be very different to what was documented in *The Collected Banshee Histories*.

In the book, they weren't considered weaker than other supernaturals or powerless. Historically banshees were viewed as goddesses by their people, a belief that spread as banshees migrated off the mainland and to neighbouring areas in Scotland and Wales. They never moved further than that for some reason, but it didn't seem to restrict their powers at any rate. They could see endlessly, perceiving death in its various forms. Yet because they were so valued by the Irish, many banshees chose only to foresee and lament the deaths of traditional Irish families.

Banshees had previously shared their prophetic knowledge with the Treize and other supernatural beings for the betterment of all. Somewhere along the line that changed. Something shifted, so they would only warn the Irish of impending doom. That decision was the beginning of the end, as eventually the people that loved them so much grew to hate the women who cried and mourned their loved ones alongside them. It was the opportunity the Treize needed, with human and supernatural governments banding together to condemn the otherworld women. Their punishment was to be dragged from the country that had birthed them and displaced to somewhere else entirely, where there was no knowledge or care for what they were.

He sat up, leaning over the book with such intensity his nose almost touched the page. Since the introduction of The Covenant, generations of banshee women had been stuck within Australia, unable to prosper, unable to leave, unable to prevent their kind from weakening, growing mad, and eventually dying out. The thing he didn't know, the thing he'd never been told, was what happened when the women of the otherworld repressed their powers. They went mad. When their gifts were turned inwards instead of outwards, it ate away at them. He thought immediately of Máire Burke, the way she had changed not just physically – the once striking woman's youth dissolving, the lines in her face deepening – but mentally, as her mind turned to mush. It was a slow, cruel fate.

No wonder parts of the supernatural population thought banshees had died out. The knowledge of what they had once been – worshipped, goddesses, beloved – hadn't made it down the grapevine to the present generation still surviving. He recognised this as misinformation that had been moulded into a lie. Maybe it was to protect the Treize at first, or even others, but the means had stopped justifying the ends *decades* ago. And with that, he thought of Sadie. Always Sadie.

Was he completely warped into believing what his family told him, what *everyone* had told him? Severing her vocal cords was the only option, they'd said. It was the only way to keep her alive and the feared banshee wail at bay permanently. He wasn't sure if that was true any more. There were so many *other* lies. And if that was a lie, the whole tower of cards was beginning to look incredibly shaky. Amongst it all, there she was: seemingly sweet on the outside, but with more teeth than people gave her credit for. Her appearance at The Wisdom trailing Denton had proven as much. Despite their time apart, he realised he and Sadie might have more in common than they initially thought as they both kept sticking their necks out in pursuit of the truth.

It was inevitable he'd end up back at the library. Even on a weekend, it was pretty busy with a few dozen people scattered throughout the space when he entered. He walked by all of the tables, gripping the handrail as he headed directly up to the third floor, slumping on the ground against one of the bookshelves as he watched Fairuza dangle from her harness in the middle of the arched ceiling. His blood was pulsing with everything he had learned and he couldn't stop his foot from tapping against the carpet as he watched her. He was jittery. It was probably half an hour before she zip-lined over to him, book in hand as she climbed the railing and slid down beside Tex.

'Didn't find the answers you were looking for?' she asked, not mentioning *The Collected Banshee Histories* but it being the ever-present subject nonetheless.

'I found some.'

'But not the ones you were expecting. Or even ones you're comfortable now knowing.'

He straightened up, back stiff as his head spun to look at her. Fairuza wasn't watching him, instead her skin glinted in the warm lighting of the library as she looked down at the floors below them, stroking her tusks as if deep in thought.

'How could you possibly know that?' he asked, voice tense as he wondered not for the first time if he was being watched in exactly the same way he'd been tasked with watching Denton.

'It's a . . . type of perception,' she said, the phrasing of her words seeming cautious and intentional to him. 'I can perceive certain *feelings*, anticipate what people need, not what they want.'

'Like the book.'

'Like the book,' she agreed.

'I guess that makes you a pretty good librarian.'

'That, and the fact I live for quite some time, means no one can fuck up my cataloguing system for a few centuries at least. Not without me drinking their marrow.'

He smirked, but the expression was wiped off his face pretty quickly when he came to the realisation Fairuza was most likely not joking. He'd wondered at the time whether the demon giving him the book was a test of sorts, to see whether he reported it to the Treize. Then he re-examined what had happened, how he'd been sprung reading his father's old Askari journals, studying the details of *that night*. What Sadie had told him about the demon knowing her older sister, Sorcha, confirmed that it had been a test – but not for the Treize. The question of 'for whom' lingered as they sat side by side.

'Right,' she said, exhaling. 'I suppose you have some queries, comments, general feedback.'

He threw her a sideways look, resisting the urge to burst out laughing at the understatement of the century.

'Just a few,' he murmured.

'You better get to it then. If there's one thing I've learned about your kind, it's that you never have as much time as you think.'

'I know the odds of Askari living past forty,' Texas replied. 'Being the first, very mortal point of contact for monsters has its drawbacks.'

'Not for your father. I heard once he accepted that immortal Custodians gig, off he skipped to immortal assholery.'

'I don't want to talk about my father.'

'Said everyone with daddy issues ever.'

'I want to talk about the Burkes.'

'I bet you do,' she murmured, her mouth twitching slightly. 'So talk.'

'Banshee abilities are echoes of what their ancestors could once do.'

'Incorrect, that's Treize talk.'

He looked around them pointedly, at the thousands of Treize books sitting in a Treize library in Treize Australian headquarters. She ignored him.

'Try again.'

He huffed, choosing his words more carefully.

'Banshee abilities are . . . echoes of what their ancestors *can* do?'

'Better,' she mused. 'Now your reading comprehension is on the level.'

'Not all banshee women could wail and cry and lament,' he said, compacting everything he had been reading over the past few days just to see if Fairuza would dispute it. 'Not all could foresee death, the same way not all could sense a growing sickness in some. Yet most banshees originally had several gifts – not one – and those are reflected in the Burke siblings.'

He'd worked through some of this stuff himself, based on what was in the family's case files as well. But there were blanks he was hoping the demon would fill.

'Máire Burke's gift is closer to curse, or was, with her being aware of specifically when a loved one is going to die. The eldest, Shannon, can see certain death scenes play out in a body of water – usually when washing clothes. It's a filtered version of a trait specific to the part of Ireland their ancestry comes from, County Galway.'

When researching this, Texas had wondered if the matriarch of the family had any sense of Shannon's gift at birth, given she was named after River Shannon, the longest river in Ireland.

'They equate her ability with being able to read tea leaves,' Fairuza said. 'But there are *old* legends of the death-messenger that centre around women seen washing the blood-stained clothes of soldiers in a river. There was even a washerwoman seen near the river on the eve of the Battle of Aughrim in sixteen ninety-one, beetling clothes just like the war goddess *Badhbh*.'

'You're saying the legend manifested in Shannon?'

'You're saying that. I'm not correcting you.'

So that's a yes, he thought, marking off a checklist in his head.

'Nora can draw scenes of death, although not truly seeing them herself.'

'She's a conduit for the visions, yes.'

'Ina can sense terminal illness. I remember when I was eight, she identified a type of cancer in David long before the doctors knew it was there.'

'Bet she regrets that gesture now.'

'Keavy can write poems that prove prophetic and Catriona can locate dead bodies when they're close, which given their line of work is often. And Sorcha . . .'

92

He trailed off. This was one of the blanks he was hoping she would fill.

'It harks back to one of the oldest and purest powers of the *bean sí*,' Fairuza said, using the ancient word for banshee. 'She can elicit some control over others with speech, but it's her movements that hold power.'

'Can,' he remarked. 'You're using present tense. She's presumed dead.'

'And yet, no body.'

'You two were friends.'

'Who told you that?'

She was intrigued by the fact Texas had this information, he could see it on her face. That didn't last long, however, as she leaned back with an interested 'huh'.

'Sadie,' Fairuza whispered, answering her own query. 'The youngest, the one brimming with possibility. I dare say what they did to her was what motivated Sorcha to break The Covenant and flee this country. Or try to, at least.'

'How so?'

'Sadie showed that if you couldn't learn how to properly suppress your powers, the Treize would snatch them away.'

'She was getting stronger?' he questioned. 'That's why she left? That doesn't make any sense, banshees grow weaker—'

'The longer they repress their powers. If they're not repressing them, what happens? And no, don't look at me like that. It's not in the book. The OG banshees never had to repress their natures simply to exist. That's a new development.'

The way she said 'development' made it clear what the intended message was to Tex. Development. Rule. Restriction.

'I need to know what happened to Sorcha,' he said.

'Why?'

'Because maybe I can prevent the same fate for Sadie.'

'You think you can just swan back into the country and fix the mistakes of a decade ago? That's not how it works.'

He didn't disagree. There were things that could never be fixed. Big things. The little things, however . . .

'You knew her,' he pushed. 'Tell me. Please.'

'She left on a cruise ship full of monsters, although you probably know that much from the files.'

'I did, yes.'

Tasmanian devil shifters had been running a trafficking operation out of Australia for nearly a century now and no matter how many the Praetorian Guard were able to find and stamp out, another always popped up. Land, sea, air, it didn't matter. They were as resourceful as they were resilient and as long as there were creatures the Treize was trying to control, there would be creatures trying to escape that reign regardless of whether it was in their best interests or not.

'A Praetorian Guard patrol had been on their foam soon as they passed North Stradbroke,' Fairuza said.

'How did they know? I mean, the devils are notoriously good at slipping under the radar.'

'Dodgy, too. Unregulated, it's hard to tell how many monsters have gone missing en route to their destinations when the devils are in charge. It's not an option you take if you have other ones at your disposal, you understand?'

He nodded. Living beings were just the beginning of things the devils were known to smuggle, with containers carrying everything from alchemist-enhanced narcotics to goblin children found dumped at ports.

'Regardless of how they knew, they knew. She broke The Covenant and they were in pursuit of her.'

'But they didn't get her.'

'They got twenty, survivors who were all rescued and swiftly thrown in Vankila. But the ship sunk off the coast of North Queensland. How? No one can say.'

'Cruise ships don't just sink.'

'They don't, do they?'

From the handful of survivor accounts they had, there were conflicting reports of *something* that got loose on board. Something terrifying. Well, more terrifying than a boat run by Tasmanian devils with a questionable moral compass, that is.

'They recovered a few hundred bodies, parts of a few hundred more, but Sorcha's was not among them.'

'The odds of her surviving . . .'

There was a long silence from Fairuza as she stared out at the library beneath them, ignoring a flag that had been raised at a desk for assistance. It wasn't until one of his uncles entered through the front doors that the demon made a move to leave.

'You didn't know her,' she said, her final words to him as she descended to the main floor. Gavino turned to watched her exit as he climbed the stairs to join Texas, the man unable to hide his curiosity.

'What are you doing talking to her?' he barked.

'The librarian?' Texas asked, getting to his feet with a sigh. 'It's a library.'

'Yeah, but you don't have to come here. Just order the books you need, they'll bring them to your office.'

'I haven't got an office yet. I've been working out of my car.'

'We're figuring that out. David's getting someone fired, so you'll have a space by next week.'

'Great,' he replied, unable to make it sound properly sincere.

'Come on, we need your help with a ghoul nest.'

Following Gavino from the library, he found it interesting how uncomfortable his uncle seemed in there. Knowledge was supposed to be a key tenant of their role as Askari. Yet it was becoming more and more clear to him just how little his family knew.

He wasn't sure what he expected, but after The Wisdom he thought Sadie and he had come through the other side of something. They'd confided in each other. She'd kept his secrets and he'd kept hers. But as he spent the next few days following the Burke sisters from crime scene to crime scene, monitoring their work and their behaviour as he had been tasked, it became apparent that she was avoiding him. He even made several efforts to get her alone so they could talk, *properly* talk.

When the opportunity finally came, it was when he least expected it. He'd been watching Sadie from a safe distance across the other side of a crime scene – giving her the space she'd so clearly indicated she wanted – when he saw it happen. He'd only read about it, never actually seen it occur in real life, so he wasn't sure what he was witnessing at first. She was carrying a green cleaning kit, the same one all of her sisters had in varying colours, but she froze mid-step. Her fingers went stiff as the kit fell to the ground, rolling on to its side with a plastic *thunk*. Her whole body went still as a statue, Tex momentarily forgetting what he had promised himself and crossing the space between them in several urgent steps.

'Sadie?' he said, voice worried as he touched her gently on the shoulder. But she didn't see him – couldn't – and he doubted whether she could even feel him. The usual hazy green-brown of her eyes was disappearing, Tex stepping back with a sharp intake of breath as red spread through the whites of her eyeballs and eventually covered her pupils.

'What is it?' Shannon said, rushing over to join them.

'I ... I think she has a burst blood vessel in her eye. Her eyes, even.'

'Get out of the way, boy scout,' she hissed, shoving him to the side. 'It's not a burst blood vessel, she's *seeing*.'

'Seeing?'

'Someone's death, right now, that's what it looks like.'

'*For the* bean sí *will have blood red eyes from the constant weeping*,' he muttered, reciting a passage from *The Collected Banshee Histories*. '*And blood will stream down her cheeks, thick with knowledge of the dead and dying*.'

'The tales all come from somewhere,' Shannon replied, the two of them standing side by side as they watched her. 'But there's no tears of blood: at least none that I've ever seen.'

'How long does she stay like this?'

'As long as the vision lasts: it plays out in real time.'

'And she sees their final moments? Whoever this person is, minute by minute?'

'Second by horrible second. The longest one I ever saw was three minutes, but they're usually a little quicker than that ... Nora! *Nora!*'

There were a series of footsteps from upstairs, the second oldest Burke sister quickly appearing in the doorway.

'Bloody what?'

'Sadie's having a vision. Get your sketchpad.'

'Shit.'

Mask resting on her forehead, she disappeared just as quickly as she materialised and sprinted out of sight.

'Take her hand, Tex, guide her to Jan the Van outside. Watch the ghoul faecal matter on the floor – they shit like cockroaches when they're dying.'

Shannon wasn't wrong, with the ruins of an industrial kitchen positively showered with what looked like black spray paint. It was, in fact, ghoul faecal matter and actually dark green when examined under the light. A contingent of Praetorian Guard soldiers had been made to raid this site, which had been a popular restaurant on the water at Glebe Point once. Yet the business had gone under and the location eventually falling into disrepair. It came on the Treize radar a few months back when natural fauna in the area started disappearing, then local cats and dogs, until finally a toddler had been taken a week ago. It all led to an investigation and eventually a ghoul hunt, with the bottom levels of this building infested by a small nest. There was a large opening for a sewer system nearby, creating the perfect environment for the creatures to slink from their usual underground dwellings and make their home in the dank, damp building.

There was truly nowhere safe to take Sadie, so he understood why Shannon had suggested their van. He wasn't sure about leading her by the hand, but he was interested to note how her limbs appeared to function as normal if given a little guidance – even while her mind was somewhere else entirely. He had to watch both of their steps carefully, lifting her knee to walk over a collapsed floorboard and taking her out of the building's main doorway carefully. They were crossing the lawn and nearly at the van when the rest of the Burke sisters swarmed, Shannon dashing past him and opening up the vehicle doors. She had a hidden mattress rolled out and laying down inside the van within seconds, placing a bottle of water, another of Fanta, and a packet of beef jerky alongside it.

'Keep working!' Shannon yelled at her siblings, Ina, Catriona and Keavy as they followed her out of the abandoned restaurant. They paused mid-step when they were told they weren't needed.

'Do as she says,' Nora punctuated as she pushed past them, 'We've got this. Finishing the clean in the scheduled time will help more, especially if we've got another job coming.'

The three figures, clad head-to-toe in their standard white jumpsuits, disappeared back inside as Tex reached up and lifted Sadie's mask from her mouth. Gently, he placed it on her head as he tugged the coveralls away from her face, the elastic that had held them in place leaving a mark on her skin.

'Get in ass first, Tex; I'll grab her other side,' Shannon ordered. Together they eased Sadie down until she was laying flat on her back, eyes still blood red and her lips parted ever so slightly as she continued to breathe. Nora had dived into the back of the van with them as well and, between the four of them, it was starting to get cramped. She slammed the roller door shut, shielding their party from the sun outside.

'Now what?' he asked.

'We wait,' Shannon snapped.

'He shouldn't be here,' Nora muttered, speaking directly to her older sister as if Tex was already absent. 'She wouldn't want him here.'

'It's a bit late for that,' Shannon responded, leaning over Sadie and gripping her hand. 'She's already beginning to come out of it.'

'All I'm saying—'

'Leave it.'

Shannon's curt response seemed to settle the issue, yet the penetrating stare Nora gave him from across Sadie's form told him he was not welcome among them. It was minutes upon minutes of waiting. And it was excruciating. He watched as Sadie's eyelids fluttered open, her face taking in the interior of the van as they huddled and waited. She slowly slipped her hand from Shannon's, reaching out for Nora instead until her fingers rested on the exposed flesh of her arm. Her sister's left hand started flying across the paper of her sketchpad almost immediately, the movements swift and jerky as she drew. Sadie's face looked grey as she described the scene, despite the fact Nora seemed to know what to sketch just by touch alone.

'It's an office building,' she signed, letting Shannon help her into a sitting position. 'It overlooks the water: I can't see the Harbour Bridge, but I can sense that it's close, maybe just out of range to my left. The space is empty, everyone has gone home for the day, so the man doesn't see the elemental come up behind him . . . he's smoke, so he shifts in and out of perception.'

'Is it night?' Nora pushed. 'Can you see a clock anywhere?'

'It's early evening, the light is red and warm but fading. The man is hit from behind, blood spraying from his nose as he whacks the keyboard. A knife slips from somewhere, it's in the elemental's hand, the gold hilt plunging into the man's back over and over again. He's making this awful, choking noise as he tries to reach for a weapon. He dies with his fingers gripped around a stapler. The elemental shifts away, but he leaves the knife wedged in the victim's back.'

'Hella Roman,' Nora muttered, not looking up from the page.

'Is the dead man human?' Shannon questioned, opening the can of Fanta and handing it to Sadie. She took a big sip, finishing half the drink before passing it back to her. Her hands moved slowly as she communicated her thoughts.

'I can't tell. Visibly he looks human, but that could mean he's a werewolf or a medium or even a well-disguised goblin. Demon, maybe. I can't feel what he is, though.'

The plastic of the beef jerky packet crinkled as Sadie opened it, eyes wide as she plopped a small piece in her mouth and chewed. It seemed like several moments before she blinked, and, as she did so, she properly realised that Tex was there. Her hand was holding a fresh bit of jerky and was on its way to her mouth when she paused. Quickly, she placed it in her mouth and when both of her hands were free again she communicated her question.

'What are you doing here?' she asked him.

'Told you,' Nora mumbled. He opened his mouth to reply, but Shannon cut in.

'Couldn't be helped, Sades. You spaced out right at a very inconvenient moment. We needed the assistance.'

'Where are the others?' Sadie asked.

'Finishing the job. Listen, do we think this has already happened or is it about to?'

'About to,' she signed, her eyes still watching Tex.

'Welp, shame we can't warn the fella. But we can be there right on time when he's axed. It's only two now so . . .'

'The time on his desktop says six fifty-two p.m.,' Nora said, sighing with contentment as she finished her drawing. He leaned forward to look at it, but Sadie stopped him.

'I need to talk to Tex,' she signed at her sisters, looking at them meaningfully. 'Alone.'

'Get fucked,' was Nora's immediate response, grabbing a rag to wipe the lead from the fingers of her right hand, which she had used for smudging.

'Please.'

Shannon flashed him a look, but he threw up his hands with surprise. He didn't know what this was about either.

'Come on,' the eldest sister said, gently shoving Nora with her.

'What? You can't be—'

Sadie's other sibling had her protests cut off as Shannon slammed the door to the van behind them, locking them into this prism of silence. *This isn't so different to my car that night,* he thought warmly. Except for the big, looming third party: death. He was surprised to see Sadie had held on to Nora's drawing and his eyes focused in on it as she held it out to him for inspection. It looked somewhat like an M. C. Escher sketch, not surrealist at all but grey and white in the colouring and meticulous in its detail. A million-dollar view stretched out from the windows of a sky-rise office building, work stations positioned in orderly cubes and all empty. Except for one, which contained the body of a man slumped over at his desk, dagger plunged deep within his shoulders. It was the background image on the desktop of his computer that gave Tex pause as he recognised both the dead and the living around him in the photograph.

'That's Denton,' he whispered, looking up at her with shock. She had seen him die in her vision, so of course Sadie knew exactly who it was.

'He's still alive,' Sadie signed at him, before grabbing his wrist to inspect the time on his watch. 'At least for another few hours anyway. My visions aren't always after the fact.'

'I didn't know that,' he murmured, making eye contact with her for the first time in almost a week. It felt like she saw right through him.

'And it wasn't an elemental who killed him.'

She had lied to her sisters. Hell, she'd lied *in front* of her sisters.

'What? I mean, if not an elemental then . . .'

He paused as she wrote down the names at the bottom of the drawing. David. Gavino.

'Y-you . . . you saw my uncles kill Denton Boys.'

She nodded. 'Today.'

'They said they were just going to meet with him.'

'And you believed them?' she signed, each word blurring into the other as her motions got faster with anger and he fought to discern her meaning. 'I thought you were smart, Tex.'

He opened his mouth to reply, but there was nothing to say. Instead, he used Auslan. He was better at reading it than using it thanks to a years-long online course, but he'd had no one to practise with. Sadie's eyes narrowed as she watched him, reading what he signed in the air. Her head snapped up.

'You know where this is,' she motioned back at him.

He nodded. 'Denton's "desk duty" is administration at a Treize hospital. Not that far from The Wisdom, actually. I can fix this.'

'How? How can you possibly fix this?' she scoffed. 'Not everything can be fixed, Texas.'

He wasn't sure what they were talking about any more.

'This can be.'

'You can't say a word,' she warned him. 'Not a peep.'

'The Covenant,' he sighed, squinting his eyes shut with frustration as he fought the headache growing there. '*Fuck.*'

'Welcome to ten seconds of life as a banshee.'

'No banshee is to forewarn others about their impending doom, upon penalty of death,' he said, the words seared into his brain as much as they were hers. 'No banshee may intervene with fate's plan, upon penalty of death. I'm not a banshee, Sadie. I don't have to forewarn him about his death, I don't have to break The Covenant, I can just . . . make sure he's not there at six fifty-two p.m.'

'And put him where, exactly? He's not going to trust you: he doesn't trust any of you.'

'I can meet him at his workplace,' he mused. 'Then just get him somewhere . . . else.'

'What if your uncles have orders from the Treize?' she asked. 'What if they've been ordered to kill him?'

'They haven't,' he said, shaking his head. 'I was under instruction to relieve Denton of his duties and monitor him, see who he might lead us back to.'

'Do they know that?'

'The first part, yes. The second part, no.'

So what does killing him achieve? he wondered.

'I have to go, get there as far ahead of time as possible. It will be less suspicious.'

He leapt forward and over Sadie, yanking open the rolling door of the van. He was slapped in the face by a gust of fresh air as his feet hit the grass below, Texas digging in his pocket for car keys. He felt Sadie's eyes on him, fixated, and when he glanced up she looked worried.

'Nobody can know this came from us,' she signed. 'Me especially.'

'Don't worry. I have as much to lose in this as you do. I won't say a word and I'd never let anything happen to you.'

Again, he thought. *I'd never let anything happen to you again.* He felt hot all of a sudden, as if he was sweating under his dress shirt and trousers. He tugged at his tie with discomfort, feeling the press of time with each passing second.

'I've got to go, I'll let you know what happens.'

'Death can't be cheated.'

'Don't tell that to the Custodians and Praetorian Guard,' he chuckled. 'Immortality is their shiniest prize.'

'They can still die though, it's just if they're left alone they'll endure.'

'Sure.' He shrugged, eyeing his car across the street.

'If you save him today, there's no saying what will happen tomorrow.'

'Hey, we've all gotta die some day.'

'Some day is better than today,' Sadie signed, her lips smirking as she did so. He smiled back at her, moving his own hands to sign a reply.

'Exactly.'

With a final wave, he offered her a farewell and sprinted towards his car. He could do something good today: he could save a man's life. He could save his uncles from becoming murderers. The idea fuelled him as he slid into the driver's seat and revved the engine. As a bonus, he could do it with the assistance of the Burke sisters and the Treize never needed to know about it. He dropped the handbrake, speeding off towards his destination.

Chapter 5

SADIE

Sadie hated silence: she loathed it with every fibre of her being. That worked out well for her, given the respective Burke households were scarcely ever quiet. But even on the rare occasions she was alone, Sadie needed noise: more specifically, she liked there to be talking. That's why she had AirPods on and the volume turned way up as she listened to an old episode of her favourite podcast, *Thirst Aid Kit*. They didn't make new ones any more and she had heard this episode about a thousand times. Perhaps it was a combination of the hosts familiar voices or that week's subject – the bangability of John Cho – that felt like a relief to her. When you were surrounded by death all the time – both professionally and personally – escapism was important, John Cho's kind eyes were *important*.

And her mind was buzzing with worries, each one aggressively flying around in her brain as she waited to hear from Texas. Twenty-four hours and one sleepless night later, there had still been nothing. No word from him about whether he had been successful or not. No word about whether Denton was dead. No words at all. The waiting made her sick and she'd spent as long as she could at home, pacing, fidgeting, avoiding the inquisitive eyes of her sisters. She had to get out, so she did. It had rained that morning, meaning the usually packed Camperdown Memorial Rest Park was empty as she walked down the footpath. Sadie was sad about it, as the main reason she chose this route for her stroll was the sheer number of dogs that were usually bounding along the grass. She desperately wanted a dog: a big, dumb boxer that dribbled over everything she loved. Or a Staffordshire bull terrier so wide it had to waddle, but fiercely loyal nonetheless.

There was no space for a dog in any one of the Burke households. She knew Nora and Deepika were planning on moving out in the New Year, but her sister was yet to broach that subject with any of her other siblings. Shannon getting her own place – even three doors down – had caused a huge fight at the time, exaggerated further when Ina sweetened the pot and went with her. It didn't matter that Shannon was pregnant and Ina had just gotten married: Aoife didn't understand why they all couldn't stay together, as they had previously. Her cousins had vocally felt the same way, along with Catriona and Keavy. Sadie and Nora had sided with Ina and Shannon, while her mother remained mute. As for Sorcha . . . well, she was gone years ago.

Mud squelched under Sadie's feet as she veered off the footpath, correcting her course as she took a right on Church Street. The wet weather had brought a break in the heat, which she was grateful for as she sipped the warm coffee in her hands. She was unsurprised to find Camperdown Cemetery deserted as she crossed through the gates that led into the grounds. The fact this place was a graveyard didn't seem to bother most people; it was usually populated with locals walking their pets or kids chasing each other around the gravestones.

On Friday mornings, the New South Wales Dog Unit used it as a place to train puppies they were hoping to turn into bona fide police dogs. It was Sadie's favourite thing, arriving a little before 9 a.m. and watching the instructors run the pups through a series of drills and exercises that increased in difficulty over the course of their training. At the end of each session, someone usually called her over and she was allowed to pet them. Few things in the world brought her more joy and she settled in at the foot of her regular gravestone, which was dry enough that she felt only a mild dampness through the tights she was wearing under her dress. Resting the back of her head against the cool concrete, she listened to the chatter coming through her headphones while she waited. And waited. Then waited some more. The podcast episode ended and she checked her phone as she clicked on another one, this time about Mahershala Ali. It was past 9.30 a.m.

Maybe the location changed because of the weather, she thought. Sadie tried to quell the rising swell of disappointment she felt in her stomach. Today was her day off, her family knew her ritual, and it was the one day she could count on being left alone. Closing her eyes, Sadie realised she wasn't so sure that she wanted to be in that moment. Starting the day with puppies just seemed right and now there was a distinct lack of them. She felt cheated, somehow. So she let her mind wander to a favourite daydream, one that involved Jason Momoa and naughty things, dirty things, followed by breakfast in bed. She felt a grin rising on her lips as her brain went there, this being an old fantasy she had visited enough times that she had all the specifics worked out.

There was a gentle touch on her shoulder and she leapt forwards, startled from her daydream and alarmed by sudden contact in the *real* world. Her eyes flew open and her alarm only increased as she digested the sight of Texas Contos crouching down in front of her. The juxtaposition of her fantasy world and reality was a weird one and her mind swam as she processed his figure. He was completely dishevelled. In fact, she had never seen him look like such a mess: his stubble appeared to have thickened in the day since she saw him last, with his black hair tousled messily and purple bags under his eyes.

'Sorry!' he exclaimed, leaning back before repeating himself in Auslan as well. 'I didn't mean to scare you; you didn't hear me when I called your name so . . .'

In actual fact, she couldn't hear his words right then either through the noise of her podcast and the question of whether Mahershala Ali invented the colour yellow. Spoiler: he did. Yet the fact Tex was signing as he spoke meant she followed along easily, removing the AirPods and sliding them into her pocket.

'You of all people should know not to sneak up on others in a graveyard,' she told him, her hands moving angrily as she mouthed the words at the same time. She hoped her frustration covered the blush she knew was colouring the pale, freckled skin of her cheeks as she prayed that what she had been thinking about wasn't written all over her face in neon ink.

'Me of all people?' he asked, looking amused.

'That should be rule number one in the Askari handbook,' Sadie continued, ignoring his outstretched hand as she got to her feet. 'Do not sneak up on people in a graveyard, regardless of what time of day it is.'

'And regardless of whether the subject of said sneaking cleans up crime scenes for a living or watches people die on the regular?'

She scowled at his comment, observing as he attempted to wipe the amused expression from his face and replace it with one more serious.

'Sorry,' Tex repeated. 'I didn't mean to scare you.'

'It's alright,' Sadie conceded, waiting a beat before she did something she didn't expect. She leaned forward, throwing her arms around his neck and enveloped him in a hug. He seemed shocked by the gesture at first, but she didn't care as she closed her eyes and inhaled the scent of him. After a moment, she felt his hands around her waist as he hugged her back. When she pulled away, putting adequate space between them again, she felt immediately awkward about the outburst.

'I didn't hear from you,' she signed. 'I didn't know—'

'It's okay,' he said, cutting her off and looking as uncomfortable as she felt. 'I mean, it's not okay. I'm okay, but I just didn't have time to . . . I'm sorry, I should have reached out sooner. And then it was a day later and I just wanted to come and find you instead.'

'What happened?'

'Ha, so much. But I'm starving, can we find somewhere to eat around here first?'

'That's not a graveyard?' Sadie signed.

'If you don't mind.'

'I know a place,' she told him, gesturing towards the church nearby that led to the only entry and exit out of the cemetery.

He fell instep beside her, Sadie unable to help but feel

self-conscious as they walked back through the park. Clouds still covered every inch of the sky, but their colouring was closer to a whitish grey rather than the earlier black. Tex was silent as they walked, his hands deep within the pockets of his trousers and a bag slung over his shoulders bumping with the movement of his thighs. A few local pet owners had emerged from their homes, bravely letting their dogs run loose through the puddles of mud that pooled in the deepest dip of Camperdown Memorial Rest Park. He must have been watching her out of the corner of his eye, following the way her attention was focused on the animals as they bounded without the restriction of a leash.

'Do you want to hear a theory?' he asked, speaking and signing at the same time. She got the impression he was trying to get better, to practise, because his signals weren't great.

'Sure,' she responded, her left hand moving down on to her right. To the casual observer it would have looked like she was indicating a karate chop rather than the Auslan meaning for a number of words depending on the context, including 'sure'.

'That graveyard you like to hang out in? Well, it used to span the entire distance of this park. And the areas around the other side too. But it got neglected and overgrown, with the body of a murdered girl being found there in the forties. So the local council decided to reclaim the space, which was taking up a little too much prime real estate in an increasingly popular suburb. They put up a wall around the church and immediate grounds, moving the most important gravestones there for display.'

'What happened to all the other bodies?'

'For the most part, they left 'em. Most of the gravestones don't actually correspond to the locations of the deceased. Instead they're everywhere, all around and beneath us. That's why I think dogs love this park so much: they can sense all the hyper chewable bones just beneath their feet. *Thousands of them.*'

She laughed, feeling the rumble in her throat but no audible sound emerging as her shoulders shook with the physical reaction.

'It's a good theory,' she signed.

'Right? I think so.'

'It also explains why Catriona never comes here: she avoids this park at all costs. She'll even walk right around it rather than cut through.'

Sadie ran a hand along the exposed skin of her arms, indicating what she was trying to tell him.

'Yeah, I imagine it would feel like her pores are alive.'

'Not pleasant,' Sadie agreed.

They passed her favourite pub on the left, the Courthouse Hotel, and came to a stop just before the local fire station. Tex looked as if he would have continued walking right past the café she gestured at, peering through the doorway with surprise as if he hadn't seen it at all. It was small, tiny almost, yet somehow it always managed to fit more people than you would expect at first glance. 212 Blu was distinctly *her* spot, the same way you fell in love with a local restaurant or corner store or book shop and emotionally marked it as your own. There were about a dozen people inside, sectioned off in small groups who sat at wooden tables each decorated with glass bottles that held a bouquet of native flowers. There were a few others drinking coffee on the bench outside, including a woman who had a French bulldog laying across her feet, limbs splayed in every direction.

'Cute,' Tex muttered, his eyes scanning the space until he picked a spot at the front window.

Sadie noted the way he took the furthest stool, with the wall at his back and the coffee machine to his right. They had a full view of the street from their vantage point, Tex looking skittish as his eyes roamed over the antique shop across the road and the pizzeria next door. If he was searching for something, she was certain he didn't find it as he let out the smallest sigh of relief. A waiter came to take their orders and she looked at him expectantly.

'Order for me.' He shrugged. 'This is your local, right?'

She nodded, tapping at an item on the menu to indicate she would like the tuna sandwich, before holding up two fingers. The staff were used to her here, with it being years since she had to write down what she wanted on the small notebook she carried with her at all times for purposes exactly like this. They'd developed a point and order system now, which was mostly useless since she pretty much always had the same thing. The waiter nodded, repeating her order back to her. Just before they were about to walk away Sadie grabbed their arm, indicating over her shoulder to the list of beverages that were written high on the wall behind the counter.

'And . . . uh, a Bloody Mary? *Two* Bloody Marys?'

She grinned and tossed him a thumbs up, the waiter grabbing their menus and heading towards the small kitchen to pass on their orders.

'Bloody Marys?' Tex smirked, when the waiter was out of earshot. He frowned as he tried to form the words in sign language, it not being a common phrase for either of them.

'You look like you could do with one,' she signed back at him. 'Or six coffees. Maybe seven.'

He laughed, running a hand over his face as if he was exhausted before staring at her appreciatively. It made Sadie uncomfortable, his gaze so openly fixed on her as she fidgeted with the cutlery.

'What?' she asked him.

'Nothing,' he answered, shaking his head slightly and looking away. But it was only a few seconds before his eyes had flicked back to staring at her. She stopped toying with the fork in her fingers, setting it down and turning to face him with an arched eyebrow.

'Okay, okay,' he said, breathily. 'It's just nice, being here in a café with you, like normal people.'

'We're not normal people.'

'I know.'

It could have been all in her own head, but she felt the weight of that admission. *I know.*

'So you did it?' she signed. 'You got him out of there?'

'Yes and no. I was halfway to the Treize hospital when I changed my mind. I'd have no reason for being there *except* to see Denton. It would just seem too out of character. I made an official request for him to come and see me at Treize headquarters instead, immediately, then I kept him there for hours.'

'Hours?'

'*Hours.* I got through some obligatory handover stuff quicker than I thought and I had nothing else to keep him there and I was stretching it and stretching it. It was just before 7 p.m. so I couldn't risk him going back to the office. I made him come to the VCC with me.'

'VCC?'

'Vampire Conservation Committee,' he said, with a flick of his wrist. 'It's not important. What is important is that thing really, truly, utterly *drags* out.'

She smiled, offering him a thumbs up. As far as half-assed plans that had been scrambled together went, that was a pretty good one.

'By the time we got out of there, it was nearly midnight. The window had well and truly passed, but . . . I don't know. I still had a bad feeling.'

'Tuna sandwiches and Bloody Marys,' the waiter announced, delivering their order in front of them. 'You guys need anything else?'

'No,' he said, speaking for the both of them. 'This looks great, thank you.'

They were quiet for the first few mouthfuls, Tex inhaling half of the sandwich, pausing only to take a sip of his drink before devouring the other. She took a few cautious bites, spending more time with her Bloody Mary as she watched him. When he was done – in what seemed like a mere matter of seconds – he wiped his hands and turned to Sadie with a serious expression.

'I suggested we get a drink at The Wisdom,' he said, picking up where he left off.

She frowned, immediately worried about where this was going.

'Wind down, you know? He said yes and . . . well, that's when I had the wombats take him.'

She nearly choked on the sip of her drink she was about to swallow, the mix of spice, vodka, and tomato juice burning her throat as she gulped it down while trying to take a breath.

'Take him? What do you mean, take him?'

'Just get him off the street for a few days, hide him, keep Denton out of the path of my uncles until I can figure out why they want him dead. And who he's working for or with.'

Sadie blinked, her mind blank with shock for a moment. Then it faded, slowly replaced with panic.

'Texas,' she signed. 'How could you be so stupid? I . . .'

She didn't know where to begin; he'd left her utterly flummoxed.

'No, hear me out,' he started. 'We have him in one place now, he's not going anywhere. And he's not dead. He's away from his family; they won't be in harm's way when my uncles go looking for him, which has probably already happened. The wombats can be trusted.'

'Why? Because you shagged Shazza's sister? This isn't a shell game, Texas. I don't think you understand how serious this: Denton is in some deep shit. That woman he was talking to was a demon from Berlin with ties to *goblins* and *werewolves*. You should have got him out of harm's way and then left it. This is too much; this is too big.'

She was worried she was hyperventilating, suddenly feeling breathless as she got to her feet to try and allow more oxygen into her lungs.

'Hey, are you okay? Sadie, you look—'

'You've spent too long in some Askari day spa. I don't know why I thought you were different, why I thought you'd come back *different*. You've forgotten what it's like out here in the real world for the rest of us supernaturals, Texas.'

'What does that mean?'

She gestured at her throat angrily, the movement looking to anyone else like she was miming choking herself. In a way, that wasn't so far from the truth.

'Blood. Death. Murder. If you're in their way, they'll kill you. You cannot get in their way, even if you're a nine-year-old fucking kid.'

She grabbed her bag, which was tucked under the chair, and threw it over her shoulder.

'Please,' he said, catching her hand.

'You can get the bill,' she told him, spinning on her heels and walking out of the café as fast as she could. He didn't chase after her, despite how much she wanted him to. She imagined his shell-shocked face sitting in the window of 212 Blu just the way she had left him. The rain had started up again as she set a quick pace for home, not bothering to wipe the tears from her face as they mingled with the weather. She was drenched by the time she made it home, the pale blue of one of her favourite dresses now dark as it carried the added weight of the water.

Sadie preferred clothing that was as far removed from the standard issue white coveralls she had to wear in her day job as she could possibly get. In a word: pretty. At least that was her aim. Sorcha had once joked that she had twenty versions of the same floral dress hanging in her wardrobe, just in different colours. She didn't have a witty retort at hand, because her sister was right. All of them were short, falling to mid-thigh in length, and the sleeves were loose and flowing. Some had discreet frills and layers, others had ornate buttons sewn into the fabric, but all were cinched at the waist and cut just low enough at the cleavage to accentuate two of her best physical features. In the moment, she wanted to rip her stupid, unofficial uniform off her body as she stomped up the stairs and slammed the door to her room. Was she throwing a tantrum? Maybe, but fear made you do irrational things.

As she grabbed a pillow from her bed and curled into a ball, she closed her eyes and told herself to breathe. What Tex had done scared her, and, in reaction, she'd run from him as quickly as she could. She was ashamed by that momentarily, yet she didn't regret it. *Please*, she begged, not sure who she was begging to. *Please don't let this be as bad as I think it is.* She repeated the mantra to herself, over and over again, as she gripped the pillow even tighter and fell asleep.

Sadie woke with a sudden gasp of pain, a sharp sensation starting at the base of her brain. The sun had set outside, with her having unexpectedly slept through the afternoon and early evening. It was testament to how bad her mood was that none of her sisters had come to wake her. Turned out, she didn't need the human alarm clock as she recognised the pain as the beginning of a vision. *Not now, please not now.* Yet her ability had never listened to her before and it wasn't about to start, the scene in her room disappearing before her eyes as something else replaced it.

She recognised Tex immediately, the pace and gait of his walk burned into her brain. He was in a park somewhere, at night, and at first she couldn't tell where it was. Yet as he passed a fountain, she recognised the figure standing at the centre of the jets of water. He was in Hyde Park, she thought, and it was late: very late. The whole place was clear except for him and a few drunks stumbling through on their way to the clubs. He glanced left and then right, before crossing the road and walking towards the towering structure of St Mary's Cathedral. Her blood was pulsing as she watched, it seeming like he was in no immediate danger but Sadie had seen these moments play out enough times to know that if she was seeing Tex like this, it wasn't because it had a happy ending.

She thought he was going to go inside the cathedral, jogging up those stairs and pushing open the elaborate wooden doors with a flourish. He didn't. Instead he walked right past the main entrance and the small balcony that sat in the courtyard, looking out on the park below as he descended a set of concrete steps. Cook + Phillip Park stretched out in front of him, the open space and lawns sitting there empty of people. It was dark and every shadow held a threat to her as she watched, her teeth biting into the flesh of her lip as he turned and strolled towards an underground car park.

There was someone waiting there for him, a figure leaning against a huge concrete pillar and smoking a cigarette as if they had watched *All the President's Men* one too many times. She saw a tired recognition cross Tex's face as he attempted to put on a smile, raising his hand in a gesture of greeting.

'Little bit heavy on the Deep Throat, aren't we?'

She saw the expression on his face falter as the person raised a gun, the weapon looking absurdly long to her as she fixated on the silencer. There was a succinct, definite sound as two shots were fired almost at point blank range. Tex barely had a second to respond or even make a grunt of surprise, the bullets hitting him between the eyes as he slumped to the ground. Face down, the figure of the first man was joined by a second as two people stood over the body. One leaned forward, checking his radial pulse.

'He's dead, David. For fuck's sake.'

'It's better to be safe than sorry.'

'It's done, then.'

'At least there's that.'

'Yeah, at least there's that.'

The vision disappeared just as suddenly as it had arrived, Sadie gasping for air as she lunged upright. Tears were swimming in her eyes as she fought to come to her senses, pushing the weakness she felt immediately after visions to the side as her mind raced. Grabbing her phone, she typed St Mary's Cathedral into the maps application and scrolled around the structure of the building, trying to follow the route she thought he had taken in her vision. And there it was: the path, the stairs, the small, blue 'P' that indicated a parking facility on the map. Sweat seemed to be drenching her body as she realised the exact thing she had feared was coming to fruition. Daydreams never came true in her world, but nightmares often did.

She had no way of knowing if her vision had already taken place or if it was yet to unfold. Something inside of her said Tex wasn't dead, not yet anyway, and if Sadie had anything to do with it that would remain so. *Please don't let me be too late*, she thought, as she grabbed the keys to Jan the Van. *Please don't let me be too late.*

Chapter 6

TEXAS

Tex should have left the library hours ago, but he was absorbed in his work. It was late and most people preferred to be elsewhere. Fairuza was the only form of company as she switched between stacking books to affixing her zip-line and zooming over the ceiling. He had headphones in his ears, the mellow sounds of The Brad Pitt Light Orchestra soothing him as he worked. After his confrontation with Sadie, he didn't know what else to do besides throw himself back into the books.

It was his coping mechanism. Was it unhealthy? Certainly, even more so when compounded with the fact he was going back over his father's journals again, taking notes, examining things he thought he'd missed. Thinking about the ritual from that night mixed with everything he'd learnt from Fairuza and *The Collected Banshee Histories* was better than giving Sadie's fears any room to bloom in his head. It was also better than visiting Denton, which Shazza had advised him strictly not to do.

'He's behaving like a complete and utter pissflap,' his friend had said in text. 'We've had to restrain him. Again. He keeps trying to escape, thinking we're going to kill him.'

It apparently didn't matter how many times Texas or Shazza explained that by keeping him hidden with the wombat shifters, they were trying to save him. The man was hysterical and completely mad with fear. Tex had nowhere else to go, not wanting to return to his apartment in case his uncles showed up and he had to pretend that everything was fine. The library was it.

At first, he'd started trying to find more detail on exactly what a banshee wail did. First-hand accounts were rare, even in the book, which just described it as 'a complete, destructive force'. Specifically what that entailed? He had no idea, yet the banshees documented with that power were feared and revered in equal measure. There was a lone illustration in *The Collected Banshees Histories* of a woman wailing, her eyes closed and her head tilted back as she cried. Bodies lay around her, while other figures clutched at their skulls in agony. He couldn't say how accurate the drawing was, having nothing to corroborate it with, but something churned inside of him. It was relief, mainly for Sadie. No one should have something this terrible at their fingertips. Even her.

He alternated between what was on paper to what was in the Treize digital database as he then attempted to look for the alchemist who had performed the 'ritual' on Sadie. He was at the point where he felt the journals could only help him so much. The key to understanding and unravelling what had been done to her vocal cords lay in the mind of the alchemist who carried out the ceremony.

With a sigh, he turned up the music on his headphones slightly and dived deeper into the alchemist database. There were a few hundred on rotation for Treize services, maybe a hundred more in full-time service, then there were the free-lancers: those who remained as insular as witches and kept to themselves. Many alchemists stuck together, with what seemed like an absurdly large number choosing to start distilleries or vineyards. He supposed there was something about the meticulous, chemical nature of those types of businesses that appealed to the alchemist mind. The woman he was looking for, however, didn't appear to be in the system. Or at least if she was, she wasn't any more. It was strange, but even if she had changed her name or appearance, Tex felt like he would know her if he passed her on the street. There was something inexplicable about the woman that he could *feel*, even though that wasn't exactly a quantifiable measure. As he flicked through faces on the screen, going over ones he had already seen and scanning their specialities, he had another thought. His mind flashed back to *The Collected Banshee Histories*, his fingers gently brushing the list of three authors who had been named at the front.

He typed 'Collette Blight' into the database, surprised to see a result returned with a Custodian file. *So she was one of them,* he thought, wondering how she had come to know so much about the plight of banshees. Maybe he could ask her? That hope was dashed as he scanned the document, noting that she had died nearly two years earlier at the age of fifty-eight in Berlin. She'd been murdered. He typed in the other two names: Iris and Geev Blight, not entirely shocked to learn they had been the woman's parents given the surname. They were dead too, having passed of natural causes just one week after the other back in the eighties. *Ah,* he thought to himself, tracking their postings. They had spent most of their Custodian roles stationed in Ireland: starting in Cork, then Dublin, Limerick, and eventually Galway.

That was likely the entry point for the banshee connection, which explained why so many extracts from the Irish Folklore Commission and their various successors appeared in the text. Whatever work they had done, their daughter had continued it. Yet Tex couldn't find any details about exactly *when* the book had been published and he had gone through it top to bottom. There was a list of published works in each of the Blight family members' files and *The Collected Banshee Histories* was not among them. He looked up, watching Fairuza in the distance as she chatted quietly with an older man leaning at the counter with a stack of books in his hands. His hair was greying, and Tex originally put his age somewhere in his late sixties, but he downgraded that number significantly the longer he looked at him.

His face cracked into a smile at something Fairuza had said, the two leaning closer together with conspirators' intent as they spoke. The gesture did something, broke some kind of shadow, as Tex realised the man was younger maybe – in his late forties, early fifties – and not as delicate or frail as he presented. In a pair of trousers, dress shoes, and a black singlet tucked tight into the waistband of his pants, Tex could see the exposed muscles on the brown skin of his wiry arms. He could see the Polynesian tattoos that wrapped down the length of his limbs, a wolf visible among the black patterns that had faded over time. He was wearing a bowler hat, which cast a shadow over most of his face. Tex thought he saw *tā moko* – the facial tattoos of the Māori people – but when he tilted his head at a different angle, the light showed nothing but bare skin on his face.

Perception, Fairuza had told him. She had a way with it and Tex wondered if her proximity to the old man was messing with what he saw and what was *really* underneath. He'd never met them properly, never dealt with them firsthand, but after the Outskirt Wars in the nineties Tex knew all Asia-Pacific werewolf packs were to be treated with extreme caution after they very nearly achieved independence from the Treize under the leadership of the Ihi pack. His phone vibrated in his pocket, dragging his mind back to the present and more pressing issues. He frowned when he saw it was a message from his uncle, Gavino.

'Are you at the office?' this one read. 'It's important, Tex.'

'I'm here,' he replied.

'Can you come meet me? It's about your father.'

What could Andres Contos possibly have done now? Tex wondered, writing back a simple 'where?'. His uncle responded immediately, dropping a pin at the location where he wanted them to rendezvous. It was just next to St Mary's Cathedral and Tex knew the spot. It was late, but not obscenely so. His phone pinged again with a follow-up message.

'Can you meet me now?'

'On my way,' he typed, immediately annoyed but knowing he had to keep up appearances and at least pretend like everything was normal. He packed up his work, unplugging his headphones and tossing everything into his satchel as he strolled out of the library at a leisurely pace.

'Night, Fairuza,' he waved.

'Tex, you got a minute? I want to introduce you to a friend of mine.'

A friend? he thought, wondering if this friend would prove to be as useful as the last thing she'd introduced him to: the book.

'Ah, sure,' he said, pausing as he joined them at the counter. *Let my uncle wait.* The man had an amused smirk on his face, as if he had heard a joke Tex wasn't privy to.

'Chester,' he said, extending a hand. 'Chester Rangi.'

'Nice to meet you, I'm Texas Contos.'

'The Greek-Aussie Askari,' Chester replied, stringing out the words as if they held some significance.

'Uh, yeah, you know me?' he asked, uncertain.

'Only of you, of course. I've met your *pāpā* a few times: he's a real *prick*.'

Tex chuckled, the gesture feeling warm in his chest but something about this whole meeting making him distinctly uneasy.

'So you work for the Treize then?' he asked.

'No.' The man smiled. 'Definitely not.'

'A contractor?'

'Nope.'

'Ah, sorry – what is it you do?'

'Cause mischief, primarily. Right now I'm just watching things in motion, shuffling cards, reassembling chess pieces.'

Fairuza didn't share the same look of amusement Chester did. Her stare was hard and almost sad, he noted.

'Well, you have fun with your chess game then,' he said. 'It was a pleasure to meet you.'

'The pleasure was all mine,' Chester Rangi responded, tipping his bowler hat at Tex.

'See you tomorrow, Fairuza.'

'Sure,' she said, the comment sounding faint as he walked out of the tunnel and into the wider, open area of the Treize offices. The College Street exit would get him there quickest and he choose the winding, metal staircase he needed and continued up it. He couldn't help the sensation of creepy crawlies running over his skin as he thought about his interaction with Chester Rangi. He paused mid-step, a word swimming to the front of his mind: *mischief*. He didn't work for the Treize, seemed extremely opposed to that idea, but knew Fairuza well enough to call her a friend. That meant he was likely a demon and more specifically, a mischief demon. They were the most dangerous kind there was and Tex had heard rumours they were out there, in circulation, and messing up other people's shit. Yet he had never met one. He'd never even met someone who had met one.

'Excuse you,' a woman said, brushing past him as he blocked the upward route of the staircase.

'Sorry, apologies,' he muttered, pushing his thoughts to the side. Meet Gavino first, sort out whatever mess there was with his father, deal with the idea of having shook the hand of a possible mischief demon later.

Hyde Park was mostly deserted as he walked through it, a group of women clearly tipsy and laughing as they lurched into each other amid taking a short cut to the clubs in the city. There were two directions that revellers headed in around this time of night: towards the CBD or away from it, along Oxford Street where the best gay clubs, drag shows, and all-night raves were. Tex wasn't destined for any of those, however. He glanced up at the cathedral as it loomed above him in the dark.

It was a clear night and stars were visible, twinkling just beyond the southern spires that stretched up into the galaxy. The air was hot, despite the fact it was close to midnight. He doubted whether the thermostat had dipped below twenty-eight degrees Celsius. He was covered in a thin sheen of sweat just from the exertion of the small walk, his dress shirt clinging to the wetness of his back.

He spotted the stairwell that led down to the pin Gavino had sent him, double checking the location before he descended. His footsteps slapped against the concrete as he moved, the sound of car horns blaring on the main road just behind him and an excited 'whoop!' of a partygoer off in the distance. He swivelled around, looking for the figure of his uncle and eventually finding it in the shadows of an underground walkway that led to a car park. A tiny, orange bead lit up in the night as his uncle sucked in on a cigarette – a habit Tex thought he had given up years ago. He felt strangely unsure as he walked towards him, hoping to ease the tension with a joke.

'Little bit heavy on the Deep Throat, aren't we?'

His smile faltered as his uncle reached into his coat, something that should have alerted him immediately as it was far too hot for that kind of outerwear. *Sadie was right*, he thought. He saw the flash of a gun for only a second, registering the clipped sound as a bullet fired, but nothing connected. Tex was violently shoved out of the way, a body colliding with his as they both painfully hit the concrete.

'WHAT THE HELL?!'

He heard his uncle yell, his voice joined by another that was familiar: David Contos.

'It's not—'

Whatever he had intended to say was thwarted by the revving of an engine, Tex wincing as he lifted his head up and watched a van mount the kerb and charge at his two uncles. David had been coming from behind him, Gavino at the front, but they were now both herded in the one direction as they ran for their lives. Someone was shaking his shoulders and he realised only by the scent of her floral perfume that it was Sadie. She was checking to see if he was shot, he realised. She was checking to see if he was conscious. Her face was still swimming into view and he wondered just how hard he had hit his head.

'Argh, I'm cut,' he said, pulling his hand back from the base of his skull and noting the sticky substance there. 'I'm bleeding.'

'You're alive though,' she signed, relief flooding her expression. It disappeared quickly as she yanked him to his feet, tucking her arm under his and pulling him towards the vehicle, which was now reversing towards them. A sharp squeak of brakes brought it to a halt and she threw open the door, shoving him roughly inside. She dived in after him, banging on the dashboard in a way that communicated urgency without a word needing to be uttered. Tex glanced up, surprised to see Keavy behind the wheel and looking tense.

'Holyshitholyshitholyshit,' her sister was muttering.

'Just drive,' Sadie signed, holding her hands in front of her sister's face so she could see what she was saying as she drove.

'Drive *where*?! I nearly committed vehicular homicide on TWO Treize officials, Sadie!'

'Your life dream come true.'

There was a beat, Keavy turning to stare at her in shock. A horn blast made her jump and she swerved to avoid colliding with the car in front of her. She let out a bark, two, which soon turned into a series of strange laughs. Tex's heart was pounding in his chest and he was breathless as he watched the two sisters squished into the van's front cabin. Sadie wasn't laughing. Instead, her face was pale as she ran her hands over face with distress. She had just saved his life. Then it hit him. His uncles had tried to kill him. They were *going* to kill him: they were both there and they had planned it.

'My uncles,' he muttered, sitting upright and strapping the seatbelt over his chest. 'The fuck.'

'They were there to murder you,' Sadie signed. 'You understand?'

'I overstand.' Tex nodded, touching his chest as if he couldn't believe he was still in one piece. 'You were right.'

She shot him a look that all but said 'of course, you dickhead' before her expression softened.

'I'm sorry,' she signed. 'I didn't want to be right.'

'I should have listened to you.'

'That's not important right now.'

'Do you think they saw it was me?' Keavy asked, ignoring their conversation as the lights flickered and they drove through an underpass.

'You?' he questioned. 'No, I mean, I don't think so? Everything happened so quickly, how could they? I don't know if they got a good look at either of you.'

'We're going back to my place first,' Sadie told both of them with her hands. 'We need to get some things then . . . I don't know what to do next. But we can't stay there.'

'Why not?' Tex questioned. He thought the Burke sisters were the perfect hiding spot: after what his family had done to theirs, it would be far down on the list of places one would immediately search for him. Sadie looked out the window for a moment, worry etched into her face as she signed her message.

'I broke The Covenant, Tex.'

Of course, he thought, wanting to smack his hand against his forehead like he was one of the three stooges. How else could she have known where he was and what was about to happen?

'You broke The Covenant,' he repeated.

She nodded. 'How long do you think it will take them to work that out?'

'A few minutes after they realise who it was that tackled me out of the path of a bullet. If there were cameras in that spot, they would have had them turned off for the crime. It could be a few hours or a few days before they connect the dots.'

The car began to slow and Tex looked out the window, worried for a moment that *someone* had caught up with them. They hadn't, rather Keavy had to decrease speed significantly as she negotiated her way through the tight Newtown streets and to the rear of the Burke property. Hitting a remote control, she barely waited for the garage door to roll all the way up before she was inching the van into the backyard, desperate to be out of the car and inside. They filed out of the vehicle, heading towards French doors that were protected with a steel grate over the top. Sadie pulled keys from her skirt pocket, unlocking one set of doors then the other as they stepped into an illuminated kitchen. Methodically, she locked and closed them behind her.

'That's our way in and out,' she told him and he nodded. They paused in the kitchen, Tex downing a bottle of water she handed him while Sadie finished two of her own. Keavy hesitated, before climbing up on to the kitchen bench and retrieving spirits from a hiding place. Twisting off the lid, she took a massive swig and Tex huffed appreciatively as he realised it was whiskey. She handed the bottle to him and he inspected the Wild Turkey Rye label for a moment.

'Fuck it,' he said. 'If you can't down hard liquor on the night you cheat death, then when can you?'

A deep frown settled into Sadie's features just as Tex held the bottle to his lips, coughing and spluttering when he pulled it away.

'That . . . ergh, that's strong shit,' he wheezed. 'Stronger than I'm used to.'

Shooting Keavy an annoyed look, Sadie held her hand out to take the bottle away from him and for the first time, Tex noticed several blood trails snaking down her arm.

'Sadie,' he whispered, moving closer to examine the wound. 'You're bleeding.'

The bullet had skimmed her, that's how close she'd been, and it had sliced through the fabric of her top.

'Take care of that,' Keavy said, peering at the injury. 'I'm going to need to wake the others.'

'We need to cut this off,' Tex said, looking around the kitchen for scissors. 'I know basic first aid; I can take a look.'

'No,' she signed, pleading with her eyes. 'This is Ina's top, she'll kill me.'

'It's her or the Treize at this point.'

'The Treize,' she told him, resolute.

'Fine, it's already ripped though – I guess you could sew it. You'll have to take this off if I'm to dress it properly.'

She pulled the top over her head quickly, like she was ripping off a Band-Aid, and suddenly Tex was staring at her ample chest. Her breasts were lifted against her chest in a grey bra that had black straps extending over her cleavage in curved arches. He knew she was looking at him, but he couldn't stop staring. Tex felt like he had to give himself a mental shake as he reached around her, turning on the tap at the sink for running water. Sadie grabbed a first-aid kit from a nearby cupboard, opening it up with her bleeding arm while her other went self-consciously around the flesh of her stomach. He wet a paper towel, telling her what he was doing as he did it and trying his utmost to keep his thoughts on the task at hand.

'I'm cleaning the wound with water,' Tex said, noting how she winced when he made contact. She hadn't shown the faintest sign that she was in pain before and he wondered if it was only now the adrenaline was starting to wear off. She leaned against the kitchen bench as he grabbed the Dettol branded bottle of antiseptic.

'I've got to pour some antiseptic on it now, this is going to sting.'

She nodded, biting her lip as he squirted some of the liquid on to it. Sadie grabbed his shoulder, her fingers squeezing hard as she dealt with the pain: pain *he* had caused, in a way. She was suffering right now because of him.

'That's it, that's the worst of it,' he said, applying a plaster dressing before covering it carefully with a bandage. 'You don't need stitches or anything.'

As he fastened the bandage in place, he couldn't help but trail his fingers down her arm. He watched the goosebumps that bubbled to the surface, adding texture to the smooth nature of her skin.

'Why did you do it, Sadie?' he mumbled, looking up at her. She was a few inches taller than him and perfectly still as he spoke. They were very close to each other, he registered that in the rear of his mind. But he didn't take a step back like he usually would. Instead, he leaned closer.

'Do what?' she mouthed, Tex unable to take his eyes off her lips.

'Save me.'

He meant to wait for an answer, he really did, but his desire to feel those lips on his was implacable. Tex let himself be drawn forward, relishing the feel of her body pressed against his as he slid his hand along the curve of her neck. His fingers brushed over the bare skin at her waist, running along her back, and followed by even more goosebumps as she reacted to his touch. He closed the last, tiny gap between them as he leaned in and kissed her. The craziest thing of all was that Sadie Burke kissed him back.

Chapter 7

SADIE

'Hag of the mist!'

The shrill tone of her sister's voice cut through the sensation of kissing Tex, Sadie having folded her body around his as she let herself get lost in the feeling of his tongue brushing against hers. She froze, their lips still pressed together, before she shoved him backwards.

'You little washerwoman!' Catriona cried, a triumphant smirk on her face as if she couldn't believe what she was seeing.

'Keening crone!' she continued, as Sadie crossed her hands over her bare chest and wished the kitchen floor would open up right there, turning into a gigantic set of teeth that could mush her to smithereens.

'Lamenting matron,' Catriona pressed, Sadie rolling her eyes as her sister truly worked her way through the banshee vernacular. Her thumb was already flying over a screen, the phone pressed to her ear in a matter of seconds.

'You're not gonna believe what I just caught your favourite *bean nighe* doing and with whom. Leave the kids with him, just get over here: you're gonna want to see this in person.'

Sadie could hear footsteps running down the stairs before Catriona hung up, Keavy's face appearing behind her in the hallway.

'What happened? I left you alone for *two* minutes.'

'All of you shut your mouths,' Sadie signed, feeling heat flushing her cheeks. She couldn't even look at Tex, who she suspected had turned away from her to hide a smirk. 'This is serious.'

'I bet it is!' Catriona exclaimed. 'Your shirt's already off! In the kitchen!'

'Ina is gonna lose her shit when she finds out you got baby gravy on her favourite top,' Nora smirked, joining them.

Sadie made a disgusted face, signing as quickly as she could. 'There's no baby gravy, no nothing; just act like adults for a second!'

As the words left her hands, she wished she had taken her own advice a few minutes earlier. *What the hell was I thinking?* It had been life and death and panic and a ticking clock and . . . he'd touched her. *Really* touched her. Then nothing else made sense. The front door slammed shut, Ina and Shannon both appearing behind the sisters Sadie could already see.

'Well, well, well.' Shannon smiled. 'Our teenage sister finally acting like a teenager.'

'Where's my shirt?' Ina called, standing on her tiptoes to see over their shoulders. Sadie was trying to sign, her shoulder on fire as she used her very best, most dramatic Auslan.

'FOR. FUCK. SAKE.'

That was Keavy, pushing her way into the centre of them.

'SADIE. IS. TRYING. TO. TELL. YOU. SOMETHING.'

Catriona's mouth was already parting, no doubt another witty retort at the ready when Tex stepped forward, his hand resting on Sadie's shoulder as he positioned himself in front of her.

'She broke The Covenant,' Keavy said, getting straight to the point. 'Twice.'

That shut them up, she thought. It was invisible to the eye, but she felt the weight that crushed down on the room, compressing the people she loved as they stood there. Shannon shoved her way forward through the others, pausing to stand in front of Sadie as she took her face in her hands, holding her there so their eyes connected. They were the same shade and shape as hers, flecks of brown and green intermingled to form an unusual hazel combination. There was so much shared heartbreak there and mutual sorrow. Now, also, this *weight*.

'Don't joke about stuff like that,' Catriona whispered, her voice small as she broke the silence.

'It's not a joke,' Tex said. 'Your sister foresaw my death at the hands of my uncles and intervened. She saved my life, nearly took a bullet for me.'

'Tell me you didn't,' Ina growled, ignoring him completely as she looked at Sadie. 'Tell me you didn't do all of that *and* sign your death sentence for him.'

'I feel the need to mention I nearly hit Tex's uncles with Jan,' Keavy said quietly.

'Only because I asked her to!' Sadie signed. 'It's important you know that. I didn't tell her where we were driving or why, just that she had to come with me.'

'It's done,' Shannon said, in a tone that was definitive and resolute. In other words: not to be argued with. She released Sadie, finally breaking eye contact to note the bandage on her arm before she turned to their sisters. 'It's done and now we work out what to do next. Nora, there's blood on his collar. Fix him up.'

Nora didn't say a peep, just moved forward and began working on the cut at the back of Tex's head. Sadie tried to get a look and see how bad it was, yet a subtle hand on her elbow directed her attention back to her sisters.

'You have to run, there's no question about it.' Ina spoke first, hands on her hips. 'Leave tonight before they have time to put everything together.'

'We all have to run,' Nora said, pressing a packet of aspirin into Tex's hand. 'And I'm done, by the way. It's not bad at all, the head just bleeds like a fucker. Not that it's going to be an issue, but I'd recommend staying awake for the next few hours just in case you have a mild concussion. And take the aspirin when the headache starts.'

'It already started,' Tex mumbled. 'Thanks.'

Sadie watched something pass between Shannon and Keavy, with her sibling slipping by the others and down the hall, out of sight, like she had a distinct purpose. It wasn't until she returned a few minutes later that Sadie learned what that was, setting down two backpacks on the floor at her feet.

'What's this?' she signed.

'It's for emergencies,' Shannon answered. 'And this constitutes an emergency. It's got supplies in there: change of clothes, tampons, toiletries, first aid stuff, some food but not much.'

'And cash,' Keavy said. 'Ten grand in rolled fifties and

twenties: the smaller bills are less memorable if you're paying for something. There's another ten grand available on a credit card under a false name and some traveller's cheques.'

Sadie open and closed her mouth, her fingers twitching as she went to sign a message. She couldn't think of the right thing to say, she was so astonished.

'Holy shit,' Tex breathed.

Shannon nodded, as if that was the correct response. 'After Sorcha, we started putting things aside. Cash from the business, bits and bobs, so that way if one of us ever had to run again we'd make sure they weren't caught.'

'How many of you knew about this?' Sadie signed, her eyes sweeping over the faces of her sisters.

'All of us,' Keavy answered. 'Except you. We didn't want to freak you out.'

'Tex, where's your phone?' Catriona asked.

He went to grab it from his pocket, but there was nothing there and he patted himself down as he searched for it. 'I don't know, it should be with me but . . . I think it's back at St Mary's Cathedral. I lost it in the scuffle.'

'Good,' Catriona stated. 'They'll be tracking you with that. Sadie, we need to put yours in the blender.'

She handed it over, watching as her sister destroyed it in front of her. Looking around at her family, she was startled to see the determined expression on all of her sisters' faces. None of them looked as scared as she felt.

'What about the rest of you?' she signed. 'This is enough stuff for Tex and me, but . . . what about all of you?'

Shannon glanced at everyone else, a few stiff nods being returned by the Burke women. Ina lobbed her phone from her standing position at the back of the group, flicking her wrists like she was in the NBA.

'Yeeeet,' she said, as it landed in the blender alongside the remnants of Sadie's.

'We go mobile,' Shannon said. 'We've planned for this possibility. Maybe not all of us at once, but . . . we've planned for this.'

'The kids,' Sadie signed. 'What about Aoife? What about Mum? What about—'

'Sades.' Shannon sighed, stepping forward again and touching her cheek affectionately. 'You two have to go now, stick together, get out of the country. We're all going to be doing the same, just . . . differently. When we're assembled and safe again, we'll find you.'

'How?' Sadie signed, trying to ignore the tears that were brimming in her eyes. She'd never had a chance to say goodbye to Sorcha. Somehow having the chance to say goodbye to her sisters wasn't any easier.

'Worry about your own shit,' Keavy answered, the words sounding harsher than the expression on her face. 'We'll figure it out, okay? You're the baby. We need to look after you.'

'That's all well and good,' Tex said, speaking up as he attempted to pace in the kitchen. It usually would have had plenty of room for dramatics, except when it was packed with six of the seven Burke sisters. 'But what do we do now? We run, but where to? And for how long? What's the endgame?'

'To get out of the country,' Shannon said. 'Sorcha had the right idea about that.'

'If we go now though,' he countered, 'I feel like that's such an obvious move. We won't make it through security before we're picked up. What kind of documentation are we travelling with? Our passports? No way, we wouldn't stand a chance.'

'Obviously you wait, dickhead,' Catriona snapped.

Tex smirked. 'Is the "dickhead" necessary?'

'Bide your time,' she pressed, ignoring his comment. 'Like a week or two, and when their guard's down that's when you bounce out of here.'

'This whole situation is fucktangular on many levels,' Nora moaned, sliding down the wall until she sat on the floor. Everyone kept talking, their voices raising and bubbling over each other as they fought to come up with a better plan for Tex and Sadie, a better solution, a better exit strategy. Nobody even seemed to notice as Sadie slunk away, taking the stairs two at a time. She stepped into her bedroom, closing the door behind her and enjoying the brief pocket of silence. Usually this space was illuminated just by candlelight, Sadie never able to settle on one scent in particular, switching up the candles in her collection almost immediately as one burned down.

She reached for the electronic fire lighter she kept by her bedside, savouring the clicking sound as she pressed her thumb down and a flame danced from the tip. She moved around the room, lighting candles as she went, and drinking in every inch of the small sanctuary she had created. Something in her bones told her she wasn't going to be coming back here. A vine stretching up from a pot plant in the corner climbed her wall, intertwining with a Chain Of Hearts and ivy as they created somewhat of a tangled rope above the pillows of her bed. Her blanket was white, with a handmade shawl from Sorcha draped over the top. Almost everything else was varying shades of green from the array of plants and succulents she had brought in.

Nora called her bedroom the greenhouse and the description was pretty fitting. Old, weathered doors opened up on to a balcony and she could see across the street to her neighbour's second storey. When it was hot, like it was tonight, she slept with the doors open in the hope of getting some kind of a breeze. Their house was too old to be fitted with air conditioning or even ceiling fans, so every room had multiple fans positioned on stands in order to cope with the Sydney summer. Her neighbour's lights were off in their bedroom and she truly didn't care in that moment if anyone saw her as she stripped out of her clothes, changing into a series of items that were more comfortable. Buckled ankle boots, sheer tights that covered the bare skin of her legs but didn't make her hot, and a floral dress in a soft, rust-like colour with green and blue flowers patterned across it.

She grabbed a small tube that contained her usual shade of lip tint and the packet that held her prescription of the contraceptive pill, slipping it into the pocket of her dress. Her short, clipped nails tapped over the wood of her dresser as she examined some of the treasures she kept there. Dainty, feminine jewellery in varying hints of silver hung from hooks, including a beautiful hair comb that had been Sorcha's with crystals set into the handle. She took the bottle of perfume that was sitting there, knowing it was illogical to pack a luxury item like that but wanting it with her anyway. There was a Claddagh ring from her high school boyfriend, which he had bought her when he learned she was of Irish heritage (as if the sheer number of siblings and redheads in her family hadn't been clue enough). She smirked, her mind jumping back to sweaty bodies pressed up against each other in the back of his car, fingers fumbling on buttons and mouths contorting with the urgency of hormones. All those years wasted on horny boys and high school hook-ups behind the sports shed had faded away when Tex kissed her. Sadie felt like she had never kissed anyone before as her skin had come alive and her body had moved with its own agency when she'd kissed him back. Of course, it was also the very worst person in the world for her to kiss and she wondered if maybe that was a big part of it.

Her fingers brushed the chain of a necklace with a decorative key on it that her sisters had all gone in on for her eighteenth birthday. She only wore it on special occasions, but what occasion was more special than running for your life? If she was going to die, she wanted to die with it on. She lifted it from the dresser, reaching behind her neck to do up the clasp. She smiled, the gesture feeling hollow as she stepped closer to the balcony and looked out. Her mother was there, in her usual chair, a blanket draped around her shoulders by one of her sisters most likely. Her eyes were shut, but Sadie doubted whether she ever truly slept. Her hand hovered on the fly screen barrier between them, like she wanted to reach out but couldn't. Máire Burke had never learnt to sign; she never knew or understood what her daughter was saying to her. So what could Sadie possibly communicate to a woman who had lost so much already? It pained her, but she wondered if her mother would even notice she was gone.

She stepped away, choosing to leave things as they were. Sadie left the candles for someone else to blow out, knowing

Ina would be in her room at some point searching for the remnants of her borrowed top. All her sisters would be, loitering in that space when they missed her presence. It's what she did when she grieved Sorcha, curling up on the bed in her sister's room and smelling her on the fabric. When she re-joined the group in the kitchen, they weren't still arguing. Instead, it looked like some kind of resolution had been met.

'Are you okay?' Texas signed, Sadie appreciating how his hands were a bit messy on the words. All of her sisters could read his message if they were looking, but there was something distinctly soft about the act, which she appreciated. Sadie nodded, touching the hanging key around her neck as a reflex.

His eyes followed her movement. 'Let's go, then.'

She bent down and threw one of the bags over her shoulders, tossing Tex the other and grabbing water bottles from the fridge. Keavy pointed a finger at Tex that would have scared any man let alone one that had been through everything he had that evening.

'You protect her,' she told him. 'You look after her, you lay down your life if it means her freedom. You hear me?'

'Loud and clear,' he muttered.

He caught the keys to the backdoor her sister threw him, unlocking it and slipping outside to give Sadie a moment with her siblings. It was a procession of hugs and whispered sentiments, ranging from 'I love you' to 'be smart'.

'Remember this email address: keaton_hazel88@xcvell. com,' Shannon said. 'You got it?'

Sadie nodded, telling her she did.

'Keaton_hazel88@xcvell.com,' she repeated. 'I'll be checking it if you need to reach us. No phones. Once yours is gone, ours aren't safe either: they could be tapping them or using the geographic pings. Email only, as that domain is automatically generated and always changing so they can't break in through a secure mailbox even if they knew what they were looking for.'

'We'll see you soon,' Nora whispered, gripping Sadie's hand tightly before she stepped out into the night.

She allowed herself one look back, just one, as her five sisters stood there and watched her leave, Catriona and Keavy clustered together in a hug, Ina bouncing slightly on the balls of her feet like she was ready to move as well, then Nora and Shannon, bookending the women on either side but looking still. And steady.

With that, she was gone, disappearing through the backyard and under the roller door as quickly as she could. Tex told her to head towards the cemetery, with the aim of being there in twenty minutes, and she set their pace through the alleyways that seemed to disorient him on foot. A cat was in their path and it meowed, slinking towards them seductively like it wanted to be patted. She saw Tex slow his steps, as if he was considering it, before increasing his pace again and following her as she turned left. It was like a labyrinth and if you didn't know where you were going even in the daylight, it was just as likely you could end up ensnared by David Bowie's mullet as arrive at your destination. Sadie's eyes caught on a syringe laying in the gutter, her steps getting quicker as she quietly wiped a tear that was streaking down her cheek. Houses backed on to these tiny, forgotten paths and she noticed Tex glancing nervously over his shoulder more than once.

'Are you sure you know where you're going?'

No answer.

'I feel like I'm about to get jumped at any moment.'

Nothing.

'Or hepatitis C at the very least.'

She snorted, signing as she walked. 'This is the quickest way, but also . . .'

Sadie pointed at the exit to the lane they were currently on, which was far in the distance. Then she pointed behind her.

'Only one entry and one exit for cars,' she signed. 'And if one does come, there's so much crap in these alleys it's a moment before they register you.'

'Then there's all these other ones,' he said. 'Too narrow for a car to get down, only usable if you're on foot.'

'Exactly.' She nodded. 'It's dirty, but it's safer. This will take us out right near the cemetery, with one quick stop on the way.'

'Stop? We don't have a lot of time.'

'It's on the way: one of those street libraries on the corner of Australia Street, near the school.'

She could tell he didn't know what a street library was, even less so when she pointed at the small wooden structure that was positioned up ahead. It was decorated to look like a cute house and they were scattered all over the suburb. They had clear doors that opened up and books inside that anyone could borrow for free, so long as they replaced them with something else. She stopped in front of it, the squeak of the hinge as she pulled the door open seeming like a siren.

'This really isn't the time to get some light reading for the road,' he whispered, but she ignored him as she reached further back into the box. Her hands tapped the ceiling, it giving way as Sadie pulled out a plastic folder from inside and put everything back the way she had found it.

'That's not one of the seventeen John Grisham thrillers from inside there,' Tex said. 'What's that?'

'Something for later,' she signed, grabbing his hand as they marched the final two blocks to the cemetery. She wanted to know who or what it was they were meeting, but she decided to trust whatever Texas and her sisters had arranged. She had to. They arrived at the meeting spot just as a battered ute turned the corner, a type of car that wasn't super common in these parts. The driver flashed their lights on to high beam and then off again, the universal sign for sneaky shit. Tex nodded at her, moving towards the vehicle as it slowed to let them in. There was no backseat and he put himself between Sadie and the driver as they all squeezed into the front cabin.

'G'day,' the man said, sliding the gearstick around Tex's knee as they moved into third gear. 'Name's Taylor Petersham and I'll be your driver this evenin'.'

Tex and Sadie shared a look, before laughter like a fog horn on fire broke through the interior of the car and Taylor cracked up at his own joke.

'Just joshin' with ya. Shazza said I'm to pick ya up and drop ya off at The Rocks, no questions asked.'

'Thanks, Taylor,' Texas said. 'We really appreciate it.'

They were silent for the rest of the drive, Taylor turning up the volume dial so Crowded House was playing loudly from the car speakers. She wondered where this man fit into the Petersham family, thinking back to what Texas had said earlier about wombat claws. Leaning forward, she tried to subtly stare at the man's knuckles as they flexed around the steering wheel. It wasn't hard to imagine massive talons shooting through the skin like X-23's claws, with shifters not restrained by the full moon the same way werewolves were. They could shift fully into their specific animal any time they wanted, no matter whether it was a full or crescent moon, and they also retained abilities related to the species. Yet unlike werewolves, when they shifted into that animal they *properly* shifted: right down to size. That meant they were as vulnerable as an everyday parrot, if that's what they were, even though they had human intelligence. She'd never seen a werewolf under the full moon, but she'd seen the diagrams: it was truly and utterly monstrous. Folks were always confusing shifters and werewolves, which annoyed the crap out of her.

They hit the hilly territory of The Rocks and Sadie knew they were close, Taylor's ute chugging up a steep incline before they rounded a corner and an old pub called The Local was in sight. The occupants of the venue had spilled out on to the street, dozens of people in clusters as they smoked and laughed and brawled within metres of the entry. Taylor drove them around the side, where Shazza was waiting as she hunched over and rolled barrels of booze along the path.

It was an excuse to be there, she noted, with the wombat shifter halting the motion as soon as she saw their vehicle. There were no other cars on the road and she walked alongside them as Taylor slowed, taking a left turn and descending down a steep driveway. The windows were open and Shazza leaned in, Sadie certain she heard the metal of the car door strain as it took the bulk of her weight.

'Twice in one week, Sadie, such a pleasure.' She grinned, her eyebrows wiggling with amusement. 'Tex.'

Texas nodded back formally. 'Thanks for this.'

'Don't mention it.'

She let go of the car to punch in a code that allowed them entry to a small, underground parking area. There were half a dozen cars already there and Sadie had no idea how they were going to fit the ute as well. With some careful wrangling, Taylor managed. Shazza had remained outside and she glanced over her shoulder as she got out of the vehicle, watching as the limited view of the street was slowly covered: one barrel at a time.

'Follow me, petals,' Taylor said, Sadie able to hear not see him. It was now pitch-black inside the loading dock of sorts, with neither she nor Tex able to distinguish any shapes let alone walk forward with confidence.

'Uh, is there a light somewhere?' Tex questioned.

'Oh shoot, sorry! I forget not everyone can see in the dark. Is that better? Can I carry anything?'

He must have hit a button somewhere, as the space blinked back into view thanks to the blinding, white light of two fluorescent bulbs overhead. They were gently swinging, adding to the disorienting effect.

'We've got it,' Tex said. 'Thank you.'

'You don't say much, do ya?' he told Sadie, looking her up and down.

Tex placed a hand on her arm. 'She can't: the Treize severed her vocal cords when she was a child.'

'Shit, I thought she was just shy. Those fucking dogs.'

Sadie held up her fingers in an okay symbol, not offended in the slightest. In truth, it was just nice to meet someone who didn't know who she was or anything about her 'condition'. It made her feel . . . regular, almost.

Taylor led them up a set of concrete steps, past a corridor of doors including one that had a metal sign nailed to it which read 'dungeon'. She didn't think that was a joke. Music was still blasting from the pub far above them, live bands having probably ended for the night as she recognised an A.B. Original track thudding through the walls. The sound dulled somewhat as they walked on, Sadie having no idea where they were in relation to the layout of the venue, which she knew about only anecdotally as one of Australia's very first. Ironically given the name, locals didn't come here; it was a tourist trap, and one that she was surprised to learn was run by the shifters. The Rocks was a historic suburb full of old pubs, winding laneways, cobbled roads, and some of the oldest buildings in the city all under the shadow of the Sydney Harbour Bridge.

She noted a subtle change in the floor below her feet from concrete to tiles and then carpet: the back of The Local seemed to go on and on. Taylor brought them into a huge living area, with worn armchairs and beds that had been folded out from couches littering the space, along with a long dining table. Denton Boys was sitting at the end of it with a handful of other faces in the room that Sadie didn't recognise. They were playing a game of Uno and passing around a joint so pungent she thought she'd get a contact high. The others barely glanced up when she entered, setting down her bag on the floor with a sigh. The Askari got to his feet at their arrival, placing his all-blue hand and a wild card on the table as he made to join them.

'I guess you've stopped trying to escape and came to your senses after all,' Texas said, the annoyance clear in his voice.

'You can't blame me for thinking you all were trying to kill me too.'

'I can't,' he replied. 'But after everything we've gone through to save your life, I think I will blame you. Just a little bit.'

'I heard.' Denton sniffed. 'I guess blood matters as much to your uncles as it does your father.'

Sadie watched Tex stiffen beside her and for the first time, she spared a thought for what he must be going through. His uncles had just tried to kill, dispatch of him like he was nothing more than Denton, an Askari who had gotten in their way. His father had abandoned him when he was a kid, choosing a promotion over his son as if there was never any choice. And now ... this. She could see he was struggling to keep his face neutral, even as she reached out and brushed her fingers against his. His hand reacted like it was a reflex, closing around her digits and gripping them for dear life. It was her only clue as to what he was really feeling.

There was a bang behind them as a door slammed shut and Shazza made her entrance into the room, looking like she had just sprinted there from her position out the front.

'You gotta put the family politics aside,' she said, swaggering into the space.

'She hasn't spent enough time with either of our families then,' Sadie signed, Texas being the only one who could understand her message and struggling to hide a sad smirk.

'We've got much bigger problems now, for everyone.'

'She's right,' said a voice, Sadie swivelling on the spot as a woman emerged from the shadows. She was short, barely more than five foot, but everything about her told Sadie she was dangerous. It was more than just the two other, equally fierce women that flanked her on either side. Or the tattoo that coloured her lip and ran down her chin.

Yet it was the man behind her that caused Sadie to lose her breath. She'd recognise him anywhere: Ben Kapoor. He wasn't a teenager struggling with the newfound weight of his pack being thrust on to his shoulders any more. He was a man, if not thirty then close to it, with a lanky body laced with muscle that hinted at the threat lurking within. He was also the head of the most prominent werewolf pack in the city, one that had been tasked with hunting her down when she was nine and Sorcha was begging her to keep running, no matter how tired their legs were. He was the werewolf who had held her still as Andres Contos maimed her permanently.

Sadie felt panic spreading in her chest, all of the years that had passed since disappearing until she was standing there in that crowd of monsters, a child. Suddenly the proximity and volume of people wasn't comforting; it was suffocating. She backed away, shaking her head slightly as Texas immediately placed himself in front of her protectively. Her back against the wall, Sadie felt trapped as she met the unflinching stare of the werewolf who towered over most people in the room at six foot four.

'What the fuck is this?' Texas was saying. 'What the fuck is *he* doing here? With *them*?'

She realised the 'them' were the women, who he seemed just as concerned about as Ben Kapoor.

'Believe me,' the werewolf growled, 'I want to be in the same room as a Contos about as much as you want to be in the same room as a Kapoor.'

'Alright, alright, everyone peace the fuck out,' said Shazza, stepping in between their two parties with her hands extended. 'Werewolves Kapoor and Ihi, chill. Askari and banshee, chill. Everyone, just keep it frosty.'

Denton wasn't clustered with them, she realised. He was standing just off to the side, but distinctly with the werewolves.

'Denton,' the wombat shifter said, clicking her fingers at the man. 'You're responsible for a large part of this mess. It's time you started explaining it to everyone who hasn't grasped the full magnitude of what's going on.'

The Askari looked thoughtful at that notion, jumping when Shazza suddenly slapped her hands together and shouted, '*NOW.*'

'What happened to being cooler than cool?' he murmured, grabbing the seat he'd left abandoned at the table of Uno players and pulling it into the centre of the room as he sat down. Sadie didn't move, nor Tex in front of her, but everyone was definitely tuned in as they started to listen.

'As I guess you two are aware now,' Denton said, gesturing at the pair of them. 'I've been leaking information for a while.'

'How long is a while?' Texas asked.

'Two years,' he answered, immediately defensive. 'And you don't understand. You're fresh outta school, kiddo. I'm forty-two. I've seen a lot of crap, *too much* crap that has compounded and compounded to the point I can't ignore it any more. I was approached by someone—'

'Who?' Texas again, getting a waved hand in response.

'*Someone*, just like me, who was on the inside but . . . troubled. They made a suggestion, I agreed, so began my brief career as a mole.'

For the werewolves, Sadie thought, her eyes flicking back to the section of the room that was heavily populated by them.

'Two years,' Texas mused. 'You worked for them for decades and they only started getting suspicious of you in the past few months, then I was assigned to take over from you. What tipped them off?'

'If I had to guess, the nature of the leaks. They started to become more—'

'The Treize were getting up to worse and worse shit,' the intimidating woman said, her New Zealand accent thick. The ladies at her side nodded in agreement. 'Small leaks are almost par for the course with this kind of operation, but when they're about the messier sides of your business? When that's more crucial than ever?'

'A death warrant,' Texas said, saying the words Sadie had signed out loud followed by her next question. 'What were the leaks about?'

'Werewolves going missing,' Denton replied. 'At first, along with information about continued monitoring of all Asia-Pacific packs involved in the Outskirt Wars.'

Her eyes flicked to Ben Kapoor and the women, understanding their involvement now. New Zealand packs, Australian packs, Japanese packs, Fijian packs, Samoan packs, Tongan packs, packs from the Philippines and all over the region had worked together once. It was back when she still had a voice and Sorcha had been obsessed with the tales of werewolves rising up and banding together to try and self-govern outside of the Treize. They had also wanted to 'come out of the woods', as it was called, and reveal themselves to the humans. She'd never understood that last part as a kid or an adult, but it was something the Outskirt Packs had fought for. They had lost, along with many of the wolves' lives and freedoms.

'Then other supernaturals started disappearing,' Denton was saying. 'At first, just a few. Then more. Too many. Too often. Too consistently.'

She glanced at Tex and he shook his head slightly, as if anticipating her question before she asked it.

'I didn't know what the leaks pertained to,' he told her. 'Just that they were classified. I asked several times for more information, as it would help how I investigated, but the clearance hadn't come through yet.'

'Even that wasn't enough to truly tip things into the red,' Denton pushed. 'Until I learned who was taking these creatures, where they were going, and what was happening to them.'

'Experiments,' Ben Kapoor said, speaking up for the first time. His gaze was locked on Sadie's as he spoke and she couldn't look away, not from his crop of dyed green hair or the snakebite piercings on his lips that glinted as he spoke. He was wearing a loose, completely redundant singlet that hung wide at his sides and exposed most of his torso, including several scars there and a pierced nipple. He looked like any other scene kid, except for the fact she knew who and what he was. 'They've been extracting DNA from all different breeds of creatures, trying to harvest their abilities and isolate their powers.'

'For what purpose?' she signed, Texas speaking her message.

'We don't know that yet. That was the next thing Denton was working on when he was reassigned.'

Several sets of eyes swivelled to Tex, who threw up his hands in an unintentionally perfect recreation of the shrug emoji. 'Hey, I had no idea about any of this. And I've been far removed from the local scene for a long time. In fact, I thought I'd been given this job because of what I knew about the Burkes, but I'm thinking now the whole reason it was tasked to me was because of what I *don't know* about everything else.'

'Well, you're in it now,' Denton said, leaning back with a smirk. 'Welcome to the shitstorm, brother.'

Their group broke apart somewhat then, Texas feeling comfortable enough to leave her as he crouched down and joined Denton. The two of them had their heads bowed as they began talking, Sadie reading their lips and hand gestures from where she stood as they began comparing notes about regimental specifics. A low hum began to build, as the others in the room with them – so many complete strangers to her – began chatting as well, dissecting everything that had been said over the last ten minutes. Shazza must have sensed her discomfort, working her way over to her until they were side by side.

'Don't be overwhelmed by these folks,' she said. 'Everyone here is on your side and would rather die than divulge information about where or who you're with.'

She'd misinterpreted her expression of discomfort for one of distrust, but she didn't interject as Shazza pointed around the room, differentiating members of the Kapoor pack from the Petershams and their extended family. She cast a glance at the three women in the corner, who were speaking in a language she didn't recognise.

'That's Tiaki Ihi; she's the matriarch of a very powerful werewolf pack in New Zealand,' she explained. 'Those women with her are part of the Aunties and you don't wanna mess with them. They're an all-female unit who vote on and enforce pack law.'

Australian and New Zealand werewolf packs in a room, working alongside shifters, and even taking a banshee and disgraced Askari under their protection; Sadie lived a strange life, but this had dipped way the heck over. Yet there was something comforting about all of this as she looked around at the present company: they were rebels, renegades, rioters. They were fugitives too, in some way. If anyone was going to be able to help get them out of the country and away from the grasp of the Treize, it was the monsters assembled in that room.

Chapter 8

TEXAS

If someone had told Texas Contos a week ago that he'd find himself hiding in the bowels of a tourist pub in Sydney, he would have told them they were dreaming. Rather, it was somewhat of a waking nightmare for the now-former Askari as he did his best to just get through the days while living in uncomfortably close quarters with creatures who hated him.

He understood their feelings, hell, he was beginning to hate what the Treize had come to stand for as well. Yet maybe he was naive, blinded by not just the fact that he was *in* the system, but *part* of it as well. He thought he'd been the best man he possibly could be within the constraints of his job – the best possible human – but Tex was quickly realising that wasn't good enough. *He* hadn't done enough: not when he was twelve and not when he was twenty-two.

There was no shoving Pandora's curse back in the box, however. There were no do-overs. He was done lying to himself. He was done making excuses for his father and the actions of his uncles. He was 'stick a fork in me' levels of done. And he knew a big part of that had to do with Sadie. The two of them stuck close to each other the entire time they were at The Local. On one level, it was because she needed him to translate everything she said as she signed it. On another, he was scared for her. He'd promised Keavy and he meant it: he was not going to leave her alone in this den of dangerous creatures. They all had a purpose and an aim, something they were trying to achieve by being there and working together. He didn't doubt their cause was noble, but he also could see how someone vulnerable like Sadie could be crushed under the machinations of it. Tex would not that let happen. The number of people who knew about their presence and were guarding that secret came to eleven in total. Tex learned all of their names, faces, and affiliations, filing away that information.

There were five members of the Petersham family, with the leadership alternating between Shazza and Taylor depending on who was around. Ben Kapoor was usually always present, slipping away only at times to manage his pack out in the real world and maintain the illusion that everything was 'normal'. Then there was Tiaki Ihi, the woman he was most fascinated by given everything he had heard about the Ihi pack and how notorious they were in the global supernatural community. He knew the Kapoors had fought alongside hers in the Outskirt Wars and it didn't take a genius to see what was going on. The two of them reunited, even though it was expressly prohibited in the treaty dictated by the Treize. Tex could recognise the start of a lycanthrope uprising when he saw one. Yet that skirmish in the nineties had been specific to the werewolves, all fighting under the leadership of Jonah Ihi. He'd unintentionally gotten the wombat shifters involved by having them detain and question Denton. They'd had little interaction with the werewolves before, but they were *in* it now that they knew the Treize had been abducting and experimenting on some of their own kind as well. He couldn't help but wonder who else had skin in the game. And when that game would be played. Those concerns were bigger than his immediate problems, at least for now.

'You can't stay in one place for long,' Tiaki Ihi told them. 'You need to get around. A moving target is hard to hit.'

'But we have to let the heat cool down first,' Shazza countered, turning to Tex and Sadie. 'You two haven't seen what it's like out there.'

'My family?' Sadie asked, while Tex spoke.

'All gone,' the shifter said. 'They vanished the same night you arrived here. I have someone watching the street and they said the Praetorian Guard raided all of your houses a few days later, hoping to catch them off guard. Gotta give the banshees credit, they haven't caught one of you yet.'

That seemed to be her primary concern, all other worries secondary. At some point a collective decision had been made to help them once they understood Sadie had broken The Covenant and what that would mean for either her or Tex if they were caught. He wasn't sure when that decision was made or by whom, he just was aware of it. It was three days into their stay when Tex realised the supernaturals had started adjusting them to nocturnal behaviour without either he or Sadie noticing it.

'It's easier to move at night,' Taylor had said with a shrug, when Tex asked him about it. 'That's more likely our element than theirs.'

So whenever and wherever they were going to move them, they'd be doing it in the evening. *Smart,* he thought, appreciating their collective tactics the longer he spent in their company. Denton was another issue altogether. Some days he was fine, playing cards and answering questions as the werewolves attempted to milk him dry of information. Other days, he was antsy: pacing and agitated as he tried to slip out and escape multiple times. It was one extreme or the other, and Tex noticed Shazza had a shifter on him at all times, day and night. They slept on fold-out couches and the creatures preferred to keep it dim, the occasional lamp illuminated on a table, but mostly just the light from the muted television as it played some dated action movie. Sadie wasn't sleeping much, preferring to stay up and flip through pages of *The Collected Banshee Histories*. He estimated she had read it cover-to-cover seven times since he finally revealed that he had it, which was a significant feat given it was some two hundred A3 pages in length.

He was sitting next to her, pillows propped under his neck as he watched Jack Black beg Bruce Willis for his life in *The Jackal*. His eyes darted back to Sadie every few minutes: that's the length it felt safest to observe her without being noticed. Her pale skin looked almost ghostly in the unnatural light, her arms and the top of her back exposed to him in a black singlet she donned for bedtime, with matching satin pants that cut off at the knees. He was compelled to reach out and touch her, feel the smoothness of her body against his once again. It felt like forever since that stolen moment in the kitchen and he longed for another. She didn't look up from the pages of the book, but she must have realised he was watching her as she started signing.

'Tell me how you got this again?'

She had to glance at him then, Tex having established without ever needing to discuss it with her that when they talked about the book it was only ever in Auslan. He'd been vague about how he'd gotten his hands on it the first few times she'd asked him. He didn't want to incriminate Fairuza, who he considered a friend – albeit a weird one. It was dangerous out there and he was uncertain who he could trust, except for Sadie.

'It was given to me by the woman who runs the Treize library,' he said, knowing that Sadie would make the connection immediately. 'Maybe guarded is a better word.'

Her head snapped up, eyes illuminated as she mouthed the word 'Fairuza'.

He nodded. 'Sorcha's friend.'

'You didn't lie about her being helpful. But this . . . this is so much more than just "helpful". You know that, right? It's just as likely your uncles could have been trying to kill you over this book than Denton's rescue.'

'Huh,' he mused. 'I didn't think about it that way.'

'She just gave the book to you?'

'Uh, she actually kind of sneaked it to me, with the dust jacket to hide what it really was and everything.'

Sadie sighed, lowering her hands as she examined the spine of the book like it was a treasure.

'Why do think Fairuza wanted you to have this book?'

'Honestly?'

She nodded.

'I think it was in the hope it would get to you, somehow.'

Sadie tilted her head, as if that thought intrigued her. It certainly intrigued him and he'd been pondering the same question for days. Yet from the moment she held the book in her hands, it just seemed *right*. Like she was *supposed* to have it. Fate, or whatever.

'There's something else,' he said, cautious about bringing up the next subject. There were actually two something elses, but he was more worried about the first than the second. That's the one he broached. 'She mentioned your sister. She doesn't think Sorcha's dead.'

Sadie's focus was laser sharp as he spoke, her interest no longer on the book and only on Tex's words.

'Tell me everything,' she signed. 'Word for word what she said.'

So he did, the banshee completely still and listening intently as he recited the whole conversation. When he was done, she reached for her backpack and retrieved the plastic folder she'd made them stop for en route to the cemetery.

'What's this?' he asked, as she fanned the documents out in front of him. It was a dumb question, because it was readily apparent what it was. There was information on Fairuza in there, along with a place called The Imperial where Sorcha had been secretly working before she fled. There was a full list of all her known and unknown associates, plus news clippings of what little there had been reported on the cruise ship sinking in the human press. There were copies of emergency service reports and maps of shipping routes.

'You think she's still alive too?'

Sadie shook her head. 'No, I thought she was dead. Just because there's no body, doesn't mean someone is alive. I never had reason to hope before.'

'Then why collect all this stuff?'

'When everything went down, I was so shocked and so . . . upset. Not surprised, exactly. Sorcha was always badass. But I realised there was a whole side to my sister I knew nothing about. She had another life that was completely secret to me, to all of us. I became obsessed with wanting to know about it.'

'You were grieving,' he said, examining what was like a very macabre scrapbooking project, minus the glitter pens.

'Maybe. I guess. All I know is I started collecting what I could, then I couldn't stop. It was like . . . if I was still learning about her, then she wasn't really dead, you know?'

'She might not be. And if she's alive, where is she? Regardless of the fact she's your sister, she's someone who has managed to stay abreast of the Treize for two years now. We could use that knowledge. We could use her contacts.'

Sadie clicked her fingers, looking excited as she pulled some documents buried underneath to the top of the pile.

'A witch?' he questioned, examining some handwritten notes about a woman called Kala Tully. 'Sadie, witches are elusive. Unpredictable. Extremely dangerous at best.'

'I know, but Sorcha was friends with this one *and* her twin sister, Willa. When the twin died, she even went to the funeral. Kala has been off the grid for years, but about six months ago she popped up again in the Blue Mountains.'

'Off the grid,' he repeated, looking at the enthusiastic way Sadie was nodding at him. 'Just like Sorcha did. Just like we need to do.'

They discussed plans back and forth, about how they might get up there and what they might find. He went to locate Shazza soon as they had a plan, his friend doing her best to hide the briefest flash of relief that crossed her features when

Tex told her that he and Sadie would be leaving. She was a good person, God bless her, but with everyone she was illegally housing on the premises her neck was exceedingly far out.

'I don't know the witch you're talking about personally, only by reputation, but she doesn't really trust . . .'

'Shifters?'

'Men,' Shazza corrected. 'I should be the one to make contact rather than Taylor or you, especially since Sadie can't. Witches hate the Treize about as much as werewolves; any chance to fuck them over is welcomed by the covens so I feel like she'll be keen.'

Hours later, Tex fell asleep where he was: movie playing out on the screen and Sadie back absorbed in the book. When he woke later, she was nestled beside him. He didn't want to shift or make any sudden movements lest he wake her. So he stayed frozen, exactly how he was, risking only the slightest motion as he reached his arm around Sadie. It was calming for Tex, his fingers gently running through her hair as she slept pressed against his shoulder. The colours were incredible, the shade of his skin intermingling with the rich warmth of her natural hair. A few of Sadie's sisters dyed theirs, but Tex was incredibly glad she didn't.

Her breathing changed slightly and he knew she was waking up. He couldn't bring himself to stop moving his fingers through the strands that fell to the base of her neck. Her lips rubbed together in a gesture he found adorable as she lifted her head and looked up at him. When Sadie's eyes registered his nearness, he felt his breath catch. She moved her own hand towards Tex, gently touching his face in a gesture that surprised him. There was a sudden bang from the kitchen, the noise scaring both of them and they jumped apart. Tex sat up, heart racing, to see Ben and several members of his werewolf pack assembling food on the counter. Their backs were to them and they chatted amongst themselves, seemingly oblivious to what had passed between Tex and Sadie in the living room.

'Set that aside, the shifters are veggos.'

'Vegetarian? Bullshit, I've seen Shazza rip a guy's ear off in a fight.'

'Did you see her eat it?'

'Well, no but—'

'Veggos, Indy. Wombats are herbivores. Doesn't mean they can't fuck you up.'

Ben turned around, a platter of cold meats and cheese in his hands.

'Ah, good – you're up. Hungry?'

'Starved,' Tex said, smirking as Sadie signed the same thing.

The supernaturals who had been tasked with watching over them were right nearby, with one of the New Zealand werewolves glancing up and unhooking the headphones that were in her ears. She'd been sitting just behind where Tex and Sadie had been sleeping, a weathered copy of *Jane Eyre* in her hands.

'Looking for your Mr Rochester?' he joked. She gave him a withering look.

'*Please*,' she responded.

Denton had been restrained again, caught attempting to escape in the night, but he was making his case to Taylor about why it was safe to untie him. Tex was jostled out of the way by one of the shifters, who descended on a third platter laid down containing a plethora of fresh and roasted vegetables. Meal times were always hectic and he usually just found it easier to wait. A plate was gently pushed into his hands and he looked up at Sadie, who smiled at him and nodded her head.

'Thanks,' he murmured, touched by the gesture.

'Everybody sit down,' Shazza called, bringing the room to order. 'We've got a few announcements to make.'

It was testament to how well all of these different beings worked together as a cohesive unit that her command was followed almost immediately.

'Firstly, Tiaki and the Aunties are leaving for New Zealand.'

'What?' said one of the female members of Ben's pack. 'Why?'

Tex saw one of the women throw her an affectionate smile. If they were in the market for one more Auntie, they might just have a new recruit.

'We've done what we came here to do,' Tiaki said.

'And what was that, exactly?' Tex asked. He felt every set of eyes in the room fall on him, reminding him without needing to vocalise it that he had absolutely no business knowing what *their* business was. He gulped.

'Besides, I'm too recognisable here for what you all need to do next. We have to return to Aotearoa and maintain the strength of our *whare*.'

She paused as Sadie signed, the wizened werewolf watching her hand movements with interest before her gaze flicked to Tex for translation.

'She asked if you're the leader of your pack,' he said.

That was something he wanted to know too and he was glad Sadie was the vessel for the answer to this question.

'No.' She sighed. 'My husband Jonah was. In the wake of his death, my nephew Simon Tianne has filled that place. Our pack is fractured at the moment, spread from the South Island to Berlin and Scotland. We need to recalibrate and solidify our standing before . . . well, just before.'

'That leaves us three bodies down in terms of security,' Ben said. 'That's the bad news. The good news is Sadie and Tex are moving on to an associate of hers.'

'Where to?' Denton asked.

'Katoomba in the Blue Mountains. Shazza will be your driver this time and she'll take you up on Thursday. Plus, it will get you out of the city and that's crucial right now.'

'Why?' Tex asked, reading Sadie's hand movements. 'What have they done?'

Nobody needed to be enlightened about who 'they' were: everybody knew.

'Seems they've gone a little bit batty for you two,' Taylor said, his comment punctuated by a loud crunch as he bit into a carrot. 'It's hard to tell which one of you is important and why, but they're tearing the CBD apart. They even raided The Wisdom.'

'The only reason they haven't come here yet is because they don't know about it,' Denton murmured, looking ill.

'And we're gonna keep it that way,' Shazza told him.

One of the shifters got to their feet, momentarily taking the floor. 'I know this could be the last time we see each other for a while, but I gotta say it has been a pleasure having you here, Ben, Tiaki and the Aunties, Tex and Sadie too. I was honestly a bit wary about a banshee on the premises – didn't want anyone dying on us or some *Final Destination* shit – but you've been a delight.'

Ben groaned loudly, the sound covering up a few of the giggles. 'Banshees don't cause death, you idiot; they only serve as a warning of it.'

'Well, I heard—'

'Sit down, Ross,' Shazza said, tugging at the back of the man's singlet.

'I was saying it as a good thing,' he muttered quietly.

Sadie's shoulders had been shaking with the physical effect of laughter even though there was no sound to back it up. Yet suddenly the movement went still, her hand jutting out to grip Tex's shoulder.

'Are you—'

'What's wrong with her eyes?' Ben questioned.

'She's bleeding from the eyes!' Ross said, jumping back to his feet. 'Someone *is* going to die!'

'Shut up!' Tex hissed, quickly grabbing the knife and fork from her hands and pulling the plate away as she stiffened up completely. 'She's having a vision.'

'Give her some space,' Ben said, urging everyone back, before quietly adding: 'Does it usually look like this?'

'I've only seen it happen once but . . . yeah. Help me lay her back on that mattress over there.'

Tex took her arms and Ben the legs, gently setting her down and propping up pillows for maximum comfort.

'Keep the food close by,' Tex said, gesturing for it with his hands. 'She needs the energy afterwards. And is there any kind of sugary drink handy?'

'Vodka cruisers?' Taylor suggested.

He frowned. 'Without alcohol.'

'There's cranberry juice in the fridge,' Shazza muttered, crouching down as she watched Sadie with the same interest Tex had the first time he'd seen this.

'Not enough sugar,' Tiaki scoffed, marching into the kitchen. 'We're trying to replenish her, not prevent a UTI.'

Tex realised without Nora around, there wouldn't be a direct visual translation of Sadie's vision. He wondered if that would be frustrating for her, yet he figured her older sister wasn't always present when one of these occurred. With the flash of an idea, he spun around on his knees and grabbed his laptop from inside his work satchel. Flipping it open, he clicked on a blank document so it was ready as soon as she came out of it.

'Is now really the time to be checking the cricket scores?' Shazza asked, leaning over his shoulder.

'It's for Sadie,' he explained. 'So she can get down all the details. When she really gets going, she signs too quickly for me to keep up. I can understand only about every second or third word, I have to piece it together from there.'

'I've been meaning to ask,' Ben said. 'Did you have a family member with hearing difficulties before or—'

'No,' Tex snapped, annoyed by the barrage of voices and questions. 'I learned it for her.'

The room was quiet around them, Tex paying no attention to it as he watched Sadie for the first inkling that she was fading out of the vision. It happened with the twitch of her index finger, then her thumb, and within seconds the vibrant red colour that filled her eye as she foresaw death started to fade. At the end of it, she blinked, her sclera looking only somewhat bloodshot as Tex and Ben both helped her sit up. Squeezing her eyes shut for just a moment, she reopened them and looked as if she was ready to say something. Tex lifted the computer and placed it in her lap, Sadie peering down at it with surprise. It took a few seconds, but realisation lit up her features.

'Clever,' she mouthed, before her hands switched from moving through the air to flying over the keys. She was a ferocious typist, her digits light to the touch but moving rapidly as she wrote four solid paragraphs before taking a breath.

'There,' she signed, pushing it away from her for the others to read. Tex watched out of the corner of his eye as Tiaki moved forward, handing Sadie a glass of apple juice with ice in it. She took it gratefully, downing half before gulping for air.

'Which one of us is it?' Ross chimed.

'None of us,' Tex growled. 'It doesn't work like that, at least I don't think so. It's, oh, a husband and wife in Bondi, she thinks, from the look of the street outside. Murder suicide ... charming. What does the sky outside look like right now?'

'Betwixt and between times,' Shazza said.

'Which means?'

'Almost dusk, transitioning into night.'

'Ah, she says it was broad daylight in her vision so it's likely this has already happened. They're human, poison for one and a bullet for the other—'

'Yada yada yada,' Ben interrupted. 'Does this concern us?'

Tex looked at Sadie for confirmation. She shook her head slowly.

'No,' he replied. 'I don't think it does.'

The rest of the room slowly began to return to normal, the werewolves and shifters circling back towards the food as Sadie sipped her apple juice. All except the Ihi matriarch, who was staying close to Sadie as she handed her pieces of freshly cut fruit.

'That could be a handy skill,' Tiaki noted, leaning back and assessing the banshee with a newfound appreciation. 'Especially if you target it, make it specific to a particular group of people likely to be in peril . . .'

'Apparently my ancestors could,' signed Sadie, as Tex verbalised her words. 'According to the histories.'

She tapped the book behind her affectionately, like it was a small child who had just done something to amuse her. Tex had read that too, along with an account of a banshee whose predicative ability was foreseeing large-scale natural disasters. It had driven her mad, with the woman eventually throwing herself off the Cliffs of Moher at just twenty-one. He didn't want that fate for Sadie.

'How old are you? Nineteen, did I hear Ben say?'

Sadie nodded, her lips red with the juice of a strawberry she was munching on.

'Werewolves have a ritual called the coming of age, which happens usually between sixteen to nineteen depending on the pack and depending on the wolf. If you survive it, you have a new appreciation of those that came before you and the mana – power – you can harness within your pack. Point is, you're not really flexing the full scale of your abilities until around nineteen. That's when you're coming into your own.'

'Did you have kids? Did your children do it?' Tex asked for Sadie.

'All except my daughter, Aruhe, who is . . . taking a bit of a gap year, I guess you could say. The women in our family have a rebellious streak. That can be hard to reconcile with when you get to my age.'

She laughed, warmth lighting up her face as it spread from her cheeks to her eyes at the mention of her family. Suddenly she was handing Sadie a piece of paper, pushing it into her hands.

'This is for you. You should make a pit stop on the way up to the Blue Mountains,' she said. 'Follow what I've written here carefully, no deviations, or it can be very dangerous. She'll be able to get you everything you need for the price written there.'

'Shit,' he said, leaning over Sadie's shoulder as he read the figure. 'That's almost all of our cash.'

'She takes card too. But you pay for what you get and in terms of fresh passports, driver's licence, birth certificates – you name it – there's no one better. And you'll need these documents to get out of the country, whether that's next week or next month.'

'Thank you,' Tex said, translating Sadie's sign before adding: 'From the both of us.'

'Chur,' she said, grabbing the empty fruit plate and glass from Sadie. 'But you should think on that other stuff, the power of that gift of yours.'

Tex watched the woman leave and he turned to Sadie, about to sign a message. Yet she wasn't watching him; she was staring at Tiaki Ihi with a sense of wonderment and the spark of something he hadn't seen before: ambition.

Chapter 9

SADIE

Even on a Thursday, the Sydney Fish Markets were packed with people. Metal of dozens upon dozens of car rooftops glinted under the morning sun, the clear-blue sky reflected in the smooth surface that was simmering to touch. It was only a few days into the official start of summer, but it was exceedingly hot for December with Sadie able to feel the heat rising up from the bitumen as she walked through the car park. It was supposed to break thirty-five degrees Celsius by lunchtime and she felt like it wasn't far off.

Tex was in front of her and she appreciated the view: he'd been supplied with fresh clothes from a combination of Ben and Taylor's wardrobes. She enjoyed the effect one of the werewolf's singlets had on him, the longline shape and dropped armholes showing off parts of his body she hadn't seen before, like the thick curve of his shoulders and the way his upper arms seemed to flex without trying. He had the kind of body guys in construction effortlessly obtained while office workers spent thousands on personal trainers to get.

He'd had to cut his hair as well, something Sadie was sad about, to be honest. He wore it shortish, but there had been enough length she could imagine grabbing a handful. Now it was shaven almost right down to the scalp, with just a fine dusting of hair. She watched as he ran his hand over it self-consciously, clearly still not used to the feeling or even how it looked as he caught a glimpse of his reflection in a car window.

'I look like Jon Bernthal,' he muttered, mostly to himself.

'That's a good thing,' Sadie signed, savouring the little spur of energy openly flirting with him gave her. It was a strange luxury.

'It's because I've broken my nose a few times, isn't? I've got that broken nose thing going too?'

Sadie just smiled, pushing her sunglasses further up her face as she shifted her attention to concentrating on the task at hand. They'd done their farewells that morning, none of them particularly emotional but Sadie had felt a reluctance to leave the company of their protectors anyway. She'd been compelled to hug Taylor, feeling the surprise in his body before he loosened and hugged her back. Sadie had been sure that he was inhaling her scent: it was a shifter thing, no doubt, and she did her best not to be weirded out by it. Tiaki and the Aunties had left a few days earlier, the Ihi matriarch pressing her nose to Sadie's as a form of farewell.

The Australian werewolves weren't much for grand gestures, but Ben had grasped her hand at one point, just as she was about to walk out the door. It had sent an electric charge through her body and she hadn't meant to jump, but she did. She could tell he felt it too, his eyes widening for just a moment before his usual mask snapped back in place.

'Be careful,' he said. 'And watch your back.'

She didn't miss the way his eyes flicked to look at Denton and Texas over her shoulder, who were conferring. The former was staying behind and the latter was going with her, but she could understand why the werewolf was distrustful of the two men even if she felt like they had proven their worth.

'You too,' she mouthed. *With whatever you're up to*, she added in her mind.

The shifters and the two werewolf packs were planning something; you didn't have to be a genius to figure that out. She'd seen their huddles and hushed tones as they'd schemed, Sadie guessing they were going to use whatever information Denton had given to locate the sites where the Treize had been conducting those experiments on supernaturals. She'd voiced this theory to Texas, who agreed with her but said 'it wasn't their concern'. He was right. They couldn't add anything to that fight. They had to focus on what they could actually do: get out of Australia, find Sorcha, reunite with her sisters, go from there.

Shazza had driven them to the fish markets in a blue Holden Barina, the woman clearly more comfortable behind the wheel of Taylor's ute as she kept muttering under her breath about the hatchback having 'no grunt'. The vehicle blended though and that was the point. The biggest risk they were taking that day was going to the fish markets, so everything else had to be calculated accordingly. In truth, it wasn't a place with a huge supernatural presence according to the shifters. It was mainly populated by humans, which made the specifics of their task all the more unusual.

They passed barbecue houses and Asian restaurants on their way towards an enormous, blue building that sat on the water.

It was huge, with massive loading docks built into the side before the main entrance opened up for everyday folk. There was a path that led down to a jetty, with boats docked there and goods being carried back and forth. A series of tents housed a fresh fruit vendor, with mangoes, Kiwi fruit, strawberries, blueberries, apples and nectarines – white and yellow – lined up for sale. A man called to her as she passed him, telling Sadie he'd do her a special deal for a pineapple and watermelon combo. *Maybe later*, she thought, before her senses were drowned in the overwhelming smell of seafood.

'The entrance is always the busiest,' she signed at Tex, who looked dazed by the whole experience. He took her hand as they slowly tried to push their way through the crush of people and into the building itself. Everyone was jostling for a better position, some people peeling off to the left or right depending on what was being sold at the vendors either side of them. A woman was shouting about king prawns going for twenty-five dollars a kilo, while directly opposite a man was loudly touting the merits of their squid which was – according to him – 'the freshest in Australia'. She wondered what a squid happily plodding along the bottom of the ocean floor felt about that.

Customers pushed and moved against her, as Tex urged them forwards; none of it rough exactly but just part of doing business here. They took a short cut through a white, tiled area as workers tossed handful after handful of ice onto trays, huge crab legs being positioned so that the orange, meaty limbs stuck up in the air. A black claw snaked over the edge of a blue, plastic box that was labelled 'live Marron' as she passed it, the crayfish looking ready to make a leap for freedom within seconds. Her stomach growled slightly as they darted by the sushi counter, rows and rows of fresh hand rolls and grilled seafood stretching out like a rainbow of deliciousness.

'Keep your eyes peeled,' Tex whispered, as they moved deeper into the heart of the markets. His hand was still linked in hers and she squeezed it gently, her eyes resting on what she thought could be the thing they were looking for. A pretty woman with hair perched on the top of her head in a long, glossy black ponytail was standing on the other side of an oyster cart. Most of her body was concealed behind it, but Sadie could still see the shiny, blue apron that was draped around her neck as she shucked oysters. The completed ones were lined up in a pile in front of a glass cabinet for passers-by to inspect, while those still being worked on were stacked in a massive, grey pile in front of her. She would lift one up, rinse it under a tap of running water, before using a tiny knife to slit it open by running the blade along the hinge from back to front. She kept her eyes down, focused on her work as both Sadie and Tex drew closer.

'Tray of half a dozen oysters, please,' Tex said, repeating the lines Tiaki had written down for Sadie.

'How do you want 'em?' the woman asked, still not glancing up as her knife cut through shell and oyster flesh. She made it look easy with smooth, confident gestures.

'Natural,' he replied, before an elbow to his ribs made him add a further comment. 'Dreckly as you like.'

If Sadie hadn't been watching her so closely, she would have missed how the woman's knife slowed for *just* a beat. She looked up at them for the first time with startlingly blue eyes that portrayed a shrewd kind of intelligence.

'Want a quarter of lime with that?'

Tex opened his mouth to reply, before glancing at Sadie for assistance.

'We prefer lemon,' he said, the words sounding somewhat robotic as he translated her sign language.

'Righto.' She nodded, gaze flicking from Sadie to Tex and back again. She called behind her to a colleague, speaking a flurry of words in Mandarin that Sadie didn't understand. The man was in the middle of filleting a fish and shouted back a one-word response, quickly wiping his knife before stepping away from the counter and heading towards them. The lady lifted the blue apron off, over her head, and looped it around the new man's thick neck. She patted him on the shoulder in thanks, before he seamlessly slipped into the spot previously occupied by her. Sadie watched as she kept the knife, moving it to a small sheath at her waist. In fact, there were several knives there and tools of various size, all dangling off a belt that hung around her hips and jiggled as she walked.

'Come with me,' she said, gesturing so that Sadie and Tex would follow her. She led them away from the busiest part of the fish markets, the trio stepping back outside into the sun again and along a wooden deck. It was a large area, but packed tight with benches and umbrellas offering some attempt at shade. There were people cramped into every available space, while huge ibises flapped their wings nearby and waited for any scrap of food that may drop to the floor at a moment's notice.

'How'd you find me?' the woman asked, glancing over her shoulder as they walked.

Tex and Sadie exchanged a look, neither one sure whether they should divulge their source.

'Oh, come on,' she cackled, with a dirty laugh. 'I assume you weren't told to just come to the Sydney Fish Markets and look for an Asian woman. As far as hiding places go, this is a pretty excellent one.'

'A werewolf friend sent us,' Tex said, reading Sadie's signs.

'That doesn't narrow it down. Male or female?'

'Female. With, uh, facial tattoos.'

The woman looked amused at the way Tex stumbled over the last part, but she nodded.

'Long-time customers,' she muttered, before pausing in front of a gate.

She pulled a key from a chain that seemed to have at least fifty different ones on it, unlocking the entry and holding it open for them as they walked through. There was a white sign hanging over their heads that said 'PRIVATE JETTY: TRESPASSERS WILL BE PROSECUTED'. The metallic structure snapped shut behind them with a clang, the woman basically skipping down the long catwalk that led to several different boats. Hers wasn't the newest or largest by any stretch, but Sadie thought there was something about it that looked distinctly homey as they neared. While her neighbours' boats were pristine white and looked more like floating toilets somehow, this one appeared to be made out of a variety of woods with dark brown, tan and a yellowish hues all mingling together like a jigsaw. A man was sitting at the stern in a deck chair, legs stretched out and resting on the railing as he watched them draw closer.

'Mind your step,' he said quietly. As they climbed aboard, Sadie caught a glance at the faded paint along the side of the boat that read: '*Titanic II*'.

'We're alright, Wyck,' the woman muttered, walking by the man who had a fishing rod propped up next to him, line trailing in the water, along with a shotgun resting casually at his feet. They were led into the interior of the boat and followed her down a set of steps into a windowless room that was decorated like an office. There was an expansive, oak desk that took up most of the space and positioned on it were several laptops, a cutting board, measurement tools, lamps with differing bulbs that she assumed did differing things, magnifying implements and a rack of ink pots. It looked like ordered chaos and Sadie's eyes ran over the hundreds of pens, paint brushes, and stamps that took up any remaining space as the woman settled into a luxurious chair. She offered them seats at the other side of the desk. A map of Australia consumed the entire back wall, with the country itself empty while all the parts that contained water were filled with intricate details about tides, currents and reefs.

'Alright, this is a safe space to discuss business matters,' she said. 'I want both of your names.'

'I'm Texas Contos and this is Sadie Burke.'

There was the slightest shift of the woman's eyebrows as Tex said her name, Sadie noticed. It was a small, almost miniscule gesture. But it was recognition.

'Pleasure,' she said, as if nothing had happened. 'I'm Dreckly Jones. Don't look so surprised: I can be both a measure of time and a person.'

Sadie liked her immediately.

'If Tiaki sent you to me and you know all the right codes, I assume you also know what I charge.'

'Yes, we have cash. And . . . uh, we heard you also take card.'

'Let's do half and half.' She shrugged. 'My safe only fits so much. What are you after?'

Sadie had written down a list and slid the piece of paper across the desk to Dreckly, the woman taking it and considering what was scrawled there.

'This isn't very specific, just documents to get *out* of the country? A passport and driver's licence will do that. Hell, I'll throw in a few tertiary ID cards like a gym membership and library card. But there's nothing here about where you're going.'

'Why is that important?' Tex questioned.

Dreckly had long, acrylic nails that were elaborately decorated. Sadie hadn't noticed them until she slipped off her gloves at the oyster cart, but now she couldn't stop staring. There was a turquoise gem stone at the tip of one and as she tapped that finger against the wood of her desk, it twinkled.

'Every country has beef with somewhere else and that somewhere else is usually on a list, with travellers coming in from those countries subject to increased scrutiny and questioning. We want to avoid that. So if you're planning on going to, say, the United States I need to know that information so I don't list you as an Iraqi national. Also, dates of travel are important: pre or post the Brexit clusterfuck, for instance. Get my drift?'

'We're leaving within the week,' Tex said. 'We—'

He paused as Sadie signed quickly, his eyes reading her message with a frown. Dreckly glanced between the two of them, looking amused.

'Get us documents for wherever my sister went,' he said, Sadie watching the woman's face intently as he spoke. 'Sorcha Burke.'

There was a beat loaded with tension as the three of them sat there, saying nothing, while Dreckly tapped her nails and created her own personal metronome.

'Londony Londony Londony,' Dreckly hummed, to the beat of a Fergie song.

She spun around, pulling some paperwork from one of several cabinets that were positioned around the office. Each had different flags on the outside of a wooden drawer. The one she targeted was a Union Jack.

'Immediate travel, entry to the UK ... I think we keep it simple. Can you do a British accent?'

Tex looked surprised for a moment, before clearing his throat. ''Ello ... Gov?'

'That's a hard no,' she said, eyes wide as she made a note. 'You'll both be New Zealand citizens and don't worry, no one over there can tell Aussie and Kiwi accents apart. You'll be a married couple, I've got some rings I can sort you out with, and you should probably dye your hair pink.'

Sadie looked over her shoulder, sure the woman had meant someone else for a heartbeat.

'Yes, you, you adorable thing. With your ginger situation, we can throw a semi-permanent supermarket box dye over the top and it will look different enough. You don't wanna go with a hard, Goth black or anything bold that looks like you're trying to hide. Sorcha could pull that off. You can't.'

I definitely won't be hiding with pink hair, she thought.

'I shaved my head last night,' Tex said quickly. 'I don't need to dye it pink too, do I?'

Dreckly smirked. 'I think we're good. Come on, up – both of you.'

They did as she ordered, the woman walking around the desk to open one of the cabinets not marked with a world flag. A myriad of things rolled out, all neatly packed and stacked on dozens of shelves. She plucked a box of hair dye from one row, which contained every colour imaginable and handed it to Sadie.

'Bathroom's down the hall. You don't need to bleach it or anything, just use the little brush in the box to lather your hair. Leave it twenty minutes then wash it out: we don't want it too dark. There are gloves under the sink and a hairdryer in there. When you're done, come back.'

'What do I do in the meantime?' Tex asked.

'Pick your wedding rings,' Dreckly answered, her hand sweeping over a shelf full of costume jewellery. 'Your girl's wearing a lot of silver, so I'd go with that.'

He reached towards one ring and Dreckly slapped his hand. 'Not that one, look at her? That's far too gaudy. You want something nice and girlie, with a little oomph.'

'Are we still talking about rings?'

Dreckly rolled her eyes, shooing Sadie away as she headed down the hall to work on her soon-to-be-pink hair.

Two hours and eight thousand dollars later, they were being ushered off the boat as Dreckly walked them up the jetty to let them out of the security gate. Not only did Sadie have a new hair colour she didn't hate entirely, she and Tex now had matching wedding rings, driver's licences, and passport photos taken. They were sharing a burner phone between them, with only Taylor and Shazza's numbers saved in the directory. It would take Dreckly two days to make everything they needed and that was expediting their order, which cost extra. When she was done, she'd send a text to the number Sadie had supplied, which was being monitored by the shifters. There were a series of lockers out the front of the fish markets, next to the booth where you paid for your parking. When their order was ready for collection, Dreckly would tell them what number they were looking for and the passcode; inside they'd find what they paid for.

'You just run this whole set-up from a boat?' Tex said, as they neared the gate. 'Don't you find an environment like this a little—'

'Fishy?' Dreckly offered, with a teasing smirk. 'Salty, maybe.'

He chuckled. 'Sure.'

'Icebergs aside, this is a pretty great escape route if I need it. I can come and go as I please, it's cheap to dock, and I have no permanent address. It's a pleasure to be my own boss, lemme tell you, especially if you've ever worked for an asshole. Sure, my clientele are usually bad people running away from bad things or good people doing the same – or not even people at all – but you need more than just bikies to pay the bills.'

She held the gate open for them, Tex extending his hand.

'Thank you for everything.'

'I don't shake hands,' she said, as politely as she could. 'I'm wishing you the best of luck though. You too, pinkie. I liked your sister.'

Sadie tipped her head, slipping under the woman's arm as they walked up off the jetty and through the fish markets. It was still busy as ever, the elapsed time clearly making no difference to people's desire to gorge themselves on seafood. Sadie and Tex were quiet as they strolled back through the car park, each one deep in thought.

'Do you think we got fleeced?' he asked. 'I mean, I know that's the price they said we should expect but I can't help feeling like we got fleeced.'

'It was a pretty cheap wedding, all things considered,' she signed, earning a hearty laugh from him. He held up his finger, inspecting his wedding ring.

'Hey, I'm Greek, so the cost of that whole experience would have barely covered our dessert table.'

Sadie smiled, glancing down at what sat on her own finger. It was a series of roses, all strung together so they overlapped in what almost looked like a Celtic design from a distance. There was a tiny, pink stone set in the middle: it was probably cubic zirconia, with the ring itself sterling silver at best. It looked real enough though and that's what mattered. Tex had fallen silent again beside her and she wondered if it was because of any perceived awkwardness that arose from joking about their wedding.

'How did you know about Sorcha?' he asked, breaking the reprieve in their conversation.

'She recognised my name,' Sadie signed. 'And I figured if Dreckly is the supernatural go-to for fake documents, it would make sense that Sorcha was a client as well. Once.'

'Do you think she was human?'

'No,' Sadie mouthed, almost immediately.

'What?' Tex responded, clearly surprised. 'Come on, just 'cos she does criminal work for supernaturals doesn't me—'

She cut him a look, raising an eyebrow that said 'how can you be so naive?'

'She looks human enough,' he murmured.

'She looks human to the humans. They think she's one of them. Our kind wouldn't trust a human with that type of work.'

'Did Tiaki tell you what she was? You two seemed kind of close. Did she mention it?'

Sadie shook her head.

'Huh, okay, let's bet five bucks on it then.'

'Make it fifty,' she signed; Tex's eyes lighting up with a real wager.

'Deal,' he said, shaking her hand as they walked. 'I'm going with . . . goblin.'

Sadie scoffed at his guess: this would be easy money. He tried to explain his choice.

'Come on, you know how good they are at anything detailed. Technology mainly, sure, but before computers it was clocks and inventions and *anything* meticulous. What's your answer then?'

She thought for a moment, trying to explain the otherness she sensed around Dreckly and where that might fit into what she knew of the wider supernatural world.

'Something to do with water,' she signed.

'Water? I didn't see any fish tail.'

'I didn't say she was a selkie. Besides, they can change form into any number of sea creatures so maybe you wouldn't know. Or at least that's what I heard.'

There was also something about the way she spoke of her boat that told Sadie she was talking around the subject, telling semi-truths among a series of lies. Dreckly needed to be near the water, she suspected. It was like a comfort blanket of some kind, but the banshee couldn't pinpoint it exactly. She'd never really met anyone like Dreckly Jones and she wasn't fool enough to believe that was her real name either. There was a curt honk and they turned their heads, Shazza waving her arm at them from out the window of the Holden Barina. She'd moved spots and – clearly glad to see them – sped out of her current one so the car pulled up alongside them.

'You get what you need?' she asked, as they climbed in.

Tex nodded. 'We'll have it in forty-eight hours, she said.'

'Grouse.' The shifter smiled, sliding into second gear as they crawled forward. 'Next stop: the Blue Mountains.'

Sadie fell asleep on the drive, waking a few hours later when the winding roads of their ascent into the mountains were enough to stir her. It was bushfire season, with the car passing an enormous hazard sign next to the road that told her how bad the threat was via a semi-circle colour wheel. The white arrow was firmly in the orange quadrant – severe – which sounded bad, but was truthfully fifty/fifty as far as things go during the Aussie summer. They were neither in the red section – extreme – or much feared red and black striped section – catastrophic – so they were fine. For now. They passed Katoomba train station, a line of tourists crossing the road as they prepared to head down the main street towards the scenic hiking trails and most Instagrammable locations. She'd been there a few times as a kid, her mind tracking back to an image of Sorcha, Shannon and her posing in front of the Three Sisters rock formation. Because they were three sisters, after all. They'd thought it was hilarious at the time.

Just thinking about her siblings stirred a complex range of emotions in her chest. She'd sent Shannon an email via the address she'd been made to memorise and used a VPN to bounce her location. The reply had been short, but it had seemed like a lifeline to her.

'Keavy and I are okay,' it read. 'So are the kids. Nora and Ina have checked in too. Waiting to hear from Catriona and Bridie, plus Aoife, Colleen and Mum. Won't say where we are, but will reach out when I can.'

She had followed it up with another email seconds later, clearly rethinking her tone.

'We love and miss you. Keavy says hi and please let us know if you *see* anything that could help.'

Their deaths, she meant. She wanted Sadie to warn them if she had a vision of any of her relatives falling into harm's way. They had all broken The Covenant now; may as well keep stamping on the smashed pieces. After her vision of the murder suicide near the beach, Sadie's conversation with Tiaki had played on her mind a lot. There was something self-determined about the New Zealand werewolves, some kind of agency that she thought might have rubbed off on her in their short time together. Her visions *would* be better if they weren't just about random people. If they were directed at the people she cared about, that could help a lot. When she was young, much younger, she used to have dreams of death and dying all the time. To other kids they might have been nightmares, but in her family they were prophetic and the first taste of what her initial ability would be.

Burke Forensic Cleaning Services had existed as long as Sadie could remember, with Shannon and Nora initially using the inheritance from their father's death to get it off the ground. It was a big risk at the time, with Shannon unable to hold down a job and Nora fresh out of university. Aoife had been against it, so too their cousins, with Sadie even remembering a document their auntie had prepared about all the reasons it was unlikely they would succeed in this very grim, very male dominated area of expertise. In hindsight, she'd made that business plan to help her nieces, not spite them. Yet it had caused a huge fight in the family. That was as far back as Sadie could pinpoint her visions, with them becoming specific to a set geographical range. Was it purely coincidental that the things she saw were helpful to her family's business? What she could foresee gave them the competitive edge, especially once they all started working together to intuit other details about crime scenes and potential jobs.

In the book that had either luckily or unluckily fallen into Tex's lap, there was a whole chapter on banshee abilities evolving around the needs of their species. They'd started off with *all* banshees having several gifts to begin with. As they'd flourished, that had started to thin down from woman to woman. Since their deportation to Australia, certain skillsets had died out completely or were just extremely rare. Even the remaining abilities were weaker, it was obvious, because banshees were weaker too.

Just something to think about, that gift of yours. The words had echoed in her mind as Sadie began to stretch it, trying to *bring on* a vision rather than wait for one to happen. She had no idea what she was doing, of course, but making it up as she went along was better than nothing. She thought of Sorcha, her beloved sister, and she tried to imagine what she would look like two full years after she'd last seen her. At first Sadie had little success, which she'd expected. Then something funny started to happen: she'd urge herself to think of Sorcha, to locate her and the events of her life, and she'd start to taste *tea*. She'd heard of people's tastebuds doing unusual things before they had a stroke, yet this was definitely not that; it was strong and it was hot and it had the faintest hint of lemon. Earl Grey, which was Sorcha's favourite when served correctly. There were other things, like a sudden coldness she would feel and the crunch of snow underfoot. She could hear accents in her head, harsh London ones. Sadie very well might be losing her mind – she knew that – but she may also be picking up on where her sibling was.

In the rare quiet moments she had to herself, and as she was drifting off at night, she was going to continue to try and push her gift to see what other results she might yield. Getting Dreckly to point them in the direction of the UK was great, but it was also somewhere with a lot of bloody people and countless places to hide. She was hoping Kala Tully would help her get more specific. There was a rough sound outside the car as the wheels crunched over loose pebbles, Shazza having turned off a residential street for a road that was only big enough to fit one car at a time. In fact, it looked better suited to a horse and cart. Huge, thick hedges lined the sides of it so they couldn't see what was through the foliage at all. Some kind of tree – tall and old – grew over the top of that, with branches drooping down and scratching the roof of the vehicle like fingernails along a chalk board.

'Can you say "witch's house" or what?' Tex muttered, leaning forward in the front seat as the hedgerow suddenly opened up to reveal a two-storey cottage. There were plants everywhere: growing from a carefully manicured garden at the front to spewing over window ledges that housed boxes of flowers, herbs, and all manner of local flora. It looked like something Professor Sprout would want to acquire if she got into the real estate market, there was *that much* green and life covering every inch. Sadie enjoyed the sound of a wind chime tinkling in the afternoon breeze, taking a moment to close her eyes and deeply inhale.

'Is it just me or can you still smell the fish too?' Tex asked, Sadie smiling as she opened her eyes.

'It's the air,' she signed. 'The air just always smells better, feels better, in the Blue Mountains.'

'That's the elevation getting to you,' he said, looking at a stone footpath that led to the front door with some trepidation. It was lined with garden gnomes of assorted size and hostility, which she thought may have been the source of his discomfort.

'Don't worry,' a voice said; 'they won't bite if you don't.'

'The . . . gnomes?' Tex gulped, looking even more cautious as a woman strolled towards them. She was in a pair of tight, ripped jeans and a black halter top, with a stunning shawl thrown over her shoulders in a variety of reds, pinks, and deep purples. Her hair was wrapped up on top of her head in a twisted bun of braids that looked heavy to Sadie's inexperienced eye. She was Aboriginal and from the hint of her bare shoulder that Sadie could see, she recognised several of the flowers from the garden inked on her skin. Somehow, the banshee felt like she could almost taste the power as it rippled off this woman with every seductive sashay of her hips.

'I'm Kala Tully,' she said, resting in front of them with her arms crossed. She added. 'The witch.'

She gave Tex only a cursory look, before her gaze fixated on Sadie.

'Thanks again for this,' Shazza said, the shifter's words eventually drawing the witch's eyes away from examining her.

'Of course,' she replied. 'A year ago I would have stayed clear of trouble like this, but things change.'

'Ain't that the truth.'

The two women were clearly in that strange stretch between shifting from acquaintances to potential friends. Tex joined their conversation, the trio exchanging details on everything that had been happening over the past week. Kala pressed for more information about the Treize's movements since the hunt for fugitives was officially on and what they knew about the experiments. That all became background noise, however, as Sadie caught sight of the second woman to emerge from the cottage. Everything the witch was, this lady was the complete opposite. Where her skin was brown and tattooed, this woman's was so pale it made Sadie look tan. Where Kala Tully was short, curvy, and endowed with a generous amount of bosom, this woman was straight up and down, thin, and small-chested. She was also incredibly tall, well over six foot, with white hair that fell past her waist. To top it all off, in place of where her right hand would be – below the elbow – was a robotic arm, complete with shining, metal fingers that curled as she walked and decorative purple lights.

She seemed as interested in Sadie as Sadie was her, with the woman ignoring the other party as she strolled up to the banshee. She stopped a few feet away from her – any closer and it would have been weird – but Sadie felt as if the lady's strange, grey eyes could see more than just her physical body. For all she knew, maybe they could.

'Hello, Sadie Burke,' she said, her voice rich with a German accent. 'My name is Corvossier von Klitzing, but you can call me Casper. My brother and I have been really looking forward to meeting you.'

A ghost materialised next to the woman: fully transparent and fully dead. It was around then that Sadie realised she may have forgotten to breathe.

Chapter 10

When Tex turned around and saw Sadie passed out, her body laying on a crumpled flower bed, he thought the ground beneath him would disappear. He had already sprinted over and lifted her into his arms before he realised there was a ghost standing right behind him. Tex hadn't even *seen* a ghost before that moment, let alone one that talked directly at him.

'Yeah, you should really put her in the recovery position,' it said. 'Just in case she vomits a little.'

'Barry!' the pale woman said, scolding.

'What? Keep the airways clear!'

'Oh Christ,' he heard the witch mumble.

'Whoa,' Shazza said, clearly in awe. 'I heard about ... but never ... *whoa*.'

'You should probably leave this to us. Those their bags?'

'Uh huh. And he's just translucent like that? You could throw a rock through him?'

'Have a safe drive, thanks again.'

Tex overheard the conversation between the shifter and the witch like it was playing on low volume on a distant

196

television. Even as he registered the noise of the car starting up and the pebbles crunching as the tyres of Shazza's vehicle spun, he couldn't quite process it.

'W-who . . .' he attempted. 'Uh, what is . . .'

'Why don't you let me start?' the woman said, the ghost hovering next to her the entire time and mirroring her compassionate smile.

'Can you carry her into the house first?' Kala Tully questioned. 'I dare say she'll be more comfortable on a couch than laying on my native rose *Boronia serrulata*.'

'Huh?' Tex blinked.

'Simple,' the pale lady said in a soothing tone, placing her hand affectionately on top of the witch's. 'Keep your words simple. Your instructions direct. Remember how you reacted the first time you met Barry?'

'Cool, calm and collected,' Kala replied. 'I was a modern day Lisa Bonet.'

The ghost laughed and she stuck out her tongue.

'Flowers,' the witch said, directing her comment back at him. 'Lift her off my flowers, follow me inside. Casper, you okay with the bags?'

'Sure thing.'

Casper, he thought, before the name repeated in his skull. *Corvossier von Klitzing, the medium!* Her ability was so rare and that set of skills valued so highly, Casper and her brother Creeper had been downright legendary among the supernatural world because of what they could do with the dead. That was until a few years ago, when something terrible had happened, but he couldn't remember all the specifics. She was German, though; Tex was certain of it. His mind was racing with questions. He was dying to know what she was doing in Australia, of all places, and clearly shacked up with a witch.

Then Sadie stirred in his arms and all queries fell away as he focused on her. Several strands of hair were covering her face and he brushed them off, leaning forward as he watched her eyelids flutter open. Her gaze was unfocused to begin with and he leaned closer, so his face would take up most of her range of vision and she wouldn't be startled back to unconsciousness by a ghost.

'Hey, you're okay. You just fainted for a moment.'

She licked her lips, as if testing to see whether they were still there.

'When was the last time you ate?'

She opened her mouth to respond, then frowned with a thought.

'S'okay, I've got you. I'm going to take you inside now, but just in case you were thinking you're crazy: you're not. You did see a ghost and I can see him too.'

He paused, waiting for a beat before leaning in and whispering in her ear.

'And he *talks*.'

'*And* he can hear you. Are you gonna pick her up like the big hero you are and bring her in already? Or we gonna leave her out here for the possums?'

Sadie half sat up, looking around Tex to examine the undead man for herself.

'Hey sweetie,' the ghost waved. 'Sorry about all that. I get a little overexcited sometimes and so rarely have the chance to just *pop* out of thin air these days. I got carried away and I apologise.'

Bracing his knee underneath him, Tex lifted Sadie in the air and began walking towards the cottage door, where the witch was waiting for them. The ghost floated along, seemingly ecstatic about having someone new to talk to as he maintained a steady flow of one-sided conversation. Sadie must have regained enough of her composure, as she told him to 'put her down' in Auslan. When he didn't, she followed that up with a 'now'.

'I'm not doing that, sorry; we're nearly inside and then you can lay down for the rest of the night if you want to.'

'Tex, I'm too heavy.'

He actually laughed at that.

'I'm taller *and* heavier than you. Put me down, this is embarrassing.'

'As the lady wishes.' He smiled, carefully lowering her on to a couch. He watched the expressions play over her face in a matter of seconds, Sadie realising that he'd kept her arguing with him just long enough to get her where she needed to go.

'*You*,' she mouthed.

'You're welcome.' He grinned.

'Here,' the medium said, slinking around him with a cup and handing it to her. 'Sip it slowly, it's just brewed. It's peppermint tea . . . helps when you're feeling nauseous.'

Sadie made a thank you gesture with her four fingers, Corvossier nodding with a smile.

'That means thank you,' Tex said. 'She thanked you for the tea.'

'And she apologised for fainting,' the ghost said. Tex turned to face him, incredulous.

'You can read Auslan? And I left that part out; seemed unnecessary to apologise for stupid shit.'

'That I agree with,' Kala said, curling up in an armchair across the room while Corvossier settled in on the couch with the banshee. The witch was watching Sadie with a neutral expression as the medium fussed over her.

'She really can't speak,' she said, after a long moment. 'I mean, Sorcha told me what they did to her but . . . seeing it is something else.'

Sadie gulped the mouthful she had, before glancing up at Tex with a look he couldn't quite decipher. That was rare, because he thought he was learning the meaning behind her every frown, lip twitch, or narrowed eye.

'I need to find her,' she signed, Texas speaking as she did so. 'I thought she was dead, I thought there was no way . . . I don't think that any more.'

'You think your sister's alive?' Corvossier asked, glancing at the ghost.

Sadie nodded. 'And if she is, I think Kala Tully might know where she has gone. Am I wrong?'

The witch waited a moment before she replied. 'No, you're not wrong.'

'She's somewhere in the UK, isn't she?' Sadie signed.

'That's what I figured.' Kala shrugged. 'That was her plan initially and if she made it out of that cruise ship disaster alive, I don't see any reason why she would have changed it.'

'And you helped her. You connected her with Dreckly?'

'The other way round, actually. Sorcha had been planning her escape for a long time before I needed to disappear as well. She spent a lot of time slowly, carefully, building up her contacts. She hooked me up with Dreckly when my sister and her husband were murdered. Without Sorcha . . .'

'You owe her a debt,' Sadie signed, while Tex stated. The witch nodded.

'Then repay it to me. Tell me where she is.'

'I don't know for certain, but London is where I'd start. She liked the anonymity a metropolis like that could afford her, plus the multiple exit routes if she needed them.'

Sadie sipped her tea, the gesture an attempt to hide her disappointment. Tex knew she'd been hoping for more information than that; after all, London was a city of more than eight million people – many of them supernaturals. Finding one banshee amongst all of that . . .

'I'm sorry,' Kala said. 'I wish I could help you more, I truly do, but that's everything I know. I'd give anything for the possibility that my sister was still alive, so I hope you find her. Until then, you should stay here. Both of you. The Treize are ripping through Sydney right now, the Blue Mountains are the safest option until you leave.'

'Can you help us do that?' Sadie signed, Texas surprised at her forcefulness. 'I know you have a way, probably several. Can you get us to London?'

The witch and the medium exchanged a look, before Corvossier spoke up. 'We know someone who might be able to help.'

'Not Tasmanian devil shifters,' Kala added.

'If this person can't get you right into London, they'll be able to get you close.' The medium smiled. 'And soon.'

'Not to interrupt,' the ghost started. 'But while we're on the subject of helping each other, just because Kala can't assist with your sister, that doesn't mean we can't.'

'What are you thinking?' Corvossier questioned, turning to her brother.

'This Sorcha's a banshee, no? Her call to the dead would be strong. Banshees aren't dissimilar to us: they're connected to the dead and death in a different way, but it leaves a thick trail through the lobby if you want me to look for it.'

She nodded. 'I do. Whatever you find, bring that information straight back. If . . . if that's okay?'

Sadie bobbed her head enthusiastically, eyes lit with hope as she mouthed the word 'please'.

'Wait,' Kala said, holding her hand up just as it looked like the ghost might vamoose right out of the room. 'There's something else.'

'Something . . . else?' Tex asked, noting how the witch's gaze shifted to focus on him expectantly.

'A book,' she said. 'Shazza mentioned you were travelling with.'

The medium straightened in her chair, if possible looking even more interested. Texas felt a flash of annoyance and he sensed Sadie stiffen beside him.

'We haven't had the best experience with evil books in the past,' the witch continued.

Sadie placed the mug on the ground, her hands quick to express her disagreement.

'Oh no, it's not evil,' Tex said, speaking for her. 'That's what Sadie's saying.'

'You get the book,' the ghost ordered him. 'I'll translate.'

Reluctantly, he began lifting items out of his work satchel to retrieve the volume.

'It's a great book,' Sadie was saying, through the ghost.

'Depressing in a lot of ways, sure, but it's full of things the Treize don't want most banshee women to know, things that used to be passed down in stories from generation to generation. But things get lost, truths get mistold, and having it all right there in a cohesive volume like this . . . well, it's not evil, that's what I'm saying.'

When she was done pleading her case, he placed the book into the outstretched hands of Corvossier.

'My God,' the medium whispered, the fingers of her non-robotic arm sliding over the scant few publishing details there were at the start of the volume. 'Barry, come look at this.'

'Barry,' Tex muttered, testing out how the word sounded on his lips.

'Full name Barastin von Klitzing,' Kala said. 'He prefers Barry.'

'I don't,' the ghost replied.

'Corvossier von Klitzing here is his twin sister, better known as Casper to you and yours. It's catchy, so you'll be surprised how little time it takes for that to stick. They were twins in life and after Barry was murdered by the same people who took Casper's arm, he has hung around in death.'

'Forgive me for being rude,' Tex said. 'But witches are very . . .'

'Private?' Kala offered. 'Secretive?'

'Yes. You tend to keep to yourselves and outsiders aren't generally let into the covens, right?'

'Right.'

'So how is it that you two met?'

Kala let out a long sigh. 'The same people who killed Barry and tried to kill Casper murdered my sister Willa.'

'Where were they?' Tex asked, shaking his head slightly as he misinterpreted Sadie's sign language. 'Sorry, *who* were they?'

'They were you.'

'What?' He blinked.

'They had been Askari, at one point or another. Before the idea of becoming something *more* consumed them. Casper found where I was hiding because she wanted to hunt them. So we did. As for the where, they're all dead now, their ashes taken out to sea.'

'The Treize covered it up,' he whispered. 'Didn't they?'

'They did,' she answered, watching him closely. 'You've got that look on your face: Casper had it too. It's that look where suddenly you realise everything you believed – everything you worked towards – was a lie.'

'I wouldn't say it's sudden,' he muttered, casting a glance at Sadie.

'Do you remember?' the ghost Barastin was saying to his sister. 'She was so proud when she finished it and then ... nothing.'

Corvossier was nodding, silent tears streaking down her face despite the fact she didn't look sad. There was even a hint of a smile there.

'I just assumed she put it back in a drawer,' she said. 'That she wasn't happy with it and wanted to make further edits.'

'I never heard her speak of it again, did you?'

'No,' Corvossier agreed, her hand running over the listed names of the Blight family.

'You knew her?' Tex asked. 'All I could find out was that Collette Blight was a Custodian, recently deceased, and that her parents were Custodians before her. There's a list of published works in her file, but *The Collected Banshee Histories* is not among them.'

'She was *our* Custodian,' Corvossier said, closing the book and pressing it to her chest like it was a physical piece of the person she missed. 'She raised Barry and I and when we were old enough, managed the jobs we did for the Treize.'

'Hauntings mostly,' her brother said. 'The occasional exorcism.'

'How did she die?' Tex asked. 'Was it suspicious?'

Corvossier snorted. 'You could say that: she was murdered the same night Barry was, by the monsters who did *this*.'

She held up her bionic arm for emphasis, the wrist rotating slightly as she wiggled the mechanical fingers at him like an exaggerated wave.

'I've just moved from Berlin,' the medium continued. 'They've shut down Treize headquarters at the Bierpinsel, which was where we all lived. I packed up her things and brought what was precious with me but this . . . I've never seen the physical, finished book before. I think it's the only one of its kind, and these pages . . . they're printed. This was manufactured at a legitimate printing press and beautifully bound. So my question is, who did she give it to and why?'

Corvossier was staring at the book in wonderment, carefully turning each page as if it contained some kind of treasure. Tex had thought Fairuza had given the book to him in the hope it would end up in Sadie's hands, yet as he watched the medium he wasn't so sure any more. It looked like it had found its rightful owner.

'Let me examine it,' Kala said, getting to her feet. 'Books can hold power, as you know. I want to go through this one thoroughly before we deem it some long-lost jewel.'

'Let me join you,' Corvossier offered, before Kala shook her head. 'Sprinkle will be home in a few hours and you're on dinner duty. It's pasta night, remember?'

'Crap, yeah. I've got my Bolognese mix brewing. Barry, can you show our guests to their rooms?'

'With pleasure,' the ghost said, ushering them onwards. 'Then I'll be off to find Miss Sorcha Burke.'

'I'll be in the garden studio,' Kala said, her footsteps punctuated by the shutting of the front door.

Corvossier gave them a small shrug. 'We've had some bad experiences with *rare* books in the past and it has taken a lot for our weird family to create a home we all feel safe in. Kala just wants to take the necessary precautions.'

'I understand.' Tex nodded, truly meaning it.

'I'll be in the kitchen if you need anything. Oh, and don't be alarmed when you see or hear an eleven-year-old child running around later. That's Kala's niece, Sprinkle.'

'Cool name,' Sadie signed.

'Just wait till you meet her. She's gonna go nuts for your hair.'

He watched Sadie smile, her fingers reaching up to touch the ends of her freshly pink locks with uncertainty. He knew she'd been reluctant to dye it and sure, he missed her natural colour too, but the magenta pink really did suit her. He grabbed both of their bags and handed Sadie a water bottle as they walked, following the semi-translucent Barastin up a set of wooden stairs that led to a second level.

'Corvossier and Kala's room is down the hall,' the ghost

said, pointing to the left. 'You'll be staying in the guest bedrooms at the opposite end here on my right, with a bathroom wedged between each of them. The madame Miss Sprinkle has the loft room upstairs, but, Tex, you're in the room known as the "games den" so she's highly likely to invade your space at some point.'

'Got it.' He smirked.

'If you follow the illuminated arrows on the floor, you'll find your nearest exit and remember, it could be behind you,' Barastin finished, in a flight attendant voice that was damn near perfect. And with that, he disappeared into thin air. Sadie and Tex both jumped, him settling her with a calming hand on her shoulder. They hesitated proceeding further for a moment, as if Barastin might reappear and frighten them as he seemed to like doing so much. When nothing happened, they continued the rest of the way down the hall, with Sadie taking one door and him the other. A single bed was covered in soft toys that Tex thought might resemble Pokémon, but he couldn't be one hundred per cent certain. There were movie posters on the walls and gaming consoles positioned neatly in an IKEA shelving structure that housed an enormous screen at the centre of it. He dumped his bag, grabbing Sadie's and heading to the room she had occupied, which looked like it was actually intended for visitors. Her back was to him and she was staring out the window, sipping the water he had given her.

'I think there's a Twix in that front pocket,' he said, as she turned to face him. He reached inside the backpack and rummaged around until he found what he was looking for.

'Aha!' He grinned, triumphant as he held up the golden

wrapped chocolate bar. He tossed it to her, Sadie catching it with a smile. She flopped down on to the bed, unwrapping it and handing him one of the sticks of confectionary.

'Nah, I'm good. That's all you.'

She waved it at him like a wand, stubbornness on her face.

'Okay, fine,' he sighed, taking it and kicking off his shoes as he rolled on to the bed next to her. A few bites in and he forgot his momentary resistance to the snack.

'God, these are good. How could anyone prefer a Mars bar to this, I'll never know.'

'Fools,' Sadie signed, before dusting of her hands. 'Utter fools.'

'What do you think?' he asked her. 'Of all this: the witch, the ghost, the medium—'

'The book.'

'The book too, yeah.'

'I keep feeling like we stumbled into the middle of a wrestling match we didn't even know was happening.'

'Ha, I understand exactly what you mean.'

'I can't decide whether we should be trying to duck punches and crawl our way out of the ring or tagging someone's hand as we pick up a folded chair.'

Sadie looked thoughtful as she lowered her hands from signing, tucking them around her chest as the two of them lay there in comfortable silence. He wasn't one hundred per cent certain what happened, but Tex felt like he closed his eyes for just a moment. Next minute, he was blinking as he opened them back up to the soft, bluish black of early evening. Sadie was asleep next to him, the pair clearly exhausted from the week of running, stressing, hiding, and puzzling over what the fuck it was they were supposed to do. *She is so beautiful*, he thought, smiling at the way her lips were parted as if she was ready to say something at a moment's notice. He inhaled deeply, looking up at the ceiling and telling himself not to think about stuff like that. *Wipe your mind*, he willed himself. *Wipe your mind*.

It didn't work very well. He felt pressure on his chest, Tex turning to see Sadie's hands skimming over the surface of the fabric there. She was awake and had propped herself up on her other elbow, the few shards of moonlight coming through the window doing enough to highlight her features. *So beautiful*, he thought, as she leaned down. He was too afraid to move at first, too afraid to react and suddenly shatter the illusion. Then Sadie's lips touched his, soft and gentle at first, before her movements grew bolder and he felt the press of her tongue. It was all he needed, Tex's mind snapping into place and his instincts taking over as if this was the grand final game his heart had been unknowingly preparing for. His hand slid over her waist, pulling her closer to him so there was no distance as their bodies pressed together. He gripped the fabric of her dress, his pulse racing so fast he worried his Adam's apple would burst out of his throat.

His pants strained uncomfortably as he began to get aroused, it taking little more than Sadie up against him before Tex was readjusting the position of his hips. She ran a hand over his freshly shaved head, enjoying the sensation as she repeated the gesture several more times. Just the scrape of her fingernails over his scalp was driving him wild, Tex having no idea how this woman was able to cause so much reaction with so little action. She hitched her leg, his free hand using it to pull around his waist as she nuzzled even closer, Tex not bothering to take a breath between kisses. It seemed like a trivial concern when she was right there, as desperate for him as he was for her, and sinking her lips into his like her life depended on it.

'DINNER!' a high-pitched voice screamed, sounding far away. Then it repeated like a siren, bringing footsteps with it up the stairs and down the hall.

'DINNER! DINNER! DINNER! DINNER!'

Sadie and Tex leapt apart as fast as they could, him watching her with some amazement as she sprung off the bed and into a standing position. She hit the switch on a lamp at her bedside, casting the room in a dull orange glow. Tex could hear how close the kid was and sat up as quickly as he could, grabbing a decorative pillow from the bed and pressing it over his lap just as a small child skidded to a stop in the doorway.

'DINNER! Oh, you're up! Hi!'

Sadie gave her a gentle wave.

'I'm Sprinkle and Casper told *me* to come and tell *you* that dinner is twenty minutes away.'

'Great.' Tex smiled, his voice tense. 'We'll freshen up and be right down.'

'Do you like board games?' she asked, cocking her head.

'Love them,' he replied, lying through his teeth.

'Coooool.'

She disappeared as quickly as she had materialised, her footsteps fading as she sprinted down the hallway. He strained to listen, only relaxing once he knew she was on the stairs. Tex let out a relieved sigh, glancing over at Sadie who was suddenly shy again as she looked down at her feet. She was smirking though, tucking strands of her hair behind her ears.

'I'm gonna shower,' she signed, before picking up one of the fluffy towels that was resting on a chair nearby. 'Unless you want to go first?'

'Uh . . . I'm going to need a minute,' he muttered. Her eyes went from his face to his lap and Tex saw her cheeks redden, but her smile grew wider.

'Come here,' he said, as she was about to step past for the bathroom. He reached out and grabbed her dangling hand, pulling her towards him. Her thighs brushed against his knees and he held her there, one hand on her waist and another tangled in her fingers. Sadie's scent was intoxicating to him, a blend of florals and spice. All he wanted to do was breathe her in and hold her close. They would need to talk about what was happening between them at some point, but as her fingers ran up his neck and eventually brushed over his lips, he didn't want to ruin the moment with words. She kissed him softly, nothing more than a peck, before she released him. He smiled at her as she sauntered off to the bathroom, Tex throwing himself backwards on to the bed with a giddy chuckle as he heard the shower start a few rooms over.

She met him downstairs, Tex joining the party after his own shower some time later. There was an elaborate feast set out in front of them, with garlic bread that smelled *so good* his mouth began to water. Electric Fields were playing over the speakers in the background, setting the jubilant mood. Kala was uncorking a bottle of red wine while Sprinkle watched her, sipping a glass of Ribena extravagantly as if it was her own adult treat. At the centre of the table there was what looked like a small cauldron, housing a bona fide mass of spaghetti Bolognese. The kid was the unofficial head of the table, with Tex and Sadie on one side and the witch and the medium across from them. Corvossier was the last to sit down, a plate of freshly grated Parmesan cheese in her hands.

'So,' she said, handing out plates, 'what have you guys been up to for the last few hours?'

Sadie's knee brushed his under the table and it was all he could do to keep a straight face.

'Napping,' he replied, thanking her as she handed him cutlery. 'Mostly.'

Sadie signed, Tex glancing at her to translate the message. 'She's saying thank you for the meal, it looks wonderful.'

'Well, there's tonnes to go around.'

'I got all my homework done,' Sprinkle proclaimed, slurping a huge string of spaghetti as she did so. 'First the maths, then the assigned chapter I was supposed to read, then Auntie Maggie and I did fire drills.'

'That sounds fun!' Corvossier beamed. 'How did it go?'

'Great! Look!'

The kid held up her hand, fingers splayed wide so you could view each of her individual digits. Then one by one a small flame danced from the tip of each of them. When her pinkie was lit up as well, she closed her fist tight and all of the flames disappeared.

'Good control, Sprinkle,' Kala muttered. 'But what did I say about practising magic in front of strangers?'

The girl sighed, looking deeply annoyed. 'That I shouldn't do it. I thought they were okay though, 'cos they're staying here? And the girl's magic.'

Kala opened her mouth to reply, before hesitating. 'How can you tell?'

'Dunno.' The kid shrugged. 'Just can. She's not a witch or anything, just . . . something.'

Tex observed an emotion akin to pride wash over the witch's features, the woman giving her niece a pleased wink as she muttered, 'Good girl.'

'How about you?' Corvossier asked her partner. 'How did you go?'

The witch's expression darkened somewhat, as she threw them all a significant look.

'We can talk about my homework later.'

Chapter 11

SADIE

'The good news is the book's not evil,' Kala Tully said, setting the tome down on the dining table in front of them. Sadie had spent the last half hour clearing the space and doing dishes alongside Tex, while the witch had put her niece to bed despite the girl's vehement protests about a 'board game session'. Now, it was just the adults: bellies full and two glasses of wine deep as they looked over *The Collected Banshee Histories*.

'Yay?' Tex replied, not sounding one hundred per cent certain with his response.

'And Sadie's right,' Kala pressed. 'All the information about banshees in here, their histories and extent of their powers, makes this extremely valuable to the Treize.'

'It undermines their narrative,' Sadie signed, Tex speaking.

'Right,' the witch agreed. 'But that's not the only reason it's valuable.'

She flipped to the back of the book, tattooed fingers running over an edge that sat out slightly from within the internal spine. One manicured nail was enough to loop under it and Sadie watched as she prised open a nearly invisible document jacket. It had been sealed with glue, the dried residue glimmering under the light. Yet somehow the witch had found it as she lifted several pieces of parchment carefully from inside.

'Whoa,' Corvossier breathed, her pale hand reaching out to touch it before she hesitated. 'Is it safe?'

'Mmm hmm,' the witch nodded. 'There's no magic on these pages; they're just very, very old.'

The medium had taken off her 'bionic limb' after dinner, the device in the corner of the room as it charged from a nearby power point. Sadie had watched, intrigued, as the woman hooked it up to a USB cable and set it down, appearing relieved when her natural limb difference was on full display.

'What are we looking at?' Tex asked, as they laid down each piece of parchment next to the other. 'Hang on, no, wait – I can see: it's a story of some kind. That's Gaelic, so we can assume this is probably Irish in origin.'

'That looks like a family crest,' Sadie signed, pointing out a symbol that was repeated over and over again. Tex verbalised her thoughts, with Kala nodding in agreement.

'That's what I thought too. And Casper, look at this woman: she reoccurs three times, always in threes, and she looks like you.'

'Not quite,' her girlfriend replied. 'She has both arms.'

'Weirdly I don't think advanced prosthetics were on the radar of the ancient Irish.'

As the witch teased her, Sadie couldn't help but think she had a point. The woman represented did bear an uncanny resemblance to Corvossier: she was painted in white, with hair that fell to her waist in the same shade. It was distinctive, to say the least.

'I'm not sure it's the one woman,' Tex said. 'I think it's three different women: each of their features are slightly different but it's repeated every time they're represented. I think it's three women, drawn over and over again.'

'Maybe not three women,' Corvossier murmured, 'Maybe it's *The* Three.'

They were all quiet then, the medium's statement more than just a tossed out theory. Any mention of The Three had weight. Allegedly, they were the origin of the phrase 'see no evil, hear no evil, speak no evil' and were supposed to be wise, immortal beings who guided the Treize. Yet there were few things Sadie thought of as more 'evil' than the Treize and her view on everything associated with them had to be adjusted accordingly. Tales of The Three often featured in her own bedtime stories as a child, but it had been years since she'd thought of them. It was akin to pondering what Santa Claus was up to in your twenties. Like, hey, how's that big, jolly guy going?

'Heath said they were interested in me, remember?' Corvossier was saying. 'And we never understood why they fed him the information about you being in Boscastle. They wanted the two of us to meet—'

'To fall in love?' Kala scoffed.

'Maybe! Who knows? We're here now, aren't we? We've built a life together and now this book is brought to us by people with a common enemy.'

'The Treize,' Tex muttered. 'But what are you supposed to get from this? What do you gain by discovering these pages?'

'I don't know. I'm way out of my depth here trying to analyse this kind of thing. We need an ancient historian.'

'Or how about just someone ancient?' Kala offered. 'Someone ancient from, say, a similar part of the world?'

'He's back in Berlin,' Corvossier said, biting her lip.

Kala had been taking a hearty sip of her wine and she paused, looking surprised by that information. 'What? He is? If they shut down all Treize ops in Germany, what's his reason for being there exactly?'

'A *werewolf*,' Corvossier said, like it was a scandalous reve-lation. 'He's tracking her, monitoring potential, according to Barry.'

'For what?' Kala asked. 'Recruitment for us or them? Or recruitment for us *through* them?'

'I met her,' the medium continued, getting up and grabbing a phone from high above a cabinet where only she could reach. 'At Phases. She's staying with the Rogues and working the bar.'

'And? What's she like?'

Corvossier was thoughtful for a moment as she used a small, metal tool to open up the phone and switch in a fresh SIM card.

'She's blue-haired, biracial, and has a path of the dead trail-ing behind her longer than I've seen for someone who isn't immortal.'

'Hmmm,' the witch murmured, before finishing the final drop of red. 'What's Heath's interest then? He never does anything without an end game.'

There was an electronic beep as the phone turned on and Corvossier began clicking her way through numbers, seem-ingly disinterested in the conversation.

'He wants a soldier, I think. Or needs one. Either way, she has powerful roots and werewolves are vicious as fuck.'

'End game.' The witch nodded.

'How about you ask him yourself?' Corvossier offered, holding up a saved number that was simply labelled 'Scot'.

Kala grinned. 'You're just gonna call him?'

'Video call, actually – so he can translate this . . . whatever it is we're looking at. First, I need someone to check if he's alone and if not, get him somewhere.'

She closed her eyes and stood still for a long moment, Sadie and Tex exchanging a glance.

'This Heath guy,' he asked the witch, 'can he be trusted? Obviously you two trust him, but Sadie and I are both fugitives right now so perhaps it's better if we don't show our faces?'

'He can be trusted,' Corvossier confirmed, eyes snapping open as she returned to present company.

Kala raised an eyebrow at her in response. The medium looked momentarily uncertain before adding: 'With this matter at least. A ghost is checking to make sure he's available; I'll know in a few minutes.'

Sadie had started to tune them out, pulling one of the pages towards her so she could inspect it more closely. The three women were drawn wearing green hooded cloaks so the juxtaposition of their white skin and white hair was stark. Tex was deep in conversation with Corvossier about The Three, the two of them comparing stories and notes from within the various structures of the Treize they had worked. Yet as Sadie stared at the crudely drawn faces of the women on the page, she thought they met another description much better.

'What is it?' the witch asked. She'd been watching Sadie without her realising it. Tex and Corvossier fell silent, their attention shifting to her as well.

'It might be nothing,' she signed, Tex saying the words out loud.

'Or it might be something,' Kala replied. 'What is it you see?'

Casting a glance around the room, her hands began to move as she signed.

'In here—' she touched the book for emphasis '—there are several Irish legends about banshees arriving in villages with flowing, green cloaks and their blood-red eyes hidden underneath from passers-by.'

She tapped a finger on each set of red eyes set inside the face of the drawn women.

'The banshee was depicted as either young and beautiful or an old woman – no in-between – but they all had long, white hair, and pale skin. A lot of legends have them carrying a comb in hand.'

She pointed at another detail the others had missed: a strange brown object always held in the hand of the creature on the left. You could see the jagged ruts of teeth, with the drawing not looking completely unlike a crude representation of a comb.

'The red eyes . . .' Tex breathed, before clarifying. 'Sorry, she didn't say that – I did. When Sadie foresees death, her eyes glaze over and go *completely* red. Like, blood red.'

Silently, they all leaned a little closer to the drawings. Corvossier's hair slipped over her shoulder, the long strands brushing against the paper, before she straightened up and tilted her head as if she could hear something they couldn't. Sadie guessed that's exactly what was happening as she smirked with amusement.

'The Great Big Blonde One is good to go,' she said, hitting the relevant buttons and waiting as the dial tone echoed out among their party. The screen switched to a crisp image of a man so bulky in frame that he took up most of the picture and nothing in the background was visible.

'Aye,' he grunted.

'Heath, you're on speaker. Did we wake you up? What time is it over there?'

'Just past ten in the morning,' he said, yanking a hoodie around his face.

'You look a wreck,' Kala said.

'Is that the witch? Swivel this shite around, lemme view the prickly bint. Let's see how you look when the Treize clear out and let the Laignach Faelad take over the city, eating wee bairns left 'n' right.'

Sadie glanced at Tex and he met her gaze, shaking his head slightly. He could only pick up every third word too, it wasn't just her. He smirked and Sadie couldn't deny the way it felt, knowing their initial kiss hadn't been a fluke. In fact, she was planning many more.

'We're off to the wrong start,' Corvossier was saying. 'We just need you to take a look at this and give us your interpretation.'

'Aight, what is it I'm looking at then?'

'Hidden pages from inside a book that Collette and her parents wrote,' the medium said, holding the screen of the phone over the top of the first page so he could see it.

'Collette?' His tone changed significantly at the mention of the woman's name. 'A book on what?'

'Banshee histories. You knew her longer than Barry and I did; she ever mention anything like this?'

'Tipperary,' he said. 'Limerick. Galway. She did a big trip around Ireland to visit Geev and Iris. When her pa got sick, she spent months there. I didn't know about the book though.'

Sadie and the others were quiet as Corvossier moved the phone down the length of the page, changing pace when Heath ordered her to go slower. He was muttering to himself on the other end, but the words were indistinguishable down the line. Every now and then, he made a loud grunt.

'Aye, take me back to the start.'

'To the border? Or—'

'Yes, there.'

Corvossier did so, repeating her slow sweep of the page.

'Firstly, not a border,' he said. 'That blue shape running around the edge of each page is a river. It's supposed to symbolise a body of water. See the way it flows over from page to page? That's how you know you need to switch the order of the fourth and fifth pages; they're in the wrong spot.'

Tex reshuffled them accordingly, earning a definitive 'yup' from Heath's end.

'If I had to guess – and that's all I'm doing here – I'd say that's the River Corrib.'

'You can tell which river it is just by looking at it?' Kala scoffed, incredulous.

'From the length,' he corrected. 'And the shape. The River Corrib is considerably short but fast moving and it sweeps through Galway in a shape not unlike that.'

Sadie's stomach twisted: Galway was where her ancestors hailed from. Another small piece clicked into place.

'We thought the women were The Three,' Corvossier said. 'But Sadie thought they were banshees. You've met The Three so . . .'

'We don't go down to the local and grab a pint,' he mumbled, his mind clearly somewhere else. 'Huh . . . that's interesting.'

'What?' Kala asked. 'What do you see?'

'It's both. The story goes as follows: three women emerge from the River Corrib, eyes red from years spent watching and crying over the deaths of the people who live on the banks. The small dots are the people, see, and the brown squares their homes. They're all-seeing, all-knowing, so they decide to share what they know. That way the women don't have to cry any more.'

Tex gasped. 'They conquer death?'

'No, you can't conquer death: just delay the inevitable. Death's drawn there, that thing following alongside the inner rim of the river. It sweeps up and takes the villagers one by one, but they're ready for it now. They have knowledge and they're not afraid of it.'

Corvossier moved on to the final two pages, Heath pausing as he waited for the image to catch up.

'The women do this for a long time. That's what the trees are showing; they're growing and their roots are getting deeper. As everyone they come to love grows old and dies, they wait patiently for their turn. Yet the river of death never sweeps them up, no matter how long they wait on its banks. So they cry again, just a small tear at first, then a flood. Until they can't see anything any more, they can't hear, they can't speak. Only then do they wither up and die, joining their friends.'

'And I thought *A Star Is Born* was bleak,' Corvossier muttered, when Heath was finished.

'That's it?' Tex asked, Sadie noting the desperation in his tone. 'You live and you die, *c'est la vie*?'

'Let's not bring B*Witched into this.' Kala grimaced.

'They die,' Heath continued, 'and three more women emerge from the river.'

'What about the Gaelic?' Tex asked, after Sadie signed the question at him.

'I can loosely translate. Not all the words are clear. Gaelic is more Lorcan's area of expertise than mine.'

Sadie smirked; that was as traditional as Irish names got.

'Where's he then?' Corvossier asked. 'Can we—'

'No,' Heath snapped. 'I'll do it, bring the phone closer. *Deirfiúr* is repeated a lot, that's sister. Yeah, that's Galway, something about "mourning death is accepting it" and, uh, here's one for your friend: *bean sí*.'

'*Bean sí*,' Kala repeated, the term sounding interesting in an Australian accent. 'What does that mean?'

'Translated literally: women of the otherworld. Anglicised though, it's *banshee*. You know, the wailing woman.'

Everyone in the room turned to face Sadie.

'What about The Three?' Corvossier questioned, her eyes still fixed on her. 'Any mention of them or even that word?'

'You have no idea how old what you're looking at is, do you?'

A penetrating silence was his response.

'Older than the name The Three is, let me tell ya. And I should know: I was fighting in the same crusade as the guy who came up with it. Fucking eejit too, but he had a knack for nicknames that stuck.'

Tex sighed, looking tired as he pulled out a chair at the dining table and slumped into it.

'So this predates them, got it.'

'No,' Heath corrected. 'It predates their name.'

Tex frowned, not seeming to understand the difference. Sadie did, however: just because they weren't called The Three on the page, that didn't mean the drawn figures weren't them.

'Any other keywords or phrases we should know about?' Tex asked.

'The women could be sisters, which works in context because The Three are literally full-blood sisters.'

Sadie tweaked, that information new to her.

'That was also a term women used to describe themselves in relation to the other: "my sister this, my sister that". It didn't necessarily mean "from the same vagina" sister.'

'Yeah sis.' Kala smirked. 'I get it.'

'Death and rebirth are coming up a lot in conjunction with each other. Or maybe it's death and birth? Rebirth fits better in the context, but as one thing leaves this plane something else must step in to fill its place. That seems to be the natural cycle of these women . . . sorry, otherworldly women.'

There was a banging from down the line and Heath's head spun around, before snapping back to them.

'I gotta go, I've got a cult of undead werewolves to hunt. That help much?'

'Uh . . .'

'Fook it, been a hoot. Always nice to see ya, Casper, Opal.'

He gave them a mischievous grin as he said that last name, Sadie having no idea who he was talking about. That was the last he said, the call ending abruptly on their end and the kitchen suddenly filled with a distinct lack of heavy, Scottish brogue.

'Well,' Corvossier sighed. 'Any questions?'

Tex raised his hand. 'I for one am certainly curious as to what an undead cult of werewolves looks like.'

Sadie grinned, the bubble of a laugh inside her chest feeling like a release somehow.

'I think we learned a lot.' Kala nodded. 'If this were a puzzle, I reckon we'd have all the edges done by now. Before, we just had a bunch of pieces dumped on the table.'

Sadie held one of those pieces in her hand, the parchment thick and rough to the touch. She looked at the story being told to them with new eyes, Heath's translation adding layers to the narrative as it took place down the page.

'You have sisters,' Kala said, looking thoughtful. 'Seven. That's the start of your own coven right there. Do you know of any banshee families with three sisters?'

'I think you're being too literal,' Tex said. 'I've studied old manuscripts like this in my training, things that are supposed to be interpreted as prophecy. Just because there's seven Burke sisters, that doesn't rule them out. This could still be about three of them, especially now that we know banshees are not these underpowered beings the Treize have been so desperate to have us believe.'

'What are you saying?' Sadie signed.

'They could be deeply afraid of you *and* your sisters because of what's illustrated here. Great power, great control. Think about it: if there has been some vaguely defined prophecy floating around for years about powerful banshee sisters bringing down the Treize—'

'Whoa, whoa, whoa,' Kala said, holding up her hands. 'Conclusions, boy. You're leaping to them.'

'Their actions don't seem so extreme, do they?' he continued. 'There's suddenly a lot more method to their madness, from the banishment and The Covenant, to severing your banshee wail before it had a chance to manifest.'

Sadie wasn't sure what he was getting at. Could he justify the actions of his uncles, of his father, that way? If they had done what they continued to do in order to maintain the Treize's survival, was that any better? She thought all of these things as she stared at him, his brow furrowed and his mind whirring with whatever theories were possessing his mind like deadly ivy.

'I think the best thing is if we mull all of this over,' the medium said, breaking into Sadie's thoughts. 'Sleep on it and see what our dreams shake loose.'

Kala smirked, reaching a hand across the table to take Corvossier's. 'That sounded like something I would say.'

'Guess you're rubbing off on me then.'

'Excuse me,' Sadie gestured as she got to her feet. 'Thank you so much for dinner, everything; I'm still exhausted and going to head right up to bed.'

'You sure?' the witch asked. 'It's barely nine o'clock. Don't fancy a night cap?'

'Only a night nap,' Tex said, chuckling over the last word of what she told him. 'Night, Sadie.'

His hands were fluid as he signed at her, asking if she was okay in a language only the two of them could understand. She nodded, telling him she was but unable to hold his eye contact for long. She tried to keep her pace leisurely as she made her way upstairs and down the hall to the bedroom she was staying in. Softly, she shut the door behind with her with a nearly soundless *click*. Sadie caught a glimpse of her reflection in an antique mirror that hung on the wall and had to turn away, the shade of her hair still too strange and too new to be any comfort. It sounded trivial, but there was a small strength to looking in the mirror and recognising the person who stared back at you.

Sadie's life hadn't been perfect by any stretch. Some might say it was stifled by the things she couldn't do, the rules that others dictated to her. But like converting a rundown shack into a home, she had made a life that was *hers*. It was constant and it was every day. Now, it felt like her grip was slippery as she tried to hold on to any sense of control she had. There was a soft knock on the door and she spun around to see Tex peeking in through a crack.

'Can I come in?' he whispered.

She nodded, angling away from him so she could sniff as subtly as possible and wipe the salty smear of a tear that was threatening to trickle down her cheeks. She felt Tex's hands on her shoulders, Sadie closing her eyes and enjoying the small relief that brought her. She leaned into him, letting herself relax as he slipped his arms around her body and held her to him, comfortably tight in a hug.

'I know this is scary,' he whispered, his lips brushing her ear as he spoke and causing her to shiver. 'I know this whole thing feels like it's spinning completely out of orbit. I'm sorry if I spoke out of turn, made you panic by bringing up some prophecy.'

She nodded her head up and down enthusiastically, his growing whiskers tickling her skin. It was the shifters' idea, to make him stop shaving his stubble and start shaving his head in order to switch up his appearance. As Sadie twisted around in his grip to look at him, she realised that she preferred it this way. She couldn't help it, her fingernails running up his neck and through his rapidly growing facial hair. *The first time I kissed him, he was clean shaven*, she thought, frowning a little at the places her mind went.

'I know this is going to sound like bumper sticker philosophy,' Tex said, his voice notably rough as she continued to touch him, 'but I really believe stuff happens for a reason. Not in a God way. Even terrible things set us on a path, shape us, solidify us. Just because we can't see or understand why something is happening in the moment or what route that's setting us on, that doesn't make it any less true.'

Sadie wanted him to shut him up, so she made him. She used her mouth to silence whatever future wisdom he was going to voice. She used her body to drag his mind away from thoughts about whether she was 'okay'. Each day was beginning to make as much sense as an episode of *Lost* and she was ready to get off the fucking island. She yanked at his unbuttoned flannel shirt, annoyed when there was a white T-shirt sitting underneath it. She disposed of that quickly too, Sadie half expecting him to gently pull back, telling her they needed to slow down or 'think' about things first. Yet as their make-out session that afternoon had proven, Tex wanted her just as badly as she wanted him.

She could taste the wine on his lips as his fingers turned into fists, scrunching up the hem of her dress and lifting it higher. Sadie felt a need pulsing deep inside her, one she usually satisfied herself with fantasies but *right now* she was living in one. His hands were running over the bare skin of her stomach, the curve of her hip, the friction of her sheer tights until suddenly, they weren't. Tex knew what he was doing and Sadie felt her lips part with a gasp that should be there, her back arching as he touched the part of her that was aching for him most. Her fingernails dug into the flesh of his chest, lightly pulling at the tufts of hair. He didn't seem to mind: he was too occupied with making her clench and twitch and contract around the hand that was inside her underwear.

She wanted to sob as the pleasure growing in her body became sharper, Tex dipping his head under her chin as he kissed her neck, her collarbone, her décolletage. Each touch was driving her wild. Reaching her own hand back, she tugged at the zipper of her dress as it fell around her in puddle of fabric. They stumbled backwards towards the bed, Tex struggling with her bra clasp and she his zipper as they attempted to do too many things at once. Tex chuckled, seemingly as drunk on hormones as she was. He yanked the blanket and tossed it over them, it feeling like they were in a cocoon of their own making. Sadie was unable to help the shudder of loss her body made as his fingers slipped away and rolled down the rest of her tights.

It was a conscious move, she realised, Tex making an effort to slow them both down as he started to kiss his way back up to her mouth. His lips brushed the bend of her knee, gently pressing a kiss there, and then the outside of her thigh, the inside of her thigh, the edge of her—

Oh God, Sadie screamed inside her head, as he proved exactly how good he was at kissing places other than her mouth. She gripped the pillow above her head, fighting the urge for her knees to lock in place as the tingles resumed more intensely than they had been before. She wanted him, desperately, inside of her and around her and a part of her. Sadie shifted her hips, forcing his head up and noting the delighted smirk that rested on his face as he licked his lips. She tugged at his arms, at his hips, pulling him towards her as his penis brushed against her body. She spread her legs wider, reaching down between them as she guided their bodies together.

'Gentle,' she mouthed, her lips brushing against his skin. She wasn't sure he could clearly read her words, but he seemed to know anyway as he hovered above her, watching her face as he slowly pushed inside. Sadie winced, unable to help it, and she could feel him begin to back out. Grabbing his ass, she pulled him deeper, urging herself to move past the initial pain. She had wanted this so badly and for so long, she wasn't going to let the moment slip away. She let him fill her up and just when she thought she couldn't take any more, he was there, holding her body with his arms like it was a treasure.

'Sadie,' he whispered, staring deep into her eyes. *I'm here*, she told him, not able to vocalise it. Whatever Tex saw as he looked at her, it was enough. He clung to her like a lifeline, guiding her smoothly through the motions as their bodies moved together, their skin growing slick with sweat. Everything that had gone wrong had led her – had led *them* – to this. *Maybe there was something to his bumper sticker philosophy after all*, she thought. It was the last comprehensive thing Sadie could process before everything else in her head was swept away.

It was far too early for anyone else to be awake, but Sadie was. She flinched slightly as she moved, her body still tender from the night before as she inched her way out of bed. Tex's arm was draped around her waist and she used her hands to carefully lower it on to the space in the mattress where she had just been. She pulled on her underpants and her dress, forgoing a bra as she just needed to tiptoe to the bathroom and she'd be right back. She might be the baby of the Burke sisters and the last virgin among them, but Sadie had never been afraid to have sex. The benefit of being the final one of her siblings to take the plunge meant she had heard their horror stories and soaked up all of their advice like a sponge.

'Drink lots and pee lots after sex,' Shannon had said.

'It always hurts initially, but it gets better: it becomes a good kind of hurt,' Ina had offered.

'Make sure you know how to make yourself cum, otherwise how can you ever expect a guy to?' Catriona had shrugged.

Yet it was Sorcha's words that floated back to her as she took care of business, flushing the toilet and heading over to the basin to clean her teeth.

'Don't lose your virginity to someone you don't give a shit about,' her sibling had said one day, as they were sitting in an empty parking garage. Sorcha was supposed to have been teaching Sadie how to drive, but they had veered – literally – off topic. 'If that person gives a damn about you and you about them, the stuff that makes sex seem scary won't be so scary.'

As Sadie splashed cold water on her face, she smiled at the thought of one day getting to tell her big sister that she had followed her advice. The house was still dark as she walked back to the guest bedroom, only faint blue light coming through the curtains providing any hint that daylight was approaching. She hesitated at the doorway, Tex's sleeping body in the exact same position it had been before she left. She looked over at the room he was supposed to be staying in, lamp still on inside and door wide open. Sadie wasn't sure she wanted the entire cottage to know they had spent the night together, so she stepped inside the space to turn off the light and creep back out. She would shut the door behind her and no one would know Tex was in her bed and not his own.

Her bare foot brushed paper and she frowned, looking down to see a whole stack of it sliding out of Tex's satchel and on to the floor. The weight of his laptop had pushed the bag over, creating a mess. She dropped down on to her knees, reassembling it all as best as she could and closing one of the notebooks that had fallen open. Sadie paused, her eye catching on a symbol. It was something her body recognised before her mind did, a cold sense of dread creeping up over her skin. She flipped open the page it was drawn on, her lips parting with a silent gasp as she poured over all the other symbols drawn there. She knew them without really knowing them, her mind snapping back to the worst night of her life.

The smells, the candlelight, the strange woman, the fear that seemed to be bursting out of her pores like a pimple ... and finally, the searing pain and the blackness that followed. When she had woken up the next day, throat aching, she had tried to ask Nora for a glass of water. She couldn't understand why she was failing at first, before her auntie swept into the room and told her news that would flip Sadie's world upside down. The hardest part of it all was that as a kid she couldn't even scream and cry about it. She did, of course, but it was silent: grief racking her tiny body but *not a sound* coming from it.

And right there on the page in front of her, in the notebook of the man she'd made love to, was the ritual for how it was all done. There was a list of ingredients he had crossed out while others were jotted over the top of and added to at a later date. The symbols were carefully charted, some clearly staying with him as he doodled their shapes in the margins. There were environmental factors that had to be right too, apparently: the moon and some other bullshit. Silver. Purification. Severance. Keywords jumped out at her and she felt like she was going to vomit right on to the page.

'Sadie? What are you . . .'

She hadn't even heard him get out of bed, hadn't registered the creak of the mattress springs or the floorboards as they groaned under his weight. She'd been too caught up in this nightmare instead. When Sadie looked up at him from her position kneeling on the floor, she knew her face was wet. Her neck was practically dripping with tears.

'What the hell is this?' she signed, letting the notebook fall to the ground.

His face dropped when he realised what she was looking at. 'I was going to tell you,' he started.

'When?' Sadie wished in that moment more than any other that she could shout. She hated his father for taking that away from her. She hated the Treize even more.

'When I knew for sure it could be done.'

'Say it,' she signed. 'Say what you mean, damn it.'

He looked like he was holding his breath. 'Reverse it. I didn't want to tell you until I was sure, no, *certain* it can be done. But . . . I think what my father did to you can be reversed, Sadie.'

'That is not information you should have kept from me. Ever!'

He dropped down next to her and grabbed a piece of paper to show her. 'I know, I mean, I know that now. But listen, I think there's a chance you can speak again. I don't think your wail ever went away, just a means of using it. If you let me—'

He reached out to touch her and she yanked her hand away, leaping up and backing slowly from the room.

'Sadie, please—'

She couldn't. She couldn't hear another word from him when she wasn't allowed to have any of her own. How long had he known this? How long had Texas withheld from her knowledge that could change her life? Her bare feet slapped against the floor as she walked then ran down the hall, her hands unlocking the front door and her will propelling her outside before she knew it. She was sprinting through the dark, the grass cold and wet between her toes as she set her eyes on the outline of trees up ahead. She heard him call to her, run after her, but she didn't slow down. For the first time in her life, Sadie wanted the darkness to swallow her up.

Chapter 12

'SADIE!'

He shouted her name, desperate for her to hear him as he ran through the bush after her. She wasn't fast per se, but Tex was bare foot, shirtless and in a very restrictive pair of jeans, sprinting through the dark in the wake of a woman whose heart he worried he had just broken. He hadn't had time to do up his fly, so was continually yanking at the waistband of his pants as they threatened to fall down around his ankles and take him out of the race. Because it *was* a race: it was a race to get to her and explain what she had just seen, before the damage couldn't be undone. It looked bad, he knew that. He just needed two minutes to spell out what he had been doing, then she'd get it.

The branches up ahead were snapping and cracking with her abrupt entry into a domain that wasn't meant for people. Not their people, anyway. The Blue Mountains was wild country and he worried that with their combined inexperience, it was only a matter of time before one of them broke their ankle. He burst through a clearing, Sadie stumbling to get up on the other side. She was panting and she was crying, the two things hindering her ability to breathe. He ran up behind her, pushing her back down to the ground. She landed on her butt, legs splayed out in front of her, eyes defiant as she glared up at him and tried to shake him off.

'*Stop*,' he heaved, '*running*.'

He let go of her, holding up his hands so she could see them and backing off as a peace gesture. He wasn't sure how far they had come, but they were both breathing hard. Sweat was dripping down his back and that was saying a lot. The sun hadn't even come up yet and the bush around them was mainly shadows.

'I won't touch you,' he said, regaining some composure. 'I won't come towards you, but you have to listen to me, Sadie.'

'Why?!' she signed, her face full of fury.

'Because it's not what you think! I know what it looks like, but *I swear* it's not what you think.'

'Just leave me to shrivel up and die,' she signed, before adding: 'Like an acorn.'

The last bit surprised him so much, he laughed. It was the worst thing he could have done and he slapped a hand over his mouth to try and hide the mistake. She didn't miss it.

'How could you not tell me?!' she signed. 'It's not permanent? How could you even entertain that possibility and keep it to yourself? How could you hold that over me and sleep with me?'

'I had to be sure! This is life-changing information, not just for you but potentially our whole world, Sadie. I couldn't give you that morsel of hope only to take it away. It would have killed me.'

'This isn't about you!'

'No, I know that,' he murmured, dropping down on to his knees so they were at the same eye line. 'Just . . . listen. When I came back to Sydney, it was the first time I had access to my father's old Askari journals. I could see what was documented there and initially it was curiosity sparked by seeing all of you again. Then Fairuza caught me, gave me *The Collected Banshee Histories*, and things started to make more sense.'

She sniffed, shaking her head slowly. 'How?'

'They heard your banshee wail, they knew you had that ability on top of already being able to foresee the last few minutes of someone's death, so they stripped you of it. My question is, why not just restrict you, huh? Or the Scold's bridle, like your ancestors? Why not have you swear that you'll never use it or bind you with magics? Why the *extreme*, violent response immediately? Especially when we've been told over and over again how banshees have no real power.'

'That we're dying off.'

'Right,' he agreed, trying not to let himself feel hopeful that she was following along . . . that the damage he'd done wasn't irreparable.

'What we've learned since is they're terrified of what banshee women can see and what banshee women can do. Maybe it's because of some prophecy. Maybe it's because there are still enough immortals around to remember what you could all really do. No banshee wail had been recorded in over one hundred and fifty years until you came along. No banshee had been documented with multiple abilities in at least two hundred years. You were the first on both counts and because of that, I don't think they knew what they were doing.'

She blinked at him, her eyelashes dislodging two errant tears that had been sitting at the corner of her puffy eyes.

'What are you saying?' she signed.

'It's temporary. You can't forcibly suppress a banshee's powers any more than you can suppress a werewolf's lycanthropy. And the purest banshee ability of them all, the wail? Not a chance.'

Her eyes narrowed, but he knew she was thinking his logic through to the same conclusion he had arrived at.

'I've spent days trying to decipher the alchemist's ritual from that night so we can break it, Sadie. The magic that did that—'

He pointed, sweeping his finger across the space at her throat.

'—it's not binding.'

He had to remind her to breathe, Tex watching the distinct lack of a rise and fall in her chest as she processed those words. Sadie gulped the air around her like a hungry fish, her hands running through her hair as she seemed to digest what he had said: *really* digest it this time. He was nervous, his stomach churning with the fear of losing something precious to him. When he was rattled, Tex couldn't stop himself from talking and he opened his mouth to continue when she held up a hand to halt him.

'Shut up,' she signed. 'Enough theories. Tell me how.'

'It's super technical and detailed,' he started. 'One wrong symbol could throw the whole thing off, one misplaced stone. It's almost like trying to recreate a meal without the recipe. And without the chef. But I'm so close, I swear I'm *so* close. Alchemist rituals and the magic that bind them are specific to the person who performs them. If I can just find the woman from that night, or even someone who worked with her, we can get your voice back, Sadie. You could speak again.'

She shifted slightly and he tried not to get his hopes up as her body leaned towards him.

'I'd have the wail?' she signed.

'Technically you've always had it, but yes. More importantly, you'd be able to use it.'

The excitement and determination he saw glinting in her eyes gave him pause. If he could help Sadie get her weapon back, he had no doubt she'd use it. That scared him.

'You don't want this, do you?' she signed.

He'd caught the movement of her hands with his eyes, missing the first half of the sentence but picking up the rest as she repeated the question.

'It's not just that you didn't know whether this could be done for certain. You don't want me to have this power.'

'What? Sadie, no! I . . .'

He went to deny it, but he felt the kernel of truth in his heart. She was right. Maybe he didn't want to disappoint her and crush her spirits, yet at the same time he was afraid of what the banshee wail could do. It was written about with such fear and such reverence, he couldn't help be frightened by it. Simultaneously, he was beginning to grasp what the Treize really was, what his uncles and father had truly become. All he had seen of absolute power was that it corrupts, absolutely. Was he worried that would happen to Sadie too? It took him less than a second to decide.

'No,' he said, voice firm. 'It's *your* power. You have a right to it. No one should stand in your way if that's a possibility. Not any more.'

He wanted her to crawl towards him, he wanted the instinct that seemed to drive both of them towards each other to return to Sadie. He wanted his arms to go wide as he pulled her towards his chest, Sadie nestling into his lap, the exposed skin on her body cold as he ran his hands over her.

Instead, she stayed sitting perfectly still: just inches away from him but it could have been miles. They didn't speak, the sounds of the bush waking up around them the conversation they weren't having, birds chirping and shrubs rustling as creatures went about their daily business. Tex was deathly terrified of snakes and he had to push the thought of one slithering up alongside them from his mind. A breeze shook the trees in the clearing, the air soothing on his skin. But it brought with it an awful scent, something pungent and sharp enough that it made his eyes water. Sadie smelled it too and she looked around, frowning as Tex tried to remember why that rank odour seemed familiar. He glanced at her at the same time Sadie's head snapped towards him, both recalling one of the last jobs she'd had before everything went to shit. The ghoul nest. The Praetorian Guard raid.

'Ghouls,' she mouthed, frantically pushing up as they both got to their feet.

'I know, I smell it too,' he whispered. 'But that's crazy, Sadie. Ghouls don't live *in the bush*. They hate wide open spaces, they hate exposed light, they hate—'

He didn't get to finish what he said, as a grey, slimy claw extended from beyond a shadow. Long talons dug into the dirt, the creature's skin moist as it crawled forward on all fours. He had only ever seen footage of ghouls in training videos, never up close like this, yet they always reminded him of a greyhound somehow. Lean and muscular with a hunched spine, they were completely blind. Their eyes were white and unseeing, but it didn't matter much: they relied largely on a powerful sense of smell, with long slits starting where a nose should be and sweeping across their face. The worst part though – the feature Tex couldn't stop staring at as he grabbed Sadie's hand and pulled her behind him – was the mouth.

They had razor sharp teeth that hung on the outside thanks to a serious underbite. They were jagged with a serrated edge and the biggest ones were at the corner of the mouth and got smaller towards the middle. They could strip the flesh from limbs, and Tex had once been obsessed with an old case where a rogue werewolf had disposed of sprite bodies by feeding them to a nest of ghouls he kept in a bunker on his property. When he'd eventually been caught, it had been very hard to establish exactly how many victims he'd had. The ghouls had done such an effective job.

'Tex,' she signed, the two of them keeping their eyes on the creature as they continued to back away. 'Ghouls aren't solitary hunters.'

No, he thought. *They hunt in packs.*

Sure enough, another emerged from the shadows at his right, followed by a third on Sadie's left. They were flanking them and without any weapons to defend themselves, Tex knew they were going to be a quick meal. But this wasn't their natural territory. You didn't usually find ghouls exposed like this and that might be the only thing working in their favour.

'If we can get back to the house,' he whispered, lips barely moving, 'we might have a chance.'

She nodded, just a slow up and down movement with her head.

'On my count: one, two, *three*!'

Gripping her hand, he pulled her after him as they both took off towards the only avenue that wasn't blocked by the feral predators. It was thankfully also the direction they had come from, even though Tex didn't know the precise route back to the house. The ground was uneven and there were mossy logs, fallen branches, and thick trees in their way. It slowed he and Sadie down, sure, but it also slowed the ghouls. He heard the crashing and banging and the God-awful shrieking that came from behind them as the creatures pursued in unnatural terrain. It was getting lighter by the minute as the sun continued to rise in the sky and Tex saw some kind of animal carcass up ahead. He veered to the left, Sadie and him having to jump over it in order to keep going. It was rotting and even with limited exposure, he could smell the stench. He knew the ghouls would as well and for a beat, things were quiet behind them as the creatures descended on the meal.

It wasn't what they were after, however, and the promise of live prey was too alluring. A shriek cut through the air, followed by an answering shriek and then another. There were at least three ghouls, but he was willing to bet there were more out there. If they'd been dispatched to hunt the two of them, the Blue Mountains was a massive area to cover. Sadie was panting and he was too, his chest burning as he urged his legs to move faster. Between his bare feet and his jeans, he wasn't in the ideal ensemble to run for his life. He had to make do. His hand was damp as he clutched on to her, willing to die rather than let Sadie go or watch her fall behind. They were in this together, for better or worse. She tripped, flying forward and pulling him with her as they tumbled, rolling in a tangle of limbs until they landed with a thud on soft grass. He groaned, his fingers gripping the ground as he pushed himself to his feet and recognised the border of the witch's property.

'COME ON!' he shouted, dragging her up with him. 'WE'RE NEARLY THERE, SADIE!'

He could see the outline of the cottage only a few hundred metres away and they got to their feet. She was limping slightly and he threw her arm over his shoulders, helping to take some of the weight off whatever ailed her. There was a snarling from behind them and he risked a look, glancing back just as five ghouls emerged from the bush, flying through the air and landing on the ground at incredible speed. There were no more obstacles between the creatures and them, nothing else to slow their rapid momentum. One was at the head of the pack and looked ready to pounce, Tex unable to take his eyes off it as he watched the muscles in its back legs flex in preparation. *This is it*, he thought. *This is how I die.*

The ghoul extended its jaws, mouth open to bite as it leaped. And then just as quickly, it was tackled from the air by a white object. It let out a pitiful howl of sorts, before one of its comrades was grabbed by – and he didn't imagine this – dozens of translucent, whitish blue hands that appeared out of the ground, holding it in place. Tex fell over in shock, glancing up just in time to see exactly what it was that was saving their asses.

Corvossier von Klitzing was walking towards them slowly, her white hair blowing behind her in the wind. In nothing more than a dark-blue nightgown that clung to her tall frame, she looked terrifying as her bare feet brushed over the grass. Her palm was facing skywards as she continued on her path, a swirling grey matter in her eyes. He twisted back around, finally recognising their saviours for what they were: ghosts. Ghosts that could maintain a *physical* form. And she was commanding them! About half a dozen of the dead had managed to occupy two of the ghouls, who were lashing and trying to fight off an enemy that seemingly couldn't take any damage. Another ghoul was still running towards them and he thought he heard a cry from Sadie, his mind truly having scrambled itself with adrenaline. Yet that creature didn't get very far, spontaneously bursting into flames. As it burned to death, it made a piercing sound that Tex would remember for the rest of his life.

There were only two more creatures and they weren't so much a threat any more as they were desperately trying to escape. Some unseen force held them in place, their legs rapidly moving through the air, but it was futile. Tex heard Kala's words before he saw her, the witch speaking so rapidly it could have been in English but he couldn't distinguish the words. She was holding two bottles in her hands and she hurled one at the first ghoul, the volume in her speech rising as she did so. The glass shattered against the creature's leathery skin and it howled, a type of smoke rolling out from the point of impact and consuming it entirely. Not even the bones were left, just a handful of ashes that collapsed on to the grass and were blown away in the breeze.

The second bottle was thrown at the feet of the remaining ghoul, with what looked like thousands of tiny, purple beetles emerging from thin air and racing over the flailing creature. This spell – whatever it was – did leave bones behind. The skeletal structure of the ghoul was all that remained, pristine and white as it lay there on the ground, the beetles picking at the bones for every last morsel of nutrients. The witch bent down, retrieving a new glass bottle from a holder draped around her neck. She uncorked it and lay it on the ground, the beetles eventually forming an orderly line and scuttling back inside it. The moment their tiny legs touched the glass, what dropped inside looked like nothing more than a dormant chia seed. With a contented sigh, Kala looked up.

'Casper, stop playing with your food,' the witch said.

The two surviving ghouls were indeed being toyed with. The ghosts were unaffected and holding them in place, while the creatures did their best to thrash around and fight for freedom.

'We can't interrogate them,' Kala continued, walking over to her. 'They're not sentient beings; there's no way of finding out who sent them.'

'I know,' the medium replied, sounding almost bored. 'I held these for Sprinkle. Thought she might want the practice.'

It was then Tex realised for the first time that the eleven-year-old witch was present too, her eyes bright and her hair bushy like she had just emerged from bed. She most likely had and he watched as she skipped over towards Corvossier, who was several feet taller than her. The older witch looked like she was about to object, before she huffed a breath and shrugged.

'That's a good point,' Kala said. 'But be quick about it: I don't like us out here and exposed.'

'Let them come,' the medium practically growled.

There was something that ignited in the witch's eyes as her girlfriend said that, a pleased smirk on her lips.

'Alright, Sprinkle,' Kala said, sidling up next to her niece. 'You did good with that first ghoul: that was a moving target and much harder. These two should be a piece of cake. One after the other, okay? Don't burn yourself out.'

The kid chuckled. 'Burn myself out. As if.'

Instinctively he threw a protective hand over Sadie as smoke, followed by flames, and preceded by an all-out blaze erupted. The ghoul couldn't escape as the ghosts held it in place, all of them unaffected by the heat that engulfed the creature.

'Good,' Kala purred. 'You've done two, a third will feel harder because you're tired now. So you need to reach down inside yourself, really coax the magic up to the surface and let it bubble out.'

Tex watched in shock as an eleven-year-old wearing Powerpuff Girls pyjamas reached out her hand and – with the power of her mind alone – set a third ghoul on fire. It was testament to the state of what his life had become that it was maybe the second or third strangest thing he'd seen that morning. When it too was ash, only then did everyone seem to let out a collective sigh of relief. With a commanding nod, Corvossier communicated with the ghosts and they disappeared once again.

'Everyone get inside,' Kala hissed. 'The closer we are to the house, the safer we are. *Nothing* will get through my wards of protection, but we're on the perimeter of them right now.'

Sadie was up before him, limping gingerly towards the house.

'Sprinkle, grab that ghoul skeleton, will you?'

'Ew,' the witch remarked, looking at her auntie as if she was joking. 'Why?'

'Because I asked you to. And because they're an incredibly difficult ingredient to get your hands on. I can think of about six different types of spells I can make with that.'

'Can I keep the skull?' Corvossier asked. 'Would make a nice incense holder.'

'Your version of nice and mine are very different, but sure.'

Once they were inside, things didn't exactly feel safer. Kala ordered them both to shower and pack as quickly as they could, Tex watching as Corvossier retrieved the hidden phone she'd used to call Heath. When they had showered, changed, packed, and dumped their bags back in the kitchen, he caught the briefest of exchanges.

'Duo? Hey, it's me. Yeah, I know. Listen, I need to bring the departure time forward ... you're a Valkyrie, thank you. I'll get them there.'

As she hung up, Tex couldn't help himself.

'So we're going?'

Corvossier tossed him a look. 'Fuck yes, you're going. You can't stay here now they've found you.'

'They were ghouls. Kala said it herself, they have no intelligence ... they can't feed back intel.'

'No, they can't,' the witch agreed, setting down several plates of oats and fresh fruit she had whipped up. 'But someone set them loose with a purpose. They were tracking your scent, like hunting dogs. The Treize might not know specifically where you are or who you're with, but they guessed it's in this area *somewhere* and they set those creatures free to hunt and kill you. They were nearly bloody successful too.'

'What were you doing out there at that hour?' Corvossier questioned. 'We can only protect you if we know where you are.'

'It's my fault,' Sadie signed, Tex frowning as he spoke her words.

'No,' he disagreed, adding his own. 'It's not her fault; it's mine and—'

'It doesn't matter whose fault it is,' Kala snapped. 'Your lovers' quarrel nearly got you eaten. And now we have to move you.'

'What?' Sprinkle said, looking up from the bowl of oats she was consuming. 'Why? They just got here.'

'They're not new playmates for you, sweetie,' the older witch cautioned. 'They're running away from people like we were.'

'That can be the best way to make new friends!' she exclaimed. 'Like me and Barry!'

'They have to leave in case someone tracks them back here,' Corvossier explained. 'And if the Treize come knocking and we're here together, hiding them, that's gonna be an irreversible tip of the hat.'

'So, what?' Tex asked. 'We have to leave ahead of schedule because it could compromise what all of you seem to be planning against the Treize?'

'Hey, *Askari*,' the witch started, pointing her finger at his chest, 'you're the one who fucked up by going for a bush walk at five in the morning! How many ghouls were let loose, huh? Say twenty and when five don't come back, that will tell somebody something. They either send out more or another line of enquiry. That could lead them back here or it could not: the bodies are gone. Now *because* of this, they will start looking a little closer at the witches who live up here and sure, there's a lot of us, but there's only one cohabitating with the world's most powerful medium.'

'Ours will be one of the first doors they knock on,' Corvossier finished, her voice calmer than her partner's. 'You can't be here then. And yes, we're working towards something bigger and we're not alone. Neither are you idiots.'

Tension crackled between everyone, Tex watching as Sadie's head swivelled from person to person, staring at each of them carefully. At least it was finally said out loud. He and Sadie were valuable to an underground web of rebels and upstarts because the Treize wanted them dead. And maybe some tattered old prophecy about banshees ending the Treize's reign. Everyone might have been shaky on the reason for that exactly, but it was enough to keep them alive.

'Before we leave,' Sadie signed, directing her question at Corvossier as Tex spoke it, 'how will Barastin know where to find us, for news about Sorcha?'

'Don't worry about Barry.' She smiled. 'He'll find you *wherever* you are. Since Duo's handling transport, that will likely be *up*.'

She pointed at the roof above them and Tex didn't know what that meant at first. When a helicopter landed on their wide, flat lawn just twenty minutes later, then he had a much clearer idea. The pilot looked like someone who had strutted straight out of a zombie apocalypse movie, with chiselled muscles, skin so dark it was the human embodiment of night, and an unforgiving facial scar that tugged at her lip. She dressed like she was once military. Tex was intrigued as he watched her interact with the medium and an envelope of cash exchanged hands. There wasn't a lot of time for big goodbyes and he didn't know these beings well enough to offer one, but he thanked them graciously for their help. They'd saved their lives, after all.

He saw Kala hand something to Sadie, realising only later that it was the carefully wrapped pages that had been hidden in the back of *The Collected Banshee Histories*. He felt pained at leaving the full book behind, especially after all he had been through with it, but it truly wasn't his to keep. He could see that Sadie thought it belonged with the medium and her dead brother, a relic left behind by a woman with a brilliant mind and a big heart. There was little to be said after that, with Sprinkle's arms crossed in a distinctly sulky pose as she huffed about losing potential new friends. With a fleeting wave to the others, he and Sadie were safely fitted into the back of the chopper. Looking down at the cottage below as it grew smaller and smaller, the bush creeping in until the residence was consumed completely, he wondered if he'd ever get a chance to go back there.

Chapter 13

SADIE

It was bizarre, flying over the city of Sydney and looking down on the place she had called home her entire life. Sadie had never flown in a helicopter before. She'd never been on a plane. Now she was about to do both, back-to-back. The tight strap of the seatbelt across her waist felt like the only thing keeping Sadie's skeleton from fleeing her worldly body altogether as the helicopter jerked and jumped through the sky. It was loud, *so* loud, as the engine and rapidly rotating blades created a cacophony of noise. She wouldn't be able to hear Tex even if he tried talking to her. After their morning though – and their evening – she guessed they were both completely spent of emotional and physical energy. He was slumped in his seat as she peered out the window, feeling sorry for the tiny, ant-like cars that were bumper-to-bumper on WestConnex – a highway they'd promised would fix all of Sydney's traffic problems. It hadn't, of course, because weirdly adding more roads to one of the most overpopulated and highly tolled traffic systems in the world was not the solution.

From the sky, it showed her their path out of the city for the next hour and a half. The office buildings and eventually houses spread out until soon it was only the train line and a highway that were visible cutting through the Australian geography like glossy, black snakes. The pilot – Duo, Corvossier said her name was – held up two fingers in the air so they could see them, then gestured downwards. They began their descent into what looked like a military airfield of some kind. The woman was speaking commands into her headset and clearly communicating with someone for clearance to land, which she eventually got. She held up another hand once they touched down, telling them to wait as the whirring of the blades began to eventually slow. It seemed she was wasn't big on words and Sadie appreciated that about her.

When it was safer to move, Duo jumped out first and opened the door for Tex, who climbed free and helped Sadie after him. They had their backpacks over their shoulders, with Tex's beloved satchel draped across his body in a diagonal line. She couldn't help but frown as she thought about everything that was inside it: the ritual. That *fucking* ritual. Duo marched ahead of them, wheeling what looked like a brown, leather golf bag. Somehow Sadie suspected it wasn't filled with pitching wedges. A man dressed head-to-toe in khaki jogged up to her, keeping pace alongside the woman as every fibre of his fabric looked like it was straining to contain the muscles underneath. He handed her a package and she nodded, thanking him, before he cast a look in their general direction. He stayed with their trio, escorting them to a bunker that housed several small planes. Duo ushered Sadie and Tex up a retractable staircase that was already lowered.

'Where to now?' Tex asked her.

'New Zealand,' she replied, curt. 'No more questions.'

She leaned across him to pass Sadie the same package the man had given Duo minutes earlier. She nodded, accepting it as they walked into the interior of the cabin. It was small, with seats for only six people, but with Duo up front in the cockpit there was plenty of room for the two of them.

'We take off in thirty minutes,' she called from outside the plane, where she remained with the army guy.

'Thank you,' Tex shouted back in response. He sighed, throwing his hands wide as he gestured to what was in front of them. 'Lady's choice.'

She took the pair of seats in the middle, dumping her bag on the chair directly behind her and Tex doing the same. Sadie touched the side of her jacket, feeling a sense of relief wash over her as she made contact with the stiff object there. It was the hidden pages from *The Collected Banshee Histories*, the witch having packaged and handed them to her just before they got in the chopper.

'I've taken reference images in case we need them, but I feel like these are supposed to go with you,' she had said. 'You're the banshee, after all. If this doesn't pertain directly to you and your sisters, then these are probably your ancestors.'

Tex was watching her, she realised, her hand still resting in place.

'She gave them to you, didn't she? The pages?'

Sadie nodded. He rarely missed anything.

'That's good, I guess.'

'Is it?' she signed. 'The Treize could have wanted you dead *through* your uncles because of these pages. We're now transporting that danger with us.'

She couldn't verbally snap, but her signed words were salty enough for Tex to get the message. They had nearly died, sure, and she was extremely glad none of them had ended up as a ghoul's brunch. But she hadn't forgotten. And she wasn't sure she could forgive just yet.

Her skin still felt hot with anger as she thought about him digging into the alchemy around the ritual that severed her vocal cords, then keeping that information from the person it was most important to: *her.* Sadie's skin felt hot for an entirely different reason when she reflected on everything they had done last night. It had been wonderful, she didn't regret it all, yet she couldn't help thinking that maybe she wouldn't be so upset if the sex had been just sex. Her emotions were already too wrapped up in him, which made the discovery of the paperwork all the more heartbreaking. Tex had his eyes closed, as if he was dozing, but it appeared his mind hadn't been too far from the same subject as hers.

'Are you, uh, okay?' he said, opening one eye to look at her.

At first she was confused. Did he mean the ghoul attack? Their sudden departure from a place she felt quite safe? The air travel? It was only after a beat did she realise that he meant the sex, her eyes going wide as she looked pointedly around them.

'We're alone, Sadie,' he said. 'Duo's out there talking to GI Jeffro and even if she wasn't, I doubt she'd be eavesdropping on the two of us.'

She thought about a harsh reply, something like, 'I'm fine – go research that.' But it was petty. And Sadie was a lot of things, but she wasn't a petty person.

'I . . . I hadn't slept with anyone before you. You were my first, Tex.'

He nodded, face full of understanding. 'I know. Are you . . . okay? This morning, I mean? I know it's different for girls the first time.'

'I'm fine,' she signed, shifting in her seat so that she was hugging herself somewhat.

'I meant it,' he said. 'I know you're hurt—'

'Hurt?'

'*Hurt* about everything you found in my bag, but I really had the best of intentions. I was trying to help you and . . . I fucked up. I shouldn't have kept what I'd learned from you, I admit that and I apologise, Sadie. I'll never stop being sorry for that. But last night? I meant it. It wasn't just sex to me. I know it wasn't just sex to you.'

'I'm sick of you knowing things about me,' she signed, turning away from him. 'Just let me sleep.'

She closed her eyes, pretending to do just that so he'd leave her alone. Eventually he did, Sadie feeling as Tex's body shifted in the seats and finally moved away, finding somewhere else on the plane to sit. She actually wished she could sleep, feeling the fatigue deep in her bones, but she was suddenly wide awake. She fidgeted, feeling a stiff object in her side before remembering what Duo had handed her as she stepped on the plane. *Of course*, she thought, opening the package and seeing two New Zealand passports. She smirked at the expression on Tex's face in the photo, inspecting a driver's licence, gym membership and library cards that came with it. Sadie's own photo made her cringe, but as far as passports went it looked incredible. It was the first time she'd had one of her very own, banshees not allowed to be issued with them given the whole ban on leaving the country thing. Yet Sadie had been obsessed with inspecting the passports of the girls she went to high school with, marvelling at the different stamps they collected over time.

She couldn't tell this one apart from the real thing: the pages felt like the right level of thickness and when she held it up to the light, she could even see the hidden hologram. After flipping through hers, she grabbed Tex's and inspected the stamps that had been marked on his as well. Turns out they had taken a lot of fictional trips together, as Mr James Lestrade and Mrs Aideen Yule-Lestrade.

Dreckly was really worth the money, she thought. If someone was able to recognise these were fakes, they deserved to catch them. They didn't even have to memorise their birthdays or anything, she'd kept them the same, and their ages. The only thing she needed to learn by heart was her home address and the trips she and Tex had taken together according to the stamps. Having never been anywhere, she was stoked to have gone to Egypt – even if it was fictitious. With a jolt, she realised soon that wouldn't be true. She was on a plane, for her first time ever, and in a matter of minutes she'd be leaving not just the state but the country. She was deliriously happy about it.

I deserve a morsel of happiness, she thought. *And I'm going to take it.* Sadie attached herself to the side of the plane like a barnacle as it rocketed forwards and then, eventually, jetted up. Her body was pushed back into the seat, ears popping as they climbed. The moment Duo switched off the seatbelt sign, she raced over to each of the dozen windows fitted into the side of the cabin. Sadie was fascinated by the ice cream clouds as they folded into the sky, their small aircraft somehow cutting through them. She felt elevated both literally and figuratively. She was finally able to access the very thing that had been denied to her for her whole life. Freedom. Escape. Sadie was soaring.

And then she was snoozing. She completely zonked out, missing their descent into New Zealand so that when Tex was gently waking her up a few hours later, they had already landed.

'I missed it?' she mouthed, more than a little crushed.

'It's okay, you'll be awake for the next one.'

'Next one?'

'We're in Wellington, on another military base. And we're hitching a ride on the next flight which is ... oh, a casual twenty hours or so. I think.'

Sadie winced at the thought: she couldn't help it. She signed for him to give her a minute, grabbing a bag of toiletries from her pack and making her way towards the tiny bathroom at the rear of the plane. As the overhead light clicked on above her, Sadie was unsurprised to see she looked like a mess. She spent the next ten minutes trying to salvage some kind of creature that resembled her previous self by washing her face, cleaning her teeth, running a brush through her hair, adding a coat of lip tint, and slapping on some tinted moisturiser. *Save me*, she thought idly. Tucking her blouse deeper into the waistband of her high-cut jeans, she gave her reflection a solid nod. *Better*. When they hit the tarmac, Duo was waiting for them.

'This is where I leave you,' she said, pointing at an enormous aircraft off in the distance. Sadie watched as a truck slowly reversed on to it, *that's* how big this plane was.

'These are friends of yours?' Tex asked.

'You'll be aight; there's a guy called Tem who will stamp off your passports on this side and check your IDs to make sure everything's legit, but this is a bit of a favour to me. Far as he knows, this is a witness protection type deal and you're grabbing a ride with a bunch of other service personnel and equipment.'

'Got it.' He nodded. 'I assume the less we talk to people, the better?'

'Definitely. And when you touch down, there will be a special gate you'll need to go through to be cleared by UK Border Force. Dreckly knows what she's doing and you'll be fine; those IDs will work. Plus, they're always slacker if you're coming through wedged among the military types.'

'Thank you,' Sadie signed, Tex speaking for the both of them. 'That's from Sadie and me, sincerely.'

Duo shrugged. 'I was paid. Thank the money.'

She walked them up to her associate, introducing Tem. He observed them both with intelligent eyes shadowed underneath the brim of a hat that had the word 'Hurricanes' scrawled over the front. Sadie wasn't sure when Duo left them exactly, but as Tem was checking off a list of names on a clipboard and stamping their papers, suddenly the pilot was no longer there. It was a wide, open airfield and Sadie's eyes searched the expanse for her silhouette as she walked away. But there was nothing.

They were directed to the front of the plane, where a cluster of about thirty seats were lined up along the sides of the craft. This was a far cry from the interiors of what they'd just flown in, yet if it got them to safety Sadie knew beggars couldn't be choosers. She and Tex took a seat towards the rear, meaning they'd only have to converse with whoever sat directly next to them. The seatbelts pulled down from above, with a harness crossing over her chest and their luggage going under their feet into a netted storage compartment. The fact they were travelling light didn't look at all suspicious, with Sadie scanning the other passengers and seeing each of them had little more than a military-issue backpack or a small, rolling suitcase.

When it came time to take off, the roar of the plane was almost deafening. Besides the powerful energy she could feel rumbling beneath her feet, there was no shortage of rattling coming from behind the massive, brown wall that separated the passengers from the machinery and whatever else was being transported from New Zealand to the UK. Nobody seemed bothered by it, so she had to assume it was normal.

After a little less than half an hour in the air, everyone seemed totally cool about unbuckling their seatbelts, stretching, strolling around, and pulling out a book or laptop. One guy even took full advantage of the space next to him, bundling up his jacket and shoving it under his neck as a pillow as he lay out horizontally. Sadie had her own ideas about what could occupy her mind, tapping Tex on the shoulder and pointing towards his work satchel. He raised his eyebrows slightly as she signed at him.

'Your notes,' she said. 'I want to read them again.'

'My . . . my notes on the ritual?'

She nodded. He looked hesitant at first, which was understandable given how she had reacted the first time she'd skimmed through them. This time, however, the Askari was out of the bag.

'They're about me and what was done to me,' she signed. 'I want to see them.'

Reluctantly, he retrieved what she was asking for with a sigh. 'Maybe there's something in there you can understand that I can't.'

Just because this is what she wanted, it didn't make reading the documents any easier. The notes on his father's journals were the most difficult to read. They made her stomach churn. Although she'd never really known the man well before the incident, in the years that had passed since she had built him up in her mind as this looming, villainous figure. That picture hadn't been so far from the truth. She pushed her feelings down, concentrating on the specifics instead: when the ritual had taken place was important, from the date itself to the environmental conditions. The symbols that had been crudely sketched by Tex on the page seem to make her mind swim, Sadie's eyes actually going blurry after she read and reread everything over the course of a few hours.

She turned her head away from the papers, choosing to watch Tex next to her instead, a pen dangling from his mouth as he chewed on the tip. His brow was furrowed and he looked deep in thought. *Did he mean it? Was it really not just sex to him?* she thought. The Contos men had proven repeatedly they were not to be trusted, but maybe – just maybe – Tex was the exception rather than the rule. She wanted to believe that, but giving him her body had been a big step. Giving him her heart was the whole damn staircase.

She wondered what it would be like growing up knowing your family didn't give a shit about you. How did that shape you as a person, when the figures who were supposed to care the most just . . . didn't? They sent you away instead. She knew Tex didn't know who his mother was and she didn't question why the woman had bounced not long after his birth. Why you'd enter into a relationship with Andres Contos was another matter altogether. Yet it was clear Tex's father had never cared about him: the most important thing in his life was the job. Always. She remembered growing up and the way Tex's uncles would behave around him at family barbecues, acting like they genuinely loved him as a son while his father never even attempted to pretend.

They were triplets and looked like sideshow mirror versions of each other. She hadn't thought they shared much in common besides their DNA and their job. Sadie was obviously wrong about that: after Andres had advanced, it was clear his uncles wanted to as well. They didn't want to be left behind, upstaged, right up until the point it likely came down to a promotion or Tex's life. She knew what they had chosen and she questioned whether there was ever a moment of doubt in their minds, as they waited in the darkness next to St Mary's Cathedral for the child they helped raise to show up. And then kill him.

She made her own choice in that moment as she watched him. Sadie slid her hand around Tex's back, touching him gently as her fingers traced shapes over the top of the material of his T-shirt. He looked up at her with surprise, that pen still dangling from his lips. She smiled at him, hoping that he felt the warmth and the understanding and the forgiveness she was trying to project. *I won't abandon you like they did*, she thought. He sat up momentarily, planting a small yet significant kiss on her lips.

'What's that for?' she signed.

'Just 'cos.'

He leaned back down and returned his attention to his laptop, but she didn't miss the satisfied smirk that stayed plastered on his expression. Her hand resumed its past activity, just the act of touching him bringing some kind of comfort to her. Closing her eyes, content, Sadie let herself retreat into her mind for a moment. She did what she considered daily stretches now, attempting to flex her powers and evolve them. It was working, gradually, with the images she could conjure of Sorcha becoming sharper. She hadn't seen her yet, but now she could get a feel for the place where she was or might end up soon. It was a club of some kind, the interior smoky and loaded with people. The music was pulsing with a slow R 'n' B beat that was down and dirty as it played. Drinks were placed on tables, droplets of condensation on the outside of the glass as a posh, British accent asked the patron whether they would like 'bottle service'.

She didn't hear their answer because she dozed off, the vision easily transitioning into a dream. This time, though, her sleep wasn't deep enough to avoid the descent. She needed to be awake and alert as they departed the plane, which wasn't hard as she was smacked with a blast of freezing air as she followed the line of other passengers across the tarmac and into a small building where they formed four queues. It was December in England, she realised, which meant right in the heart of their winter and the exact opposite season to what it currently was in Australia. At best there was maybe one hoodie in her backpack and she was grateful for the fact jeans were at least covering her legs. With her hand wrapped in Tex's, they walked towards the Border Force official together. *He's good at this,* she thought, watching as he did the talking for the both of them. He charmed the middle-aged woman as they made small talk, the lady chuckling as she idly glanced at their documentation before stamping it and letting them through.

As they followed the illuminated arrows to the exit, it was a bizarre feeling as they stepped back outside and into the frosty weather. There was a car park in front of them and a drop-off area directly to their left where several of their fellow passengers were having emotional reunions with family members. And then ... nothing. There was a road that stretched away from the building and rolling fields, with Sadie surprised at the crunching sound underneath her feet. Looking down, she realised she had stepped on a patch of snow – one of the last, as it was quickly melting into a brown puddle. The moment was too close to what she had seen trying to conjure up images of Sorcha, it feeling like more than déjà vu. This was the right path and she was on it. Two cabs were idling nearby and they climbed in the first, Tex asking the driver to take them to the nearest Holiday Inn.

'Thought it would be somewhere we can reliably get a room before we figure out our next move,' he whispered to her.

She nodded in agreement, the hotel only a brief twenty-minute drive and just one exit off the A40 highway. Sadie felt like she might fall asleep on her feet as Tex checked them in at the reception desk, her head eventually dropping on to his shoulder as the clerk scanned the credit card they had between them. It was weird, she thought, having done little more than sit still for the past twenty-four hours. Yet she was completely and utterly exhausted, not to mention desperate for a shower. They took the elevator up to their room on the seventh floor, the tiny space not much but it looking like a literal palace to her in that moment as her eyes fixated on the enormous king-sized bed.

She threw herself down on it like a starfish, luxuriating in the clinical smell of the sheets beneath her and the abundance of pillows around her head. No two people needed ten pillows and she enjoyed throwing the majority of them across the room and on to the floor.

'Hey!' Tex laughed, ducking one that flew dangerously close to his head.

'Get better reflexes,' she signed, quickly rolling to the side as he attempted to surprise her with a sneak attack of his own. The pillow impacted with an empty mattress as Sadie rolled off, landing ungracefully on the ground. Tex half-slid, half-fell on top of her as she helped yank him down to her level. Pushing his chest down so that his back was against the carpet, she straddled Tex and attempted to hold him in place with the strength of her thighs alone.

'Alright, Xenia Onatopp,' he wheezed, but Sadie could see the thrill in his eyes. She could feel it within her own body too.

Slowly, she unbuttoned her blouse, starting at the top button and working her way down. He reached out to stop her, his hand resting on top of Sadie's.

'Wait,' he said.

'Wait?'

'Do you want to do this again? I mean, we don't have to.'

'Because of what happened last time,' she signed, sighing as she leaned back and climbed off him.

'Hey, don't go anywhere,' Tex said, following after her as she curled up on the floor next to the bed. He wrapped his arms around her, pulling her closer towards him so she could nestle against his chest. She was opposed to the idea at first, but then instinct took over. He smelled *so* good, despite all the travel. He had that man scent. She nestled.

'I'm not saying ghouls are going to burst out of the woods every time we have sex,' he was saying, causing Sadie's shoulders to shake with laughter. It was soundless, but if she could have she would have been in hysterics at that very sentence.

'Stop,' she mouthed at him, putting her fingers over his lips so the next crazy thing wouldn't slip out. 'I want to do it again.'

'Sex.'

She nodded, resisting the urge to roll her eyes. What else could they have been talking about?

'I want to do it again too,' he said. 'Hell, I only ever want to do it again with you for the rest of my life.'

She watched as he caught his own words, as if he'd said too much.

'I'm ready to do it again, with you,' she signed. 'To learn more and get better and—'

'Sadie, stop, we're in no rush, okay? We have time to learn from each and try different things, if that's what you want.'

She grinned enthusiastically.

'Okay, good, I was hoping you felt the same way because I would have a tough time keeping my hands to myself.'

'I'd really prefer if you didn't.'

He gave her a lopsided smirk, one that sent her pulse racing as it somehow hinted at everything he knew how to do to her.

'Then I won't.'

His gaze was so powerful she could almost feel it, his eyes running over her like hands as she reached for him. *This is dangerous*, her brain said. *The stakes are too high; you need to protect your heart.* Sadie knew what she should do, but what she should do and what she wanted to were not the same. So she gave in to the latter rather than the former, embracing the strength she felt as her body intertwined with his. It was like a call and response, her limbs knowing it was Tex's touch and his touch only to which they wanted to react so viscerally.

'Sadie,' he whispered.

Texas pressed his face to hers as he whispered her name, over and over, Sadie wanting more than anything to be able to call out his. Somewhere in the back of her mind, she registered the dull burn of the carpet as they rolled around, but any slight pain was dominated by the pleasure. Of all the imagined scenarios she had crafted over the years, she realised that nothing was better than the real thing.

There was a man running, his face wet with sweat as he sprinted towards an illuminated EXIT sign. He slammed against the metal bar across the door, pushing it open as he hit the concrete stairwell and plunged down it as quickly as he could. When he burst out on to the street, it was daylight and the sun was blinding at first. Yet he kept running, not slowing for a second as he sprinted through an open gate and down what appeared to be a road. White and grey landmarks were streaking past, before he took a sharp right turn and began dashing through them, darting around them, attempting to dodge his pursuers.

There were gravestones, thousands of them, stretching out over a green hill that sloped towards a glittering blue sea in the distance. It was difficult to tell where the cemetery began and the sea ended, as it looked like one bled into the other. The juxtaposition of a graveyard with a postcard view would be enough to stop most people in their tracks, but it made this man only sprint faster. Suddenly he let out a cry, flying forwards with tremendous force as he collided with a headstone. The impact was so hard that granite flew outwards, cracking off a chunk from the wing of a headless, white angel that looked down upon a nearby grave.

The man didn't move at first, blood dripping from a ghastly head wound. There was a low moan and his body twitched, the urge to stay alive and stay *moving* continuing as he attempted to crawl forwards. He was on all fours and truthfully not that far away from the perimeter of the cemetery, a protective fence just up ahead. A figure stepped over him, walking around the damaged body with interest.

'You got further than I thought you would, I'll give you that.'

'Gavino, *please*,' the man croaked. 'My family—'

'If you cared about your family, you'd give up the others. You know there's no way you're making it out of this alive. So just tell me *who* you shared the test results with and *why*. That's all the Treize want. Actually, I want to know who's helping you as well, who hid you for so long. Throw that in as a bonus for me, will you?'

'Helping me?' he coughed, almost laughing. 'Does it look like anyone's helping me?'

'You were meant to be taken care of weeks ago. Yet you weren't where you were supposed to be and we haven't had an opportunity since. Somehow Texas knew, tipped you off . . . how? We need these questions answered, Denton.'

The man's eyes widened slightly, as if something clicked into place for him, some kind of understanding. Yet his lips remained shut. There was a swift kick to his ribs, a crack audible as he cried out and rolled on to his back in agony.

'You know it won't work, don't you?' he said, each word strained as he panted. 'Their unnatural long lives are coming to an end no matter how many demons, goblins, or selkies they try to cut apart looking for an answer.'

He laughed, rolling back on to his stomach so that he almost landed on the shoe of another gentleman.

'I can see it in your eyes even *you* didn't know, not until I just told you then.'

David and Gavino walked alongside the crawling Denton, one on either side, hands resting on guns strapped to the holsters at each of their waists. They were silent.

'The Treize's reign is coming to an end no matter how hard they try to clutch on to it. And soon, every supernatural creature in the world is going to know their truth and the truth of all the little cretins who have been blindly carrying out orders for centuries. Including me.'

He spat a mouthful of blood, the substance landing on the toe of a shiny, black shoe.

'And there's nothing you can do about it.'

The movement was swift, with Gavino aiming his weapon and firing it in a matter of seconds. The bullet entered through the back of Denton's skull, exploding out the front of his left eye as his facial features became all but unrecognisable. He was dead immediately. As he bled out on the grass of the graveyard, David looked up at his brother with a flash of annoyance.

'What?' Gavino shrugged, gun still gripped in his hand. 'I think it's clear he wasn't going to give us the answers.'

'Question him first, then execute.'

'We were unsuccessful on the first count, may as well be successful on the second. You know we can't afford another failure.'

'No, we can't.'

Wordlessly, they moved together as one unit. There was no one nearby, not a single other soul in Waverley Cemetery to watch as a body was dragged to the fence line and lifted over. No one to witness as two men swiftly climbed it as well, carrying the corpse the final distance to the edge of a cliff. With one person placed at each end of the body, there was a loud grunt before Denton Boys was hurled over the steep drop-off. They watched as he sailed hundreds of metres downwards, landing with a wet *thack* on the jagged rocks below. Blood mixed with the running sea water momentarily, before a wave crashed over the corpse and dragged it along the uneven surface. A few more sets and the body would be submerged altogether, before no doubt washing up on a nearby beach in a few days depending on the current and whether a shark took care of it first.

The two figures on the Bronte clifftop turned away, pulling their short but bulky frames over the fence once more. Their eyes followed the very visible trail of blood left behind in their quest to drag the body from the origin of death to the point of disposal.

'I didn't expect him to be a runner,' David muttered, reaching into his jacket for supplies.

In a hotel bed across the other side of the world, Sadie Burke jerked upright with a gasp. Her hand flew over her naked chest, the skin damp with sweat as she tried to control her breathing. The vision had pulled her in, *deep*, and it was taking a moment for her to adjust to the mental whiplash of being somewhere else entirely. She cast a look beside her at the sleeping man, gingerly getting out from underneath the blankets and tiptoeing away from the bed. Her hands were shaking as she shrugged on a blouse and a pair of underwear that were strewn about on the ground. There was a room service tray resting on a nearby desk and she picked at it, shoving several cold fries into her mouth as quickly as she could. Glancing over her shoulder to make sure she hadn't woken him, she pulled out a chair and sat down, grabbing one of the hotel pens and writing furiously on the Holiday Inn notepad nearby.

She continued to munch on the leftovers of what had been a post-coital meal, Sadie and Tex both needing the sustenance. She was so consumed in her task, it took her a moment to realise there was an unearthly, blue glow coming from behind her. She sat up, back stiff as she turned around slowly.

'If you look like you've seen a ghost before I've shown up, that takes the fun out it,' Barastin said, floating around so that it appeared as if he was sitting next to her. She didn't crack a smile at his joke. She barely flinched at his words.

'I didn't mean to creep in,' he continued. 'Just looked like you were having a nightmare, so figured I'd wait until you woke up to tell you that I've found your sister, Sorcha. Returning once you had a moment of privacy seemed like the right thing to do.'

He gestured to her attire, or lack thereof, and she glanced down, hurriedly doing up a few buttons on the blouse. The ghost looked like he was about to open his mouth to make another joke, but paused when he fully assessed her expression.

'That wasn't a nightmare,' he murmured. 'That was something much worse, wasn't it? A vision.'

Sadie was hesitant to acknowledge the comment.

'Honey, I can smell the stench of death *through* you. And your skin is lit up with it. Who died?'

She glanced behind her nervously.

'Please, I think you shagged him into a coma,' Barastin said with a snort. 'Or it's the jet lag. Truthfully, I don't really understand how heterosexuality works.'

A hint of a smirk looked like it wanted to emerge as her pen slid across the notepad, Barastin leaning over as he read it.

'Second attempt at Denton Boys' life, this time in broad daylight, crime scene a graveyard – Waverley Cemetery, eastern suburbs. Executioners David and Gavino Contos, ugh, Tex's uncles . . . that family. Treize testing supernaturals, that we know, in order to save "them". Who's the "them"?'

Sadie tapped the page, writing something additional down.

'You want me to check to see if he's dead?' Barastin asked, before looking back down as she wrote. 'Need to know if the vision was of the past, present, or future. What details do I need?'

He huffed, crossing his arms.

'Not a single one: you've given me a name and location. Let me dip into the lobby and see what I can find.'

She tapped her wrist, specifically the spot where a watch might be.

'Ah, how long?'

She nodded.

'Should take me a beat. See you in a jiffy.'

He disappeared and Sadie was left in the hotel room, sitting at the desk with a pen still poised in her hand. There was enough light coming through the window from the highway down below that she could clearly see her notes. She scrawled another one, worry etched into her features as she ran a hand through her hair, which was still damp from having washed it just before bed.

'Annnnd, I'm back,' the ghost announced, her eyes lighting up with hope. 'And he's dead. Only minutes ago, I'd say. Your vision was showing you something in the present.'

Her face dropped, Sadie trying to push down the sense of panic she felt curdling up inside of her.

'Sweetie,' Barastin said, tone soft as he observed her reaction. 'I'm so sorry. He was a friend of yours?'

She shook her head, mouthing the words 'not really'. The ghost looked surprised.

'Oh, well, I mean it's obvious he was important to the cause but . . . what has you so upset?'

'He was meant to die weeks ago,' she signed. 'But I had a vision that *saved* him. I thought we'd changed his fate by stepping in. Instead the end result was the same, just a different path to get there.'

'Oh,' the ghost said. '*Oh.*'

He turned around, following her gaze to a sleeping Tex. He was flat on his stomach, head twisted to the side on one of the enormous, fluffy pillows. One hand was laying on an empty part of the mattress, his fingers still curled up into the shape they had been when they were gripping Sadie's.

'You predicted his death,' the ghost said quietly.

She nodded sadly, unable to tear her eyes away from him.
'Are you going to tell him?'

Sadie twisted around, pushing the chair back as she got to her feet. Pacing over the stiff carpet didn't make her feel any better or enlighten her mind. When she looked up at Barastin, the answer was clear in her eyes.

'No.'

Chapter 14

When Tex woke in the morning, he could tell there was something wrong with Sadie. She was upset about *something*; he just couldn't tell what. It definitely wasn't the sex. He knew she didn't regret that due to the fact she wanted to keep having it. Yet there was clearly an issue weighing on her mind. They ordered room service again, indulging in a rare luxury, and ate breakfast quietly. She picked at her food, taking a bite and nibbling, followed by long stretches staring out the window. Finally, after a quiet, mostly unresponsive hour, he opened his mouth to ask what was wrong. As if sensing his question, her hands began moving as she signed a message.

'Barastin is coming.'

'Barastin? Oh, *Barry*. Right. Jet lag brain.'

'You need more sleep.'

'Well,' he smirked, 'whose fault is that?'

A smile played on her lips and she glanced down at her plate, almost blushing but not quite. They were getting past that point.

'When is he coming?' Tex asked, cutting a slice of pork sausage. She turned around, looking at the alarm clock next to the bed.

'Now,' she signed.

'Now?'

'Now,' a third voice said, appearing suddenly. Tex had been taking a sip from his tomato juice and nearly snorted it out of his nose as Barastin materialised.

'Fuck,' he scoffed. 'Do people ever get used to that?'

The ghost seemed to think for a moment. 'No.'

'I think that makes me feel better. How'd you know he was coming?'

'He checked in when you were sleeping,' Sadie signed.

'Ah, so – wait, did you see—'

'Nothing past your lower back,' Barastin said, with a sigh. 'Unfortunately.'

'He found Sorcha,' Sadie told him. 'But I wanted to wait until we were both awake for the debrief.'

'Good.' He nodded, grabbing his notebook. 'What's the plan?'

'We're not far from London,' Sadie signed. 'So I think we get the train into the city and find a place to stay in Shoreditch so we're closer. I've already looked and there's some nice Airbnb joints.'

'Cute flats,' Barastin added.

'Closer to where?' Tex asked.

'Hue.'

'Hue? The supernatural strip club?'

'I think they prefer the term adult entertainment venue.'

'That makes it sound like porn,' Sadie signed, before adding. 'Which would be fine. Long as she's happy. And safe.'

'She seems both,' the ghost noted. 'And rich: she's one of their top earners. A neo-burlesque star, if you will.'

Sadie frowned, before signing. 'Neo . . . burlesque?'

The ghost's expression lit up. 'Oh yes, there are two different types, I've learned! A striptease, which is more of your classic, cabaret style – fans, feathers, jazz horns. And what your sister does, neo-burlesque, where there's a character or a storyli—'

'Hey,' Tex interrupted, waving his hand to try and get everyone back on topic. 'Can we stay focused? You're saying we go there, just rock up to Hue? I'm not sure if that's the best idea; anyone could recognise us.'

'Who?' Sadie replied. 'I've never been overseas before; the Treize still think I'm in Australia probably. The odds of someone recognising us are incredibly low.'

'And the people likely to are Askari,' Barastin remarked. 'It's not the kind of establishment they frequent. It's largely creatures mostly. And Praetorian Guard soldiers.'

Tex didn't like this: he felt like they were walking right into the lion's den. Yet he knew how important it was to Sadie.

'So?' she signed.

'Let's do it. It's Sorcha: she risked everything for you once. Very least we can do is take the risk to see her.'

He knew he'd said exactly the right thing by the way Sadie's face illuminated. Barastin threw him a thumbs up over her shoulder, mouthing the words 'good job'.

'Right,' he sighed. 'What do we need to do to get in?'

'I'm so glad you asked,' the ghost replied with a smile, sitting down at the table with them. 'Hue is in Shoreditch, with the entrance down Brick Lane just beyond the Cereal

Killer Cafe. It's called Hue Lingerie on the outside and looks like any other Agent Provocateur rip-off. You enter through the change room on the far right with the black, satin curtain. Cover charge is fifty quid and you'll be searched: all weapons must be cloaked.'

'What weapons could we possibly carry with us?' Tex scoffed.

'It's obviously not a policy put in place for people like you, moron. Anyway, Sorcha's dancing on the third floor for the next two nights and that's when I'd recommend you go. She's on the main stage Friday to Sunday, which are the busiest nights of the week. It will be harder to get at her.'

'How exactly do we get "at" her?'

'Easy,' Sadie signed. 'We go in like regular customers and sit in the audience.'

'And just hope she sees us?'

'She'll see us. Well, she'll see me.'

He wanted to ask her how she was so sure, how she could take such a massive risk on a fleeting glance into the crowd. Yet he didn't. The world was full of more things he couldn't explain than things he could. The connection Sadie and the Burke sisters had was one of them. Whether it was a super-natural element or just their family, he couldn't say. He'd sure as hell never had that kind of reaction with any of his blood relatives, but he also wasn't a banshee.

'There's something else,' Sadie signed, 'before Barastin goes.'

He watched the two of them exchange a glance and immediately Tex knew he had to brace himself for bad news.

'Denton,' she started. 'He's dead, Tex. He was killed while you were sleeping.'

'He ...' His throat felt dry as he digested her words, processed the sympathy sitting in those big eyes of hers. 'He can't be. We stopped that, didn't we?'

'You stopped an attempt, but it wasn't enough. They were determined to kill him. I'm sorry, I'm so sorry.'

'It's not your fault,' he half-laughed, before pulling himself together. 'Sorry, I'm not laughing I just ... are you sure? Like, really sure?'

'I saw it,' she told him.

'Uh,' he murmured. 'That's why you seemed sad this morning. You had a vision, didn't you?'

She hesitated for a moment, before slowly nodding her head up and down with confirmation.

'You said *they*: they were determined to kill him. Do you mean ...'

Tex held Sadie's gaze as he said it, searching for the answer.

'Your uncles,' she signed. His stomach dropped.

'Tell me everything,' he whispered, running his hands over his face. 'I want to know how it happened, where, everything.'

Sadie's face looked pale as she made him wait, before finally replying.

'No.'

He blinked. 'No?'

'No.'

'You're not going to tell me?'

'That's correct. There's information that might be helpful to the network and Barastin has already passed that on to the people who need it but Tex ... there are some things that are better off not knowing.'

He opened his mouth to argue, unable to help the heat building under his skin as he felt a flash of anger. It was the news of his death, he told himself rationally. That's what he was reacting to. That and the fact his uncles had *murdered* Denton. They were coming for him next.

'We should get moving,' Tex said, knowing that his voice didn't sound like his own. 'We need to check out by ten. If we're going to find a place in Shoreditch—'

'Got it,' Barastin said, springing to his feet. 'I'll leave you to it. I've got things to . . . haunt.'

Sadie signed a thank you.

The second he was gone, the silence in the room felt pressing. He could feel Sadie watching him, examining his face. He didn't want to talk. He couldn't. If he stopped moving, if there was a moment of inaction, he'd be forced to think about it. And Tex would do anything not to be left alone with his own thoughts currently. So he maintained forward motion: first, he found a tiny, self-contained studio apartment on Shoreditch High Street. He booked it for three nights at the bargain price of one hundred and fifteen Australian dollars per night, while Sadie mapped out a route that would get them there using inexpensive public transport. He was conscious of the fact they were down to the last of their cash and wanted to space out using the credit card if he could. They didn't have much to pack, so he was showered and dressed in fifteen minutes with Sadie already assembled and waiting at the door for him.

They checked out, left the Holiday Inn, walked over a highway bypass, and waited patiently for a Central line train. Tex tracked their progress via the map of twisted, coloured lines with the names of famous and not-so-famous locations called out over the speaker system at each stop. His eyes followed the red path as they passed Oxford Circus, St Paul's, and Liverpool Street as they got closer to their destination. It was mid-morning and he was grateful they were on the other side of the peak hour commute. Inside, he felt like the pressure was building.

The owner of the apartment lived in the same building, Tex following the instructions in the confirmation email and buzzing up to his floor once they reached the right address. He was a nice enough bloke, an entrepreneurial sort who apparently worked from home and 'loved' their Kiwi accents. It took all of Tex's last remaining effort to politely get through the chitchat. It started with whether it was their first time in London, continued with where they were going next, and when it got to asking if they wanted to know where the nearest Walkabout pub was he had to politely cut him off.

When they were finally alone, the walls felt like a prison. He strolled from the bedroom to the living room and the small kitchen that split off from it. He thought maybe taking a moment for himself in the bathroom might help, but although it was clean and modern, it was little more than the size of a wardrobe. He needed to walk. He needed to be alone.

'I need to get some clothes that are better suited for the weather,' Sadie was signing. 'I was going to take a stroll if—'

'That's good.' He nodded. 'You should do that.'

'Well, do you want to come? You have maybe one jacket more than I do and if we're going to Hue, we need to look the part.'

'Grab me something, you know what I like. The credit card's there, we've got a little cash ... I need to get out. Meet back here at six? Head to Hue around eight?'

'Sure,' is what she signed, but he could see the worry on her face.

He walked forward, taking her face in his hands and pressing a light kiss to her forehead. She barely had a moment to react before he grabbed one of the two keys and dashed out the door.

Tex had no idea where he was going at first, the only clue that he was walking down different streets being the murals that were painted on the sides of walls. From a building splashed entirely in lush, dripping flowers to an enormous black and white crane that seemed to stretch for storeys, it wasn't until he came face-to-face with a colourful portrait of Stan Lee that he stopped. He pivoted around on the spot, looking past a collection of carts nearby that were selling different types of cuisine on the street and observing two women as they posed for a selfie next to a storefront.

A bar, he thought. *I need to find a bar.* Tex was a social drinker at most and despite the situation being anything but social, he wanted to drown himself in alcohol. He started walking again, seeing yet not truly observing what was around him. This was London after all and he figured he'd come across a pub or a bar or a tavern or an entire God damn distillery sooner rather than later. At some point he hopped on a train, blindly tapping his Oyster card before slipping it back into his pocket with the other cards that were labelled as belonging to a man that wasn't him. There was a woman with a bright purple coat, the velvet texture of it drawing his eye, and before he knew it he was out on the street again. This place didn't seem familiar. It was noticeably affluent, with each of the streets looking the same as they bled into each other.

He was unable to tell one tall, thin, white house from the slightly less white, tall, thin house next to it. A dog walker struggled to rein in eight different, expensive-looking breeds as he used their leashes to guide them across the road and towards a gated dog park. Yet this place was decidedly human and he realised with a start that's what he had been seeking. Tex was craving the company of everyday, regular civilians who were unlikely to be brutally murdered by monsters or hunted by blood relatives.

'Hey,' he said, stopping a man around his age who was walking past him. 'Do you know where the nearest bar is?'

'Nearest? Scorpion and The Hog's on the corner. If I were you, turn left on Earls Court Square and go ta Evan's & Peel Detective Agency.'

'A private dick?'

'Nah, bruv, it's a gimmick, innit. There's a speakeasy on the other side. That's my bet, just look for the sign.'

'Thanks,' he mumbled, the lad offering him a square nod as he strutted off on his journey.

Tex followed his directions, searching for a sign so small and insignificant he nearly passed it. Rather, it was a doorway instead, numbered 310 C and the words 'Evan's & Peel Detective Agency' scrawled across it. He tried the door handle at first, only to find it was locked.

'Press the buzzer.'

He jerked back, looking around to see where the voice came from. Tex craned his neck upwards, seeing a small camera.

'The buzzer,' the voice repeated. 'To your left.'

There was a small, silver panel set into the wall. Tex glanced at the camera, but no further instructions came. He pressed the lone button on the buzzer, listening to the sound of an electronic crackle.

'Evan's & Peel Detective Agency, do you have an appointment?'

It was the same voice from just seconds earlier.

'No,' Tex said drily, glowering up at the camera.

'Is there a case we can help you with?' the voice chirped.

'The case of let me the fuck in?' he muttered.

'What was that?'

'I'm here for a drink,' Tex corrected, thinking quickly about the kind of alcohol one would come to a speakeasy to consume. 'A friend recommended the, uh, rum . . .'

Rum? You idiot, he scolded himself. *You're not a bloody pirate.*

'The Rum Runner? Well, come on in then; it's one of our cocktail specials. Ahem, I mean, please step into the agency and we'll see if we can assist with your case.'

The door clicked open, Tex pushing inside and walking up half a dozen stairs until he had reached what looked like a private detective's office straight out of *The Maltese Falcon*. There was even a Humphrey Bogart lookalike sitting on the edge of a desk, beaming at him as he buried his hands deep within his pockets.

'You should have seen the doll that walked in here before you,' the man started. 'The gams on her, who-eeeee.'

'I just want to get drunk,' Tex said, not slowing down as he walked past the man and to the bookcase behind him. 'Which one of these is it, huh? If I just pull enough books down one of them will be the – uh, this one.'

Of course it was a copy of *The Great Gatsby*. Unlike the other books on the shelf, it didn't lift out. He could tell from the moment he touched it that it was *the* book. There was a snapping sound somewhere, then the bookcase split apart and rolled back as if he was about to enter the Batcave. Instead, there was a dimly lit bar on the other side.

'Hey man, that's not cool. We've got a job we're trying to do, you know? We work really hard on maintaining the illusion and I'm just trying to work my way through acting school.'

Tex left him to yammer, walking down through a line of tables where patrons were illuminated by flickering candlelight. Everyday people, he noted. No one with horns or tusks or the ability to control earth elements. Just regular, boring folk.

'Asshole,' the guy muttered behind him, pulling the bookcase doors shut as he presumably returned to his desk to wait for the next appointment.

He took a stool at the bar, asking for the Rum Runner since it was supposed to be the special after all. It was better than he expected, but to be honest he couldn't remember if he had ever properly drunk rum before. Once, he thought back. When he was fourteen and underage. He and his roommate had broken into the alcohol cabinet in the teachers' quarters. He didn't understand portions at that age, assuming that half the bottle of rum mixed with the Coke they had in the fridge would do the trick. It had. They'd been caught practically vomiting up vital organs in the seniors' bathroom, sickly drunk for the first time. Tex wondered why he remembered that, of all things, before he ordered another rum.

'You sure you don't want to try something else after that?' the bartender said, setting down his drink in front of him. 'Get a little more adventurous. We've got endless options, really. I can even make The Commonwealth.'

Tex frowned, glancing up at the barman. 'The Commonwealth? How do you *make* The Commonwealth? Didn't you Brits already manage that?'

'Touché but no, this is a cocktail: technically the hardest cocktail to make. It has over seventy-one ingredients and is fairly new, only invented in two thousand and fourteen in Glasgow to commemorate the Commonwealth Games – hence the title. It's quite fruity.'

There was something to the way the man spoke that caused Tex to narrow his eyes as he took a big swig of his drink. For the first time, he focused in on the rest of the bar. It was structured like an elaborate filing system, with tiny wooden draws extended and the names of various cocktails labelled on the outside. They were recipe cards, thousands of them, and above that were dozens of bottles containing coloured liquid. It wasn't just alcohol, although he did zero in on the label of a spirit that sat slightly in front of the rest and kept recurring: 3Souls.

'This is an alchemist bar, isn't it?' he breathed.

The barman was drying a glass and paused mid-motion, staring at Tex intensely.

'I'm not sure I know what you mean, sir.'

'Only an alchemist would give a shit about making *technically* the most complicated cocktail. Only an alchemist establishment would organise their cocktail recipes like it's the New York Public Library. Only an alchemist joint would stock that many bottles of 3Souls, a single malt that just so happens to come from a distillery run by a Scot in Adelaide. Oh yeah, and they're an alchemist too.'

Tex slammed back the rest of his drink, finishing it with a harsh cough as the full impact of the rum hit the back of his throat.

'Just my fucking luck, you know? I'm trying to run away from this crap and in a city of *eight* million people I end up in a damn alchemist bar.'

'You're . . . Askari?' the barman questioned, his eyes flicking to the bandage around Tex's wrist. It had been Sadie's idea, to keep it hidden once they left The Local. The alchemist symbol tattooed there marked his position within the Treize and it would only be recognised by people within the community. Those were people they didn't want to be recognised by.

'Like it matters,' Tex murmured, slapping down more cash than was necessary on to the bar. 'There's just some things you can't run away from, it seems.'

He burst out the back door of Evan's & Peel Detective Agency as quickly as he could, stumbling on to the street and directly into The Scorpion and The Hog. They had beer there: cheap and horrible and human and simple. Nothing complex about it and nothing that would appeal to the alchemist mind-set, he figured. There was a cab ride among all of that, Tex knowing it was a waste of money when he should have gotten the train back to Shoreditch but he was feeling reckless. He practically tripped into the apartment, dropping his keys on the ground as he did so. Sadie stepped out of the bathroom, hand poised in the act of putting on make-up. She was half-dressed, wearing what looked like black, lacy lingerie to him. Or maybe that's what he wanted to imagine it was.

'Are you . . . drunk?' she signed, stepping towards him.

'Yeah nah,' he replied. 'Nah yeah?'

He reached out to touch her, his fingers brushing the mark on her arm that was now little more than a red line. It was where the bullet had grazed her, his careful packing of the wound now no longer necessary as it continued to heal. He should have died that night. His uncles had wanted to murder him too, just like Denton. And she had stopped it. Her perfume was almost too much for him, entirely intoxicating as he leaned against her and breathed in deeply. She was touching him, soothing him with every gesture, and he was so desperate for it he couldn't find the courage to pull away.

'I need you,' he said, sniffing. 'I need you right now.'

She was taller than him, something that had never concerned Tex but he knew usually bothered other girls. She ducked her head so they were at the same level, her gaze penetrating as she touched his face. Her fingers were wet, he realised with some surprise. He was crying. *Gross*, he thought. *I'm an emotional drunk: the worst kind.*

'They killed him,' he whispered. 'It was horrible, wasn't it? What they did to him? That's why you won't tell me.'

He wanted the comfort of her huge lips. She had lined them with colour and they seemed even bigger to him as she moved closer.

'They want to do that to me, they'll keep trying to. How can someone's own flesh and blood want to hurt them?'

She was *heaven*, her hands running over him and through his hair as the weight of everything finally broke him down. He voiced something he'd always known, but never said out loud due to how much it physically hurt him.

'They don't love me, Sadie. My own family, my dad, my uncles . . . they've never loved me.'

Tex was descending into despair and Sadie saved him as she enveloped him, holding him tightly in her arms as he cried.

'You don't need their love,' she signed, Tex pulling back so he could read her words. 'You have mine.'

He held his breath for a moment, almost in disbelief. He didn't deserve her love; he knew it as surely as he knew getting into a fight with a werewolf was a bad idea. Tex ran a hand over her cheek, trying to commit every single one of her freckles to memory like they were a constellation. He didn't deserve her love, but he desperately needed it.

Chapter 15

SADIE

Sadie was so nervous, she thought she might throw up. She wished she was as tipsy as Tex at her side, his hand linked in hers, but he was sobering up quickly after the episode in the apartment. She had all but told him she loved him and frankly, being drunk might have dulled the mild panic she was feeling about that. Thankfully, there was an important task to distract the both of them. It might have been closer to midnight than midday, yet Brick Lane was even busier than it was during the day when she'd visited, trying to obtain new clothes. It had been a successful mission, with Sadie getting several items more appropriate for winter and outfits for both Tex and her that evening. She caught a glimpse of herself in Hue Lingerie's highly polished window, the dark red of her dress clinging to every one of her curves and lines smoothed out by the control underwear she had on underneath. Her breasts were lifted high against her chest, the bust of the dress ending a little lower than she would like but Sadie considered it ideal for the venue. You were supposed to dress a little sexy when coming to a strip club. She'd added a pair of dangly, silver earrings to her usual collection of necklaces and the choker that sat around her neck.

A bell above the doorframe jingled as they stepped into the storefront, mannequins positioned every few metres in different poses that showed off the custom lingerie in fabrics like silk, lace, satin and organza. None of it looked particularly comfortable to Sadie's eyes, but that wasn't really the point of the product. There was a shopgirl standing nearby, dressed in what looked like a Hervé Léger frock that had sheer panels cutting across her body. Sadie registered the scent of her perfume, Chanel No. 5, a classic for a reason as it communicated a certain type of high-class elegance. Yet she wasn't fooled, noting the grace with which the woman moved. Sure, she'd likely sell anyone a bustier if they wandered in off the street. She could also probably kill you with her bare hands in a matter of seconds. The supernatural world was full of things presenting as they weren't.

'Good evening,' she crooned. 'Can I help you at all? Perhaps you'd like to view our couple's collection? It's just in: there's something for her *and* something for him.'

'No, thank you.' Tex smiled, speaking for them both.

'Oh,' she said, with some understanding. 'Please then, proceed.'

The change rooms were just behind the register and Sadie thought that was clever, meaning no one could get in or out without crossing this woman first. The black, satin curtain that Barastin had told them about was billowing slightly in a breeze, the only hint there was something else back there besides a full-length mirror that would make you feel crap about yourself from every angle. Tex positioned himself to step through first, giving her a look that made Sadie know it was intentional. She followed, the pair of them proceeding down a dark hallway. It was mirrored and she had to quell the notion that another couple who looked *just like them* were following alongside in a scene straight out of a Jordan Peele movie. There was a cloakroom and a security desk on opposite sides of each other, a woman in a bright pink slip with black lace trim patting them down before they proceeded further.

'No weapons then, loves?' she asked.

'No,' Tex replied.

'Shame.'

She stared directly at Sadie as she spoke that last word, her eyes running slowly up and down her body in a way that made her feel naked. They paid the entry fee to a butch man whose head went directly from shoulder to chin – no visible neck at all – and they followed the sound of the music deeper into the club.

'Hey sweetie,' another woman whispered as she passed them with a drinks tray. Again, her focus was on Sadie.

'You know,' Tex said, leaning close. 'I thought if anyone was going to leave here feeling jealous, it would be you. Now I'm ready to scratch someone's eyes out.'

She grinned, wondering if he was joking with her to ease the nerves. She'd felt twitchy all day due to a combination of the lingering effects of such a visceral vision and watching Tex spiral afterwards. Then there was the whole getting to see her sister for the first time in two years thing. All of it right now was a lot.

Hue was packed full of people and she scanned the venue, intrigued by what looked like a tunnel filled with water that wrapped around the perimeter just above people's heads. They started to make their way up to the third floor, where they'd been told Sorcha would be dancing. The crowd thinned out the further they climbed up one of several staircases that twisted around like metal tornados. There were poles that started high above them and went down the length of the entire building, Sadie leaning over the railing and watching with interest as a man with more abs than she could count spun around one of them at a rapid pace. His body was a blur – he was moving *that* fast – and she was worried for him as he dropped metres at a time. Yet he landed in the splits, looking like the impressive physical feat was nothing more than a hair flick.

His performance was met with cheers from the side of the stage he was working, the dancer thrusting up on to his knees and stroking the horns that grew from the base of his scalp in a beautiful, twisted formation. The screams increased and he was showered in twenty-pound bills, his clientele clearly pleased with the show he was putting on as he vogued closer to their general direction.

'Sadie,' Tex said, gently touching her elbow.

'Sorry,' she signed, continuing to follow him up to the third floor. 'I got distracted.'

'I can understand why.'

She followed his gaze to a different raised platform that was separate to the main stage and had its own audience gathered around it. Men and women were staring up appreciatively at a fire elemental as they shifted in and out of form. It was fascinating to watch, the flames undeniably seductive as they licked at the ceiling before merging into the shape of a full-bodied woman whose very movements looked like an extension of the fire itself. The third floor was cast in a different kind of light, purple and pinks that shifted to the darker end of the colour spectrum and back again in time with the pulse of a George Maple song.

There was a creature grinding at the railing of the balcony, their hands clicking in time with the music as they mouthed the words to the track. Their eyes appeared to glow as they followed Tex's path towards the bar, where he got a glass of water for himself and a vodka, lemon, lime and bitters for her.

'What's the best spot up here tonight?' Tex asked the barman casually.

'The diamond stage over there.'

'The one with the hoops hanging from the ceiling?'

'That's it. There are still plenty of seats left, club doesn't usually fill up for another hour or so. But it won't stay that way for long.'

'Yeah?'

'Pumpkin Spice is up in five minutes. You're not gonna want to miss her. This is just the appetiser: she does a Wonder Woman set later that's brilliant.'

They took their drinks and made for the area the man had pointed out, settling into a comfortable duo of chairs two rows back from the front.

'Pumpkin Spice?' she mouthed, incredulous.

'Sure.' He shrugged. 'Everyone here probably dances under a fake name, why not really go for it?'

'Maybe her act is that she comes out and carves pumpkins with artisan knives.'

Tex laughed, Sadie pleased with the reaction she got out of him as she sipped her drink.

'To the *Halloween* theme,' she added, 'slowly crumping to John Carpenter's keys.'

'Naturally.'

Suddenly the lights dimmed and the song ended, the percussion on a new track building the audience anticipation as someone cheered. She had been expecting Sorcha to strut on to the stage with purpose, maybe Rihanna's 'Work' playing in the background, but the entrance was made from above as another hoop was lowered from the ceiling. The silhouette of a woman was illuminated by a spotlight, long legs draping around the curve of the equipment as she slid half her body to the floor. Her arms stayed attached to the hoop above her, muscles visible as she pulled her form back up and flipped herself over. Sadie registered the lyrics of the song she was performing to with amusement, the hook 'the bigger the hoops, the bigger the hoe' repeating over and over. The routine was moving faster now as she swung from hoop to hoop, using the momentum of each to elongate her body and put it on full display.

With each item of her costume that was being shed one by one, she seemed to encourage a larger cheer from the audience. It was one that was only matched when she displayed another impressive feat of flexibility or strength. She blew a kiss to a man in the front row, crawling towards him before spinning around and arching her back at the last second. In the process, she yanked at the slit of her layered skirt and threw it away, it landing on the adoring gentleman. Her hips swung and she twirled as the silk gloves were tossed, then the bustier she was wearing unzipped as she dangled with one leg from a hoop, her body rotating in a full three-hundred-and-sixty-degree angle. Tex looked down at his feet beside her, not able to watch any more as she danced around in a thong and glittery, orange pasties with black tassels covering her nipples.

The audience around them couldn't stop staring; Sadie watching the crowd as they leaned forward in their seats, completely hypnotised. She grinned, thinking about how terrified the Treize seemed to be of the banshee wail. Yet there was her sister, up on that stage with almost every person in the room eating out of the palm of her hand as she disconnected one of the ceiling hoops and spun it around her waist like a hula hoop. Sorcha's gift was being able to enchant people with her movements and, occasionally, speech. Sadie couldn't help but feel something bordering on pride as she watched her sibling exploit it for every dollar she could.

The song swelled to a crescendo just as she was spinning the tassels – hands-free, of course – in opposite directions, Sorcha throwing herself through a hoop at the last minute and swinging out over the stage. As her feet made contact with the surface once more, she slid to a stop and threw one hand up in the air, triumphant. Her chest was rising and falling with the exertion of her act, a sassy smile plastered on her face as she delivered a final wink to anyone who was looking. Sadie was. In fact, she was staring so intently that her sister's head swivelled as if feeling the heat of her gaze. Their eyes met for just a moment, Sorcha's diamanté eyebrows twitching with surprise, but like a true professional she otherwise held her composure.

'That was Pumpkin Spice,' an announcer said. 'Performing to the appropriately titled "Hoops" by Willam. She descended from the heavens above, so show her how much you love her.'

There was another enormous round of applause, with cash appearing out of thin air.

'Pumpkin is available for private dances in the champagne room, just see the bar for bookings, and will be back on this stage in half an hour so stick around. Next up, you saw her on Drag Race struggling to keep her wild instincts in check. Yes, it's the werewolf who has everyone howling – Mercy McSnuggletits!'

Sadie was already on her feet, her drink downed and left empty on the table behind them as she tracked Sorcha along the length of the stage. There was a discreet staff entrance that Mercy appeared from, her sister slapping the drag queen with a high five as she passed. When the horns of a new song took over and the spotlight fixed on the latest performer, Sorcha's sultry walk shifted immediately. She slid off the stage, clearly keeping her emotions in check as she fell instep alongside Sadie and Tex.

'Come on,' Sorcha said, jerking her head towards the staff entrance. 'Both of you.'

The door opened on to a slightly smaller door, Sadie feeling like she was in a Lewis Carroll story or an acid trip: both being weirdly the same thing. This one was guarded by a woman who could be described by a single word: *babe*.

'It's okay, LaToya,' her sister said. 'They're with me.'

'Both of them?'

Sorcha looked back at Tex reluctantly for a moment. 'Yeah, the guy too.'

Another beat passed as the woman stared at them, before she eventually twisted the handle and let them inside. They were bombarded with a barrage of noise, not just music but people shouting at each other – some of them laughing – while a voice off in the distance gargled along to the words of a Kelis song that was blasting. It was manic, with fully naked people dashing between doorways while others strutted past in elaborate costumes.

'This is a safe spac—'

Sorcha didn't get to finish what she was saying, Sadie launching herself at her sister instead. She blanketed her in a crushing hug, Sorcha's hands gripping her hair as she hugged her back. She couldn't care less that it was her sister's nearly naked body as Sadie closed her eyes and drank in every part of her. She didn't ever want to let her go or move apart, she just wanted to stay exactly as they were forever, her skin affixed to her sibling's like glue. Eventually they did separate, Sorcha wiping away a tear as she sniffed and glanced around them.

'I can't believe it,' she whispered. 'I can't believe it's you! And . . .'

'It's Texas,' Sadie signed, looking over at him. 'Sorcha, there's so much going on. I've got so much to tell you.'

'Come on then,' she said. 'It's safe back here, but . . .'

She trailed off, Sorcha's caution clearly one of the things that had helped her get this far. She led them with purpose towards a closed door that had a huge pumpkin on it, along with a crude drawing of breasts underneath and a fish.

'Those are some mixed messages,' Sadie signed.

Sorcha grinned, tapping each image. 'Me, obviously – the pumpkin. Mercy is the tits and the fish . . .'

She opened the door, Sadie and Tex stepping inside to find an enormous tank fitted into what otherwise looked like a fairly regular dressing room. Sorcha shut the door behind them, smiling as she threw on a dressing gown and observed their reactions. Sadie inched closer to the glass, pressing her fingers up against it as a woman inside placed her own hand in the same spot. Her skin was grey and thick hair that must have extended well past her waist billowed behind her like a storm cloud. She wasn't sure if it was rude to stare, yet she could not pull her eyes away from the long, muscular tail that extended from the woman's hips like a pair of low-rise jeans. Except these were scaled, shiny, and unbelievably beautiful to gawk at.

'A selkie?' Tex muttered, the awe in his voice mimicking the awe she was feeling. 'I've never . . . oh, sorry.'

He turned away quickly from the tank as the creature lifted her arms up, pushing herself through the water and exposing a small pair of perfect, perky breasts. Sorcha cackled, the selkie's teeth flashing too as she laughed underwater.

'Little Texas Contos,' her sister started. 'They're just *breasts*. Christ, you saw mine only a few minutes ago!'

'Please don't make this any weirder for me,' he muttered.

'Ugh, here: Atlanta, throw this on.'

Sorcha tossed her a bra that had novelty seashells sewn on to the front of each cup, the selkie half-leaping out of the tank to catch it as it sailed through the air. Sadie stepped back as water splashed at her feet and she realised the floor of the dressing room was actually tiled. There were even several small drains built in every few metres. Sorcha struck a match from a small packet that had the Hue logo printed on the front, lighting two cigarettes held between her lips. She handed one to the selkie when she was done clasping the bra. Absentmindedly she started making herself a cup of tea, offering Sadie and Tex one as they shook their heads to tell her no. There was a pretty cup and saucer set that Sorcha was using and it matched the teapot, butterflies painted along the sides of the porcelain. Sadie watched as the brown water was poured into the receptacle, along with a thin slice of lemon. *Earl Grey*, she thought to herself. *Exactly the way Sorcha likes it.*

'I didn't realise selkies were so . . .' Sadie signed, not quite able to find the phrasing '. . . mermaid like?'

'Me neither,' she admitted. 'I hadn't seen one until I left Sydney. They can change shape depending on where they're from. Apparently back home they like to stick closer to the top end. Water's a little too cold down south for their liking.'

'And too many people,' Atlanta added.

'Sorry,' Sadie signed at her sister. 'Can you apologise for me? Tell her I can't speak?'

'She knows. I've told her all about you. Atlanta, my sister wants me to apologise on her behalf so you don't think she's rude for not speaking.'

The selkie reached a hand out of the tank, lightly touching Sadie's shoulder. 'Honey, my whole act at this club is recreating *The Little Mermaid*: a story about a teenage girl who gives up her voice for a fucking man. You don't need to apologise for a thing; I heard all about what those Treize bastards did to you.'

'You talk openly to her about all this?' Tex asked. 'She knows who you are and everything?'

'It's safe,' Atlanta said. 'I'll take Sorcha's secrets with me to a watery grave. She saved my life.'

'You did?' Sadie signed.

'It's a long story, later. Right now I want to know what the fuck the two of you are doing here. I wasn't sure what shocked me more: the fact my baby sister was watching me strip or the fact you dyed your hair pink!'

Sadie smiled, self-consciously touching her locks again.

'Oh, don't do that,' Sorcha said, slapping her hand away. 'It looks great, *you* look great in this red wine vixen number. And Tex . . . I wanna know what he's doing here, hell, what you're both doing at Hue.'

Atlanta made a gesture behind Sadie, catching Sorcha's eye as she wiggled a finger. Her sister's gaze immediately flicked to Sadie's wedding ring, before she pivoted and grabbed Tex's hand forcefully.

'Whoa, what the fuck? *Are you two married?!* Sadie, you're nineteen!'

'No!' she signed, a grin creeping on to her lips as she enjoyed the shock on Sorcha's face. Her sibling was used to being the shocking one in their family.

'It's a cover,' Tex explained, snatching his hand back.

'Speaking of long stories,' Sadie started, looking over at him. 'You tell her: it's easier for everyone if it's spoken aloud.'

So he did, Sadie feeling weirdly voyeuristic as she leaned up against the tank and listened to her life over the past month recounted in audio form. Tex went right back to the start, divulging how he had been assigned to the Burke sisters and returned to Sydney, Australia, for the first time to replace Denton Boys who was under suspicion for leaking Treize secrets. He spoke about how Sadie had followed him, learning those suspicions were correct, and how once she'd predicted his death things had gotten messy as they attempted to both hide and save him. There were Sorcha's old friends popping up in cameos, from Fairuza handing over *The Collected Banshee Histories* and Dreckly with their fake identity documents, to the witch Kala Tully helping set them on a path to find her and get out of Australia. Then there was the banshee specific stuff, as they properly began to understand their power as a species, even if the Treize had done their best to isolate them in Australia and let them die out. And Tex's belief that what had been done to Sadie wasn't permanent, that the power of the banshee wail couldn't be stifled if they could just understand the specifics of the alchemist's ritual. The potential prophecy was brought up and the banshee sisters predicted within it: their suspicions being the Treize had seen this same document once and interpreted their end as coming at the hands of banshee women. He ended on Denton's death and Sadie breaking The Covenant when she foresaw the attempt on Tex's life at the hands of his uncles, followed by her sweeping in to save the day.

Sadie maintained her focus on Tex when he got to that part, feeling her sister's gaze on her as she sipped her tea but refusing to meet it. Instead she let her eyes wander to Sorcha's array of costumes that were hanging in the corner, including several iconic superhero outfits with thigh-high leather boots positioned underneath and masks dangling from the hangers. She vaguely listened to Tex talk about how all of the Burke sisters were mobile, the banshee family still successfully evading the Treize in small groups, while they had fought some ghouls and come in search of Sorcha, hoping she could help them stay alive. When he was done, he shook his head slightly with disbelief. It was a lot just to hear, let alone to live. Sorcha got up from her spot and held out the ashtray for Atlanta, the selkie putting out her cigarette before positioning the top half of her body over the tank.

'So you came to England for me?' Sorcha asked, resettling herself.

'We had to,' Sadie signed, before correcting. 'I had to. When I learned you were alive . . . it was something I'd never dared let myself hope before. I couldn't live another year, another two, without seeing you again.'

Her older sister sprung up, pulling Sadie into a crushing embrace once again. She planted a kiss on each of her eyelids for added effect.

'I'm so glad you did,' she whispered. 'But coming to the club is a risk, you must know that.'

'It's likely they're still looking for us in Australia,' Tex said. 'The Blue Mountains was only a few days ago: Kala said that's where they'd concentrate their search. Anywhere out of the country is good. Somewhere really far away and loaded with people is even better.'

'Welcome to London,' Atlanta murmured, Sadie picking up what she thought might be a mild South African accent.

Sorcha snorted. 'Funny, those were the same reasons I chose London. That and the sheer number of Aussie ex-pats here: the accent doesn't stand out so much. Plus, I tried putting on a fake one and I was terrible. Could never hold it for longer than a few sentences.'

'Aren't you worried about working here?' Sadie questioned. 'Barry said not many Askari frequent this place but still, what about Praetorian Guard soldiers? Even a random Treize official or someone from back home?'

'Firstly, look at the amount of fake tan I'm wearing. I don't look like a Burke sister any more, bless our pale hearts. I have a sleeve of tattoos that I'm trying to add to constantly to distance myself from how I presented before. I'm platinum blonde with a pixie cut, shredded, and *even* if all of that didn't throw the person, when I'm up on that stage they're in my control. I can sense if they're harbouring ill will towards me, I can sense authentic recognition. That's how I knew you were there tonight. Most importantly, I can manipulate it.'

She twirled her finger through the air for emphasis.

'Truly, there couldn't be another job better suited to me.'

'Politician,' Tex answered.

There was a knock on the dressing room door and Sadie froze.

'It's fine.' Sorcha waved, wandering over to answer it. She opened it just a crack, peeking her head out.

'Tell Atlanta she's on in ten,' a voice barked from the other side.

'Atlanta, you're on in ten,' Sorcha repeated, before turning back to the speaker. 'Happy?'

'Delirious.'

She shut the door, waiting an added moment before she decided to lock it too.

'It was lovely to meet you both,' the selkie purred, grabbing a red wig that hung from a hook just above her. 'If you're still here once I'm done, we should grab a drink. If not, I'll see you around.'

Sadie waved as the woman dived back under the surface, her body squeezing through a hole at the side of the tank she hadn't even realised was there.

'She has to do a few laps of the club first,' Sorcha explained. 'Give people a taste tester, lure them to whatever stage she's on that night.'

'That's what the tunnel is for?' Sadie signed, with realisation. 'The one I saw when I walked in.'

'Yup. Gotta make the most of every star, especially one as rare as Atlanta.'

'You have her tattooed on you,' Sadie signed, noting with surprise that what snaked around her sister's left arm was Atlanta's tail. Or at least the tail of *some* selkie. However, the face of the creature bore a striking resemblance to the woman she'd just met.

'And what of it?'

'Are you dating? Are you together? How does that even work?'

'How do you two even work?' Sorcha replied. 'Oh yeah, I'm not an idiot: "cover" my ass. My moves barely affect him, Sadie; ask me why that is?'

'No.'

'Because those that are really in love, *deeply* in love, can't be swayed.'

'I think I might go to the bathroom,' Tex murmured. 'Down the hall, was it?'

'On your left,' Sorcha said, not looking away from the daggers Sadie was shooting at her. The moment the door was shut behind him, they were straight back into it.

'It's not just Tex in love with you, you're in love with him too!' her sister screeched.

'You're thinking of the kid, Sorcha. Not the man. You don't know the kind of person he has grown into, everything he has done for our family, everything he has risked for me.'

'Fine, whatever, I'm missing the "previously on *The Adventures of Sadie Burke*" stinger. Bone him if you have to, get a good dicking and get it out of your system. But falling in love, Sadie? Oh, *oh* please tell me you didn't?'

'Didn't what?'

'You lost your virginity to him. Don't even deny it, I can see it on your face. Shit, you're never pulling yourself out of that dicksand now.'

'Hey, remember when I kept your secret? Remember when I covered for you when you were going on dates with girls and were afraid to be the only gay in the family? You lost your virginity to a chick who worked the Supré counter and I never once made fun of you.'

'Except for right now.'

'I'm not making fun; I'm pointing out hypocrisy. It's not a fling, Sorcha: I love him.'

'That is fucking clear as day. Sure, he has risked everything for you. That doesn't mean you two are good for each other.'

'Why not?'

'Because of what his family did to you! How can you even stomach him let alone—'

'He's not his family, Sorch. His father's a bastard and his uncles tried to murder him. He's not that guy.'

'No, he's just a dead guy.'

Sadie's hands were ready to sign a reply to whatever Sorcha was going to throw at her next, but they weren't ready for that. They fell at her side, shocked at what her sister had just said.

'Take that back,' she signed eventually, when she felt like she could. The anger was so intense as it coursed through her, her fingers felt stiff.

305

'No.'

'Take it back, Sorcha.' Her skin was growing hot, her very blood feeling like lava as it seemed to vibrate in her veins.

'He said it himself: you had the vision of Denton ahead of time and he intervened, saved him, but it didn't last. He died anyway.'

'Shut your mouth.' She ground her teeth together, ignoring the horrible sound it made in her skull.

'You can't change fate, Sadie. You can't mess with death's plan: Mum knew that and it nearly killed her.'

'You don't know what you're talking about.' Sadie's throat tingled like bugs were crawling down it and she closed her eyes, trying to shut out the face of her sister that was driving her mad.

'A banshee doomed to love a dead man. You can't say it's not poetic.'

Sadie balled her hands into fists, unable to do anything else with them as her eyes flew open and she stared at her sister. The teacup resting on a saucer nearby started to vibrate, the sound rhythmic as it rattled on the spot. Sorcha turned around and watched it, frowning with confusion before she spun towards Sadie.

'Sis . . .'

The water in the tank was sloshing too, as the glass vibrated with the same energy. Sadie could barely focus on her sibling as she felt her rage take over, her anger at everything hurtful Sorcha had just said bursting out of her. She screamed, a sound erupting from Sadie's throat for the first time in years. It was piercing, Sorcha dropping to her knees as she slapped her hands over her ears and tried to block the high-pitched cry.

The mirrors in the dressing room shattered one by one, shards of glass falling like confetti and smashing on to the floor. The tank was next, the glass unable to take the sheer power of her frequency as water burst from its previous restraints and washed into the room. The door flew open, Tex momentarily knocked off his feet as a wave washed him back down the hall. Debris was blocking parts of the drain and the fluid was seeping out of any gap, exit, doorway available. Sadie screamed until she was out of breath, the bizarre sound dying in her mouth like a strangled cry.

She blinked, eyes finally seeing what had happened around her for the first time. The mess, the destruction, Sorcha scratched and bleeding from broken glass while a semi-drowned Tex crawled through the door, coughing up mouthfuls of water. Her eyes were wide as she stared around, a shaking hand covering her mouth. She had caused this. This had been her doing. Sadie had wreaked all of this havoc with . . .

'My voice,' she said, the sound ringing in her ears as she spoke. They were the first words she'd said in nearly ten years.

Chapter 16

TEX

Tex knew they needed to run. Yet he couldn't stop staring at Sadie Burke as she stood there, soaked to the bone and eyes wide with shock at what she had just done. He was shocked too: she had wailed, proper *banshee* wailed. And she'd nearly brought the whole room down around them. Suddenly nothing made sense. He scrambled to his feet, sliding as he struggled to find his footing in the shallow water that had poured from the tank.

'Sadie,' he said, grabbing her hand. It was as if the mere act of saying her name shook her out of it. Her head snapped towards him and she started blinking rapidly as his fingers curled among hers. 'We need to get out of here.'

'The fire exit,' Sorcha managed to mumble, Tex noting with surprise that she was covered in scratches. The water made the cuts look worse than they were, blood expanding as it mixed with the fluid.

'Where is it?' he asked, frantic. The music in the club had stopped and he could hear raised voices out in the hall. The dancers backstage had begun to react to the vibrations that had rocked the building and the strange noise that followed. Then there was also the matter of the tank water, which was flowing out of the open doorway and towards any number of dressing rooms. Tex's eyes were already darting towards their only exit when the security guard from earlier appeared in the doorway.

'What the hell is going?' she asked, eyes wild. 'Are you okay?'

'LaToya!' Sorcha cried. 'Can you take them to the fire exit? They've gotta get gone.'

The woman looked like she was ready to protest.

'*Please*,' Sorcha begged. Tex felt as if he could almost sense the power Sorcha infused into those words. It wasn't a request; it was a supernatural command and one that had to be obeyed.

'Come with me then,' the security guard barked, taking a moment to process the order. 'You have minutes, barely, before the rest of the crew is up here investigating.'

'I live in a converted warehouse on Winchester Lane, number thirteen,' Sorcha said, as Tex pulled Sadie from the room. 'Come find me.'

Soon they were out of the space and dashing through a crowd of performers.

'What was that, LaToya?' a man wearing a floral crown asked as they scooted past him.

'Every bulb on my mirror has burst!' somebody else shouted. 'Every single one!'

'That's fine, Winsome; you look like you do your make-up in the dark anyway!'

'Shut the f—'

'Ewwww, why is the floor wet?'

It was chaos out there and they were able to use it to their advantage, LaToya muttering to each person she passed about how she was 'looking into it' and 'management had been called'. All the while she was shuffling them closer to an illuminated sign that hung above their heads and depicted a white man on a red background running down a set of stairs. She thrust open the door, revealing an industrial stairwell that led both up and down. She pointed in the direction they needed to head, downwards, and slapped on the light switch set against the wall.

'Go,' she ordered. 'Take it all the way to the bottom and you'll end up in a corridor that will take you to the station.'

'Thank you,' Sadie said, her expression unsure as she spoke again.

Tex couldn't stop staring at her lips, fascinated by the fact *audible* words were coming from them. He pushed her through the door as LaToya slammed it behind them.

They descended the steps as quickly as they could, their feet falling into a rhythm as they took flight. They kept going until there were no more stairs and just a dented, steel door. He yanked it open, the gesture taking most of his strength due to the sheer weight as Sadie flew through it. The fluorescent lights above them were flickering as they ran, throwing the tight space in and out of darkness. Their breaths were shallow and they sounded loud as they echoed off the tiled walls and floor. Tex felt like they were rats in a maze, racing blindly down a tunnel that turned and dipped and rose. They skidded to a stop in front of an elevator, Sadie slapping the button and the two of them diving in and hitting the upwards arrow. That was the only option: there was no downwards arrow. They were yanked upwards and when the doors slid open a few seconds later, they were standing at a little-used side entrance to a train station.

'I have my Oyster card, do you?' he asked, as they walked with purpose towards the barriers.

She shook her head, but didn't slow down. Sadie planted a hand on either side of the barrier and swung herself over, stumbling slightly on the other side. She kept her pace as if nothing had happened, not glancing around for a ticket officer or anyone who might have seen what she just did. He tapped his card and walked through, jogging after her as they strolled right to a platform and through the open doors of the first waiting train. The loudspeaker told them where they were going, but Tex knew neither of them really cared. As long as they were moving away from Hue and any evidence that a banshee had been there, then they were okay. He glanced over at Sadie and found her big, bright eyes watching him. There was the shadow of a smile on her face, but it was soon replaced by a frown as she touched her throat.

'Does it hurt?' he asked, worried as he reached behind her neck to undo the choker she always wore fastened there.

She shook her head, her fingers running along the shape of her scar.

'Is it still there?' she signed. 'It feels like it's still there.'

'It is; you still have the scar.'

'Then how did I . . .'

'I don't know,' he admitted, leaning forward as he examined the old wound more closely.

'What is it?'

'I . . . here, see for yourself.'

He grabbed the back-up phone they had been sharing, flipping the camera so she could see herself. She pushed the device closer to her chin, eyes scanning what she saw there.

'It's not silver any more,' she whispered, verbalising words. 'The thread of silver through the scar . . . it's gone.'

'I thought it was just in my mind,' he muttered. He noted how uncomfortable she looked, how uncomfortable she sounded, with the 's' on all her words dragged out like a lisp somehow.

'It's not,' Sadie confirmed, reverting back to Auslan, which she clearly preferred. She twisted her head from side to side. 'When did it go?'

'I don't know . . .' He dropped his voice, looking around the train carriage. It was mostly empty, save for a father and daughter sitting at the opposite side and a middle-aged woman who was bopping her head along to the music coming from her headphones. 'You take it off when we have sex, usually. All of your necklaces.'

She tilted her head with interest. 'What does that have to do with it?'

'It's the only time I see your neck bare,' he whispered. 'When we're having sex. Or when you're sleeping.'

'And it was there then?'

He thought on it. 'The first night definitely, back at Casper and Kala's in the Blue Mountains. After that, I'm not so sure.'

The train stopped, the last remaining person in their carriage getting off.

'How long do we stay on for?' she signed, eyes glancing up at the tube map above them.

'Till the end of the line,' he said, settling back in his seat. 'We take this train all the way to Epping and then figure it out from there.'

She rested her head on his shoulder, Tex enjoying the sweet familiarity of the gesture. She was damp, they both were, but it was at least warm inside the train. It wouldn't be when they got out. He would worry about that later.

'What did it feel like?' he asked, unable to help himself.

He thought the gentle rocking motion of the train might have lulled her to sleep, but Sadie stirred at his words.

'To speak?' she signed. 'Or the wail?'

He was looking at the movement of her hands as she used Auslan to communicate, Sadie following his gaze until she realised what she was doing too.

'Oh,' she whispered, voice sounding raspy.

'You don't have to sign any more.'

'It feels weird not to,' Sadie spoke, still creating the words with her hands in the air.

'Then do both.' He shrugged. 'Do whatever makes you comfortable. Shit, you know I just realised I've never heard your adult voice.'

'*I've* never heard my adult voice,' she countered.

'Is it what you expected?'

She sighed, shaking her head. Sadie was quiet for a moment, thoughtful, before her back stiffened and she sat up.

'*Tex*.' She practically purred the word, wrapping it around her tongue. 'Texas Contos. Do you know how long it has been since I said that?'

'Yes, because it's the ten-year anniversary of what happened next month: the end of January.'

'Could that have something to do with it then? A time thing?'

'I don't really understand how,' he admitted. 'Then again, I don't even understand how we're having this conversation.'

'Oh!'

'What?'

'You know what I just realised? All these *bad* words I didn't know as a kid, I never got a chance to say them.'

He laughed, enjoying the complete and utter delight in her eyes.

'Fuckstick,' she said, drawing out the sound verbally as she spelled the word physically as well. 'Cunt. Motherfucker. Ah, motherfucker's nice to say. Dickhead.'

'Okay,' he chuckled. 'Let's maybe slow down on the cussing; an old lady just got on-board.'

'Please, she's British: they basically invented swearing. Plus, she's far away and probably has a hearing aid. Piss, fuck, shit.'

He tried to put his hand over her mouth, but he was laughing too hard.

'Sssssh, let's not get thrown off this train. We need to circle back to the apartment in Shoreditch safely before dawn. You know, 'cos of that whole running from a supernatural strip club thing?'

'I think I remember it.' She smirked. 'Bullshit is still better.'

'What?'

'Bullshit. It's better in sign.'

She demonstrated with a smile and he couldn't disagree. Her hand reached up to touch his face, smoothly running along his jawline as she stared at his lips.

'What are you thinking right now?' he questioned. 'You have a look on your face that's worrying me.'

'I'm going to whisper something dirty in your ear.'

'Sadie!'

'Let me try it.'

He couldn't wipe the smile off his face as she leaned in and kissed him so deep that if there had been more people on the train they might have blushed. She placed smaller kisses on top of the big ones, sending shivers down his spine and to other places as she gently kissed her way to his ear. She gently bit his earlobe, her wet tongue touching the skin there and he felt his body pulse with desire.

'*Texas Contos,*' she murmured. 'I'm going to—'

'Stop.'

'What?' she asked, switching back to signing immediately like it was a reflex. 'Why, don't you like it?'

'No, I mean, yes – I do, obviously.' He gestured to his lap. 'But look: we're not going to Epping any more.'

'Huh? Oh, so? The train is just stopping at South Woodford instead. That's no big deal.'

'That's not what it was saying on the display thingy before.'

'*Thingy,*' she said, her lips moving more than was necessary to pronounce the word. 'That's fun to say.'

The train slowed, the two of them getting up as they followed the old woman from the carriage and out on to the platform. It was a tiny little station, there not being many options for them other than waiting to see if the next train that arrived took them further or risk their chances on the train after that, which would take them back towards central London. Tex wasn't sure what to do, his mind whirring through the possibilities as Sadie curled up next to him.

'It's freezing out here,' she signed, not speaking the words.

'I know,' he mumbled, wishing he had a jacket to throw over her shoulders. 'As soon as I work out . . .'

He trailed off, eyes fixing on the lady they had shuffled out behind. She had settled on a bench at the end of the platform as she waited for the next train. There was a floral headscarf wrapped around her hair, with grey curls sneaking out the bottom. That wasn't what alarmed him though: she was texting rapidly on a smartphone and as her wrist moved, he caught just the tip of her tattoo as it was exposed from under her cardigan. *Askari*, he thought to himself. As if on cue, she glanced up and stared in their direction. She pretended not to be able to see them, affixing glasses over her eyes as she squinted and then adjusted her view to the digital board above that was displaying the next set of train times. Whether she knew who they were or just that she had found the two beings that had sprinted from the club, it didn't matter. It would all end up in the same place.

'Come on,' he said, grabbing Sadie's hand as they rushed down the stairs of the train station and towards the exit. There was a sharp, blind corner and a mirror affixed midway down the staircase so commuters wouldn't collide bodily with someone they couldn't see coming. It was the only warning Tex had as he saw out, past the empty interior of the train station, and to the car park as several cars screeched into it. He practically dragged Sadie the rest of the way down the stairs and across the space into the male bathrooms in front of them.

'What are you doing?' she croaked. 'The exit's back that way!'

The bathroom was disgusting, with dirt and dried piss caking the tiles as he shoved them into one of only three cubicles. This one was the least gross of the lot, but that wasn't saying much as he hoped the brown stain on the floor wasn't faecal matter. His mind was racing with ideas about how they could get out of this, yet he could only come up with one. He closed his eyes, resting his forehead against hers. The closeness quieted her and he kissed Sadie softly.

'I love you,' he whispered.

'I . . . I love you too.'

'I love that you're the girl who wears floral dresses, even when it's winter,' Tex said, suddenly desperate to get this out. 'I love that your lips are always pink, which I don't understand, especially after a meal. I love that you're kind to people who don't deserve it, but you're not a pushover – especially where your sisters are concerned.'

Her eyes were wide and he could tell she was confused about why he was telling her all this *right now* in a festy train station bathroom. If it sounded like a goodbye, it's because it was.

'I love that you have freckles I find myself thinking about when I should be doing *literally* anything else. I love that your words all bleed together when you try to sign while excited or angry, yet somehow I still know what you mean. I've been in love with you since I was ten. That's who you are to me, Sadie Burke. You're all those things *and* you're the love of my life.'

He was immediately sorry about what he had to do.

'I love you and I need you to stay here, completely quiet, for as long as you can. Please. I have to ask this of you.'

He emptied his pockets, tucking his cards and cash into her dress as he spoke. Tex could hear orders being shouted from outside the toilets and he knew he had to hurry.

'I'm so sorry,' he signed, unwilling to even risk the noise it would take to whisper. 'Askari are here, probably Praetorian Guard too at this point. They'll follow me, I can lead them away if you just stay here and stay quiet.'

She shook her head, tears spilling down her cheeks as she moved towards him. He leaned in, kissing them away.

'You said you love me too, so promise me you'll stay – okay? You can't come after me. Promise.'

She looked like she didn't want to, her head refusing to nod up and down. But eventually, slowly, she signed the words he was waiting for: *I promise.*

'They're after you, not me: I'm just in the way. They'll take me, but they won't kill me if they think I can give them information on where to find you. So there's a window of time, alright?'

She opened her mouth to protest, but he stopped her, desperate for her to understand.

'It's important they don't get you. You can wail now, Sadie. Their attempt at stopping that has failed for whatever reason and they won't hesitate to kill you if they work out what you can do. I can't let that happen, I can't let them hurt you again.'

His fingers were aching it was such a massive burst of words and he hoped that he hadn't stuffed it up, that she understood what he'd told her as his lips mouthed the sounds as well. From the look on her face, she had. He locked the door to the cubicle they were in, signing one last phrase before he climbed underneath.

The Wailing Woman

'I love you.'

He slid over the tiles on his stomach, his heart so raw he wasn't even thinking about the myriad of germs he was probably picking up in the process. A rumble overhead told him the next scheduled train had arrived as he opened the door to the bathroom just a crack, peering out on to the ground floor of the station. He was right: he could just see two men at the top of the stairs, speaking with the old woman. She was gesturing wildly and leading them down the platform. She must have thought they dived on to the tracks and tried to make a run for it when her head was turned. Behind them, there was a short man, dark man. He was joined by a tall woman and just from glancing at them he could tell who they were: soldiers. The Treize had sent the Askari and Praetorian Guard like he suspected they would.

'Ennis, if you'd just let me bring Fluffy, I could have tracked them,' the woman was saying as Tex inched from the bathroom.

'Nice try,' the man scoffed. 'I heard about what happened in Kokand. That ghoul tracked an Askari instead, nearly ate him entirely when you idiots showed up at his door.'

'Fluffy is still learning,' she mumbled.

'We're trying to pass for civilians, Venus. This is suburban London: your pet ghoul won't allow us to do that.'

'Fine.'

The train had stopped and Tex was counting the seconds in his head as he waited at the bottom of the stairs. Soon as the Praetorian Guard crept around the blind corner, he followed. When they were on the platform and facing towards the empty side of the track, that's when he sprinted up the stairs. The doors began making that electronic beeping sound they do when they're about to close and he urged himself to sprint faster.

'RUN!' he cried, making sure their attention was on him as he dashed for the closing gap. He dived, sliding through the doors just in time. There were a group of teenagers in the carriage and they looked at him like he was a mad person as he waved and made hand signals at a woman he was pretending was there with him.

'STAY LOW!' he shouted, knowing they'd hear him on the platform. 'KEEP MOVING, GO GO!'

He spun around as the train began to inch forward, the woman named Venus banging on the doors that had now sealed shut. The other Praetorian Guard soldier even withdrew a sword that was short and thick – kind of like him – and looked as if he was about to try and slice it between the seam in the doors, but the train had too much momentum. He watched as they yelled commands at each other, the two Askari jogging up behind them and Tex getting a proper look at their faces for the first time. He was unsurprised to see his uncles, but it made his blood boil nonetheless as Gavino and David Contos threw their hands up in the air in frustration.

'Come on, come on,' he whispered to himself. 'Take the bait.'

It was the guy with the sword, Ennis, who clicked first and pointed at the digital display board. Their figures were growing smaller as the train put more distance between them, but Tex observed keenly as they sprinted from the platform and disappeared down the stairs. The car park was below the train tracks and the lights of vehicles came on as they took off. They'd taken it: hook, line and sinker. Everyone who posed a threat to Sadie was now in those cars and trying to race him to the next station.

'Off his rocker,' someone was saying as he finally stepped back from the door and proceeded to walk into the next carriage.

Maybe he could make it, he dared to think for a moment. Maybe that would be enough distance to get a head start on his uncles and their hunting party. They'd catch him eventually, he didn't doubt it, but Tex knew the longer he kept them running the worse they'd look. If his execution meant they would get a promotion, they'd failed at that. If hunting Sadie and him down was part of the mess they were supposed to clean up, things were still very messy for the Contos brothers. Now that they had him in their sights, he was going to milk it for as long as he could. *You could get lucky*, a voice was saying inside his head, allowing him to hope. *They might never find you.*

He was dumb enough to believe it as he moved all the way up the train, cutting through each carriage so that even if they did make it to the next station in time, they wouldn't know where he'd be stepping off. He had nothing on him that would lead back to Sadie and that was comforting: he'd left everything with her. The look of betrayal on her face as he left her locked in that dirty stall was enough to make him nearly turn back. Yet he knew he couldn't. Crouching low so as not to give his position away, the train slowed as it pulled up at the next station. Nobody stepped on to his carriage and he waited patiently, his ears clued for that ping that would signal the closing doors. When he heard it, he burst out of the blocks and on to the platform. He leaped the gap and thought he was in the clear, until someone shoved him hard enough in his chest that he was sent flying. Landing painfully on his back, he looked up at a figure he hadn't see in many, many years.

'Texas Contos, we're taking you in.'

'Sure,' Tex replied, not resisting as two Praetorian Guard soldiers pulled him to his feet. 'Whatever you say, *Dad*.'

Chapter 17

SADIE

Sadie was fully aware she looked like a crazy person, but she was beyond caring as she stormed through the streets of Shoreditch. It was barely past 7 a.m. and she was barefoot, with her fishnet stockings in tatters and mascara streaked down her face. A businessman had his head down, texting on his phone as he walked, and at the last minute he glanced up and caught a glimpse of her. He practically yelped as he darted out of her way, Sadie taking a right turn down Winchester Lane. When she reached number thirteen, she banged on the door so hard she thought it might give way thanks to sheer force of will.

Her sister answered, Sorcha staring at her for a full ten seconds before Sadie disposed of niceties and stormed inside. It was a converted warehouse like she had said, with wooden dividers being the only thing that split up one 'room' from another. There was a quadrangle of couches assembled in the middle of the space and Sadie marched towards them, noting that her sister's place was heated. She was so cold, she'd actually stopped feeling it and she shuddered with relief.

'What the hell happened to you?' Sorcha questioned. 'You look and smell like death.'

'They took Tex,' she signed, before realising her sister couldn't see what she was saying with her back to her. Spinning around, she repeated her response.

'They as in . . .'

'The Treize,' Sadie whispered, still struggling with the newfound sensation of being actually able to vocalise her thoughts.

'*Fuck*. I'm going to get you a drink.'

She returned from the kitchen a moment later with a bottle of water, just blindly handing it to Sadie along with a glass of something else. She downed the H20 first, then took a swig of the mystery liquid. She nearly choked.

'Gin?!'

'It will do you good,' her sister encouraged. 'Just finish the glass, and shut the fuck up about it. You need something to calm your nerves.'

'Not this early in the morning, I don't.'

'Hey, you're here and you seem safe. The Treize didn't take you so that's something to celebrate.'

'Only because Tex used himself as a diversion,' she growled. 'He put me somewhere out of sight and then made himself the bait. Where do they have him? Have you heard anything?'

Sorcha hesitated in her response, Sadie immediately sensing when her sister was holding out on her.

'What? What is it? What do you know?'

She said nothing, just reached into her pocket, tapped away at her phone and handed it to Sadie, the screen open on to Twitter.

'Lookit this guy getting grabbed fam!' the tweet read. 'These bloods crazy.'

It was a nine-second video and she hit play, watching as a man who was very clearly Tex got dragged off a train station platform. Her blood chilled as she played it again, examining the faces of the other people present.

'I see you recognise Mr Contos as well,' Sorcha said, bitterness in her voice. 'Prick.'

'Not just him,' Sadie replied, hitting play again. 'His uncles are there in the background too.'

She felt anger pulsing through her blood at the very sight of them, Sadie closing her eyes as she attempted to squash the feeling deep down inside herself.

'You're not going to wail again, are you?' Sorcha asked quietly.

She shook her head, but truthfully she wasn't sure how she had done it the first time. Her sister's expression wasn't any less wary, but she took Sadie's hand as she forced her to sit down on the couch next to her.

'Take me through everything that happened after you left Hue: top-to-bottom, side-to-side, front-to-back.'

'We left the club,' Sadie started, 'took the exit LaToya led us to, jumped on the first train. We were gonna take it to the end of the line, I think, but it stopped early, leaving us stranded at South Woodford. I don't exactly know what happened, but Tex obviously saw something or someone that alerted him to the fact we were being followed. I dunno. He took me to the bathroom, made me promise I wouldn't come with him, then left me there. He said he was going to make sure they followed him and I could get away.'

'He must have been able to get on another train,' Sorcha muttered. 'Made it a few stops further before they caught up with him. And it worked: you got out of there fine and you made it here, that's the most important thing.'

'No, it's not,' Sadie growled, getting to her feet. 'They have him! Who knows where they took him or if he's even still . . .'

Her voice broke on that last part. *He's still alive*, she told herself. She hadn't seen him in a vision yet, so that meant he had to be alive. Even as she thought it, she could see the holes in her argument. She didn't see visions of everyone's death. Maybe she wouldn't see his. No, she knew she had a window of time. Tex had told her as much. He'd remain alive as long as they thought he could lead them to Sadie or *any* of the Burke sisters.

'Just stay calm,' Sorcha whispered.

Sadie wanted to slap her. 'Stay calm?! Are you kidding me right now?'

'Getting mad or upset isn't going to help anyone. Remember what happened the last time you and I had an argument?'

She took a deep breath in and out, repeating the process four more times before she sat back down. Sorcha left and returned with a cup of tea, which Sadie sipped slowly.

'You think our *argument* brought on the wail,' she whispered, swallowing the warm liquid.

Her sister looked uncertain. 'I don't know. But you were emotional and angry and then . . . boom! It happened. Now you can speak again? I had to move Atlanta to my bathtub because the tank is completely busted. Mercy spent the last few hours plucking glass from my skin with tweezers. I don't know about you, but this has been one of the wildest nights of my life.'

Sadie felt guilty for a moment. 'I didn't mean to hurt you. I didn't mean to break Atlanta's tank.'

'I know,' her sister said, gripping her hand in support. 'I know all of that, just like you didn't mean to slip backwards off that playground and wail the first time. Yet it happened. And unlike back then, we're not kids any more. We can fight adults *as* adults and you have undeniable power now. I know you're worried about Tex, but put that aside for a minute: this is bigger than him. When was the last time one of our kind could wail?'

Sadie met her sister's hard, penetrating stare. She wanted to feel that same excitement and thrill she could sense pulsing through Sorcha. She truly did. Yet Sadie was consumed with thoughts of Tex: where he was and what they were doing to him. Her sibling leaned back, as if understanding what was going through her mind.

'We need help,' Sadie signed.

'Speak,' Sorcha said. 'You'll get stronger and better at it the more you try. Confident.'

'It's still . . . weird,' Sadie replied, verbally this time.

'I know, hun. But also? My Auslan is out of practice; I can't follow you as clearly as I used to.'

She nodded, agreeing to her sister's request. 'Alright. I'll speak if you do something for me.'

'What?'

'Call someone. I know you have contacts, I know you used a network to get out of the country: Fairuza, Dreckly, Kala. We need help, sis. We need to find Tex and we need to speak to someone who might know where they'd take him.'

The moment she said it, she knew who that person was. Or formerly a person, rather.

'What?' Sorcha asked. 'Your eyes just lit up. Who are you thinking of?'

'He said we're easy to find because we're very well connected to the dead . . .'

Barastin, she thought, saying his name loudly in her mind. Hell, was this how that worked? She closed her eyes, concentrating, and said his name over and over again. When she opened them and the room swam back into focus, there was nothing.

'You do it,' she said, turning to her sister. 'He already tracked you down once, so maybe he's . . . in tune with you or something.'

'In tune?'

'And your speech has power. I need you to think this name: Barastin. Keep thinking it in your mind, loudly, on repeat.'

'Is he the motherfucking Candyman? I don't want to get hooked like some dumb babysitter.'

'Just do it,' Sadie begged.

'Fine, but I'm saying his name out loud too. Feels weird to just do one way and not the other.'

'Whatever,' Sadie signed, knowing her sister wasn't that out of practice not to pick up on a dig.

Sorcha started saying his name, while Sadie continued to think it. When it got to five minutes, both sisters stopped.

'How long are we supposed to do this for?' Sorcha asked with a huff.

'Not for another God damn minute, *please*,' came the voice of a man. 'I don't even have a head any more and I feel like you two are about to split it open with all that yelling.'

Sorcha jumped at the appearance of the ghost, who materialised on her coffee table. He was laying across it horizontally, extremely dramatic. Sadie grinned.

'Holy—'

Sorcha's expletive was cut short as her phone started to vibrate, Sadie watching as her horrified sister glanced down at the 'unknown' number.

'It's for you,' Barastin said, adding an elaborate gesture.

She looked down at the device as it vibrated on the table, acting like it was possessed.

'I don't answer unknown callers,' she murmured.

'You're going to want to answer this one,' the ghost replied. 'After all, you two were calling me for help, I presume?'

Sadie nodded furiously.

'Well, it often comes in the most unusual of forms.'

Sadie lunged forward, making the decision for the both of them as she hit the green 'receive' button followed by the speaker, so they could all hear it. There was a long pause, before a voice crackled down the line.

'This the fookin' banshee?'

'There's two banshees in the room.' Sorcha frowned. 'This is one of them, yes.'

'A smart ass, I love it. Just what I need: another one of those in my life. You know who this is?'

Sadie answered for them. 'I recognise the voice.'

The thick, Scottish brogue was pretty damn unique.

'Aye, speaking of voices, I hear you have one now. That's an interesting development.'

She said nothing: what was there left to say? The 'man on the inside' called Heath chuckled down the line.

'Listen, I got your information from Creeper.'

'Creeper?' Sorcha asked.

'The ghost, Barastin,' Sadie said, pointing.

Heath pressed on. 'Everything you told him from your vision was passed on through the necessary channels.'

'To you, I take it,' Sadie muttered.

'To me, to Casper, to Kala, to the Petershams, to other people you don't need to know about just yet. You might have met some of them, you might not. My concern now is what we do with you.'

'Do with me?'

'The whole supernatural world is blowing up right now,' Barastin said, sitting up. 'Rumours of a banshee that can *wail* over a century after the last reported case of that happening. An entire banshee family breaking The Covenant in the same month and still AWOL despite the Praetorian Guard sent out to find them. The Treize popping up, acting wild, all but confirming the rumours with their actions.'

Sadie glanced at Sorcha, who raised her chin slightly in a stiff nod.

'They raided the club half an hour ago.'

'Looking for you?'

'Not yet, but it won't take long for them to figure out who the "banshee" was there to see. They'll put the pieces together. Atlanta and I will be gone by then. And you're coming with us.'

'I'm not,' Sadie affirmed. 'Not without Tex.'

Heath cut in. 'Your boyfriend's only alive right now because they'll be torturing him to find out where you are or what he knows.'

'Do you know where he is?' Sadie snapped.

'No. And I only have limited time as I'm in transit right now to Treize headquarters in Transylvania. So you listen carefully: you need to get out of the country, both of you. Barastin is going to help. You should go to Galway; that's where your folks are from, isn't it?'

'Yes, but why—'

'Creatures are always strongest on their ancestral lands. Werewolf packs know this, so do shifters, so do selkies, so do witches: it's one of the big reasons they moved banshees as far away from Ireland as possible.'

'I'm not going to Galway.'

'You are.'

'I'm not. I'm not leaving without Tex.'

'You're possibly the most valuable thing to the Treize right now so we need to make sure you're nowhere near them, not trot in to save some mortal—'

'Ask my sister what happens if you try to make me do something I don't want to do. Ask her what happens when I wail.'

Sorcha looked nervous as Sadie stared at her, the resolve thick in her blood as she committed to what she was intending to do. Barastin glanced between the two of them nervously.

'Listen, ya wee bint—'

'You help me find and free Tex. Then and *only then* will I gladly let you hide me wherever you want in Galway.'

He must have held the phone away from his mouth for a moment, as Sadie was able to hear a string of muffled curse words.

'Fine,' Heath said, back on the line and sounding as if it killed him. 'But, girlie, when I meet you, we're going to have a long, hard chat about why this war is more important than one person.'

'I'm not in your damn war.'

'Love, you're right at the heart of it and you don't even know. I swear, I'm going to throw myself off a cliff made entirely out of the corpses of stubborn women.'

Her scalp itched with irritation, but this was the help she needed.

'There's an alchemist speakeasy,' Heath said. 'Near Notting Hill.'

'I know it,' Sorcha answered.

'Tell Barastin everything you know about it. The woman who owns it is likely to be called to wherever they're holding Tex within the next few hours.'

'Why?' Sadie asked.

'At some point, when they're done with the initial round of questions, they're going to want to know about you,' the immortal soldier answered.

'How I can wail,' she whispered.

'Yes. It's likely they think Tex worked out how to break the ritual and they'll want this alchemist to answer some questions herself.'

'The rituals are specific to the alchemist who performed them,' Sadie answered. 'Only the alchemist who . . . *oh.*'

'Wait.' Sorcha blanched. 'The alchemist who did *that* to my sister lives in this city? Why the fuck do we need her?'

'She lives in an apartment above the bar,' Heath corrected. 'Barastin, you need to intercept her. She'll tell you where we need to go.'

'Why would she do that?' Sadie asked.

'Money,' the ghost scoffed. 'It's always money with them.'

'Then what?' Sorcha scoffed. 'We just storm in there?'

'Holy fucking.pissflaps, you're monsters, aren't you? If two banshees and a selkie can't figure it out . . .'

There was a long sigh.

'I give Barastin full permission to help you however he can. Don't die. Then get to Galway. I'll meet you there soon as possible.'

With that, he hung up, the phone returning to Sorcha's lock screen as the call was ended. Sorcha ran a hand through her short hair, intentionally messing up the strands as she did so.

'So . . . now what?' Sadie questioned.

She hadn't finished the rest of the gin her sister had given her and Sorcha snatched it up, downing the remaining alcohol in one go. She turned to Barastin, words spilling out of her mouth as she divulged every detail on the alchemist speakeasy that she knew. The woman who owned the place was a mystery to her, few people had met her in person, but Barastin seemed to get what he needed from Sorcha's recounting. With a wink and a thumbs up, he dematerialised in front of them saying that he'd return with details when he could.

'Come on,' her sister said, taking Sadie's hand and pulling her along with her.

'Where are we g—'

She used her hip to bump open a half-closed door, revealing a bathroom on the other side and a mermaid lounging in the tub. Sadie could only see her tail at first, before water splashed over the side of the ceramics and slopped on to the floor. Her face emerged from the other side, a lollypop stick dangling out of her mouth. There was a Tesco shopping trolley next to the bath and Sadie assumed that's how the selkie had been moved.

'You need a shower,' Sorcha said. 'Do that and get changed while I speak to Atlanta. And leave me the address and key for where you're staying. It's safer if I have a friend collect whatever you've left there.'

Sadie nodded, laying down both keys and the apartment details before stepping into the tiny shower cubicle fully clothed and closing the curtain behind her. Her sister had seen her naked a thousand times, but stripping off in front of a selkie was something just a little too strange for her after the night she'd had. When she stepped out of the shower twenty minutes later, leaving her clothes in a wet pile near the drain, Atlanta wasn't there. Neither was Sorcha. Neither was the trolley. With her skin and hair washed, the warehouse was eerily quiet as her bare feet tiptoed through the space. She found Sorcha behind one of the many dividers, a bag laying open on her bed as she threw clothes into it. Sadie set down her things on a small table that was scattered with make-up, adjusting the towel that was wrapped around her body.

'Where's Atlanta?' she asked.

Sorcha didn't look up as she continued to pack. 'The street runs parallel to a dirty but well-linked canal.'

'Oh,' was all Sadie managed to say.

'That outfit's for you, by the way.'

Sadie glanced at an ensemble that was laid out on the bed with some scepticism.

'Sorch, I know we have the same shoe size but—'

'But what?' her sister snapped.

'I'm a size fourteen. You have a stripper's body. That stuff isn't gonna fit me.'

'Yes, it will,' she huffed. 'Just shut up and try it on. I'll accept your apology later.'

Sadie did as she was told, wiggling into a pair of faux-leather leggings that – sure, okay – actually fit her. There was a black T-shirt there and an olive-green knitted sweater, which she both threw on, the latter falling to mid-thigh. She examined herself in the mirror as she zipped up a pair of ankle boots that could have been plucked from her very own wardrobe.

'Apology accepted,' Sorcha murmured from behind her.

'Are you packing for Ireland?' Sadie asked.

'Yes, for the both of us. First, we go get that idiot Askari. Then we get to Galway. I assume you have a way to reach Shannon?'

Sadie smiled, loving that Sorcha knew immediately Shannon would have taken the lead. 'I do, yes.'

'Good. When we're safe and in Galway, when we know we haven't been followed, we reach out.'

'A family reunion,' Sadie signed, feeling a surge through her body that she didn't understand at first. She thought it was excitement at the possibility of seeing her siblings again, but then she realised what it really was: *power*. The knowledge that they'd be together again made her feel powerful.

Sorcha sighed, finally taking a break from packing as she flopped down on to her bed. Sadie joined her, the two laying side by side. There was an enormous canvas that hung on the wall and took up most of the space there, Sadie frowning as she realised it was several panels from a comic book featuring the same white-haired woman over and over. Sorcha followed her gaze, smirking.

'You like that?' she asked.

'Always such a nerd,' Sadie muttered.

'Hey, show some respect. That's Jeannette from *Secret Six*, I'll have you know.'

'Is that supposed to mean something to me?'

'Oh, only that she's an immortal banshee who suffered cruelly at the hands of men and set out to get vengeance.'

Sadie laughed. 'Okay, now I understand why she has prime real estate on your wall.'

'She's going to have prime real estate on my body one day: a tattoo sleeve of Jeannette. That's the dream.'

'I wish I got to see your Wonder Woman act,' she said, with disappointment. 'It's *so* you, the whole nerdlesque thing.'

Sorcha smiled, propping herself up on her elbows. 'Thanks, I'm pretty proud of it, to be honest. I used to do a lot more stuff in the kink community when I started out but transitioning to neo-burlesque made a lot of sense. Whips can be surprisingly versatile in an act.'

Sadie laughed, watching as her sister made a flicking motion through the air and controlled an invisible whip with her wrist.

There was a knock at the door and both sisters sat up, Sorcha placing a hand on Sadie's arm to calm her.

'It's okay, I'm expecting someone.'

She left Sadie where she was, marching from the room and returning a short while later with two backpacks over her arms, along with Tex's work satchel. She set everything down, Sadie quickly going through it all until she located the rough edges of the plastic she had the ancient papers wrapped in. She wasn't sure why, but as long as they were there with her and safe, that was important.

'Boo!'

Both women jumped as Barastin popped back up and chuckled with glee at having scared them. Sadie slapped a hand over her heart, feeling the rapid beating there.

'Do not *do that*!' she yelled at him. 'It's a terrible idea to frighten a banshee who can't control her wail, Barastin! You could kill someone!'

'Who am I going to kill?' He laughed. 'I'm already dead.'

'I hate ghosts,' Sorcha whispered. 'I really hate ghosts.'

'You're not gonna hate me when I tell you I've got an address.'

'Thank God,' Sadie breathed. 'I've been trying to focus my visions on him, see where he is but ... I'm getting nothing except greyness.'

'You just described most of England,' the ghost replied. 'He's being held on a houseboat about an hour out of the city, in the countryside on a river.'

'Let's go then,' Sadie said, bouncing on her toes. 'What are we waiting for?'

Barastin crossed his arms, a frown set on his face. 'There's two Praetorian Guard soldiers at that location: if you want to take him, you'll have to kill them. That's how it works for those people. I'm not including the Askari – three of them – and one Custodian.'

'That will be his father.'

'Those are just the bodies we know about. Now they don't expect anyone to be hunting them, so you have that going for you. Oh, and the houseboat thing.'

Sorcha smiled at that. 'They probably thought it was smart, to have him on the water and mobile. Easier body disposal too.'

'Their mistake,' Barastin replied. 'Shall I go speak to your selkie friend out back? I've never met one before, you know.'

She nodded, the ghost slipping away and leaving the two of them behind.

'I can't take all of those people,' Sorcha started. 'I can manipulate not maim some of them. Atlanta can help. But you ... I don't know what you can do and neither do you, which concerns me. We're vastly outnumbered but I don't know if we're outgunned. You think you can do it again, wail?'

Sadie nodded. 'I ... I think so. I'd need to practise.'

'Then we start practising.'

'Here?'

'No. We'll need to strike at dark, which leaves us a good ten hours or so. Once we drive out there, we'll find somewhere isolated to practise.'

'Hone my weapon,' she murmured.

'Exactly.'

Sadie wasn't sure what it was about the English countryside that made her hate it. Once they were out of the city and powering towards their destination in Sorcha's second-hand, pink VW Beetle, she found herself agitated. She knew that in other circumstances, she would probably find the wide, green fields appealing or even the lanes they were driving down quaint and adorable. Right then, though, she hated it. She hated the other cars they passed, she hated the white pubs on the side of the road that resembled barns, she hated the music her sister was playing on the radio. She'd tried turning it off, but Sorcha had snapped at her.

'Allow me Siouxsie and the Banshees,' she said. 'Or I'll bite you.'

Her hate was a good thing, she guessed. She could use it to channel something inside herself that everyone else seemed so afraid of. She bumped up and down in her seat as Sorcha took them off-road, having found what she called 'the perfect practice location'. They were going to remain there until dusk. It had been a cake factory once, with the shell of the building now left in disrepair as parts of it crumbled into the growing wilds.

Sadie was glad to stretch her limbs as she climbed out of the vehicle, brushing off the crumbs on her lap from a sausage roll they had picked up from Greggs en route. She couldn't remember the last time she ate something, so Sorcha had practically bought out half the bakery as she insisted Sadie needed her strength. Her older sibling followed her as they picked their way through the ruins, a huge pair of noise-cancelling headphones in her hand as they searched for the perfect spot.

'Nowhere that looks particularly vulnerable,' Sorcha said. 'Infrastructure wise, that is. We don't want to bring the building down around us.'

'Why don't we just practise outside then?' Sadie asked.

''Cos I don't think you're strong enough to bring down an empty factory on the first go. Cocky, maybe.'

Sadie opened her mouth to argue, deeply annoyed. A bulk of that emotion could probably be attributed to a lack of sleep as well. She saw Sorcha quickly slide her headphones on over her ears, hands pressing down on the outside.

'I see what you're doing,' she signed, understanding that her sister was attempting to make her mad. Why not? That's what had worked the first time. So Sadie rolled with it, letting all the tiny irritations in her life build up and annoy her until they felt momentous rather than small. She grew angry, curling her fists as she thought about Andres Contos. She focused on the blurry image of his face that she'd seen in the video footage from the train station. Sadie recalled how much she hated that man, how he had taken so much from her and now he was attempting to take something else. Texas didn't belong to that asshole; he belonged to her in heart and body and spirit. She felt her cheeks flush with heat and her eyes sharpen. She opened her mouth and used the voice she wasn't supposed to have.

Sadie screamed; it sounding human at first before the pitch rose beyond that of any normal civilian. She pushed further, digging deeper, as the few errant pigeons inside the factory took off. There were still a few unbroken windows and they shattered above her, one after the other in a procession. She squinted her eyes shut, feeling the ground underneath her rock slightly as she peeled her lips back over her teeth. And then she was done, her wail disappearing on the breeze as a small whimper escaped her lips instead. Sorcha was on her knees, hands pressed over the headphones and eyes closed. She opened one, peering around with interest at the damage. There was an internal wall just to their left, which had probably been a hallway once. It crumbled to the ground, the bricks looking more like grains of sand than a previously solid mass.

'Shit,' Sorcha muttered, getting to her feet as she slid the headphones around her neck. 'Take that, Ariana Grande's whistle register.'

Sadie was still standing, her breathing slowly returning to normal as she let the anger dissipate. She didn't feel tired or spent in any way: she felt like there was more inside of her, like she was just beginning to feed a flame. If female rage was all it took to summon her abilities, she was grateful she had a lot of it. Glancing at her sister, she jerked her head towards the exit.

'Let's go outside,' Sadie said. 'You can watch me bring this building down.'

Chapter 18

TEX

Tex was looking at his tooth as it lay there on the floor, it having bounced off the figure of his father as he spat it at him. He concentrated on the small, white fragment that was speckled with blood as he continued to ignore the questions. *My blood,* he thought. *My blood drawn out by my blood.* He giggled, the idea amusing him in the moment. The gesture turned into a full out laugh. He was delirious and he knew it, but the belly chuckle at least distracted him from his present situation. His father and cronies had dragged him from that train station and thrown him into the boot of a car. He was bound and gagged, which he guessed was some pretty solid instant karma for what he'd done to Sadie. They'd driven fast and they'd driven far, Tex unsure of where they took him. His restraints were too tight for him to wiggle around and access any of the tools that were usually kept under a spare tyre in the car boot.

He was yanked out and smelled fresh, salty air for all but a moment, before being hauled somewhere else. Once his blindfold was removed, he guessed it could have been a basement but there was no way to tell. The interior was just a sad grey room, with a

342

tiny cot and toilet in the corner. There were no blankets and no window, but there was a chair with shackles fitted into it. There was also a fixture above his head, which they sometimes alternated between hanging him in. He had lost all concept of time and without any natural light, he couldn't estimate what hour of the day it was or even how long he had been there. *Days*, he thought, no more than two, given the level of hunger and thirst.

'I'll ask you again, Tex,' his father said, setting down the bloodied pliers that had been deep inside his mouth only minutes earlier. 'Tell me where the banshee is.'

'And I'll tell *you* again,' he replied, his words sounding funny due to the amount of fluid in his mouth and the missing teeth, 'I have no idea. You can't even try to trick it out of me, because I genuinely don't know. I just hope she's far enough away from wherever you fucks are looking.'

It wasn't even a lie, that was the beauty of it. He had no idea where Sadie was and given his ongoing torture, it was clear they didn't either.

'We went back through the footage, Texas. She wasn't on that train like you made out.'

'Wasn't she? Does the CCTV get *every* angle?'

It might have, for all Tex knew. Yet he was just planting seeds of doubt and that was enough.

'When we find her—'

'You'll kill her, yeah, Dad: I know. She knows. Everybody knows. You've never exactly been quiet about the things you want.'

'Oh, here we go again. Poor little orphan boy, left to be raised by his uncles because his father had an opportunity for greatness.'

'Eh, have you achieved greatness though?' Tex quizzed. 'I certainly haven't heard much about you. I mean, you've got that shiny necklace of immortality dangling around your neck like all the immortal Custodians. An ankh, cool, it's very hip. Very now.'

His father backhanded him, the hit hurting more than the previous ones just because of how sore Tex's mouth now was. He would never let him know that, though. He squinted his eyes open and shut, waiting a moment as the small bursts of light eventually faded to nothing more than dull stars.

'See, now you're making me nostalgic, Daddy,' Tex said, conscious of the fact he was drooling. 'Keep hitting me like that and I'll start believing you didn't abandon me as a kid after all.'

His father grunted with frustration, storming from the room and slamming the door behind him. He left Tex restrained on the chair he had been tortured on for the past few hours, the former Askari forced to observe the tray of tools that had been used on him. There were many that hadn't been touched yet and he knew the strategy: make sure the implements were in full view, that way the subject can imagine any number of horrible possibilities. Often times it wasn't the physical pain that broke a prisoner, but their imagination. *I've done the same entry-level course in interrogation techniques as you, Dad*, he thought. It was compulsory for all Askari, in case they had to assist the Praetorian Guard in such a scenario.

The position Tex had found himself in was a special circumstance, however. The two Praetorian Guard soldiers, Venus and Ennis, were left to watch on as the three Contos brothers went to town. His father must have done something significant in his time as an immortal Custodian, much as Tex hated to admit it, because he was clearly in charge of their small operation. The soldiers took orders from him, Tex able to read their discomfort as they did so. His uncles for the most part were pretty useless: his father barked commands and they followed them. They weren't very good at the torture and their primary duties seemed to be relaying any updates to Andres about the search for Sadie. David sometimes took notes during the interrogation, in case Tex said anything valuable. Rather, it had been his captors who had been better at providing information.

'There's nothing,' he'd heard David say at one point, his voice audible under the crack of the door. Tex had been left to rest at the time, the broken rib his father had given him being a step 'too far', according to Ennis. Tex had silenced his pained groan as he slipped from the bed and pressed himself against the door in order to listen, just like when he was a kid.

'What do you mean nothing?' his father barked. 'She can't just disappear.'

'Can't she? We don't know what she can do. By all reports, what was heard and witnessed at Hue was a banshee wail. She was there and she was vocal.'

'It must have been weak,' Ennis remarked. 'In my day, I heard banshees could bring a man to his knees, burst his eardrums until brain matter and blood trickled out of the ears.'

'Cool,' Venus chirped.

'She's weak for now,' Gavino noted. 'But I'd imagine it's like anything: when you haven't used a particular muscle for a while, it takes time for you to build up strength.'

His father huffed. 'You imagine nothing. That book is fuck knows where and without it, we have no recorded documentation of exactly what a banshee wail can do or how long it will take her to get back to full power. Outside of the vague whispers of a few.'

There was a loaded silence after. Tex hoped Ennis was shooting a look at his father that told him as soon as he no longer had to take orders from him, that man would be buried in the ground.

'Get me the alchemist,' his father said after a long beat. 'She was supposed to make sure this never happened. I want to know why her ritual failed after nearly ten years of working perfectly.'

He knew his father well enough to sense the desperation there, and Tex couldn't help but wonder if his continued position in the Custodian ranks was under threat. It was a notion that brought him a little bit of comfort as he dragged himself back to that lame excuse for a bed, only to be woken and questioned again a few hours later. From that exercise, he'd also learned exactly why his uncles had been sent to kill him. They had been following orders, obviously: the two of them didn't share the same streak for evil ingenuity as his father.

'Denton Boys,' David had asked. 'Why did you help him, huh? When did he recruit you?'

'Recruit me?' Tex had scoffed. 'He didn't. And like it matters. He's dead now anyway.'

'How does he know that?' Gavino had questioned. 'How could he possibly know that?'

The removal of a fingernail was supposed to give them the answer, but Tex stayed silent despite the sweat that drenched his body.

'The banshee,' his father correctly guessed. 'That was her primary ability, before the wail. If she saw you two kill Denton, she likely told Tex everything.'

She hadn't, but she had told him enough.

'Listen.' His father smirked, leaning in. 'The Three are sick: they're dying. We can't have that kind of information filtering out to the rest of the supernatural world, you know? Denton was leaking information to someone about the tests being done to save them; we just want to know who. Now it's likely a member of the species grouping who were being harvested, that's all he had to tell us: goblins, werewolves, shifters, selkies, elementals, demons, whatever. Give me a name and this whole mess can be cleaned up.'

'I don't have it,' Tex said, trying to keep his face neutral.

Everything was starting to make a lot more sense to him though: if The Three were dying, the Treize would be doing everything in their power to save them. They were very much their most powerful weapon, helping the Treize anticipate danger and – he realised now – quash rebellion before it started. Without them, the supernatural government would be weak. For anyone planning to overthrow them, the timing for that couldn't be more perfect. He thought hopelessly of Ben Kapoor's werewolf pack, Tiaki Ihi and the Aunties, the wombat shifters, Fairuza, Casper and Kala Tully, their combined network of players ... this could be the information they needed, but he had no way of getting it to them. He'd die with what he knew trapped inside his head. After all, the only reason his father would relay such valuable information to him was because he knew Tex was never leaving this place. Like he had doubted it anyway, but that was one hundred per cent confirmation they were planning on killing him. He couldn't go back out into the world or even into the bowels of Vankila knowing what he knew.

They had left him for a prolonged period after that, Tex remaining restrained in what he now dubbed the 'torture chair'. This was usually an indication they would be back soon, with more questions and more pain. When the door to his cell was unlocked, he was surprised by the overwhelming scent of sage that came wafting in. He let out a groan as a black robe swept over the floor, Tex looking up at the woman he had been searching for. He'd never forgotten her face and suddenly he was staring at it, the alchemist he'd seen as a boy sitting down in a chair in front of him. He'd watched her slit Sadie's throat with calm contemplation. Now she was studying him with that same look, her face this time etched with the lines of age and teeth fading with blackness as they died in her mouth.

'You,' he whispered, knowing how weak he sounded.

'I speak to him alone or not at all,' the alchemist told whoever was waiting over her shoulder. 'And no hovering near the door. I'll know.'

There was a grumbled response, before the door was shut again and they were left alone as she had requested.

'Have you been in London this whole time?' he asked.

'No. I moved here fairly recently, about four years ago. My business partner and I opened a bar.'

'*No*,' he breathed, unable to believe his terrible luck. 'A fucking detective agency with a gimmick?'

'We're an award-winning establishment, I'll have you know.'

'Fuck you.'

'It seems fate has fucked you, rather. Of all the places you could have wandered into, full of despair . . .'

Tex felt it in his bones for the first time: he was doomed. Generally he thought of himself as an optimistic person, but pessimism was slowly creeping in from the edges of the frame like a fade to black.

'Your father asked me here, of course. He wants to know how you two broke the binding ritual.'

'It doesn't matter now.' He smiled. 'I've read *The Collected Banshee Histories*. You can't suppress an adult banshee wail; that's why my father had you do it to a child.'

He watched her face with interest.

'But he doesn't know that. He doesn't know you can't do the ritual again. That's why you're here: he still thinks you have value.'

'And I do,' she replied, offering the slightest shrug of her shoulders. 'I can tell him anything I want and he'll believe it.'

'You want to make a deal,' Tex realised, disbelief coursing through him.

'Too much time has lapsed between when she first used her wail at the club and now. She will have grown too powerful for anything I can do to stop her, let alone the fact she'll be motivated by anger and heartbreak and vengeance.'

'And love,' he spat.

'Ah, that's what I feared,' she murmured, sitting back. 'All of that makes for a deadly cocktail.'

'What's the bargain then? Make your offer and I'll consider it.'

She chuckled. 'You're a smug little one, aren't you? Barely in the position to negotiate. Alright, here's what I want: tell me how you broke the ritual. I'll tell your father that if Sadie is taken alive, it's safer for everyone and the ritual can be performed again.'

'Bind it,' he said, through gritted teeth. 'I know you can bind it with your words.'

'You have done your homework.' She smiled, considering him for a moment. She slid back the hood of her robe, letting it rest on her shoulders so he could see her full face. She pulled a small dagger from her sleeve, pricking just the tip of her finger. When there was a droplet of blood, she smeared it with one of the many cuts on his bare chest.

'You have my word,' she said. 'I bind my promise and I bind my exchange.'

He exhaled deeply, feeling something surge through him that could have been her magic or his own relief. It was hard to tell.

'I don't know,' he said. 'I don't know how we did it; it just happened.'

'It just happened?' she scoffed. 'It doesn't just happen.'

'Well, it did. We only realised after she wailed that the silver on her scar was gone. I know she'd been testing her powers, pushing at the limits of them because of the book and what some werewolf said back in Syd—'

'The silver was gone?'

'I – uh, yes. Why, is that important?'

'You weren't joking about the love thing, were you?'

'No,' he said, his lips pressing into a hard line.

'She clearly loves you back then.'

'What does . . . I don't understand.'

'Silver is a pure metal, which is why I used it in the ritual. Sadie Burke was a nine-year-old child and few things are purer than a child. In alchemy, you work with the elements available. Her birthday is July eight, is it not?'

'Yeah, it is.'

'She's a Cancer. The night of the ritual was a Monday morning and the moon was visible: all things that heighten the properties of the element you're working with. In my case, it was silver, something that even has a gender if you will: female. So I used all of that to achieve the end result your father desired. Alchemy is a combination of science and magic, both of which can be undone in various ways. That's nature: for every animal, there is prey. And for every ritual, there is a backdoor. It can be something seemingly small and insignificant, or something momentous.'

'Okay . . .'

'Was Sadie a virgin until fairly recently, Texas?'

'That's entirely none of your business.'

'I'll take that as a yes. And it's clear you were the deflowerer.'

'Hey—'

'It takes an act of pure love to undo an act of pure hate.'

Tex's mouth dropped open, his various aches and pains dulling somewhat as he processed the woman's words.

'Are you saying . . . because we had sex—'

'You didn't just have sex. She loved you, and you her, and the physical act of your love undid the knot I had so carefully tied many years ago.'

Tex truly didn't have anything left to say, his mind whirring back to the days that followed after their time at the cottage. Nearly a full week had passed since and she was silent for most of it. Had she tried to use her voice? No, she hadn't: why would she? She would have had no idea the ritual balance had been broken. She'd signed as she always had, a fight with her sister after years apart finally bringing her powers to the surface. He'd wondered then if emotions, heightened ones, had been the trigger. Turns out the gun was already loaded and it had just been waiting for a target.

351

'How very interesting,' the alchemist said, as she slid her hood back over her face and got to her feet. 'I expect she'll be coming for you now. You won't have long to wait.'

Tex watched her leave, the woman knocking on the door and waiting for a moment before it was opened and she disappeared through it.

'You need to let him rest,' she was telling his father. 'He'll give you the answers you want, but the body can only take so much.'

'Did he tell you what he did? How did he break it?'

'The important thing is when you have her, let me know. I can perform the ritual again and make the necessary changes so it cannot be broken this time, no matter what. I feel that if you kill her, now that so many are invested, the ramifications will . . . well, let's just say I can imagine that news making its way right way up to the top.'

'You'll do it again then, yes? Shackling her is better?'

'It is. And I'll expect your call, Andres. Along with my fee for today.'

'The money is already in your account, thank you again. As always.'

There was a shuffling of feet as the waiting party moved away from his cell, his uncle returning a few minutes later and dragging him to the bed. David seemed relaxed almost, chilled enough that as he bent down to undo the restraints at his ankles Tex was able to lean forward and swipe a scalpel from the torture tray. It was the only thing he could reach that was small enough for him to hide, Tex pretending to rest his hand on his hip as he was hoisted to his feet. He slipped the weapon into the waistband of his pants, laying down carefully so he didn't stab himself. The cart of implements was wheeled out as his uncle left the cell, Tex feeling the cold metal of the scalpel against his hand as he positioned it properly.

Now, all he had to do was wait. The alchemist, for whatever reason, wasn't exactly helping him. Yet she definitely wasn't helping his father. Whether it was money or curiosity, her motivations were entirely her own. Tex closed his eyes, his body in too much pain for him to be physically able to sleep. And his mind was racing with everything he had learned, all of the scraps of conversations he'd overheard and ones he'd been a part of whirling through his brain as he tried to save whatever energy he had left.

'Pssst.'

Tex thought he imagined the sound at first, annoyed that he had clearly slipped off to sleep. Then it repeated.

'*Psssssst.*'

He opened one eye, a testament to how injured he was that he didn't jump out of the cot entirely. After all, Barastin was floating just inches above his face and watching him intently.

'Oh thank God,' the ghost said, genuinely relieved. 'I could tell that you weren't dead, but you *look* dead and I thought "if he's in a coma, that banshee is going to kill me . . . again".'

'Is she here? She okay?' he whispered.

'Okay is . . . not the word for it, but you should be more worried about yourself right now. Can you get up? Can you run unassisted?'

'Yes to the first, no to the last.'

'Hmmm. I see you have a handy tool for stabbing, great. Hold on to that. I'm going to have to lead Atlanta to you so if anyone comes—'

'Shank them.'

'My, you have been in London too long. Hang in there, Tex; help is coming.'

'Wait!' he urged. 'I need to tell you something as quickly as I can – in case I don't get a chance later.'

'You'll get a—'

'Please,' he begged.

'Fine,' the ghost whispered. 'Word vomit.'

He offloaded everything he had heard, seen, been asked about, as fast as he possibly could. He could see Barastin growing dimmer, there clearly being a pull towards somewhere else that he needed to be. However, the ghost listened to it all, telling him he had it down and offering a swift nod before he disappeared entirely.

It was only when Barastin was gone that he realised what the dead man had said. *Atlanta?* he thought. *How on earth were they going to be able to bring a selkie here?* It was then that it snapped into place for him and he re-examined the room he was being held in. The low ceilings, the salty smell, the near-constant motion, which he thought was actually dizziness at first. It was water. He was on a boat, somewhere, and Atlanta was coming to get him. No doubt Sadie and Sorcha weren't far behind.

The floor seemed to vibrate beneath him and he jumped, wondering what the hell that was. It happened again, but this time louder and louder until the banging sound was coming up right underneath the floor beneath him. He watched with fascination as part of the wood started to splinter apart, hearing a surprised shout from outside and then several others. Feet came running down the stairs, someone unfortunately tasked with grabbing him from his cell. They would be on the move again, fleeing from whoever was laying assault to their hideout. He limped to the other side of the doorway, bracing the scalpel in his fist just as a figure burst into the space.

Tex let his own momentum do the work for him, jutting out his forearm towards the person's neck as the blade sunk into flesh smoother than he could have imagined. He repeated the gesture, stabbing quickly as they grabbed his shoulders and pulled him down to the ground with him. Their hot blood spurted out, covering Tex as much as it did themselves and only then did he realise it was his uncle, Gavino. His eyes were wide, eyebrows twitching as Tex removed the scalpel and watched an ungodly amount of red liquid spurt from his artery. He felt his body dry heave just a little, but there was nothing in his stomach for him to empty as the physical act of killing his uncle – the same one who had tried to kill him – reverberated through his body.

There was a splash of something and he yelped, thinking that it was more blood. It wasn't. It was water instead as fluid began to bubble up through an opening in the floor that was growing larger by the second. Atlanta's face appeared like Jack Torrance through the door, Tex slipping and sliding over to help her. He flinched at the pain in his body as he exerted himself, the selkie's long wrist reaching through the opening and handing him a crowbar.

Don't think about anything, he told himself, as he used the steel to wrench up more of the wood. *Don't think about the fact you just killed your uncle. Don't think about the fact you just accepted hardware from a mermaid. Don't think, just get out of here.*

When there was enough space, Atlanta punched a few rougher edges free before pulling herself through the hole and up into a sitting position on the floor next to him. Gavino's blood was mixing with the water of the river, the whole floor now slick with pinkish fluid that he tried to ignore. Her eyes looked less than human as she registered the presence of the body, narrowing into slits before they flicked back to him.

'It's going to hurt,' Atlanta said.

'What is?'

'When you get in the water, every cut on your body is going to sting like hell.'

'I have a lot of cuts.'

'I know. How long can you hold your breath?'

'Uh, maybe a minute, usually. But in this condition . . .'

'Don't fight when I pull you under. Don't be fearful.'

He was trying to ignore her serrated teeth as she spoke, her instruction of not being afraid contradicted by what was in her mouth.

'We're meeting Sadie and Sorcha on the shore.'

'Where are they now?'

There was a yell from above, followed by a shudder that seemed to rock the entire boat. Atlanta glanced upwards, thoughtful.

'Currently they're firebombing the outside of the boat,' she said, like it was the most normal thing in the world. 'And creating a diversion for us. So we need to—'

She was cut off by the sound of more feet stomping down the steps, David rushing after his brother.

'Hurry the fuck up, what is—'

David was in the open doorway, freezing as he saw the sight of Gavino dead on the floor and his nephew sitting next to a selkie. However he intended to react, there was no time for it as Atlanta leapt – *literally* leapt – from her position on the ground. The sheer muscle of her tail propelled her forward, the selkie using it to throw herself off the ground and on to the unsuspecting man. There was barely time for him to cry as her mouth extended wide and locked down on his jugular, the creature all but ripping out his throat as she moved her head from side to side like a crocodile.

Tex watched with horror; he couldn't help himself, as his uncle's fists weakly tried to beat her off. The movements grew softer and softer, until he stopped moving altogether. There was a horrible panting sound and it took Tex several moments to realise it was actually coming from him. Pulling her head back, Atlanta turned to him with blood coating her lips and dribbling down her chin.

'Water,' she ordered, pointing at the hole they had made together. '*Now.*'

He jumped with fright at her second command, dumping the crowbar and pushing himself legs-first into the river. He bobbed there for a moment, shocked by the cold of the water, before Atlanta slid herself along the floor above him and used two hands to push him under. With his last moment above the surface, he took a big breath. It was impossible *not* to panic after what he'd just seen her do, but he tried. Squinting his eyes shut, her weight pushed him deeper and deeper as she dove on top of him. When they must have been submerged enough, her two hands gripped around his torso and they were propelled forward at incredible speed. They were going under the boat and away from it, the two of them bursting through the surface a short time later.

He was coughing and spluttering as she held him up, Tex taking a moment to get his bearings. His eyes were immediately drawn to the light, a huge, orange ball of it illuminating the night sky. It was the houseboat he had been held on, he realised, with the entire top deck now aflame. He watched as the silhouette of two people dived from it, landing in the water on the other side with a splash. There was an explosion from somewhere and one side of the boat disintegrated completely. He saw a metal dinghy circle the boat, two crouched figures inspecting the damage, before it turned and tore off in the direction of the shore. The sound of the motor drew closer and he realised they were moving again, Atlanta following the boat as she dragged him through the water. Something slippery ran over his bare feet like thin, slimy fingers, and he jerked his legs upright towards his chest.

'They're just reeds,' Atlanta chuckled. 'You should be able to stand up now.'

He extended one foot and then the other, feeling not just the reeds but a coarse type of sand mixed with pebbles. He stumbled, half-wading, half-walking as Atlanta helped him along. The dinghy had pulled up on the shore only metres ahead of him and he recognised Sadie as she sprung out of it. She landed in the water at knee-depth, jogging along until she was in his arms, hugging him, kissing him, holding him. He nearly collapsed against her, feeling her body strain against his as her weight propped him up. Pulling back, he examined the face he never thought he'd see again. It was illuminated by the burning houseboat off in the distance, the flames dancing in her eyes as she stared back at him.

'Texas,' she whispered, the words somewhat shaky. 'I'm so sorry, I tried to get here sooner. I—'

'You're sorry?' He laughed. 'I'm sorry! I left you in that bathroom! I'm just glad you came after me at all.'

'You're bleeding, there's so much blood—'

'Only half of it's mine.'

And then he was kissing her, unable to stop himself despite how much it hurt his mouth full of missing teeth. She didn't seem to care either, both of them now completely drenched as they held each other.

'Come on,' she said, sliding his arm around her so he could lean against her body as they limped from the river. 'The car is through that field and then we're out of here.'

He turned to thank Atlanta, but there was just a splash and several ripples where the selkie had once been. Sorcha wasn't stupid enough to let herself get wet, waiting for them on land as they inched their way towards her. He was so badly injured that it was slow going, which annoyed Tex because more than anything he just wanted to be out of there and in a warm car next to Sadie. There was long grass as tall as they were in the field and they needed to pass through it, Sorcha pushing ahead of them and trying to create a path with her hands. Sadie and Tex ran into her back as she suddenly came to a stop, both of them wondering what had halted their progress. Peeking around the older Burke sister, he realised what it was: Venus, one of the Praetorian Guard soldiers, and his father. They were standing directly in their path, drenched and looking worse for wear. The woman had burns on one side of her face so bad that her left eye had swollen shut. His father was bleeding from a small cut on his cheek.

Tex dropped to the ground, unable to remain on his feet. Lifting his head up, his eyes met the bloodied gaze of Sadie. She wasn't looking at him, she was staring directly at his father, but her hands were moving slowly.

'Get out of our way and we'll let you live,' Sorcha was saying, as Sadie moved to stand beside her. They were partially blocking Tex, he realised.

'Let *me* live? You've gotta be fucking kidding; you Burke bitches have truly lost the plot.'

'Put something in your ears,' Sadie was signing to him. His father wasn't paying attention to the message she was delivering to Tex and even if he was, he would never have understood it. The long grass around them was being whipped up by the wind and Tex began to realise this wasn't a natural breeze. It was localised, specific. It was Sadie. He grabbed some of it, shoving as much as he could into his ears and repeating the process. He could see Sorcha swaying her hips, moving forward in an almost serpentine-like fashion as she attempted to sway his dad with the power of her movements. It was working on the woman, who lowered the blade she was carrying, but he knew the weaker the person's will, the more efficient her ability tended to be. Andres Contos was a strong-willed asshole.

Words were being exchanged, heated ones, and his father let both of the women see the gun he had resting in his hand. Tex felt like a chess piece in the middle of them, waiting anxiously to see who would move their pawn first. He felt it rather than heard it, most of the noise now blocked out from the tuffs of grass shoved in his ears. He pressed his hands over the top for extra pressure. The earth started to rumble and he watched a field mouse sprint past him across the ground. It was clear

Venus knew what was happening before his father did and she attempted to run. Yet you can't outrun a banshee's wail.

He watched with fascination as Sadie opened her mouth and screamed. The Praetorian Guard soldier dropped to the ground, clutching at her ears as she attempted to block out the sound. She was too late, her body twisting and contorting with pain as she rolled around on the grass. Blood was pouring from her ears, just like Ennis had said it would. It ended up being an eerily prophetic death for the once immortal soldier. Her skull looked like a soda can being squashed by an invisible hand, bursting in a cloud of gore that splashed around her. Her body lay still, but his father was still going, his own mouth open as he screamed as well. His arm was stiff as he lifted the gun to his head, desperate to end what must have been extreme pain. His skull exploded first, Tex only registering the sound of the weapon after the fact in what he assumed was a reflex action as his father fell backwards.

He reached towards his ears, ready to pull out the grass but he hesitated. Sadie's eyes were still blood red, her lips still parted as if she would wail again at any moment. Sorcha slid a pair of noise-cancelling headphones from her ears, reaching across and holding her sister's hand. Just like last time, the physical contact seemed to stir her. Her natural pupils broke through and she blinked, eyes refocusing on Tex's position on the ground. She ran towards him, skidding down in front as he yanked the last of the grass from his ears so he could hear her voice again. Her hands were all over him, touching his skin for a moment and then pulling back as if the flesh was too tender.

'Is my father dead?' he asked. 'Can someone check his vitals? I don't want to feel relief until I know he's really gone.'

'He has no skull,' Sadie murmured, panic etched into her face.

'Oh. Good. You can't come back from that, yeah?'

She shook her head, trying to smile. 'No, you can't come back from that.'

'She was right, the alchemist was so right,' he murmured, not understanding why Sadie looked so worried. 'She said once her ritual was broken, there was no way to dial down your powers. You'd just get stronger and stronger a—'

She shut him up with a kiss. Tex's words – which had seemed so important to him in the moment – disappeared from his lips as she consumed them, practically crawling into his body. *It takes an act of pure love to undo one of pure hate*, he thought to himself, the alchemist's voice floating back to the forefront of his mind as he kissed her back. He must have flinched slightly and Sadie leapt backwards, tears on her cheeks. It was at that moment he realised he'd been shot, shock stopping the pain from coming to him until minutes after his father's weapon had been discharged.

Tex had always thought it was a stupid gun, an outdated Smith & Wesson revolver that only took five bullets at a time. His father had coveted that pistol, even though it looked better suited for a cowboy in a Western than actual use in real life. As he glanced down at himself, he heard a weird giggle escape his mouth as he realised it didn't matter how the weapon looked. It had done the job. *She's okay though*, he thought happily, seeing not a scratch on her. There was a lot of blood, but it didn't matter so much if it was his. The dirt under his head felt like the most comfortable pillow in the world as he let himself relax into it, the night sky falling in and out of focus as he stared up at it.

Suddenly his view was blocked by Sadie, the only thing in the world more beautiful than the stars. Her face was contorted in pain and he wondered if she was hurt after all, the banshee looking at him with agony as she said his name, louder and louder. There was something about getting him to a hospital, if only they could just move him a little further. Her hands were touching his body and he could feel the physical pressure of it, but not register much else. That probably wasn't a good sign, he figured. If Sadie was touching him and his skin wasn't alive with the sensation, then he didn't know what to think. Her hands came back bloody as she held his face between them, keeping his gaze focused on her.

'No no no no no,' she was saying, repeating the words in a constant thrum.

'I'm okay, s'okay,' he tried to say, the words slurred.

'Please no, I'll do anything, anything!'

He didn't know who she was talking to, but she was begging someone for something.

'I didn't see this! It wasn't supposed to happen like this!'

'Sadie,' he whispered, touching her bottom lip. It was so big, that lip. It was his favourite. 'I love you, it will be fine.'

Tex was lying: he knew it wouldn't be. As the woman he loved looked down at him, he saw the truth in her eyes as well. He was dying. He was about to die. The entire Contos line was ending that night and as he searched inside himself, Tex came up with the realisation that he was okay with it. It made sense to him, somehow. All of it. He was meant to be there that day nearly ten years ago, he was meant to yell at her to run and pray that she made it. When she didn't, he was meant to witness the true nature of his family as they had maimed a

363

nine-year-old girl. He was meant to fall in love with her, just as she was meant to fall madly back in love with him. They were meant to break the ritual together. Most importantly, he understood with his final breath that he was meant to die that night so Sadie could live.

'Fate's plan,' he croaked, unable to finish the thought as Sadie's tears fell on to his face like raindrops. She faded from his vision completely, but it was alright. He could sense she was present and if there was one thing he finally realised after a lifetime surrounded by banshees, it was that you couldn't outrun death.

When he opened his eyes again, he wasn't expecting to see a familiar face.

'Hello, Texas,' Barastin said, offering him a friendly smile as he stood in front of him. His eyes scanned their surroundings, and for a moment he thought he might have survived. They were back in Kala and Corvossier's cottage in the Blue Mountains: he was even sitting on the bed in the spare room he and Sadie had slept in together. Her things weren't there though. The space looked just like the one they had been in, but there was something missing. It was a feeling rather than key details.

'Why am I here?' he asked.

'The lobby shifts and changes around the needs of the . . . person. You're here in this room, I'd say, because it holds memories that made you very happy.'

'The lobby . . .'

He was looking down at his hands, which were no longer dirty and cut from his fight to escape that houseboat. They were clean, pristine, and slightly translucent. Tex jerked his head up to meet the eyes of his ghost friend.

'I'm dead,' he said, there being no question about it.

Barastin nodded sadly. 'I'm afraid so. We were hoping it wouldn't come to pass but . . .'

'You can't cheat death.'

'You can't,' Barastin agreed, gesturing to himself. 'But you can have a handy tour guide, if you're lucky.'

Tex smiled, unable to feel grief for himself just yet. He wanted to miss Sadie, but the very thought of her name just brought a warm feeling to the surface of his chest. It began to spread, growing stronger and pulling him to his feet like a magnet. It was as if Tex had a sense of direction, like he knew there was somewhere he needed to go.

'Alright then, Barry,' he said, letting himself be tugged towards that growing sense of contentment. 'Show me the sights.'

Chapter 19

SADIE

It was Saint Patrick's Day in Galway and absolute chaos. Sadie felt like she was the only person in Ireland who wasn't drunk and she desperately wanted to be. She sensed a concerned glance from Sorcha beside her as they walked down Quay Street, navigating around tourists and singing locals who all seemed as sloshed as each other. A man dashed in front of her, Sorcha instinctively appearing from Sadie's right and stepping in his path. The guy didn't seem to care though, just pivoted to the left and bent over as he threw up right there on the street.

Sadie felt her own throat grow dry with an urge to do the same, just the scent and sight of his puke enough to send her rushing towards a nearby alley. There was a half-empty bin there and she leaned over it, retching into the receptacle. Sorcha's hand was on her back, soothing her as she felt tears streak down her face like a complimentary reaction.

'Ooph,' the guy from earlier wheezed, wiping his mouth as he stumbled away from them. 'Glad to see I'm not the only one. Better out than in, love.'

Sadie ignored him, taking a moment as she panted and tried to collect herself. Sorcha passed her a water bottle and she took a swig, gargling and then spitting out into the bin. She went to hand it back and her sister grimaced.

'Ick, I don't want your vom bottle. Keep it.'

She knew her sibling was trying to make her laugh, but it had felt like a long time since she had done that. Sorcha handed her a stick of gum and Sadie chewed it, the peppermint taste and scent immediately making her feel less queasy.

'Come on,' her sister said. 'We're nearly there.'

Sorcha had chosen this day for them to leave the safety of the place they'd been holed up in for over three months now. They'd journeyed outside on Christmas Eve and New Year's Eve as well, all days when the city was positively packed with people. Numbers brought safety and anonymity. Coloured flags fluttered in the wind above them, draped from the edge of one building and over to another. It was just past 2 p.m. and she knew from staring out the window at night that fairy lights would flicker on once the sun set. The buildings were just as bright, each one a vibrant splash of green or blue or yellow or even the shade of pink her hair had been once. It was back to its usual colour now, with just a pastel rose tint under certain light. *Tex would love it*, she thought, immediately trying to suppress the notion as quickly as it popped into her brain.

Texas Contos had been dead for months. Sadie lived with the grief every day, it seeming supremely weird to her that the rest of the world wasn't mourning as well. She had been around death most of her life – seen it; been raised by women who could sense it; cleaned it up for a living – yet the thing that was most baffling to her was how it went by unfelt. The people closest to the deceased mourned intimately, but the ripple effect was small, almost entirely self-contained. Her world had been flipped upside down, yet everything was still on the same path – still completely normal – for the women who danced in front of her as part of a bachelorette party that had spilled out on to the street.

Tex had died and Sadie had been left with nothing except the memories. She had a few errant items of clothing and his work satchel, complete with his laptop and his notebooks. She gently touched the necklace her sisters had given her, fingering the key as it hung around her neck. It was joined by two rings on the chain now, one the wedding ring she had been wearing and the other Tex's. It was a pithy remnant of the person and what he had meant to her, but it was all she had. The house-boat he had been held on was at the bottom of a river now, the whole thing burning down and sinking the evidence along with it.

Atlanta had made sure the bodies of David and Gavino Contos hadn't been left to float ashore, along with that of the elderly Askari woman who had been on-board and first spotted them at the train station. The other Praetorian Guard soldier Ennis had escaped in the chaos somehow; where he'd gone no longer their concern.

Sadie had found herself immobile as she'd crouched next to Tex's body in the grass. It had been wrapped in black tarpaulin, just his face and the top of his chest visible as she'd sat there and stared at him. She had refused to let his body be dragged into the river with that of his father and Venus. She hadn't wanted that watery fate for him. Sadie had known it was stupid, and once you were dead, you were dead: nothing remained with your corpse. Yet there had been something disgusting about the thought of his body resting alongside theirs. So she'd sat alone in the grass, the night sky pressing down on her, while Sorcha had doused the field in enough fuel to ignite any remaining evidence. Flames were the great destroyer.

She'd sensed the presence of someone beside her before she'd registered the illumination over her shoulder. Sadie had been touching the grooves of Tex's face, running her fingertips over the shape of his nose, which was permanently wonky.

'Just tell me he's okay,' she had signed, not looking up to face the ghost of Barastin who she knew was now sitting beside her.

'He's okay,' he'd whispered, voice soft. 'He's more than okay. He hasn't lingered; he's gone where he needs to.'

She'd nodded, her throat feeling thick as she'd tasted a hint of salt on her lips. Tears had been streaming down her face in a steady flow for what had felt like hours. When Barastin had met them at the cake factory, Sadie had been positively tingling with power. Their practice session had yielded more than satisfactory results and the alchemist had just entered the houseboat with their double agenda. She'd asked him to warn Tex and if it was safe, let him know they were coming. She hadn't known his presence would be required for another reason.

So as she'd sat there in the dark with Tex's body, waiting her sister to return, Barastin had remained with her. He'd spoken to Sadie quietly about the last conversation he'd had with Tex, the things he had urgently told the ghost, knowing full well the chances of him making it out of there alive were slim. Even up until his last moments, Tex had been trying to protect her. He had tried to make sure that even if he wasn't around, Sadie would be armed with all of the knowledge he could possibly impart. That's not to say it was easy sitting next to the body of your dead lover while hearing from a ghost that the act of losing your virginity was what undid the ritual designed to smother your banshee powers. Yet it was something Sadie *needed* to know.

'Only an act of pure love can undo one of pure hate,' Barastin had said. 'That's what the alchemist told Tex.'

Those were words that stayed with her over the coming weeks. She heard them in Tex's voice echoing through her head when she sat up at night, unable to sleep through the physical ache of missing him. She thought about them when she risked visiting the grave of one Edward Wollstone at a small cemetery just outside of Bletchingley. It was where they had buried Tex's body, digging up a grave in the middle of the night, burying him under the coffin of the long-dead Mr Wollstone. It was the biggest risk they could take, with no family left to send Tex's body to, even if they could have managed it. No one remained to care about him except Sadie. At least now she knew of a physical place where he rested.

'Only an act of pure love can undo one of pure hate,' she had whispered to herself, setting a small bunch of daisies down in front of the gravestone. They were her favourite flower. She didn't know what his was; she had never asked.

It seemed like everything in the supernatural world was being driven by fear and hate. From what the Treize were doing in their experiments with supernatural creatures to try and save The Three due to their fear of what they would be without them, to mindless lackeys carrying out the orders of beings they believed to be better than them purely because the people in charge hated the idea of an equal playing field. Sadie didn't have to be soft and she didn't have to show mercy in order to be nothing like them. She'd spent so much of her life being told she was powerless and now she wasn't. It was a bizarre feeling of levity to mix with what seemed like the unending spiral of her grief. So she poured herself into what she could.

Speaking to her sisters on email, wishing more than anything that she was with them, but eternally grateful she was at least with one of them. Practising the power of her wail in abandoned spaces, trying to cause maximum amounts of destruction but also make the sound waves more specific. Organising a place for Atlanta to meet them in Galway once they'd made it there. Following every crazy instruction Sorcha dictated as they left London behind, alternating between driving and even a ferry at one point so that it took days to get to Ireland when it should have been an hour. They had both come too far to fuck up on something trivial and let themselves be followed to Galway. So they had taken every precaution, found somewhere in the city where they could hide and blend safely in equal measure, and then they'd waited.

The good news was the Burke sisters weren't the only set of banshees the Treize were looking for any more. Sorcha had heard the news first, then Shannon when she filled Sadie in on more details over email. Since their family had successfully escaped and evaded the Trieze, other Australian banshee families had started dropping off the grid. It was eleven at last count, with two having being caught but another nine still in the wind: that was some forty-two women free and thriving *somewhere.* She had to guess that, just like her siblings, they too were growing stronger as they stopped repressing their powers.

'We started something,' Shannon had written. 'Well, technically you and Sorcha started something. But don't tell her I said that.'

Fire crackers made Sadie jump as someone let them off in the street, everyone around them cheering appreciatively as Sorcha guided them past with a deep frown. Her hand had reached for something at her hip that Sadie couldn't see, yet she could guess it was a weapon of some kind. Her sister didn't go anywhere without one now, even though the greatest weapon she had was Sadie. It was an invisible, intangible thing, but despite all her grief and all her sorrow, Sadie felt different as she walked through the crowd of people. She felt powerful. If she wanted to, she could bring everyone around them to their knees. She could turn the pub on her left into rubble. Yet no one had any clue about the threat in their midst as a man skipped past her, launching into a rendition of Ed Sheeran's 'Galway Girl'. The chorus of singing voices only grew louder as they broke through the cluster, the spacing of pubs now enough that a few shopfronts were popping up in between. Leaning in the doorway of one was an enormous man, his body hunched over as he took a long drag from a cigarette. His hair was tied in two buns on top of his head so that he looked like a Spice Girl. There was an Irish flag draped over his shoulders and a pair of glittery green, heart-shaped sunglasses completed the look.

'Happy Saint Paddy's,' he said, in a Scottish accent so thick Sadie recognised it straight away.

'Heath?' she questioned. The blurry FaceTime footage on Corvossier's phone did not do him justice.

'Aye, nice to meet ye finally.'

'You look . . . festive,' Sorcha said.

'It was either this or come as a four-leaf clover.'

'At least you're camouflaged.' Her sister shrugged.

The doorway opened behind him, revealing a staircase and a blue-haired woman at the bottom of it.

'Camouflage is a little hard when you're eighty-two fookin' feet tall,' she said, with a Scottish accent that matched Heath's. 'I tried to talk him into a leprechaun outfit, but he said it was too conspicuous.'

'No bawbag of mine is squeezing into sequinned hot pants, you're having a laugh.'

'Technically we'd *all* be having a laugh, but sure – hold out on us, Heath.'

It felt strange to Sadie, the sensation of a smile creeping up on her face. She truly couldn't remember the last time she'd done it, her face being like a veil for the misery she had been feeling. The woman gave her a small wink, stepping outside to join them. She held open the door for them, Sadie unable to stop staring at the muscles as they flexed along the skin of her bare arm. There was a bruise along her jaw that looked as if it was a few days into the healing process and turning green, plus several long scratches that started at her shoulder and disappeared beneath the material of a singlet that was knotted to expose part of her midriff. Sadie had met a lot of dangerous people in her life and every one of her senses was loudly communicating that this woman was right up there with them.

'Go on in,' she said, smiling. 'She's waiting for you upstairs. The surgery's closed today so it's just us.'

Sorcha went first, as she always did, with Sadie following behind her as Heath stamped out his cigarette. She spared a glance behind them as she walked, watching with interest as the lumbering giant slid the sunglasses onto the face of the much shorter woman.

'You put that flag round my shoulders and we're gonna have words,' she warned. He grinned, doing exactly that, and even adding a green top hat on her head.

'You couldn't even dye your hair green for the occasion?' he teased. 'Now we have to cover it up.'

'The hair stays blue.'

'Yeah, alright. Remember what I said? Headphones in.'

'And Charly Bliss all the way up, bruv,' she replied, adjusting the sound on her phone before wedging two headphones into her ears. Her attention immediately shifted from him to the people milling about on the street below. Sadie noted the flash of a weapon, maybe a gun, tucked into the waistband of her jeans where her tailbone was. Heath caught her looking as she reached the landing.

'She's not coming?' she asked.

He shook his head. 'Tommi's a solider, one of the best. And we need a good guard out there just in case.'

A good guard that can't hear, Sadie thought to herself.

'Take no chances,' Sorcha said, repeating a mantra she had said a thousand times over the past few months.

'Go on then.' Heath gestured, pointing out an open door. 'You're safe here, get on with it.'

Sorcha tossed him a look that very clearly told him what she thought. 'God, for all the help you've provided, you're a bit of an asshole, aren't you?'

'Listen, *Pumpkin*, you have no idea how much it took just to wrangle this situation together. Me and the blueberry were-wolf are in the middle of a kill mission that's taking us all across Ireland just so I had adequate cover to set this up. Think I'm an asshole all you want, but I'm an effective asshole.'

'It's okay,' Sadie said, touching her sister's arm. 'Let's just get this over with.'

They left him glowering in the empty reception area, the two banshees entering a doctor's office where a woman was tinkering around with equipment. She looked up as Sorcha shut the door behind them, offering both girls a steady smile.

'Afternoon, ladies. I'm Doctor Sue Kikuchi. Now I'm a Paranormal Practitioner so don't you worry, I'm well versed and ready to handle anything.'

Sorcha and Sadie shared a significant look.

'How about you all sit down and we have a chat first?'

They did as she asked, Sadie taking a moment to introduce herself and Sorcha. The woman nodded, saying it was nice to meet them but keeping it brief and professional.

'Now,' she said, opening a folder. 'I know you did several home kits, but after going through the samples you sent me I can confirm you're definitely pregnant.'

Sadie didn't react. Although it was the first time she'd heard those words out loud, she'd known the truth for a while. Her period could usually be up to a week late, but after December became January and January became February, she could feel the changes in her body. She was simultaneously starving and nauseous. Her boobs were hypersensitive and sore at all times.

She'd risked getting a DIY pregnancy test in a convenience store on New Year's Eve, the second time they'd dared to step out the front door since they arrived in Galway. She had waited another week until she built up the courage to pee on a stick, the little blue lines sealing her fate. She had long gone past the point of panic that Sorcha had entered into when she'd told her, her sister running out and getting three more kits for them to try. All positive.

'I'm sorry,' Sorcha said, speaking up. 'How can this happen exactly? Sadie has been on the pill since she was fourteen to regulate her period. Even if they hadn't used protection—'

'The contraceptive pill isn't always effective,' Dr Kikuchi said. 'Its effectiveness also comes down to the user, taking it every day and as close to the same time as they can.'

They'd been on the run, hopping from safe house to safe house, crossing oceans and country lines as they'd fled from one place to the next. Sadie knew she had missed the occasional pill and as for the timings, well, she had barely known what time zone she was in, *let alone* when she should be taking it.

'Condoms aren't always effective, just like the Catholic method, so even with both used properly, accidents happen. We can discuss other forms of contraception going forward once you make up your mind—'

Sadie wanted to tell her contraception wouldn't be an issue. If Tex wasn't around, she couldn't fathom the idea of having sex with someone else let alone being attracted to them. She'd voiced that opinion to Sorcha, who had delicately told her she wouldn't always feel that way. Sadie wasn't so sure, especially if she was about to be reminded of the man she loved by looking into the face of his child every day for the rest of her life.

'I'm keeping the baby,' she said, cutting off the doctor's speech.

'Sadie,' Sorcha murmured, reaching across to grab her hand. 'Think about this for a moment. Having his baby is not going to keep Tex alive.'

She knew that her sister meant it from a place of love, but she couldn't deny that her words stung. Her older sibling had joked about a teenage pregnancy harking back to Aoife's greatest fear for them and made frequent comments about how Sadie wasn't exactly 'overly maternal'. She'd let her, keeping her lips sealed shut and her temper in check as Sorcha had projected her own feelings on to her. The truth was, she might have been the baby of their family and raised by her sisters, but Sadie worshipped the ground her nieces and nephews walked on. She had always planned on having children someday with someone. The *someday* had arrived a lot earlier than she expected and the *someone* was buried in a grave with another man's name on it. Sadie had thought about it for endless hours, there not being much else to do in a house that felt claustrophobic at times. She knew what it meant, to have this baby while on the run, and she knew that although she had a support network around her, she'd be a single mother by her twentieth birthday. That scared her shitless, but it didn't stop every fibre of Sadie's being telling her the same thing.

'It's my choice,' she said, feeling the resolve in her voice as she spoke up. 'I'm having the baby and I'm keeping it.'

She met Sorcha's gaze, staring at her in such a way that told her sibling not to push her.

'Okay,' Dr Kikuchi said, pointedly ignoring the tension in the room. 'I'd like to take another set of bloods and run you through a few other tests, then we'll get you up on the bed. The father wasn't a supernatural being like yourself, was he?'

'No,' she replied. 'Just human.'

And amazing and brave and smart and incredible in bed and the most important person to her. *And dead,* her mind added. Sadie followed the woman's instructions, Sorcha nervously biting her fingernails as she stood in the corner of the room and watched as blood pressure was taken, along with blood and several other physical exams. When Sadie lay down on the bed, sliding her dress up to her breasts, she couldn't help but run her hands over the significant bump that was already growing.

'Uh, I see you're showing quite a bit,' Dr Kikuchi said, surprise evident in her voice.

'I've been eating my feelings,' Sadie murmured, beyond the stage of freaking out over how her body had began to shift way sooner than she was expecting.

Dr Kikuchi looked thoughtful. 'With the estimated range of conception, I'd say you're only at the four-month mark.'

'Is that too early to be showing this much?' Sorcha asked, drawn back in as she positioned herself at Sadie's side.

'Some women show late, some women show earlier. It's more important what's going on in there.'

She tapped Sadie's belly with one finger, reaching behind her to wheel over an ultrasound machine.

'We can take a look now, if you'd like?'

'You'll see something?' Sadie questioned, unable to ignore the flutter she felt in her heart.

'Oh yeah.' Dr Kikuchi smiled. 'Might even be able to tell the sex if you want to—'

'I want to know.'

The doctor chuckled. 'Fair enough. Now this will feel a little cool . . .'

The gel was squirted on to her belly, the paddle moving it around and spreading it over the surface area. Her eyes were fixed on the small screen next to her, but Sadie felt her sister's hand brush against hers, her nails weaving their way among her fingers so that she was no longer gripping the edge of the bed. It was just a blur of black and white images, neither of the Burke sisters sure what they were supposed to be looking at as the doctor made a humming noise to herself. She was nothing but professional, even if she wasn't dressed like a regular doctor in an oversized Los Angeles Lakers jersey and jeans instead.

'Excuse the attire,' she muttered, as if reading Sadie's mind. 'No need to dress like I'm on *Grey's Anatomy* when this is all supposed to be under the table anyway. Oh, there it is . . . ah, one second.'

'Is everything okay?' Sadie questioned.

'It's fine, just a little more activity than I was expecting so it's taking a moment to get a proper read.'

There was a throbbing sound that filled the room, Sadie and Sorcha both glancing at each other. Her older sibling might have been opposed to the idea of her becoming a mother so soon, but she could see the tears welling up in her eyes.

'Okay, so if you look here that's the heartbeat,' Dr Kikuchi said, pointing to the screen. Truthfully, it looked like little more than pulsing shapes to Sadie.

'Boy or girl?' she asked.

'That's a difficult question, since it's quite crowded in there.'

She turned to stare down at Sadie, the doctor meeting her gaze.

'Crowded?'

'Let's call this one Baby A, shall we? That there is Baby B and . . . at the top, that's Baby C.'

'Doc,' Sorcha whispered, 'that's basically the alphabet.'

'She's carrying triplets.'

Sorcha's hand tightened. 'Fuck.'

'Triplets,' Sadie repeated. 'As in . . . three? Three babies?'

'Yup, which brings your estimated delivery date forward a bit. Most triplets are at full term around thirty-five weeks but we need to be monitoring things closely as soon as you hit thirty.'

'She's going to have to deliver them in a hospital, right? Like, this cannot be a home birth situation?'

'There are a lot of things we're going to—'

The screen glitched out, turning to static and then switching to black altogether. The bed rattled just slightly and Sorcha glanced down.

'Sadie . . .'

'I need a moment,' she said, her voice sounding unlike her own.

'Of course,' Dr Kikuchi said, quickly wiping down the handle of the ultrasound equipment and handing Sadie a box of tissues. 'Your sister and I will wait out in reception for you.'

Sorcha looked like she was reluctant to go, but the doctor put a gentle hand on her elbow and guided them both from the room. Sadie sat up, using the tissues to wipe her belly free of the glop as she slid her dress back down and stared out the window. She placed a hand over her heart, closing her eyes as she felt the dull thud against her skin. If Sadie had bothered to put on make-up in the last several months, she knew mascara would be running down her cheeks like Alice Cooper. *Thud thud, thud thud, thud thud.* Her heartbeat, along with three others. *Only an act of pure love can undo one of pure hate.* It had done so much more than that, she realised. Triplets, just like his father and his uncles had been. Triplets, just like The Three. If only Tex could see this, she wondered how he would feel.

Sadie remained sitting there for a long while, wrapped up in her thoughts. She knew time had passed as she watched the light shift from day to early evening in the sky outside. The door opened behind her and clicked shut again shortly afterwards, the bed she had been laying on sinking with the weight of the man who took a seat next to her. They were both quiet, sitting shoulder to shoulder even though Heath's were closer to her head than regular shoulder height. He was only going to break the silence when she was ready. It was a small thing, but Sadie appreciated it.

'Do you believe in fate?' she asked.

'Mmmm, that's a hard question. My people didn't really believe in things like that, but then again, my people are very old. They had no concept of sin or fate; that shite came later. I've been alive long enough to know that things often run in cycles and can go beyond our understanding. That can look like fate, I guess, but no . . . I don't believe in it.'

His answer was thoughtful and she considered it for several beats before she spoke again.

'You know The Three; you're personally acquainted with them.'

'Aye, we immortal PG soldiers can get offed just like regular folk. But I'm quite old. You stick around long enough, ladies like them take an interest.'

'The Three are banshees, aren't they?'

'Ah . . .'

She turned her head to face him, catching the surprise on his features.

'Hear no evil, see no evil, speak no evil . . . they're the original immortals that emerged from the River Corrib. That's why you recognised the story.'

'I had never seen it on those pages. It was only ever whispers, you understand? Whispers that died on the lips of the people who spoke them. And the less banshees knew about themselves – the less banshees existed – the more valuable The Three were to the Treize.'

'The most powerful banshee women ever,' she said. 'Unable to take the pain of watching those in the world around them die. Did they volunteer their services to the Treize? Or were they detained?'

'I think the former, originally. They genuinely believed in what the organisation stood for, as did I, for centuries. Then if you spend enough time removed from reality, you lose any notion of how to be a part of it. The Three live in their visions; I don't think they could survive out in the real world any more.'

'Now they're not,' she whispered, running a hand over her round stomach, which had been strategically hidden under a layered, floral dress.

The Three were dying and Sadie was carrying triplets. She didn't need another ultrasound to tell her what she already knew: they would be three, healthy girls and gifted with banshee abilities stronger than anything seen in a millennia.

'The heirs apparent,' Heath said, staring at her belly. 'That's what you're thinking, isn't it?'

'Am I wrong?'

'As *The Lion King* would say, it's the circle of—'

'Don't.'

He held up his hands in surrender. 'Fine. But this changes everything, potentially our whole world. Maybe even theirs out there.'

He jerked his head at the window, where the sounds of Saint Patrick's Day celebrations could still be heard.

'If the Treize's thinking aligns with your theory, you know they'll do anything to have those children. They're the replacements. They'll keep you alive as long as they have to, with whatever incentive they need, then as soon as they're born they'll kill you. It's easier to get you out of the way.'

'They're not touching my babies and they're not touching me. They already took the father, that's enough.'

He nodded, seemingly agreeing.

'What will we do?' she questioned. 'How do we hide this? What if The Three see—'

'The Three aren't seeing anything. They started suppressing their visions once they saw the arrival of a certain werewolf.'

'The girl outside?'

'Aye, she was the last true vision and from there . . . they've said nothing, predicted nothing. I heard from a source the running theory is their ailing health is a result of their choice not to speak on what they see, that holding it in is proving toxic.'

'Banshee minds degenerate if they repress their powers.'

'Sure.'

'You don't agree?'

'I think everything has a balance. They're ready to leave, craving it, and they're ready for the world to be different. With their absence, something else needs to exist on a similar power spectrum.'

'Baby A, Baby B and Baby C.'

He lurched to his feet, the sudden movement surprising her as he slapped his hands together.

'Okay, let's work through this. Galway is good for now, but it's not a permanent solution: it's too close to the Treize's power structures in Europe, England, Scotland ... being this close to Vankila makes me nervous. It's too hard to defend and there's too many people, too many variables. We can't just throw you into the sea with Atlanta if things get dicey. And you can't deliver here.'

'So ... where?'

'The bulletproof solution is killing as many people who know about this as possible, which eliminates the chance of leaks.'

'NO!' she said, getting to her feet.

'Ease up on the blood-red eyes, banshee. I'm not going to do that; I'm just saying it's what a smart person would do. As it stands, the only people who definitively know you're pregnant and carrying triplets are myself, your sister, the selkie, and the doctor.'

'What about the werewolf downstairs?'

'Tommi? I asked her to wear headphones for a reason. Her werewolf hearing would have meant nothing that happened in this office was secret. She doesn't know your name, what you are, or what has happened to you.'

'Then why is she here? Why is she helping?'

'I needed someone to watch my back, someone I knew wouldn't flinch if things got bloody. It helps that she doesn't entirely trust me, so when I called to collect on a favour she owed me I told her the less she knew, the better, and it wasn't a lie. Plus, she's a raging feminist and I said there was a young woman who needed help. She's totally a sucker for that.'

Sadie bristled at his description of her, but 'young woman who needed help' wasn't inaccurate.

'Go on,' she muttered.

'The only other people I trust are Tommi, Ludwig, Yu, Stilj, Gaea, Casper, Creeper and the witch – but don't tell her I said that.'

She only recognised a few of those names. 'What about the shifters and Ben Kapoor?'

'Eh, werewolves are sketchy.'

Sadie threw him a look.

'Tommi's different. And Ben's sister Sushmita is locked up in Vankila: they have leverage on him.'

Sadie nearly slapped herself on the forehead, she felt so stupid about not having jumped to this answer immediately.

'My sisters,' she said.

'Huh?'

'My sisters, my auntie, my cousins: they're all in the wind. They're resourceful and cunning and would die trying to protect me. You couldn't buy better protection than family.'

'Family,' he said, repeating her word slowly.

'Yeah, and?'

'Just . . . hold on, I'm having a thought. Sorcha isn't enough, we need more than one person on you full-time and you've made the case for your sisters, I don't disagree. But we need fighters as well, those who are physically equipped to defend you in a place that is geographically sufficient to hide you.'

Sadie tried to be patient, really, but it was difficult when her future was being workshopped in front of her.

'I know the place. It's somewhere safe, somewhere remote, somewhere the Trieze would never expect to look for you even if they knew what you were carrying. Most important of all, it's somewhere *very* well guarded.'

As Sadie strained to pull herself out of the seat after such a long flight, she couldn't help but note the nervous energy she felt tingling along her skin. It was more than just pins and needles, which Dr Kikuchi had told her was completely normal over and over again. The Paranormal Practitioner was assigned to Sadie permanently, along with her wife, with both of them travelling together with the group from Ireland. It was easier that way, Heath had said, to 'disappear' them both so there wasn't anyone the Treize could use against the doctor if it was discovered she was helping them. It made Sadie feel better, knowing the woman was with her and in an ever-changing roster of NBA jerseys whenever she needed. She had just passed the six-month mark and her growing belly was immense.

'Baby got *front*,' Sorcha had said, in her best impression of Sir Mix-A-Lot. 'We gotta protect this pregnancy like a Jenner sister.'

She was right. In a pair of exercise tights and an oversized jumper worn for maximum comfort on the long flight, Sadie suspected she could pass for regular from a front angle. If she turned side on, however, the jig was up. She looked like she was smuggling several watermelons.

It was evening as she stepped off the plane, Sorcha telling her that it was a little past 9 p.m. in Auckland. They had landed on a private airfield owned by the Ihi pack, the tarmac slick with rain that had stopped falling just before their descent into New Zealand. She held on to the railing as she climbed down the stairs, not looking where she was putting her feet as her eyes settled on a familiar figure. Several of them, in fact. Shannon Burke's face was grim as she stood there, before dashing forward to take her hand as she made it down the last step. There was a moment of awareness, just a moment, before she pulled her into an all-encompassing hug. She closed her eyes, leaning hard into the gesture as she gripped her sister back.

Sorcha herself had been enveloped, a sea of Burke sisters and cousins descending on and around her. To them, she had come back from the dead. Sadie understood exactly how they would be feeling, as she'd felt it too. That's what she attributed the tears to, she told herself, as she pulled back and quickly swept one away.

'Aw, come on now: don't get mushy on me,' Shannon teased.

'It's the hormones.' She sniffed. 'I swear.'

'Well, yeah, I mean . . . just look at you.' It was a genuine smile as she glanced down at her belly, Sadie self-consciously placing her hands over it. Shannon placed hers on top. 'I'm here to protect you and those kids. I swear, those Treize fucks aren't gonna get anywhere near them.'

She nodded, appreciating the fierceness of her family more than words could formulate right in that moment.

'I'm so sorry,' Shannon was saying. 'About Tex, about everything you lost . . .'

'It's okay,' she said, squeezing her hand. 'I gained a lot too.'

She looked up from her belly, her hand going to her throat, which was still draped in several necklaces and her moonstone choker.

'Which is great for the rest of us.' Her sister smiled, before Sadie replied in Auslan.

'And terrible for them.'

Glancing at the cluster of Burke women, she could barely see Sorcha's peroxide pixie cut among them she was still being swamped. Sadie knew Shannon would want to join them as well and she jerked her head, telling her to go on. She left them all to get reacquainted, sensing she was needed elsewhere. Her eyes scanned the open space and settled on an assembly of vehicles that had been parked nearby. A group of ten women were walking towards her slowly. Everyone else was varying degrees of tense, but these women were comfortable, sure of themselves. They looked like they owned the night, and, in a way, Sadie guessed that they did. This was their land, after all, and they could see better, smell better, hear better, and hunt better than any other creature on this island. Tiaki was at the head of the pack and it was literally a pack, the Aunties behind her ranging in age from a girl who didn't look much older than Sadie to a woman with white hair that was plaited long down her back.

'Kia ora,' the werewolf said, grasping Sadie on the shoulder. 'I knew we'd end up back together somehow, although not with you knocked up, aye? *Too* much.'

'Believe me,' she sighed. 'Wasn't part of the plan.'

'I see you found that voice of yours. And worked out how to use it.'

'Hone my weapon, right? That's what you said.'

'*Ka pai*, been a long time since they've had to face a proper banshee. Let alone a *family* of them. Glad you're on our side and not theirs.'

'It's a little difficult not to be,' she murmured, glancing around her.

'So listen,' Tiaki started, 'you landing here is safest 'cos we control who comes in and out. Usually this airfield is just for business, private freighters and import/export, that kind of thing. They're not gonna know you're here but we're still taking precautions anyway, the same ones we took as your sisters began to arrive.

'Hence the road trip'

'Exactly. I've got three caravans for your travelling party and you'll look just like any other group of tourists driving around Aotearoa in those things. I'm assigning two Aunties to each van, but unfortunately that's all I can spare.'

'That's amazing, thank you.'

'You'll be well protected. Plus, you need the Aunties to get you through the North Island and across to the South. We might be in charge of the territory here, but there's other Māori packs and Pākehā packs that need to be addressed as we pass through their land.'

'That sounds . . . dicey.'

'Nah, it's fine,' Tiaki scoffed, looking almost bored by the conversation. 'We're all working towards the same goal here, and, because of that, everyone gets along. They let something pass unnoticed through their territory, we deal them in on a percentage of a new development. You know how it is.'

She didn't, but she nodded enthusiastically as if talking business was entirely in her repertoire.

'Got you staying in a property in Arrowtown, which is small and off the grid. When I say the last big thing that happened there was the gold rush, I really mean it.'

Sadie laughed. 'Hey, I'm taking your word for it at this point.'

'It's the Dawson pack down there. They're all bushy redheads and farmers, but they're good folk. They'll make sure you're set up and then leave you be. I gotta pull the Aunties out after that, but we'll replace them with someone from the Kapoor pack or the Petershams so the numbers line up. Plus, the Dawsons have a direct connect to us if anyone weird or new shows up in town.'

'Is that likely?'

'No. They'd need to a) find you b) get through us and then c) face the Dawsons. My late husband liked to keep them onside largely because he never wanted to come up against them: they're very into axes.'

She felt a small squirm inside her, as if one of the babies had somehow sensed their home for the next few months was in a deserted town surrounded by axe-wielding werewolves. Come to think of it, the idea actually comforted Sadie. *If it's good enough for your mother, it's good enough for you*, she told them, a hand running over her stomach.

'The caravans have got a lot of the medical equipment that was requested stocked in there already, it's just a matter of getting it out and setting it up once you're there. I'm sure the doc knows what she's doing.'

'I hope so,' Sadie whispered.

'Tiaki,' an Auntie called, the woman looking over her shoulder and nodding. 'Listen, I gotta go but the Aunties going with you have all the contact numbers you could need hooked up with a burner so just call. About anything.'

She handed Sadie a small, woven basket, pressing it into her hands. As she took it, she realised there were actually three of them stacked on top of each other.

'What's this?' she asked, surprised.

'It's just a few wee things we put together, me and the Aunties: wahakura for the babies to sleep in, and you can rest next to them safely; kiwi fruit seed oil for the stretch marks; chocolate fish for the cravings.'

'Tiaki, this is . . .' She could barely speak, she was so touched by the gesture. At the same time, a part of her mind was wondering why 'chocolate' and 'fish' would ever go together.

'The Aunties are the Aunties for a reason: we've all had our pēpē and seen them grow up. Some of them, anyway. But we don't do it alone: we have the whole pack. Now you have yours too.'

Sadie pressed her lips into a hard line, trying not to cry. *These God damn hormones.* Tiaki must have seen the expression on her face and at the first sign of tears, the woman looked ready to sprint for nearby mountains.

'Too much,' she said, waving a hand at her. 'Too much.'

It was her form of farewell, she guessed, the werewolf spinning on her heels and rejoining the cluster of women from her pack. A few of them were looking over at her and Sadie smiled, offering a wave. She wasn't sure what the right gesture was for mostly strangers hiding her in their country just because they all shared the same enemy. A few of them nodded back and she gripped the baskets a little tighter.

'Let's move,' Shannon called, their bags on a trolley as she began splitting them up into the groups they'd be travelling in. 'It's a long drive, a ferry, then another longer drive, and we're gonna keep our breaks to a minimum. Let's get where we're going.'

Everyone divided into their specified clusters, moving towards where the Aunties were gathered at the caravans. Tiaki had mentioned the medical equipment, but Sadie could see weapons had been loaded too. Everyone there was taking a massive risk for her, mainly because they believed it would result in a better world not just for themselves personally, but for all supernatural creatures. They were willing to fight for that belief and Sadie was too. She realised with a start that, in a way, she'd already been fighting for a long time. It was just now she had better weapons and better friends.

'Banshees, demons, werewolves, witches, ghosts, mediums and immortals working together,' Sorcha said, falling in step beside her. 'This is not normal.'

Sadie smiled, looking up at her as they walked. 'Maybe it can be the new normal.'

Glossary

Alchemist Those who have the ability to infuse and convert materials with magical properties through a combination of symbols, science and ceremony. Alchemists were instrumental in the founding of the Treize, particularly the Askari themselves. Obsessed with immortality, it's rumoured their formula is responsible for the prolonged lives of Praetorian Guard soldiers and Custodians.

Arachnia Traditionally considered a nightmarish vision from Japanese folklore, arachnia emerged from the shadows relatively late compared to other supernatural species and were discovered to have existed worldwide. Their natural state is comparable to a large, spider-like creature, with traits similar to the arthropod.

Askari Foot soldiers and collectors of ground truth. The first point of call in the supernatural community, they simultaneously liaise and gather information. Mortal, yet members often work their way up into the Custodian ranks. Identified by a wrist tattoo, which is the alchemist symbol for wood to signify a strong foundation.

The Aunties A pack within the Ihi pack, this fearsome all-women group are responsible for voting on and enforcing pack law.

Banshee Thought to be extinct by the wider supernatural community before re-emerging in Australia, a banshee is a supernatural being cursed with the ability to sense death or impending doom in its various forms. Exclusively female.

Bierpinsel A large, colourful tower in the centre of Berlin: the Bierpinsel is the base of Treize operations for Germany and much of Europe.

Blood pack The family unit a werewolf is born into by direct descent, usually operating on a specific piece of geographical territory.

Coming of age A ritual all werewolves must complete before they're considered mature members of their blood pack. A wolf can only choose to go 'rogue' once they have survived the coming of age.

Coven A grouping of witches within a particular area, covens can include members of the same biological family as well as women of no biological relation. No two members of a coven have the same magical ability, with similar powers spread out over other covens as an evolutionary defence mechanism. Members of a coven can draw on each other's powers, giving them strength and safety in their sisterhood.

The Covenant The series of rules established for banshees to follow once they were deported en masse from Ireland, Scotland and Wales in the seventeen hundreds. If The Covenant is broken, the penalty can range from imprisonment in Vankila to death.

Custodians The counsellors or emotional guardians of beings without other help, assistance or species grouping. Immortality is a choice made by individual Custodians, with those choosing it identified by a necklace with an Egyptian ankh.

Demon One of the oldest forms of supernatural beings, pure-blood demons are known for being reclusive and rarely interact with those outside of the paranormal world. Certain species of demon have a fondness for the flesh, leading to half-blood demon hybrids usually identifiable via physical traits like horns or tusks (often filed down so it's easier to blend in to society).

Elemental Originally thought to be those who could control the elements – earth, air, fire and water – elementals are paranormal beings descended directly from nature. Able to physically become the elements if they so desire, they share a strong allegiance with shifters, werewolves and selkies.

Ghost Translucent and bluish grey in colour, ghosts are the physical manifestation of one's soul after death. Their presence in the realm of the living can be for several reasons, ranging from an unjust demise to a connection with a person or place. The strength of any particular ghost varies case-to-case.

Ghoul Usually found in underground sewer systems and living in nest formations, ghouls are considered a lower class of paranormal creature due to their lack of intelligence or individual personality traits. With razor sharp claws and serrated teeth, they can be deadly in numbers.

Goblin Highly intelligent and supernaturally agile, goblins are known for their speed and lethal nature if provoked. Although not immortal, they have exceedingly long lives and prefer living in urban environments such as cities or large towns. They are one of several paranormal species impacted by the lunar cycle.

Medium A being that can communicate with and control the dead, including spirits and ghosts. Extremely rare, the full range of their abilities is unknown and largely undocumented.

Outskirt Packs The collective description for werewolf packs from the Asia-Pacific region who fought against the Treize – unsuccessfully – for the right to self-govern and expose their true nature to the human world. Formed in 1993 and disbanded upon defeat in 1998, key leaders included Jonah Ihi, Sushmita Kapoor and John Tianne. This conflict was known as the Outskirt Wars.

Paranormal Practitioner The healers and medical experts of the unnatural world. Usually gifted individuals themselves, they wield methods outside of conventional medicine.

Praetorian Guard A squadron of elite warriors that quell violence and evil within the supernatural community. They're gifted with immortality for their service. Founded by a member of the original Roman Praetorian Guard.

Rogue A werewolf who chooses to live and operate outside of their blood pack.

The Rogues Comprised of rogue werewolves who have decided to leave their blood packs, this group functions from within the nightclub Phases in Berlin and includes global members who have come of age.

Selkie The source of mermaid and merman folklore, selkies are aquatic humanoids that inhabit any large body of water. Despite some human features, tribes of selkie from certain parts of the world have been known to take the form of marine animals like seals, dolphins and sharks.

Shifter Found globally, shifters have the ability to transform into one specific creature depending on their linage. Often confused with werewolves due to their capacity to take animal shape, shifters can transform outside of the full moon both fully and in-part.

Spirit Incorrectly compared to ghosts, spirits are their more powerful counterparts. A term used to describe the dead who can travel between pre-existing plains and occasionally take some physical form, they usually preoccupy themselves with the business of their direct ancestors.

Sprite Said to be the result of a union between selkies and earth elementals, sprites are highly secretive and rarely identify themselves to other supernatural creatures. They struggle being around members of their own kind and prefer to live close to nature.

The Three A trio of semi-psychic women who guide the Treize with regards to past, present and future events. The subject of the phrase 'hear no evil, see no evil, speak no evil'. Origin and age unknown.

Treize The governing body of the supernatural world comprising of thirteen members of different ages, races, nationalities, abilities, species and genders. Given their namesake by four French founders, they oversee the Praetorian Guard, Custodians, Askari and Paranormal Practitioners.

Vampire Rodent-like creature who lives off the blood of animals or people (whatever they can get). Endangered in the supernatural community due to widespread disease.

Vankila The Treize's supernatural prison, located in St Andrews, Scotland, and built hundreds of metres below a Cold War bunker.

Werewolf Considered one of the most volatile and ferocious paranormal species, werewolves are humans that shift into enormous wolf-hybrids during the nights of the full moon. Outside of the lunar cycle they retain heightened abilities, such as strength and healing, with the most powerful of their kind able to transform at will and retain human consciousness. Often found living in blood packs, they are resistant towards most forms of paranormal government.

Witch A woman naturally gifted with paranormal abilities that can be heightened with study and practice. Although the witch gene is passed down through the female line, skills vary from woman to woman regardless of blood. Witches believe their power is loaned to them temporarily by a higher being, who redistributes it to another witch after their death. Highly suspicious and distrustful of the Treize due to centuries of persecution, they are closed off from the rest of the supernatural community.

Acknowledgements

Firstly, thank you to all the IRL wailing women out there, the otherworld sisters and what not. This book is supposed to be about finding your voice and using it, so hopefully that's what you take away from it. Of course, thanks to Anna Boatman at Little, Brown for helping bring to life another chapter in this shared supernatural universe. It's wild to think we started with werewolves and now have a glossary worth of monsters. Merci merci to my agent, literary whore himself Ed Wilson, my long-term publicist, Nazia Khatun, and the combined eyeballs of Eleanor Russell, Sandra Ferguson and Donna Hillyer.

Special thank you to Blake and Sam Howard, plus Hazel Hermione and Keaton James. I wouldn't have been able to get through the past year if it wasn't for your emotional support, hospitality, and casual mocking of my ability on crutches. Huge chuuuuurrrr sis to my network of girlfriends, the murderino m'ladies, who were there without question when it felt like everything else was imploding (you know who you are).

Always thank you to Nicola Scott for her enduring wisdom and support, but in this case an extra big thanks for creating one of only a few pop culture representations of banshees with Gail Simone. Long live Jeannette and long live *Secret Six*.

The intimate She Pack: Casey Zilbert, for being fierce and fearless in her pursuit of feminist storytelling and supporting others to do the same. The OG Auntie, Kath Akuhata-Brown, for the wahakura and helping inform this world just a little bit more. Here's to endless rooftop swims in lightning storms.

Una 'toiling' Butorac, for her in-depth research on Auslan users in Australia and taking the time to educate me on the intricacies. Kaylee Hottle and the Hottle family, for helping steer me through ASL as a shoddy beginner. To Dr Jodi McAlister, using her PhD for the powers of good and helping me access the rare few academic journals on banshees that are out there. Team Vampire Academy fo lyf (VA!).

To the legacy of proofreaders who gave me early and great feedback on *The Wailing Woman*: mana wāhine Anna Gough for enduring my frequent use of the word panties, Ramona Sen Gupta, for proofing this book in less than 12 hours and adding reaction gifs (which are obvs very important), Caris 'teary' Bizzaca, for continuing to trust me even though the last thing I made her read had terrifying giant spider-people in it, Angel Giuffria, who permanently lives alongside Casper in my mind now as a supernatural entity not to be messed with, Kate Czerny, for starting on the police beat together more than a decade ago and proofing that first Tommi draft (and every draft since), the keen eyes of Janna Zagari, Denise Pirko, Jill Pantozzi, Robin and Ron Cobb, and the supportive sisterhood of Jean-Anne Kidd, Rae Johnston, Caitlin Jinks, Maddie, and Laura Murphy-Oates.

Everyone who let me sleep on their couches last book tour and more: Juanita, Mark, Claire, Skye, Missy, Ineke, Hayley and Kieran, legal and medical experts respectively Yen and Dr

Cocks, the entire Hancock clan, and the plethora of creative sounding boards in Sonja Hammer, Mariko Tamaki, Lexi Alexander, Lynette Noni, Tom Taylor, Dionne Gipson, Keri Arthur, Alison Goodman, Candice Fox, and cigar-smoking comrade Angela Slatter.

The Hoodlum team and Tracey Robertson, plus the Screen Queensland BAMFs of Tracey Vieira and Jo Dillion for believing in women and supporting me from day one even though I'm deeply suspicious of authority figures.

Assorted thank youse to Bettie Bandit, for letting me into the nerdlesque universe and Imogen Kelly, for helping inform Sorcha and her world at Hue with her years of experience on stage. Kallel Zimba, for the VPN bouncing and secure email tech advice – even if it was for a family of fictional banshees. Kodie Bedford, for letting me invade her space and finish off *The Wailing Woman* at her mountain sanctuary. The Auslan Signbank, for being an incredible resource, and the Irish Folklore Commission. My family of three Ts: Tom, Teresa, and Tania, plus Jolly Jingo.

The city of Sydney, which I love so much despite the ridiculous house prices, dumb-as-fuck lockout laws, and complete lack of road infrastructure. You finally got to be the setting for a published book, rather than all my dusty manuscripts.

Most importantly, to the readers and booksellers and bloggers and journos who have stayed with me five books into this series of supernatural sisters. Thanks for continuing to believe that stories about female monsters in all their varying forms are worth telling. Grrrr argh etc.

Praise for Maria Lewis

'Journalist Maria Lewis grabs the paranormal fiction genre by the scruff of its neck to give it a shake' *The West Australian*

'Author Maria Lewis has created her own pop culture universe' *Daily Telegraph*

'[Maria Lewis] easily weaves the magic into each page of this spin-off to her already successful Who's Afraid series with another strong female lead' *The Daily Nerd*

'Gripping, fast-paced and completely unexpected . . . Maria Lewis is definitely one to watch' *New York Times* bestselling author Darynda Jones

'If you love a strong female lead, then *Who's Afraid?* by Maria Lewis is a must-read' Buzzfeed

'If you want a fresh, funny, sexy & downright sassy take on the werewolf genre then this series is for you' Geek Bomb

'She writes kick-ass monsters and things that go bump in the night with a flair for the awesome' Reviewers of Oz

'Truly one of the best in the genre I have ever read' Oscar-nominated filmmaker Lexi Alexander (*Green Street Hooligans*, *Punisher*: *War Zone, Arrow, Supergirl*)

'It's about time we had another kick-arse werewolf heroine – can't wait to find out what happens next!' *New York Times* bestselling author Keri Arthur

'*The Witch Who Courted Death* is an unashamedly feminist story about a woman out for revenge' *Readings*

'A feminist take on two well-known classic ghosts and witches – giving them the Lewis makeover and throwing them into her renowned supernatural world' *Aurealis*

'It's Underworld meets Animal Kingdom' ALPHA Reader

'The next *True Blood*' NW *Magazine*

'Lewis creates an intriguing world that's just begging to be fleshed out in further books' *APN*

'Definitely worth reading over and over again, as well as buying multiple copies. Great stocking stuffers, those were-wolf books' Maria Lewis' mum

If you enjoyed *The Wailing Women*, look out for the rest of Maria Lewis' novels

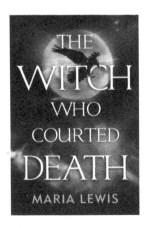
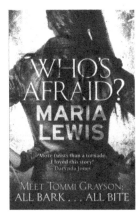
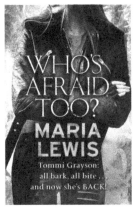

Available now from

piatkus